Three in One
Magical Mystery Stories

THE CONJUROR'S GAME

Alick is fascinated by Luke Ferris – the Conjuror!
Where does he get his strange powers of healing?
Why has he got six fingers? What is his connection
with the sinister goings-on in the wood? Then
Alick follows the Conjuror and discovers something
which will soon unleash dark and terrifying forces
on to the world.

THE THIRTEENTH OWL

Taunted by the village about her scarred face,
Imogen feels very alone. And then she sees the
white owl who stares long and hard at her before
swooping into Mr Balik's barn. But when Mr Balik
torches the barn, Imogen's nightmares about the owl
begin. Soon she and Mr Balik are drawn closer
together through a chain of very strange events.

WORDS OF STONE

Ever since the death of his mother, Blaze has
developed many phobias. He finds it hard to talk
about his fears with anyone except his imaginary
friends. Then strange messages start appearing on
the hillside, spelt out with stones, and Blaze's life
takes an unexpected turn.

Other Red Fox Story Collections

Cool School Stories
More Cool School Stories
Three in One Animal Stories
Completely Wild Stories
Three in One Ballet Stories
Three in One Pony Stories
Brilliantly Bad Stories
The Charlie Moon Collection
Doctor Dolittle Stories
The Willard Price Adventure Collection

THREE IN ONE
MAGICAL
MYSTERY
STORIES

RED FOX

A Red Fox Book

Published by Random House Children's Books
20 Vauxhall Bridge Road, London SW1V 2SA

A division of Random House UK Ltd
London Melbourne Sydney Auckland
Johannesburg and agencies throughout the world

The Conjuror's Game first published in Great Britain
by The Bodley Head Children's Books 1990
Red Fox edition 1991
Text copyright © Catherine Fisher 1990

The Thirteenth Owl first published in Great Britain
by the Bodley Head Children's Books 1993
Red Fox edition 1994
Text copyright © Nick Warburton 1993

Words of Stone first published in USA by
Greenwillow Books 1992

First published in Great Britain by
Julia MacRae 1994
Red Fox edition 1995
Text copyright © Kevin Henkes 1992

This Red Fox anthology first published 1999

Phototypeset by Intype London Ltd
Printed and bound in Norway by Ait Trondheim AS

Random House UK Limited Reg. No. 954009

ISBN 0 09 940262 9

CONTENTS

THE
CONJUROR'S GAME

Catherine Fisher

To My Parents

'And as they looked they could hear a rider coming towards them, to the place where Arthur and Owein were over the gaming board. The squire greeted Arthur and said that Owein's ravens were slaying his bachelors and squires. And Arthur looked at Owein and said, "Call off thy ravens." "Lord," said Owein, "play thy game." And they played. The rider returned towards the battle, and the ravens were no more called off than before.'

From 'The Dream of Rhonabwy' in the Mabinogion (translated by Gwyn Jones and Thomas Jones)

1

THE BROWN OINTMENT

'There he is,' Mr Webster said.

'Who?'

'Luke Ferris. The chap I was telling you about. The conjuror.'

Alick stood up and had a look. Out in the street, on the opposite pavement, a thin, dark-haired man was looking in the shop windows. Just behind him trotted a white dog.

'Is that him?' Alick sat down again, and picked up the pen. 'I've seen him about before. He looks just like anybody else.'

'Ah, yes. I expect that's just what he wants you to think.' His father's mouth twitched. Alick knew something had amused him. 'Anyway, he's coming over, so you can find out for yourself.'

They watched the man cross the street, weaving between the cars. He came up to the window of Webster's Secondhand Bookshop and paused, looking in at the bright display of Christmas books and posters that Alick had spent the morning arranging. Then the bell on the shop door jangled as he came in.

It was nearly five o'clock on a late December

afternoon, and the shop was already quite dark. Down at one end, the fire had smouldered into embers, and the three shelves of musty, leatherbound books that never sold, gleamed in the warm glow. Mr Webster switched on the lamp near the window. 'Cold enough for snow, Luke,' he observed.

The conjuror nodded, and gave Alick a quick glance. His face was white with cold, and a gold earring glinted in the fire light. He wandered among the shelves, picking a book up now and again. Mr Webster searched the desk for his glasses, and Alick leaned his elbows on the counter and watched their customer.

A conjuror. And in Halcombe Great Wood that meant the real thing – not the man you saw on the television doing tricks with cards and white rabbits. And they said he was good. Well, he certainly looked at you in an odd way; as if he could see what you had for breakfast, if he wanted to. But *he* wouldn't be able to do anything about it either, Alick thought bitterly. No one could. The whole thing was hopeless.

A movement by the door caught his eye, and he saw that the white dog was lying there, watching him. Chin on paws it lay, and there was an odd smirk about its mouth, as if it found something funny.

The ashes of the fire crackled. The lights in the butcher's opposite went out. Finally, Mr Webster straightened up and slid the accounts book back to

Alick with a satisfied nod. 'Good. All done.' He looked up.

'Anything you want, Luke?'

'Just these, I think.' The conjuror came and put two books on the counter, and Alick took a sideways look at the titles. *The Medicinal Properties of Herbs and Simples* was the first, and the other was a small paperback called *Poisons*. He swallowed. Perhaps it would be better not to ask after all. But it was too late; as he wrapped the books his father had already begun.

'I'm glad you called in, Luke, I've been wanting a word for a while now. It's about Alick.'

'Oh?' Alick felt the man stare at him. 'What's he been up to?'

'Nothing.' Mr Webster laughed, pressing down a piece of sticky tape. 'No, it's his hands. Show him, Alick.'

Feeling foolish, Alick put both hands on the shop counter and stared at them gloomily.

Warts!

They looked horrible, and dirty, and they itched like mad. There were four on one hand and three on the other, including a big hard one like a knob of dried glue on the end of his thumb. He'd had them since he went fishing with Jamie in the Green-mere, but his father didn't know about that. The Mere was strictly out of bounds – a man had drowned in it last year. The kids at school had been calling him Frog-face ever since. He was just about sick of it.

The conjuror looked down at the warts thoughtfully. 'How long have you had these?'

'About three weeks.'

'And did they just appear?'

'Sort of,' Alick stammered.

'I see. You hadn't been anywhere wet? Mucky pools? Ponds?'

'No.'

Luke Ferris nodded. 'I see,' he said again. Suddenly he smiled at Alick; Alick felt himself go red. He knew!

'I've tried everything,' his father put in, pushing the parcel of books across the counter. 'Calamine, chilblain cream, every wart paint you've ever heard of. Then the doctor gave him some nasty, white burning stuff. None of it's done the slightest good . . . That'll be eight pounds fifty, please, Luke.'

'I think,' Luke said evenly, 'that I may be able to help. It'll cost you . . . eight pounds fifty. Payment on results.'

Mr Webster laughed. 'Fair enough.'

The conjuror gave Alick another grin, and reaching into his coat pocket, pulled out a few, small, round boxes which he scattered along the counter. Then he spread out a clean, white handkerchief and told Alick to put his hands on it, palms down. Warily, Alick obeyed. The warts itched like crazy. Mr Webster bolted the shop door, turned the sign to 'Closed' and came and leaned on the counter, filling his pipe and watching the proceedings with interest.

Humming, Luke opened one of the boxes.

Immediately a sharp, pungent smell began to fill the shop, making Alick's eyes water. The dog by the door made a small noise in its throat.

'It's all right, Tam,' the conjuror said, without turning his head. Dipping one finger into the sticky, brown ointment, he carefully put a small dab of it on each of the warts, and two dabs on the large one, all the time humming and muttering words that Alick, close as he was, could not catch.

The smell made him feel dizzy, but the ointment did not sting as the doctor's had – it was just cold, like chocolate ice-cream. At last, the treatment seemed to be over; the shop was dim with a faint smoke. Luke wiped his finger clean on the edge of the handkerchief and replaced the box lid. He gathered the others up and dropped them in his pocket. Alick watched the brown blobs of ointment harden into crusts. 'Can I move now?'

'Not yet. Let it dry.'

Impatient, he kept still. Luke and his father began to talk about people they knew, and he had to wait. The smell bothered him, made him think of deep woods and wet, mushy leaves. And he felt daft, with his hands out flat like someone at a seance.

'I hope it works,' he said when the talk had stopped.

Luke did not answer.

'It's horrible having people stare at your hands all the time.'

For some reason this seemed the wrong thing to say. His father glared at him angrily. He couldn't see why. But then the conjuror took his hands out of his pockets and laid them down flat beside Alick's.

'I know,' he said.

It was all Alick could do not to shout out. The long, brown hand next to his had, not five fingers, but *six*! He glanced at the other. It was the same.

Luke was watching him. 'Not so easy to cure as warts,' he said.

Alick felt foolish. 'I'm sorry,' he stammered. 'I didn't know.'

'I didn't think you did . . .' Luke paused, as if he was about to say something else, then, changing his mind, picked up the handkerchief and swiftly rubbed away the brown crusts from Alick's fingers.

Mr Webster gave a whistle of amazement.

The warts were gone. Just a crumble of fine dust lay on the counter.

Alick couldn't believe it. He stared at his fingers as if they did not belong to him, then touched them, carefully. No pain, no itching – not even a scar. Nothing!

Luke had already picked up his parcel of books and turned towards the door, nodding at Mr Webster's astonished thanks.

'Oh, that's all right. But if I were you, Alick,' he added, turning suddenly, 'I'd give up fishing at the Greenmere. It's not the sort of place you'll catch anything fit to eat. Besides, it's dangerous. Your father will tell you that.'

'Indeed I will,' Mr Webster said in a meaningful way.

The conjuror smiled. 'Goodnight, Tom.'

'Goodnight, Luke. Thanks again.'

And the door closed behind him.

Mr Webster turned around and took the pipe from his mouth, but before he could mention the Greenmere, Alick changed the subject.

'I never thought he could do it!' he announced, holding up his fingers to the light. 'It's magic!'

'It might look like that to you,' his father said, instantly sarcastic. 'Luke knows a lot about folk medicine and such. But it's true I've never seen warts done as fast as that, though there was an old chap down at Swinder's End used to do them, once. Didn't you feel anything?'

'No,' Alick plumped himself on to a stool. 'Dad, why didn't you tell me about his hands?'

'Well, I didn't know you'd come out with a tomfool remark like that, did I?' his father said. 'Besides, everyone knows. Or I thought they did. Odd, isn't it?'

Alick nodded.

'Mind, he's an odd sort is Luke.'

Alick clasped his knees. 'How do you mean?'

'Well, it's not just warts.' Mr Webster crossed to the fire and began to rake it out. 'You know McCarthy, the baker? He had arthritis last year, very bad. The doctor told him he might be in bed for the rest of his life. Then his son called on Luke, and the next week the old man's in the Crown and Fiddle drinking pints. I'll bet he charged more than eight pounds fifty for that.' He straightened up and dusted his hands. 'Well now, I think we'd better go upstairs and have some tea, don't you? And a nice little chat. About the Greenmere.'

2

GREENMERE

'And he did it just like that?' Jamie stared at Alick's hands. 'Get out! It's impossible!'

'It's not. Besides, Dad was there – ask him.' Alick was annoyed. 'You never believe anything I say.'

'Too much imagination,' Jamie said. 'It's all those batty old books, it is.'

'Oh shut up.' Alick felt guilty. He shouldn't be here, not after the row he had got last night. They were in the Combe, a narrow lane that ran deep into the wood; their heads bent against the bitter breeze. He pulled his gloves back on. 'It is true. And he does have six fingers. And what's more he knew I'd been at the Mere too.'

'Lucky guess.'

'No. He knew.' Alick kicked up the leaves. 'He said it was dangerous. And Dad knew then, of course.' He pulled a face.

'Was it bad?'

'Not really. Said I ought to think of other people.' And yet, he thought, here I am going there again.

Jamie must have guessed what he was thinking. 'Well, we're only going to walk past it. There's nothing wrong with that, is there? And I *must* have dropped that reel there; I've looked everywhere else.'

The Combe had been getting narrower for some time; now it was just a deep, gloomy cutting in the very lowest part of the wood. On each side, steep banks of earth towered over their heads, as if a knife had cut a deep slash in the ground and they stood at the bottom of it. In summer the banks were a riot of flowers, but now, in bleak December, only a tangle of tree-roots and frost-bitten brambles poked out of the soil. High above, crowding to the edge as if to look down, were rows of golden beech trees, their leaves filling the Combe in deep drifts to the boys' knees.

They climbed up by the usual way; a zig-zag staircase of roots that stuck out of one bank. At the top, the forest was silent all about them; a faint breeze rustled the tree-tops. Far down the ranks of trees a crow 'karked' noisily and flew away.

Briskly, Jamie started down the path. 'It's all non-sense, all this stuff about the Mere. I mean, I know that chap was drowned in it, but that's just because he fell in, or went swimming and got stuck. There must be acres of mud in there. You'd never catch me swimming in it!'

Behind him, Alick shook his head. 'That man had all his clothes on. You don't go swimming like that.'

'Well, he fell. It's just the same. But these yarns about the Mere being a bad place, and people who go into the wood and never come out again – that's just stuff! Stuff to keep little kids away from the edge.'

It sounded sensible. Jamie usually did – and he was always sure he was right. Alick said nothing.

'Are you listening?'

'Yes.'

'Good!' Jamie jumped on a fallen log and raced along it, arms wide. 'There's nothing here but rabbits, and squirrels, and birds, and, er . . .'

'Foxes,' Alick put in quietly.

'FOXES!'

The thin, red shape Alick had seen, loped off at the sudden shout. All at once they both burst into a fit of giggles, shoving and pushing each other and crashing noisily through the drifts of leaves.

Around them, echoes rang in the trees for miles.

Halcombe Great Wood stretches for fifty thousand acres, most of it rarely visited. Only four roads come into the Wood, meeting in a crooked X at Halcombe Cross. One of the lanes leads to Halcombe village; the other two are roads towards Gloucester and Monmouth; and the fourth, far more spindly and lost under its leaves, is the Combe, which goes only to the house at Swinder's End and then peters out in the trees. It is an ancient wood, a wildwood, riddled with lumps and humps, ruined cottages, and a maze of bridleways and tracks and paths.

Halcombe village is surrounded by trees. From the church tower, all you can see in any direction are endless dark green branches, and the cluster of red roofs like an island in the middle. And, if it is a fine day, you might see the sun glittering on the pinnacles of Gloucester Cathedral, thirty miles away.

You would also see Tolbury Tump. All the forest is hilly, but Tolbury Tump stands out; a high round knoll, bare of trees, the only bald spot in the whole of the wood. And at the foot of the Tump, hidden in a gloomy hollow of dark pines, lies the Greenmere.

As Alick and Jamie trod the thick layer of pine needles towards it, their footsteps were muffled, and the reek of weed and rottenness seemed stronger than ever. Alick pulled a face. 'Yuk!'

The Mere stank. It was always green; a scum of algae lay on the surface like a heavy velvet cloth. It never seemed to break, either – even when you threw a stone in, it was just gulped down without a ripple, and there was no sign of that sudden opening and closing. It was a mouth; it swallowed things. No one in their right minds would go swimming in there.

The boys paused right at the edge.

'Now if I listened to you,' Jamie said slyly, 'I'd be waiting for some slimy hand to come out of that lot, grab me by the ankle, and haul me in.'

Alick laughed, but it wasn't funny. 'Forget the reel. Let's go up the hill,' he said. 'It's worse down here than usual, and darker.'

'Tut–tut. Scared of shadows.'

Alick ignored that. He looked at the trees. The leaves were black and heavy; glossy. Small bright lights glinted among them. He caught Jamie's sleeve.

'Look!' he whispered. 'In the branches!'

The trees were black with birds. Every twig, every branch, bent with their weight; a feathered host, a shadow of wings and beaks and bright eyes. Alick glanced from tree to tree. There were rows of them, sitting perfectly still, looking at him.

Jamie whistled. 'Crows. Where did they all come from?'

'Don't know.' Alick's eyes moved uneasily along the branches. 'Perhaps it's some kind of migration.'

'Crows don't, daft. It's weird.'

The breeze rustled. Black barbs of feathers rose and fell.

Suddenly Alick turned. 'Let's go.'

'They're only birds.' Before Alick could stop him, Jamie picked up a handful of grit and flung it into the Mere with a tremendous splash. 'Go on,' he yelled, waving his arms. 'Clear off! Shoo!' But the birds did not move. Rank on rank they perched, hunched up in the wind.

Jamie backed away. When he spoke again his voice was quieter than usual. 'I don't get this. Let's get out of it.'

They turned, but Alick stopped so suddenly that Jamie slammed into the back of him. 'Hell!' he said.

Across the lake, sunlight was slanting into the trees, lighting up the wood. In the golden glade stood a line of horses, snorting and shifting, their pale manes lifting in the cold wind. One bent its long slender neck to the water, clinking its harness.

And on the golden horses, golden riders.

23

There were men with long cloaks and tunics to the knee, helmed, with spears slung at their saddles. There were women with long ropes of hair twisted with braid and gold thread; and minstrels with harps; grooms and huntsmen; falconers with their hooded hawks flapping and screeching on their wrists. Between the horses' legs, a pack of slim greyhounds twisted their leashes, growling and snuffling in the bushes.

'Mad,' Jamie muttered. 'That's it. I'm going mad.'

Alick shook his head. 'Then it must be both of us.'

Birds and horsemen eyed each other coldly.

'I'm not going to be scared of this lot.' Jamie thrust both fists into his pockets. 'Just walk slow. Back the way we came.'

'I don't think so.' Alick glanced back at the birds. 'Look at them. The way they're lined up. It's as if they're waiting for a battle. And we're in the middle.'

'Down here then.' Jamie pushed through the bushes at the edge of the Mere. 'We can get through.' The bank began to crumble gently at his feet.

'Be careful.'

'Oh, it's all right.'

Soil slipped and splashed into the water.

And then, in the wood, a horn rang out – an eerie, alarming, shattering of the stillness – and in answer, every bird in the trees opened its wings and screamed!

Jamie turned too quickly, slipped, flung out his arms. For a second he hung on the lip of the lake, then, with an enormous splash, he fell. The birds screeched; water cascaded over Alick's face.

'Jamie!'

The green carpet of the Mere was foaming and boiling. Hands and a face floundered and disappeared, bubbled up again, shouting. Desperate, Alick ran along the edge and yelled at the horsemen.

'He's drowning! For God's sake!'

Silent, unmoving, they stared at him. Their eyes were cold. One horse chewed grass, quietly.

Swearing, Alick tore off coat and boots and gloves. The water was ice round his knees; the mud of the Mere soft and cold around his feet. 'Swim!' he yelled. 'Keep up!' But the white face gasped and turned over and under, and without another thought he threw himself forward and the Mere opened its cold mouth and swallowed him.

After a black second he came up, gasping. The water was a solid weight on his clothes, pulling him down. He kicked towards Jamie; a dark commotion in the ripples somewhere ahead. Blue-lipped, breathless, he forced his arms and legs to move. They were lead weights, the effort to raise them exhausted him. The cold bit him; its teeth pierced through his fingers and bones and lungs. He grabbed at the dark heavy shape in the water, sank, swallowed green scum and vomited it out, caught a glimpse of pale sky far up over the trees.

Then the Mere put its hand over his mouth and dragged him down.

3

THE FIDCHELL

Choking, kicking and struggling, Alick sank into blackness. But the hand held him; a thin, firm hand that heaved him up by his shirt, out of the sucking grip of the water, out into sudden wind and air and an explosion of roaring trees.

Luke dragged and shoved him to the bank. 'Get out,' he commanded. 'Hurry up.'

The birds and the horsemen were gone.

Confused, wet and gashed, Alick stumbled out on to the pine needles and slumped against a tree, gasping for breath in the bitter cold. The conjuror was waist-deep in the water; he had both arms under Jamie's shoulders and was half-dragging him to shore. Slowly they staggered out together and collapsed, breathless.

There was a moment of coughing and spitting and wiping of eyes.

Then Alick got his breath. 'We'd have drowned!' he yelled furiously.

'They wouldn't help . . . they just sat there!'

He pushed the wet hair out of his eyes and crouched down, shivering. The conjuror coughed, and the gold of his earring glinted. 'Who did?'

'The horsemen . . . those people . . . riders. And all those birds screaming at us . . .'

'Were they?' Luke looked at them both. 'Then you must have frightened them. Birds don't just scream at people.'

'Ordinary birds don't.' Jamie scraped green algae from his ears. 'These weren't ordinary. They were weird. Gosh, I'm frozen.'

He rubbed his face and arms furiously.

'It was as if they could think,' Alick said firmly. 'Not like birds at all. And who blew the horn? Who were those people?'

Luke stood up and tugged his wet shirt off, then picked up his coat from the floor and flung it on, shivering. Then he whistled. As the white dog came out from the trees, Alick said, 'You must have seen them.'

Luke did not answer. Angry now, Alick persisted. 'Jamie did.'

'Thought I did.'

'You know you did!'

Jamie laughed, despite the cold and the pain in his leg. 'Yes, all right. But I was too busy drowning.'

Alick turned to Luke. 'Did you see them?'

Luke shook his wet hair. 'I think you'd better come home with me. It's too cold to hang about.' And as if he had not heard, he hauled Jamie to his feet and started off with him through the wood.

Thoroughly annoyed, Alick trailed after them. They had seen those people, the horses, the strange gold colour of their clothes. What's more, Luke had seen them too. He must have. So what was going on?

Talley was a small woodman's cottage, among the trees on the north side of Tolbury Tump. It was quite isolated, and only a narrow, overgrown track led down to it from the main road. By the time they reached the house, they were all shaking uncontrollably with the cold, and Alick's clothes stuck to him, wet and stiff with the smelly algae. He was very relieved to see smoke rising from the chimney.

Luke lifted the latch and hurried them in. While they huddled numbly over the fire, he dragged out some dry logs and tossed them on, stirring the blaze up rapidly; then disappeared into the kitchen. A few minutes later he came back with a huge bowl of steaming water and some dark blue towels.

'Here. Get the worst off – and those wet clothes. I'll see if I've got anything you can wear.'

It was glorious to feel the hot water on their faces and bodies after the icy wind. They got as much of the green scum off as they could, then spread their clothes to dry and sat huddled up in towels next to the blaze. Jamie's ankle was swelling fast. He touched it, gingerly.

'Ouch.'

'Does it hurt?'

'Like hell. My throat is stinging too. I swallowed pints of that muck.'

'And me.' With the stinging of his hands and face, Alick had forgotten his annoyance. 'It'll be a wonder if we're not poisoned.'

'We'll catch something worse at home, anyway. Or I will.' Jamie sighed and wriggled his toes. 'I can just about feel my feet now. Funny sort of place this, isn't it?'

Alick nodded. It was a small, dark room with scraps of rug on the floor and bare rafters above. There was only one window, and the light that filtered in was dim and green from the trees outside. A dresser stood at one end; its shelves and drawers crammed with boxes and jars, dirty dishes, papers, shells, stones, books. Bunches of herbs hung from the ceiling; some were so crisp that their leaves had dropped off and lay crushed on the floor. The window-sill was jammed with dusty books, and muddy wellingtons and a spade leaned by the door. Around the walls hung branches of holly and mistletoe, and a white cat walked along the back of Jamie's chair. It was all rather untidy, but warm and comfortable. Alick liked it.

But Jamie had caught sight of something else. 'Alick,' he said. 'Look at that!'

On a table in the corner was a large black and gold chequered board, and on it was what seemed to be a chess set, but with bigger pieces than Alick had ever seen. And different. The black pieces were made of a dark stone. There were no pawns or bishops. Instead, as he noticed with a shock, there were three rows of hunched black birds with diamonds for eyes, each barb and feather accurately carved. Sightless, they glared at him.

The opposite pieces were the same size, but made

29

out of what seemed like gold, and they glistened with emeralds and rubies and bright enamels. On this side were knights on horseback, ladies, minstrels with harps of jasper. Each was different, frozen in movement, their shields and surcoats blazing with colour; before them a row of greyhounds, cats and twisting serpents. Even the falconer was there, with his hooded hawk.

Jamie whistled. 'It's Them! Just like in the wood. And they must be worth a *fortune*! Real gold, I'll bet . . .'

'They can't be.' Alick stood up, gathered his towel about him, and padded over to the table. He picked up one of the horsemen. 'Gosh, it's heavy though.' Thoughtfully he put it down, and picked up something else. 'I wonder what this is for?'

It was a piece that stood by itself in the middle of the board. A golden tree. Tiny leaves of metal hung from it, and made a quiet, tinkling noise as he raised it. The leaves nearest the gold army were gold, and those on the other side, nearest the black army of birds, were black. He turned it round, and gasped.

'What's up?' Jamie could only see his friend's back.

'Nothing.' Alick stood very still. How could he say what he had seen – that as he had turned the tree, the black leaves were now gold and the gold, black! Was it a trick of the light? No . . . there it was again. No matter how much you turned it round, the gold leaves were always by the gold pieces. 'Come and look at this,' he began, but a growl silenced him.

Luke's dog had come into the room. It growled again, teeth bared.

'Better put it down,' Jamie muttered.

Nervously, Alick's hand moved an inch towards the board. An explosion of barks nearly made him drop the piece.

'Tam! That's enough!'

The conjuror raced down the stairs, pushed the dog aside, then came and took the tree swiftly out of Alick's hand. His six fingers closed around it, tight.

He gave Alick a peculiar look. 'Like it, do you?'

'Yes . . . I was just looking . . .' Alick could feel himself going red. 'It's not chess, is it?'

'Fidchell,' the conjuror said, putting the tree gently back on its central square. 'A very old game. Not played much now.'

And then someone laughed.

Alick looked round, astonished. It hadn't been Luke, or Jamie. The room was dark; there was no one else in it but the dog, watching him with that same smirk it had had in the shop.

'What was that?' Jamie asked.

'Owls. You hear them all the time.' Luke tossed a bundle of clothes carelessly towards them. 'Here, try these. They'll be a bit big, but they're all I've got.'

While they were dressing and giggling at the rolled-up trousers and large shirts, he stood leaning against the table, watching them. Alick felt uneasy. Surely Luke didn't think he'd have stolen that tree?

31

And how were the pieces the same as those people . . . and the birds?

When they were dressed, Luke laughed at them, and strapped Jamie's ankle with a tight, white bandage and some stuff to stop it hurting. Then he gave them a hot drink that wasn't tea or coffee, but whatever it was it drove the cold right out, and Alick suddenly felt warm and glowing to his finger-ends.

While they were drinking it, Luke went out, and when he came back he said he had been down to the telephone box on the road and phoned Jamie's father. 'He'll be here in about five minutes.'

'Thanks. I'd never walk it.'

'Where's the dog?' Alick asked, glancing round.

'Outside.'

Alick was glad. He didn't like it. He kept thinking it was the thing that had laughed.

There was silence for a while. Alick stroked the cat. Jamie was moving his ankle, testing it. Alick noticed Luke's eyes move across the room, from door to stairs, as if he was watching someone cross the room. There was nothing there. Then, upstairs, a door slammed.

At the same time, the conjuror leaned forwards and poked the fire. 'Didn't I tell you yesterday not to go near the Mere?'

Alick was tongue-tied.

'It was my fault,' Jamie put in. 'I lost a reel. Still haven't found it either.'

Luke made no comment. Instead, he said, 'The Mere is a bad spot. There are places like that – places that have a bad effect on animals, and birds, even people. I suppose you do physics at school?'

They nodded.

'Well, there are physical causes for it,' Luke went on, staring into the fire. 'It may be something to do with magnetic forces in the earth. They affect people's nerves, make them ill, uneasy. The Chinese have a science called feng shui – it means they find out these places and then they keep away from them. I advise you to do the same.'

Something's going on, Alick thought. Something queer, that he doesn't want us to know about.

The fire made a row of strange shadows walk down the wall.

'But you live here,' Jamie objected.

'I do.' The conjuror gave him a look that wiped the grin off his face. 'But I'm different.'

Alick glanced at the hands holding the poker. He must have seen them, those riders and those birds – gold and black, like the Fidchell.

But the purr of a car up the track interrupted him. Luke got up abruptly and went to the door. 'It's your father, Jamie. Come on.'

4

THE HOLLOW HILL

When Alick walked into the bookshop ten minutes later, Mr Webster nearly fell off his stool with laughter. 'Where on earth did you get those clothes! Oxfam?'

Alick scowled. 'They're not mine. I fell . . . well, I got wet. In a stream. Your friend Luke lent me these.' And he hauled himself up on the counter and told his father about the strange riders, and the black birds, and Luke, but took care not to mention the Greenmere.

'Talley, eh? I've never been inside,' his father said curiously, filling his pipe. 'What's it like?'

'Scruffy. All right though. All sorts of odd things. That reminds me, how do you play Fidchell?'

'What?'

'Fidchell.'

'Never heard of it.'

'It's a game,' Alick explained. 'Like chess. Luke's got a set. Jamie thought some of the pieces were gold.'

'Gold!' Mr Webster snorted as he put the bolt across the door. 'Oh, I'm sure. I suppose you want a set for Christmas? Gold, my eye!'

While his father laughed and smoked and struggled with the accounts, Alick ran upstairs and changed. He put his wet clothes in the bottom of the basket in the bathroom, hoping his father wouldn't find them. Then he came downstairs and went along the 'Natural History' shelf until he found a good bird book. That was one advantage of living in a bookshop – you had your own library.

He looked up crows. The picture showed two black, rather scruffy birds, but they weren't right. But on the next page was a raven – big, hunched, with a beak like a nutcracker. That was it, ravens. Not crows. But according to the book they were very rare. It was odd. The whole business was odd.

He put it back and looked for something on Fidchell. It was that tree that had fascinated him: he couldn't forget the way the leaves had changed. But none of the books made any mention of the game at all, until finally, in a battered old encyclopaedia without a cover, 50p in the bargain box, he found this:

FIDCHELL (or WOODEN WISDOM)
A board game, probably similar to chess, consisting of two armies of men on a chequered board. Known to have been played by the Celts, this game is mentioned in several ancient texts, and is known to have had magical meaning. No known pieces have been found. The rules are nowhere recorded. Pronunciation: *Fee*-kell.

Puzzled, he asked, 'Dad, how long ago were the Celts?'

'Oh, hundreds of years,' his father said absently. 'Before the Romans. Now don't start reading down here. We're closing.'

Hundred of years. No pieces found. It didn't make sense. Even more puzzled, he put the book back in the box, then took it out.

'Can I keep this?'

'If you want. 50p.'

Jamie telephoned that night. 'My ankle's the size of a balloon,' he moaned. 'Stay off it till Christmas, the doctor says. *And* I'm having a bike! What's the use if I can't ride it?'

Alick laughed.

'Shut up, heartless. Listen, that Luke character is *weird*!'

'Well, I told you, didn't I!'

'Ah, but I still don't swallow all that about the warts. But those chess pieces, that was uncanny . . .'

Alick nodded. 'He saw them too . . . in the wood, whatever he said. I know he did.'

'Yes. And that means you'll have to find out what's afoot, my trusty sidekick.'

'Me?'

'Well, I can't, can I?' Jamie demanded. 'It's easy. Just watch him. Follow him. Use your brain.' He giggled, 'What there is of it.'

It was when he was crouched behind a tree outside Luke's cottage, and trying to edge his cramped feet

36

into an easier position, that Alick realized that finding things out was cold, uncomfortable and, up to now, boring.

He ate his last-but-one bit of chocolate, and counted the chimes from Halcombe church as they rang out over the tree-tops. Five o'clock. He'd been there an hour already. Around him the forest was dark and silent; far off in the trees, a patch of moonlight showed. And it was getting colder. He thought about his supper, hot in the oven.

Then, the light in Luke's window went out; a figure came down the path, opened the gate, and moved off among the trees. Alick slipped after him, without a sound. Whatever Luke knew, he would find it out.

The moon striped the wood black and silver like a great badger. Far down the path, Luke's figure glimmered across a patch of light and vanished into darkness again. There was no sign of the dog – which was just as well, Alick thought.

He tried to get a bit closer. It was hard to see in the dappled wood, and if Luke left the path he might miss him altogether. The conjuror was a flicker of movement ahead; he seemed to be heading straight for Tolbury Tump.

Once he was sure of this, Alick could concentrate on keeping quiet. He had cracked two twigs already, and once, Luke had looked back as if he had heard something. Flattened against a beech bole, fingers gripping the smooth cold sides, Alick watched the conjuror turn and walk on. He was more careful after that.

A few minutes later he had a shock. It was starting to snow. Tiny grains floated in the air like scraps of paper; his breath smoked as he walked. By the time they reached the bottom of the Tump and had begun to climb, there was a fine powder underfoot, crunching as he stepped on it. Luke went up the hill and Alick, back in the shadows, wondered why. The path was steeper now, twisting through tree-roots and old rabbit burrows. Finally, he came to the very edge of the trees and looked out.

The top of Tolbury Tump was a grey dome, gleaming faintly with snow. Under the precise silver ring of the moon, Luke was walking up the slope. He came to a small hollow in the hillside, where a few scrubby bushes clung out of the wind, and stopped. He looked around, cautiously. Then he turned aside and went down into the hollow.

There was a ditch along the wood's edge. Alick jumped down into it and squirmed along until he could see between the bushes. Snow swirled in his eyes. Between the flakes he saw Luke stoop. There was a noise. He listened, intently.

Tap. Tap. Tap.

The knock of stone on stone.

More snow. He wiped his eyes. What was Luke doing? And *what was that!*

It was light; bright and golden. As he stared, a great slot of light was swinging slowly open in the hillside, reddening his face and making the falling snow glitter like golden grains.

Then the conjuror stepped inside, and with a click the door was shut.

In the cold moonlight, Alick's breath made a slow cloud. He took the last piece of chocolate from his pocket and ate it, automatically, tasting nothing. Then he crinkled the silver paper. Ideas were flooding into his head. Tugging his feet out of the mud, he watched the moon as, agonizingly slowly, the cloud drifted over it. Now it was a dome, now a fingernail, now a faint line closing up at the edges. As soon as it was gone, he leapt up, ran up the slope and jumped into the hollow. Brambles whipped round him; the hole was full of thorns and scrubby rowan; a steep earth cliff overhung it. The snow was settling, but he groped round till he found a stone, and then crouched down by the one big grey boulder. Brushing the snow away he pulled a glove off and felt the surface: spirals and circles, old zig-zag lines. Then he raised the stone as Luke had done, and knocked.

Tap. Tap. Tap.

The light caught him before he could move; a dazzling slit, widening in the hollow, reddening rowan berries to globes of fire.

Crouching, he turned to face it.

Behind him a small door stood open in the hill-side; the light shone out of it. He saw a long tunnel. The walls gave out the light; they glimmered golden, and hundreds of thin, golden pinnacles and pillars upheld the roof. They were not smooth, but twisted and spindly like young trees. Their roots spread over the floor, and they even had stony branches – nets of fruit and leaves on the cavern roof. There was no sign of Luke. Far ahead the tunnel turned a corner.

Alick stood up, bit his lip, and stepped inside.

5

FIRST MOVE

He was standing in pitch darkness.

Alick swore in surprise; he hadn't even heard the door shut. Carefully he stretched out his hands into emptiness. Then he moved – and crack! his head hit something so hard, the tears jerked into his eyes.

'Damn!' he hissed, clutching his head in both hands. It was the ceiling. It felt cold and knobbly through his gloves. It shouldn't have been so low. Hurriedly, he felt in his pocket, found a box with three matches in, and struck one. Then, shielding the glow, he gazed around.

Slabs of grey stone, and a litter of bones and rubble on the floor. No sign of a door. There were spirals and squiggles carved on the rocks, like the boulder outside. Then the match scorched his fingers. He threw it down, bewildered. Where were the golden pillars? And where was Luke?

'Luke?' he whispered.

Echoes whispered back. He began to move, cautiously. It was difficult, shuffling a few inches at a time, trying not to make any noise on the loose stones, and keeping one hand on the clammy, invisible wall. As he went deeper into the hill it got colder, and the air grew earthy and unpleasant. Then he stopped.

He could hear voices.

They were low, and far ahead, but they were there.

He went on, carefully, and at each twist of the tunnel the murmuring grew louder, until it sounded like a few men talking quietly. One of them must be Luke. Then Alick realized he could see his hand, and the tunnel wall. And round the next bend the tunnel ended.

It was closed by a glimmering, golden curtain that fell to the floor. His hand reached out to it, and had almost touched it, when a sudden uproar of laughing and clapping froze him with terror, his heart thumping loudly and his hands clenched in his gloves.

But no one came through, and the talk went on. Music was playing too; low, subtle and strange, it drew him to the curtain – he could see a few blurred forms through it; the glow and crackle of a fire. He heard chairs being pushed back, and somewhere a door opening and closing. A smell of flowers, an impossible summery smell, wafted out.

Then there was silence.

He waited a few minutes, then carefully reached out and pulled a corner of the curtain aside.

A large hall lay before him, with a fire burning in its centre – the flames were sweet smelling and strangely smokeless. The walls were golden, the floor chequered with huge squares of black and gold, and the same pillars he had seen in the tunnel held

up the roof — their trunks twisted like ice, tinkling
with frosty fruits and leaves.

Alick stepped further into the hall. At the far end,
he saw three doors, all closed, and in front of them,
near the fire, were two chairs facing each other across
a small table. There was nothing else.

He padded across the cold floor, feeling snow drip
from his shoulders. The table had a board on it. The
Fidchell pieces stood there, gleaming gold and black
in the firelight.

He was beyond surprise; anything could happen
now. Carefully he picked up the tree and turned it.
Just as he'd thought — the leaves changed colour. It
was inexplicable . . . magical.

Suddenly he noticed something lying on the floor
by one of the chairs. It was a fruit, like a cherry, but
pure white. He picked it up and smelled it; felt its
soft juiciness under his fingers, imagined its sweetness. The next minute he had eaten it.

He knew at once it was a mistake. There was no
delicious taste, it was just like water in his mouth —
rather sour water too. It made him feel sick. The
room looked different, shadowy, in the corners, and
he felt dizzy, like the time he had drunk a whole
tumbler of his father's port. And there must be something wrong with his eyes, because the Fidchell
pieces had all turned their heads and were looking
at him; the knights amused, the ladies laughing, the
dogs and horses shifting, the black birds in ominous
silence. He backed towards the curtain, watching
one raven unfurl its wings and stare.

The curtain was a rag of cobweb. He tore it down and plunged into the tunnel, banging and bumping himself in the darkness as the noise rang around him; laughter, low and mocking, cat-calls, whistles, the beat of wings. He ran so fast and so carelessly that he had crashed into the smooth surface of the door before he realized, and it swung open without a sound, spilling him out into the bitter cold of the hollow. Breathless, he crouched, and looked back.

In the distance, down the tunnel, shadows moved. Black, golden, they flickered towards him. He flung himself on the door and heaved, but it stayed open, unmoving – the golden light bathing the rowan bushes – and when the first horn rang faintly in the distance, he turned and fled, leaving it wide.

He crashed to the lip of the hollow, took a deep breath, and let it out in amazement. He had forgotten the snow! The hillside was a white sheet; the air full of flying patches that muffled the moon. Reckless, he jumped knee-deep into the drifts and struggled for the wood.

Noise pursuing him, he raced along the path, coughing and spluttering. Snow stuck to his hair and eyelashes, branches tripped him; he was sure that his noisy crashing run could be heard for miles. And perhaps he was half a mile down the path before he realized what he had in his hand.

Small and enigmatic, the tree from the Fidchell board shimmered and tinkled. Without stopping, he stared at it, taking in the truth. What an idiot he was! But it was too late to worry about that now. He shoved it into the pocket of his coat, and ran all the faster.

Even so, after ten more minutes he had to slow down, clutching his aching side. He was so breathless and dizzy he hardly recognized where he was before the earth fell away suddenly in front of his feet, and below him the Combe lay silent and leaf-littered in the moonlight.

He slipped and slid and slithered to the bottom. Only then, when the sudden silence fell, did he look up. High overhead, crowding among the trees, a host of shapes gazed down at him. He saw glints of metal and gold; horses and men. And in the branches, the birds.

He said nothing. The horses clinked their harnesses; the rows of eyes did not move from him. Both sides were there, and he knew they wanted that tree. That damned tree.

It was about a mile to the village – it might just as well be ten, he thought, bitterly. He tried a step forward and nothing happened. He took another, then yelled in fright and leapt back.

The spear quivered in the leaves by his foot. There was no sign who had thrown it; the dark ranks were silent and unmoving.

Alick rolled his hands into fists. 'Listen!' he shouted, and then stopped, ears catching that new, deep purr behind him. A car!

But the listeners had heard it, too. With a cry and a hiss the thin sinuous shapes of hounds and serpents poured over the lip of the hollow. Alick turned and raced along the lane, waving and shouting as the humming in the air grew. Something grabbed his coat, wrapping round his ankle; in a flurry of leaves he fought and kicked and struggled.

'Alick? Alick Webster?'

Bewildered, he opened his eyes. Snowflakes swirled in the glare of two large headlamps. Someone was leaning out of the car.

'It is you, isn't it? Have you hurt yourself?'

'Er, no. Thanks.' Alick climbed stiffly to his feet and glanced around. The Combe was empty.

'Going home? Hop in then.'

The passenger door jerked open, and Alick slid hastily in and slammed it tight. The warmth of the car, its smell of tobacco and leather, wrapped him like a blanket. The driver switched on the light.

'Hello, Vicar.'

'You're a bit wet,' the vicar remarked, releasing the brake. Alick realized that water was dripping all over the seat.

'Sorry. It's snow.'

'That's all right. Just take your coat off and put it in the back. On top of that big box will do. It's just stuff for decorating the church. That's better.'

It was. Alick felt the warmth prickle his hands and cheeks. The snow had soaked his trousers though, and the tips of his ears ached.

The car droned up the Combe in a flurry of snow. He gazed out of the window, but only saw himself and some flying branches.

'Coming to the Carol Service?'

'Yes . . . probably.'

'Good, good. That's what all those boxes are for, to decorate the little chapel at Ashton Bailey – it'll be there this year as usual – though the place is so old and damp, I wonder how the Lord keeps it up. You've seen the old tombs there? Mind if I drop you here?'

Alick nodded. The street lamps were on in Halcombe, and the bookshop window was bright with red and gold. As they pulled in, the vicar asked, 'How's the coin collection?'

'Oh fine, thanks.'

'You don't want any old halfpennies, do you?'

Alick shrugged. 'If you've got any rare ones . . .'

'Oh, I don't know the dates,' the vicar laughed, fishing Alick's coat out of a box. 'Just found a bag of them in a cupboard. Come and get them sometime. You never know, they might be worth something.'

The light was on over the bookshop. As Alick waited for his father to open the door, he wondered what time it was. And he was half-way up the stairs when he realized the pockets of his coat were empty. He had lost the little tree.

6

INQUISITION

'Six ninety-five, please.' Alick pushed the book across the counter and then dropped the money in the till.

'Merry Christmas,' the woman said cheerfully.

Then the shop was empty, the first time that morning. He went over and poked the fire, and fetched more coal. Then he noticed one of the decorations had fallen down, and pinned it up with a drawing pin still bent from last year. Still no customers. He went to the window.

Halcombe High Street was full of shoppers slipping on the snow. Outside most shops it had been scraped away, but some still lay outside the houses and the empty shop, trodden down flat like dirty marzipan. A lorry was gritting the road, and the butcher was putting up a sash saying 'We wish all our Customers the Compliments of the Season.' Alick was wondering what they were, when the shop door opened with a loud jangle and Luke Ferris walked in, glanced around, and flipped the sign over to say 'Closed' in one deft movement.

'Hey! You can't do that!'

'Can't I!' The conjuror's eyes were black and he

did not smile. The dog padded to the fire. Luke
followed it and warmed his hands.

'Was it you?'

Alick was nervous. 'Was what me?'

'You know very well.'

Alick reddened. 'The shop's open,' he stammered,
going to the door and changing the sign. 'Do you
want to buy something?'

Luke drew himself up and leaned on the mantelpiece. But just then a young woman with a baby
came in and asked Alick for books on Italian cookery.
He tried to be polite, showing her the shelf and
taking out books, and all the time watching the
conjuror from the corner of his eye. Luke did not
seem to move, but after a few minutes something
changed in the shop. It was mustier, dimmer. Alick
counted the girl's change for the third time – the
coins seeming to multiply and slither from his suddenly clumsy hands. She smiled, gave him back a
pound, and went to the door. The cold draught
swirled the strange blue sparks in the fire to a glittering fountain. It was hard to breathe. He leaned
on the counter, sleepily.

After a moment, Luke went to the door, locked
it, turned the sign, and pulled the blind down on
the window. Then he pushed Alick into a chair.

'Can you hear me?' he asked coldly.

Alick nodded. The voice came from a dark blur
standing over him.

'Tell me how you got into the hill.'

'. . . I . . . followed you,' he mumbled.

'Me!' Luke crouched down and clutched the chair arm. 'Last night?'

Somebody tried the door handle. Luke ignored it.

'What did you see?'

Alick didn't answer.

'Tell me!'

'Chairs. A table. A game like yours. And three doors.'

'Did you open any of the doors?' the voice asked softly.

'No.'

'But you took the tree, didn't you?'

Alick nodded, miserable. It was easier to breathe now. His sight was clearing. 'I didn't mean to. I didn't know till later. I suppose I got scared; starting to think those . . . things were after me.'

Luke was watching him carefully. 'So you ate something too. You've been very stupid, Alick. It's a long time since the Fidchell was played. And it's no game.' He drummed his fingers on the table. 'Go and get the tree. We might still have time.'

Alick felt sick. 'I've lost it,' he said.

Luke was silent for at least a minute.

Suddenly scared, Alick tried to explain. 'It might have been in the Combe . . . or in the vicar's car – it must have fallen out of my pocket. Is it . . . that important?'

Luke laughed, harshly. 'Important!' For a moment he seemed lost for words. Then he straightened. 'Alick, by taking the tree you've started the game. Both armies – the Black and the Gold – will be after it, anywhere, wherever it is. They'll spill out into the wood, into the villages, searching, hunting, letting nothing stand in their way.' He stared at the fire. 'Last time it happened here was in 1561.'

'The Black Winter?'

Luke nodded. 'Blizzards, famine, trees falling, unexplained migrations of animals, flooding. Fires, that started for no reason. Dead men, found in ditches. Portents and strange signs in the sky. That's the Fidchell, Alick. And now you've started it again.'

For a moment they were both silent. Then Luke sighed, rummaged in his pockets and brought out a small wax candle, pale green and about an inch high. 'We must find it, that's all. Have you got a mirror?'

'Upstairs.'

'Get it. Tam, go with him.'

The white dog raced up the stairs before Alick. Then it went into the bathroom, jumped on to the bath, and stared into his father's shaving mirror.

'Get down!' Alick snapped – then stared. For a moment he had seen a different face in the glass. A pale, thin, laughing, dangerous face. Then it was just the dog, ears pricked.

He took the mirror downstairs, thoughtfully.

'Your dog's one of them, isn't he?'

Luke laughed. 'What dog?'

A small white cat lay by the fire, washing.

Luke lit the candle and put it in the middle of the mirror. It had an unpleasant smell.

'This may help us,' Luke said. 'Don't speak, and don't touch the mirror.' Then, muttering something, he picked up the candle and poured the hot wax on to the glass.

The small pool was almost white; faint smoke came from it. Alick expected it to go hard, but it didn't. Bubbling and hissing, the film spread. Then he saw things come into it. First, dark, meaningless quivers, then a house, a tree, moonlight glinting on some water. Luke was staring at it, waiting.

Suddenly, the picture changed. Faint and grey as a cobweb, he saw a stone figure of a man, lying on its back. The man's legs were crossed at the ankles. His face was covered in dust. A spider ran over his chest, and a dead leaf gusted by. Then the wax was white and cold and smooth.

'It looked like a tomb.'

'Yes,' Luke said quietly. 'And I think I know where.'

The doorhandle rattled. A loud knocking startled them.

'Alick! Open up!'

'It's my father,' Alick said, but Luke pushed him back. 'Wait. Be at my house this afternoon. Two o'clock. Right?'

Alick nodded. 'Yes, but . . .'

The letterbox rattled. 'Alick!'

'Just be there,' Luke went on, shoving the candle into his pocket. 'We've got to sort this thing out.'

'ALICK!'

'Coming!' he yelled, opening the door. Cold bright air struck his face.

'Give us a hand, then.' Mr Webster began to tug

in a few heavy boxes. 'It's damn cold out here!' He stalked to the fire. 'And the shop shouldn't be shut yet, and it's as smoky as . . . Oh, hello, Luke.'

'Tom,' said the conjuror, thrusting his hands in his pockets.

'Tam Lin, too.'

'Yes, we just dropped in.'

'His warts haven't come back, you know.'

'They won't.' Luke called the dog and went to the door. 'Merry Christmas to you both.' And with a meaningful glance at Alick, he went out and walked swiftly up the snowy street.

Alick watched him go. 'He's a daunting sort of person, isn't he? Always seems to know much more than you do.'

'Very,' said Mr Webster. 'Alick, isn't this my shaving mirror? And what's this muck all over it?'

7

THE HOSTING

At ten to twelve, Jamie phoned.

'Listen, Sunshine,' said the testy voice, 'how about visiting a poor invalid? I still exist you know. It's not the Black Death.'

Alick grinned. 'How's the foot?'

'Sore. Why didn't your magician friend give me some magical cure?'

'Perhaps he thought you deserved it.'

'Found anything out?'

Alick thought about it. 'Not really,' he said. 'And if I do, I'll tell you.' He knew just how much Jamie would believe of all this. Nothing.

'That reminds me,' Jamie said. 'Those birds were ravens. Did you hear it on the radio?'

'No. What?'

'About the ravens. A bird-watching chap was talking about them. All sorts of reports they'd had, of these huge black birds. Ouch, my cat's walking on my leg!'

Alick laughed, and promised to go over the next day – Christmas Eve. Then he went thoughtfully back into the sitting-room.

His father was sitting by the fire. Large boxes of

books were piled by his feet; he was writing prices on the front pages.

'1878,' he remarked. 'First Edition. Very good. Might get fifteen pounds for that. Your dinner's hot, and I got you one of those ghastly sticky things you like, from Thomas's.'

'Good.' Alick sat at the table, picked up his fork and switched the radio on.

'Today has seen the worst blizzard conditions in the west of England for sixteen years,' said a woman's voice briskly. 'Four feet of snow fell overnight in some parts. Roads in the Mendips and Cotswolds are impassable, and helicopters from nearby RAF Arlington have been dropping supplies and fodder to outlying farms . . .'

'Oh, very nice,' Mr Webster muttered. 'Look, Alick, if it's too bad for me to get back tonight, lock up and go to Jamie's, all right?'

Alick nodded. He had forgotten his father was going to the book fair.

'And finally, on a lighter note,' the announcer continued, 'at Halcombe Great Wood, in Gloucestershire, several curious phenomena have been reported. Flocks of large, unidentified birds have invaded farmers' fields, and residents claim to have seen packs of spectral hounds and riders streaming across the sky.'

'Ha!' Mr Webster grinned. 'After closing time!'

Alick said nothing. It's all starting, he thought. He felt rather cold.

'Oh, I saw 'em all right,' said a loud local voice.

'Great white cloudy things, like dogs, like, and horses. Tops of the trees all cracking under them. Streaming down from the Tump they were, and the whole of the wood shaking, and full of wind, and noise . . .'

Mr Webster stared at the radio. 'Sounds like Jacky Harris. I thought he was teetotal.' He poked the fire. 'Well, well. Seen any spectral hounds, Alick?'

'I thought I saw one,' Alick said thoughtfully. 'In your shaving mirror.'

On the way to Luke's he had to pass the vicarage, and on a sudden impulse he knocked at the door. He could have dropped the tree in the car; it would be easy enough to find out.

The door opened with a jerk; the housekeeper glared out. When she saw Alick, her frown cleared. 'Oh, sorry, love. We've had a few queer callers round here this morning.'

She left him in a big room with lots of bookshelves and potted plants. A clock ticked in one corner. Alick sat on the edge of the settee and twisted his scarf, nervously. Out in the snowy graveyard a black bird landed on a tombstone. He looked at it suspiciously. Was it one of *Them?*

The door opened.

'Alick!' the vicar said, dumping a pile of books on the piano. 'I thought it might be you. Now let me see, where did I put it . . .'

For a glorious moment, Alick thought he meant

the tree, but the vicar dumped a small plastic bag on to the table. Coins spilled and rattled and rolled.

'There. Anything interesting?'

Alick swallowed his disappointment and sorted through the coins. 'The Maunday sixpence is nice – early, and almost mint, too. Most of the halfpennies I've got . . . um, and halfcrowns. None of it's worth much, I'm afraid.'

'Never mind,' said the vicar. He smiled nostalgically as Alick gathered up the coins. 'Used to collect moths myself, at one time. Had to stop though; takes up too much room – all those cabinets and boxes. Display yours, do you?'

Alick nodded. 'I've got a room upstairs.'

'Ah! Big old house.'

Alick buttoned his coat slowly. 'Um, there was one thing I wanted to ask. I think I may have dropped something in your car. A little tree . . . a piece from a game.'

'Tree? Can't say I've seen it. Come on, we'll go and look.'

The car door was open. The vicar stared at it. 'Damn it! I locked that . . . someone's been in here.'

Hurriedly, he checked his car radio and glove box. 'Nothing gone though. You look for your tree, and I'll go back and ask Mrs Hughes . . .' Still talking, he went back up the drive. Alick dived into the car and scrabbled under the seats, then ran his hand down gaps and crannies. Nothing. Nothing but a few golden hairs, strangely stiff and bright. He was wondering about them when the vicar came back.

'She didn't open it. Says there've been people hanging about the place though. Strangers. Still, no harm. Did you find it?'

'No.'

'It may have fallen in the boxes.' The vicar closed the door. 'I've taken them over to Ashton Bailey chapel. You're welcome to look.'

Ashton Bailey. Famous for its tombs. Stone knights, crusaders. Like the picture in Luke's mirror. 'Thanks,' Alick said, starting up the drive. 'I will.'

Twenty minutes later he was standing in Luke's house.

'They've moved!'

Luke nodded, both hands leaning on the corners of the table. On the Fidchell board the pieces were scattered, black and gold, in a confused huddle. Some had fallen over. Alick wanted to pick them up, but Luke warned him not to touch them. He was studying their positions carefully.

'I should say,' he murmured, 'that they've got the scent. See how they are gathering together?'

'You talk as if they move themselves.'

'And so they do. Not that you ever see it, however long you look. See what I mean.' He pointed to a golden knight. Alick blinked. A minute ago it had been on the other side of the board.

'So . . . who decides the moves?'

'They do. There are two players,' Luke said, 'but they can only watch. That's their fate. The game cannot be stopped till one side or other gets the tree,

58

or . . .' he put his thin extra finger on the empty square in the centre of the board, ' . . . or we put it back here. Then the board will be balanced.'

'Your tree has gone, too.'

'There is only one tree.'

Alick frowned over that. 'But I saw two. One here and one on the other board.'

Luke shrugged. 'You may have. But there is only one, and that is the one you took. This board,' he waved a hand at it, 'and the other two like it, merely show us what happens. The board in the hill is, if you like, the master board, the real game.'

'So there are two others?'

'Only three left in the world; each guarded.'

'By whom?'

Luke smiled slowly. 'And wouldn't you like to know! By others like me, those that are half of one world and half of another.' He looked closely at Alick. 'You must have guessed?'

Alick shrugged. 'I suppose so. You mean . . .' he struggled for words, 'you're related to Them?'

The conjuror grinned. 'Sort of. We have strange blood in our family. But we must get on.' He went to a drawer in the dresser and pulled out a small round box, like the one the ointment had been in. He threw it to Alick. 'Here. This is only for emergencies. Don't open it unless you absolutely can't do anything else. I'll have this.' He put a thin wand of peeled hazel in his pocket. 'I've been working on it all night. It will have the power to scatter Them over the board, and they'll take time to regroup. It may help.'

Alick pocketed the box and watched the conjuror wind a scarf round his neck. Then he said, 'I've been to the vicar's. The tree isn't there, but I found these.'

Luke took the hairs and held them up to the light. 'Well. This means they're ahead of us.'

'It's at Ashton Bailey, isn't it?'

Luke nodded. 'Now don't say too much when we get outside. The wood is full of movement; we're bound to be watched.'

Rather unhappily, Alick followed him out into the snow, the slam of the door echoing ominously in his ears. They took a short cut through a thick larch plantation that would bring them out on to the main road beyond the village. It took only ten minutes steady walking for Alick to feel uneasy. He glanced around.

'Oh, they're here all right,' Luke muttered. 'Since we left the house.'

Alick couldn't see anything, but he believed it. They began to hurry. The going was wet and difficult, the path sometimes clear and sometimes blocked by drifts as high as Alick's knees. And it got dark. The darkness closed in – it seemed to ooze out of the trees, so thick that it seemed Luke was forcing his way through a black, solid resistance. The branches creaked and swished, invisible above their heads.

The feeling of oppression, of hidden watchers, was getting on Alick's nerves. 'How far to the Cross?'

'About ten minutes.' Luke sounded worried. 'I

didn't think they'd start so soon. Keep close, and don't look behind you. *Don't!* Understand?'

He nodded. But from the corners of his eyes he could already see the shadows moving with them, just out of sight, like reflections that move and flicker in a grimy mirror. And then he began to feel it – the soft touching on his shoulders, a light tapping, something brushing his hair, soft and cold and clinking. He was shivering and couldn't stop.

'Luke . . .'

The conjuror stopped, clenched his fists, then turned around. He looked straight over Alick's shoulder, staring at whatever was there, calmly. At once Alick felt the coldness loosen from his neck. Something backed away.

'Further,' Luke said.

A rustle.

'Get in front of me, Alick,' Luke said quietly, and he obeyed, keeping his eyes firmly ahead.

It was an incredible relief to have Luke behind him, but as they went on, the snow splashed in his face, and he didn't know the path. Luke muttered instructions, but Alick kept his eyes ahead. Finally, the trees ended. They stepped out on to the road at Halcombe Cross.

Gaunt, misshapen, the finger of stone marked the heart of the wood. It was old, it had been a trysting-place, a market, a gallows, but the original purpose was long forgotten. Strange marks and carvings adorned it; a rough cross, and under that, pagan rings and spirals and letters from forgotten alphabets.

Alick leaned on it, breathing hard.

'Don't stop,' Luke warned.

The roads were deserted, already thick with snow. On the modern fingerpost a bird was perched, black and silent.

'Come on!' Grabbing his elbow the conjuror strode with him roughly down the road towards Ashton. Alick gasped for breath, but Luke would not slow down, and he constantly glanced over his shoulder.

And then Alick knew why. The certainty came in the silence and tension of the forest. A great host was moving after them down the white road; a crowd of shapes, creaking, and rustling and padding. Their shadows, long and black, stretched out before him. Fingers touched him again, icy coldness closing at his neck.

Suddenly, Luke shoved him ahead and whirled round on his enemies. Surprised, Alick stumbled and fell his length in the wet snow, and at once the road was aflame with an astounding brilliance and a rumbling and roaring that rang in the trees around him. He jerked his head.

Two huge white eyes roared through a torn mist. Luke stood before them, his figure small and dark, half lost in the eerie swirling smoke and the dark bulk screeching down on him.

Then the lorry swerved. With a scream of brakes it careered past them down the road and slithered to a stop.

The cab door was flung open and a head poked out. '*What* the 'ell do you think you're doing, mate?'

Luke grabbed Alick's arm and hauled him towards the lorry. Mist snaked after them.

'You drunk or something?' the driver asked, seeing them loom up in the dimness.

'No. Listen, can you give us a lift along the road? To Ashton?'

The man laughed. 'It's barely five minutes walk!'

'I know. Will you?'

'Oh, all right. Get in round the other side.'

As he climbed up the step, Alick glanced back. Something misty hung there, hardly visible. In the cab the radio was playing loudly. The driver whistled the tune cheerfully through his teeth. With a great hiss and shudder the lorry started. He changed gear noisily.

'Could've been killed, in the road like that!' he yelled above the music. 'Snow, patchy fog. Dangerous!'

Luke nodded. His face was pale; his fingers deep in pockets.

The lorry dropped them half a mile further on. When it had roared away, Alick looked at the conjuror.

'Are you all right?'

'Quite.' Luke climbed the fence. 'But we'll have to take more care. I can see how they're moving. With me out of the way, you'd be on your own, and easy prey for them.'

Alick didn't like the thought of that at all.

8

ASHTON BAILEY

Along the road ran a metal fence, old-fashioned and bent. Luke jumped over and began to push through the undergrowth. Alick followed, getting snow flicked all over him from the springy branches. Soon they stepped out on to a track, very straight, running into dimness. The trees above were thick and black, and withered grass poked up between frozen puddles.

'Gloomy,' Alick muttered.

Luke crossed the track and tugged ivy from what seemed to be a rock. Half smothered in the leaves was a standing stone.

'There's another,' Alick pointed ahead. 'And one over there. It's an avenue.'

'It is. This will help them; it's their sort of place.'

The weight of oppression, of being watched, had lifted from Alick. He felt careless of danger.

'Feng shui,' he said suddenly.

Luke laughed. 'Yes. A lot of good trying to tell you that, though. You and your sceptical friend!'

'Oh, Jamie's all right.' He stopped, struck by a thought. 'You made his leg worse, didn't you? On purpose!'

Luke had the grace to look confused. 'Well, a bit. Not much, though. I wanted him out of the way. Stupid of me, but I thought he might be the one to go poking his nose into things. How wrong can you get.'

Alick thought about that for a while. Then he said, 'I've always thought . . . the wood has more in it, than you can see. It's a special place.'

'It's Their place, Alick. The wood is a web of danger. We're just trespassers.'

'Like that man who drowned?'

Luke sighed, and was silent. Ice splintered under their feet. Then he said, 'I was too late that day.'

As they walked on, it grew darker. Waxy laurels sprouted on each side, their berries black and poisonous. The ditch stank of fungi and stagnation. Alick pulled the scarf over his nose in disgust, and then noticed the small square tower ahead.

'There's one thing in our favour,' Luke said, blowing on his cold fingers. 'The church.'

The gate clanged noisily behind them. Alick followed the conjuror up the path and stood close behind as Luke turned the great round handle. The door rumbled, and swung slowly open.

The chapel was quiet and empty. Bunches of fresh holly and mistletoe were piled in the middle of the floor, and next to them three large boxes that Alick recognized from the vicar's car. There were no benches; the church was derelict, and only used for the candlelight carol service on Christmas Eve – a tradition that went back to medieval times. It was bitterly cold. The famous tombs, with their figures of knights and ladies, lay under a coating of frost.

Luke went in, snow swirling behind him. 'Come on.'

He tipped the contents of the first box out, and began sifting through them. Echoes ran around the walls. Alick opened the next. Candles, hymn-books, hassocks and papers, jammed together, damp to the touch. It was as he tugged a sheaf of papers out that he heard it, the tiny, melodious tinkle.

'It's here!' He groped about at the bottom. Then, with a laugh that rang in the roof, grasped the edge of a stone tomb and hauled himself to his feet, the gold and black tree glittering in his hand.

Luke sat back on his heels. He looked relieved.

Then Alick gasped, jerked his head. The stone hand of the knight on the tomb had closed around his wrist.

'Luke!'

'Be quiet!' The conjuror was already there. The knight lay on its slab, eyes closed. It was stone. Its hands were stone. This was impossible.

'It's holding me! I can't get out!'

'Quiet!' Feverishly the conjuror searched his pockets. Then suddenly he turned around.

'What's the matter?'

Luke ignored him. 'Show yourselves!' he said to the empty chapel. Nothing seemed different. But now there was a shadow outside the windows; a mass of shadows.

Luke took a step forward. He had the hazel wand

in his hand. 'There's been a mistake,' he said quietly.
'You should go back. The game is over.'

'The game is just begun.'

Alick jumped. The whisper had come echoing
round the walls.

'No.' Luke's eyes travelled round the room, as if
he saw things Alick could not.

'Friend, it begins here.'

A rustle in the corner. Alick twisted, shouted, the
door slammed open. In a whirlwind of dust and
leaves, a cascade of black and gold shapes arched
over them, hung, crashed down.

'Luke!' Alick squirmed in the stone grip. Stones
and leaves fell on him, stuck to his hands and face,
knocked him to his knees. Arms over head he clung
to the effigy, handcuffed in stone, under the uproar
of wind and dust. Luke reeled backwards – was
slammed to the floor – but as he fell he raised the
wand and swept it before him. Vivid white sparks
stung Alick's eyes.

It ended as quickly as it had begun.

When he was ready, Alick uncovered his face.
Dust and dead leaves coated the floor, and rose in
clouds from his clothes. Luke was lying by an over-
turned box.

'Luke!'

The conjuror was still, crooked. Alick knew he
would not answer. Fiercely he tugged at the stone
hand. 'Let me go, damn it!' The tree was in his
pocket. What if they came back for it now? But no.
He had time.

Then he saw the white rod. Luke must have dropped it – it lay on the floor nearby. However he stretched, his hand couldn't reach it . . . but perhaps with his foot?

He pushed himself as far out from the tomb as he could, stretched towards the stick. Inch by inch his foot strained for it; cramps attacked his toes, the stone grip seared his skin. Another inch – and he touched. Would it roll away? Painfully, he rolled the wand, dragged it, scooped it in, until it was close enough to pick up.

A peeled hazel stick, white and thin. Now he had got it, he didn't know what to do with it. How did it work? He touched the stone glove with one end. Nothing happened. Tugging was no use; his wrist was sore and bleeding from that. A stone. Get a stone and smash it. Putting the stick in his trapped hand he bent down to fumble for a broken tile – and fell over! It had let him go! Or rather, he thought, rubbing his aching wrist, he had gone through it as if it was sand.

He turned to Luke. The conjuror's eyes were closed, his forehead lay on the stone floor. He was cold, and shaking his shoulder had no result. Alick bit his lip. His fingers felt the conjuror's pulse. He didn't even know if it was fast or slow. That first aid class, he thought. Sat at the back and talked. What a fool.

He would have to go for help. Cautiously, he went to the door. Outside it was snowing again. The wood was a web of white driven flakes. He was on his own. They'd got what They wanted.

Alick went back. 'Please, Luke! Wake up!' No use. He didn't seem hurt, perhaps it was some sort of spell. Finally, Alick found a pencil and a scrap of paper, wrote 'Gone for help' and pushed it under the conjuror's cold fingers.

When he turned, the white dog was sitting in the doorway. It padded softly past him and sat down, then looked at him.

'Tell him I've gone on,' Alick said suddenly. The dog lay down, chin on paws. He felt stupid, and yet . . . 'I'll take care of the tree. Look after Luke.' Then he marched out into the snow, pulling the door behind him. After about ten steps, he remembered that the hazel twig was still in his pocket. Should he leave it? No. After all, They were probably still about.

Plunging hands in pockets, he began to plough up the long avenue. Gloom seeped into him with the cold and the wet. What a mess. Where was he to go? What should he do? Ahead, the standing stones began, a tall one loomed at the side of the track and a shorter one leaned opposite it. Among the flung blurs of snow, their edges seemed like faces, hook-nosed, gaunt. After a moment's consideration, Alick stepped off the track and plunged into the wood.

9

THE OAK TREE

He had once been a Boy Scout for two years – he knew all about compasses and guiding yourself by the stars and blazing your trail. Despite that, in ten minutes he was totally lost. Everything was black and white, straight trees and flying snow; the sky, when he glimpsed it, a horrible dead yellow. The blizzard was almost horizontal, blinding him, soaking the front of his clothes and numbing his face and hands. He had tried to cut marks in the trees with his latchkey, but it was useless. Stumbling, he struggled on. If he kept this way he was sure to get back to the road, sure to.

The snow lay in humps and hollows; often he sank knee-deep in drifts. Blackthorn and bramble spread nets to tangle him. At one point the snow suddenly collapsed. He found himself gasping ankle-deep in an ice cold stream, and as he jerked his hands out of his pockets to balance himself, the white stick fell out and into the water. Wordless, he watched it float swiftly away.

On the bank he wrung out his socks, stamped about to get his feet warm, and put the tree in his shirt pocket inside his pullover. As he moved it, the tiny leaves tinkled, and he closed his hand over it quickly. For a second he had sensed the wood listening. The sudden silence was enormous. All around him, nothing for miles and miles but the trees, their humps and hollows, their boughs and boles and branches. He was all alone in it, and small.

It was then he heard the bang. Not very far ahead. Familiar. Normal. It took him a second to pin it down. A car door, slamming. After a second's astonishment he shouldered through the snowy bushes to his right and almost fell out on to a narrow gravel track. There in front of him, solid stone and with a warm comfortable light in its windows, was the last thing he had ever expected to see – a pub.

Where on earth was he?

Puzzled, he limped through the car park and stopped under the sign.

It creaked and swung under its coating of ice. The Oak Tree. He really must be lost. Still, he thought thankfully, they're bound to have a telephone or something.

He made his way round to the front and peered in through the window, rubbing snow from the glass. There were only about nine or ten people inside, most at the bar or sitting down, two playing darts. Boldly, he pushed the door open and went in.

The smell of beer and cigarettes struck him, and the drowsy, airless warmth of a hot room. Heads turned. He felt suddenly small, and wet and scruffy.

'Well! What happened to you!' The barmaid laughed and put down her cloth.

Alick felt the snow slide off his boots. 'I'm sorry,' he muttered.

'*And* you're under age.' She winked at a man at the bar.

'I haven't come in for a drink.'

The customers chortled. 'Don't mind her, son,' one of them said. 'She's just kidding you.'

Alick smiled, uncomfortably. He went up to the bar, hoping they'd stop staring at him and carry on their talk.

'How far am I from Halcombe?' he asked quietly.

'About four miles.'

He groaned, silently. 'Have you got a phone?'

'I'm sorry, my love,' the barmaid said. 'It's out of order. Snow, I expect. We're waiting for the engineer.'

He might have known. Nothing was going right – perhaps 'They' had even pulled the lines down. He had hoped to get help for Luke, but now he saw he was on his own.

He must have looked as dejected as he felt.

'Come over and sit by the fire, love,' the girl was saying. 'You're wet through. Take your coat off and have a nice hot cup of tea.'

He shouldn't stop; he ought not to waste time. And yet ... After a second's hesitation, he pulled off his gloves and undid the wet thongs of his duffel coat. He needn't stay long; just to get warm.

He gave her the coat and wandered across the room to the fire. There was a comfortable armchair next to it, but he did not sit down. Better not get too cosy. As he warmed his face and hands, he thought hard. Luke had said the tree had to go back on the board – presumably that meant to Tolbury Tump. He must be six miles or more from there. In the snow and growing darkness, it would take him hours – even if he got to the road it would be choked with snow-drifts by now. Traffic must have all but stopped. Well, at least that meant his father would have to stay in Gloucester . . . if only he didn't phone Jamie's house!

Alick sighed. He would have to walk to the Tump – there was no other way. He was beginning to wish he had stayed with Luke.

The fireplace was wooden, carved with old twisting snakes and stems. Above it, a large mirror reflected the room. He looked up at it. The barmaid was hanging up his coat on a peg by the door. And as he watched he was sure he saw her hand slip out of his pocket. She hung the coat up, and went into the kitchen.

Despite the fire, he felt cold. The tree, small and hard, was in his shirt pocket; he could feel it against his chest. Was that what she was looking for?

Some of the customers were looking at him; two men at the bar. They had hard, black eyes, and high, hooked noses; somehow familiar. They leaned easily on the bar, but did not drink. They pretended to talk, but their eyes were on him. The hairs on the back of his hands bristled with tension. He knew now. 'They' were here! He wasn't certain how many, but they were here all right; watching.

A few more men came in, laughing, and went to the bar. Some dogs slipped in behind them. If the roads were blocked, how did they all get out here? Sixteen, seventeen now. Was it all of them? The fire crackled cheerfully. Steam rose from his damp knees.

'Now then, how about some tea?'

The barmaid was at his elbow, with a tray. On it was a large mug of steaming liquid and a plate of cakes – small sponge cakes with buttery icing.

'How much will it cost?'

'Oh, never mind that,' she said. 'Go and sit down . . . sit in that armchair there by the fire.' She nodded at the big chair with its soft, enticing cushions. He sighed, thought, Why not? and was about to step towards it when he glanced in the mirror.

Every eye in the room was on him.

The drinkers were not drinking, talk had died, the dart players had forgotten their game. Even the landlord was leaning on the bar, studying him.

'Go on,' said the girl, impatiently. 'What's the matter?'

He looked at her. Her eyes were black, bird-like. Something bright sparkled in her hair.

'Sit down!' she commanded.

Suddenly, overwhelmingly, fear washed over him. He could not move – No! Keep still, think! Knight, minstrel, king, lady and bird; they were all here. From the corner of his eye he saw the carved serpents on the fireplace rustle. He did the only thing he

74

could think of; plunged his hand in his pocket and brought out the conjuror's box.

At once the girl dropped her tray and grabbed at him with a scream. The men at the bar leapt from their stools and flung themselves forward. But the lid was off.

It was dark, and cold. Snow settled slowly on his pullover. He was standing six inches from the edge of a sheer cliff. It plummeted down into the forest, bushes springing out from its side. As he stood there, a rock slipped and bounced, crashing down endlessly into emptiness. One more step, that's all it would have needed. One more step . . .

Ten minutes later he realized he was sitting on a stone in the snow, staring stupidly at nothing. Shock. He had to pull himself together. Getting up, he stamped about, shivering. The box was still in his hand. It was empty, but the inside was coated with black powder, like soot. He touched it gently, then realized that the stuff was all over his hands and clothes, and was blowing about in the wind. Black smudges darkened the snow.

He put the lid back on and put it in his pocket, then washed his face and hands with snow, rubbing vigorously until his skin tingled. His coat and scarf hung on a bush. He pulled them on and gazed around.

It was a small clearing in the wood, that was all. Where the door had been was a crushed trail of nettles. The whole thing, pub, fire, chair, had been an illusion, made for him. One more step and he would be lying down there now, badly injured if not worse, and those Things pawing him for the tree. No wonder Luke had been worried.

He began to march in what he hoped was the right direction. Things were bad – he must hurry. They knew where he was, but he was hopelessly lost, and had used up Luke's box. He was also cold, tired, and hungry – the memory of those cakes was a torment. And it was almost dark. He *had* to find the road.

An hour later, leaning on a tree-trunk to catch his breath, he knew he could not do it. The wood, they said, had twenty million trees, and he was blundering further and further into the middle of it. Down here among the aisles of trunks, the snow lay in drifts; dark branches overhead hid the stars. And the silence was the worst – the unbroken winter stillness. As he moved on, even his footsteps were muffled. The snow stopped, then began to freeze slowly on the ground. He was walking into trees now, and bushes, it was so dark, and the tiny threads of path led him nowhere. Worst of all, he began to imagine he was walking in circles; was sure he recognized trees he had passed ten minutes ago. Trees, trees, trees.

Until he saw the light.

Yes! There it was! Ahead of him, a little way off to the left.

A warm, red light, flickering.

But Alick was wary. Once bitten . . . he thought,

and stood still in the silence, watching it. When he moved at last, it was as slowly and quietly as he could, slipping from tree to tree without a rustle in the wet undergrowth. Soon he was close enough to see.

It was a fire. From behind a thick holly bush he took a good look. The fire lit a small clearing. In the centre of the clearing was an ancient oak stump, rotten and hollow, with a great gash down its side. For five minutes he watched the flames burn and nothing stirred – finally he crept out and warmed his hands. It might be a tramp's fire. A tramp would be a relief.

Then he noticed the tracks, trampled in the snow around the oak stump. A dog's? Or a fox? He got down on hands and knees and looked closer. The crack in the tree was wide. He slipped his head in and waited to get used to the blackness. He saw the outline of a heap of straw, a huddle of what looked like fur. And then the voice spoke, close by his ear in the darkness.

'I've been waiting for you, Alick Webster,' it said.

10

TOD-LOWERY

Alick froze.

The bundle of furs twitched, stretched out a long thin arm, and grabbed the end of his scarf as it dangled on the floor.

'Come in, sonny. I don't bite – much.'

Tugged suddenly forward, he fell on his hands and knees into the hollow tree, and the bright light of the fire flooded in behind him. It showed a thin weaselly face, straggly hair, rusty whiskers. The creature hugged its knees with bony arms, and the fingers that held his scarf had sharp nails and were covered with short, reddish hair.

'Got the tree?' it asked casually, turning its head sideways and laying it on its knees.

Alick nodded, speechless.

The creature grinned, showing sharp white teeth. 'Good.'

There was nothing else to do. Alick crawled in and leaned back against the damp bark. The tree was dingy and smelt of wet fur and leaves.

'Tod-lowery,' the thing said, with a wink of one eye. 'That's what you call me. Chicken?'

'What?'

'Chicken. From a farm over Minsterworth way. A bit stringy, but chewable.'

Bewildered, Alick watched the creature fish something out from a corner. It was a chicken leg, badly singed.

'I don't usually bother myself, but I thought you might not like it raw. Take it then!'

Alick took it, rather unwilling.

'Eat it,' the Tod said slyly. 'It's real enough.'

It was. And delicious, since he hadn't eaten for what seemed hours – *was* hours, by now. As he chewed, he watched the creature and the creature watched him.

Finally, he tossed the bone outside and licked his fingers.

'Thanks.'

'And now, a drink.'

It was a murky-looking liquid, in a carved wooden cup. Dubious, he sipped and felt the warmth spread through his chest. As he downed the rest he tried to remember where he had tasted it before, and as he put the cup down it came to him. At Talley. It was the same stuff.

'Now,' the Tod said, 'we can speak. Tell me how you got it.'

'Got what?'

It smiled. 'The Fidchell tree, my innocent.'

The narrow eyes shone in the firelight. Whoever it was, it knew too much already. To his surprise Alick found himself unafraid. He explained how he had gone into Tolbury Tump.

79

The Tod nodded wisely. 'And on that day of all days. So you're the one who started it – the Fidchell.'

'You know about that?'

'Everybody does. It happens.' Seeing Alick was uneasy, it grinned, and wrapped long bony arms around its knees. 'But not for a long time now. *What* a naughty boy we've been. No wonder there's all this fuss.'

'Fuss?'

'Out there.' It nodded towards the opening. 'The wood is alive with them; swarming, like a tipped-up hive. I've heard there's been no end of trouble already.'

'It's not fair!' Alick said suddenly.

The Tod looked surprised. 'That's the game, sonny. Gold and black, sunshine and shadow. They have to be in balance.'

'And who are the players?'

The weaselly face turned sideways. 'So you don't know that either. We are innocent, aren't we? Well then, long ago, little cub, two kings played Fidchell. They played it in an iron-grey fortress, while outside their two armies tore each other to pieces. It was a battle they could have stopped, but neither of them would lose the game.'

Alick stared. 'So what happened?'

'It's said that their punishment for causing all those deaths is that they must play Fidchell until Doomsday, and only on one night in a hundred can they leave the board. Which, I suppose, is where you came in!'

'So they move the pieces?'

'Oh no. Nothing's that simple.' The Tod winked slyly. 'The Fidchell armies play their own game; the players must sit, and watch, and suffer, and not a finger can they raise to help – whatever happens.' He hugged himself gleefully. 'They'll be in a fine state watching this.'

'So am I,' Alick thought. 'What about you?' he asked aloud. 'Aren't you in it?'

'Ah, well, I'm just me. I keep out of it, no one bothers me.' He licked his sharp white teeth. 'Just as well.'

A gust of wind crackled the flames. The Tod's nose wrinkled. 'You smell of wizardry,' it said slowly.

Alick remembered the box. 'I can't smell anything.'

'But I can. What is it?'

He took the box out of his pocket, but kept hold of it.

'And who gave you that?'

'A conjuror.'

The Tod-lowery narrowed its eyes. 'Ah! That'll be the sorcerer at Talley.'

'I thought you might know Luke!'

'I know him.' The Tod grinned. 'And he knows me.'

Perhaps it wasn't such good news. Still, Alick explained about the attack in the ruined chapel.

'Oh, he'll not be hurt, not that one. He'll be about by now.'

'Can you help me to find him? Or to get to Tolbury? I'll never get through by myself.'

'Well now,' the creature scratched idly, 'I might.'

Suddenly Alick wondered if it could be trusted. After that business at the pub he should be much more wary. He put the box away.

'Forget it. I'll go myself.'

'The last one who tried that,' the Tod said casually, 'didn't get far. I found him hanging on a tree, not ten paces from where I left him. Not a pretty sight. Bloody as a dead fox.'

It pulled a flea out of one ear and cracked it.

Alick fidgeted. Then he said, 'Can we start now?'

'No,' the Tod shook its head. 'We'll wait for the moon. They're more than a handful in the dark. You go to sleep now over there. I'll call you.'

Its white teeth glittered. After a moment, Alick shuffled down into the straw. He felt tired, but didn't want to sleep; he wanted to get it all over. But the Tod was in no hurry. It lay down again, yawning and scratching and fidgeting itself into a comfortable hollow. 'Can I ask you something?' Alick said after a long while.

'Surely.'

'Well, all the time we've been here, you haven't put a bit of wood on that fire, and it's as bright as ever. There's no smoke, either. And how did you know my name?'

But the Tod turned over, and began to snore.

Alick sighed. He hadn't really expected an answer. Through the crack in the tree he could see the snow, falling softly again, smoothing out his footprints. He had lost all count of time; it must be late, after midnight. Where was Luke by now? Was he out there in the wood, or in Halcombe, banging on the bookshop door? Or was he still lying in the cold chapel? Wondering, Alick fell asleep.

When he woke, the Tod-lowery was gone and the fire was out. A wand of moonlight came down through the branches. He sat up, stiff with cold, and felt anxiously for the tree. It was still there, chiming faintly under his fingers. Outside, something howled, long and melancholy. A fox, he thought. After a while it stopped. Then, in the silence, he heard paddings and rustlings in the wood.

He crouched, warily, watching the crack of darkness. Now he could distinguish the sound of hooves; a low thudding in the leaves, that grew louder and closer. The clinking of harnesses began to fill the clearing. Silent, his hands and knees deep in the straw, he watched them pass the crack in the tree; the pale hooves of the horses gleaming in a strange light, the paws of dogs padding past. Someone was playing a harp. The soft notes tugged at him, but he sat still, hardly breathing, every hair and muscle stiff with dread.

It took them at least five minutes to pass – all that silent, jingling troop – and once, to his dismay, a golden dog put its nose to the tree and sniffed, so that the hair prickled on his scalp; but it padded on, and the whole glinting, shimmering army rustled away into silence.

After a few minutes he looked out. The Tod was standing in the glade, a lean shadow. As Alick crawled out he saw the wood was made of black columns rising from a white carpet. And far above the branches, like gems in a net, shone the brilliant frosty stars of December.

'Ready?' The Tod held out a hand – almost a paw, Alick thought – and helped him up. 'Right. That was too close. Now we go my ways, and very odd ways you'll find them. Don't say a word . . . not for anything. If you see anything more of Them, give me a poke in the back, but doubtless I'll have seen them before you. Remember, not a whisper!'

'But where are we going?'

The Tod glared. 'That's a daft remark. Tolbury, where else?'

'Luke might need help.'

'*You* need help!' The Tod grinned. 'Luke can look after himself. He's had plenty of practice. Come on.'

It was a journey Alick never forgot. They walked for hours, under great plantations of trees, in a black and white world. The Tod loped ahead, squeezing through gaps in bushes and under sharp, overhanging rocks, climbing over scree or following invisible threads of paths through the hummocky snow. Often they crossed small streams that had frozen into ice; underfoot the glassy slabs splintered; and bubbles of trapped air slid and creaked.

Many things paused to watch them go by. Badgers, snuffling in the undergrowth; a startled deer; a white owl that twisted its head silently as they passed. The

Tod winked at it and it flew off, hoo-hooing gently. And there was a woman, dressed in green who came up to them suddenly out of the trees and spoke a few low words to the Tod. As she passed beside him, Alick shivered at the iciness and the cold sweet smell that hung about her. But he was careful not to ask any questions. When they went on again the Tod grinned at him strangely, eyes and teeth a-glitter in the moonlight.

After that things grew confused. Alick lost himself; walked in a dream or a spell, vaguely aware of wading chest-high through snow (or was it leaves?), of entering tunnels and moving through holes – dark narrow holes littered with branches and rubble and insects that were too large. Size and shape seemed to change; sometimes he was sure the trees were miles above him, bushes were like forests about him, or that he was bent over, long and lean and running on hands and feet. Glimpses of his own hands showed them strange, unfamiliar. Once, at the end of a long ride of oak trees, he saw a dark bird flap ahead of them; its feathers brushed a scatter of snow from the branches. He tapped the Tod and pointed, but the Tod just laughed and shook its head.

Finally, they came to the end of the trees. With a rush, recognition came back to him, and he straightened, easing a strange ache in his back. He knew now where they were. Before him the moonlit fields dipped to the railway line where it ran deep in its cutting into the great tunnel under Corsham Chase.

Beyond that, somewhere in the wood, was the Greenmere, and the bald dome of Tolbury Tump.

'Right,' said the Tod. 'You can talk now. We have to cross the field and the silver lines, and this is the hard part, for I have no power once out of the trees. They'll see us for sure.' The foxy face grinned at him. 'Good runner?'

'Sort of. Not very fast though.'

'Isn't that a pity. Well, take a deep breath, and do your best . . .'

'Wait!' Alick said. 'Before we start, was that one of Them, in the wood?'

'No.' Alert, the Tod rubbed its long nose. 'That was just folk, moving. Things are restless. Everyone knows the Fidchell is on. The Ellyll told me.'

'Who?'

'The Ellyll, the icy lady. She said the wood is sealed tight. Nothing can get in or out. And she's heard the sorcerer is looking for you.'

Alick's eyes widened. 'Luke!'

'Ay. I told you, didn't I? He'll be making for the Tump. Now, are you ready?'

'Yes.'

'Let's go!'

They leapt into the white field, floundering rather than running; snow to the knees. But only half-way across, and they heard the whirr of wings above them. Something blotted out the stars.

'Hurry!' the Tod yelled. Ahead, the field was sliced clean. Alick shouldered through the bushes and saw, below him, the railway lines – two tracks of silver in the moonlight. Shadows wheeled over him. He plunged over the side and slithered and scrambled after the Tod, through the stinging nettles and brambles, hitting the bottom cut and sore. The Tod loped over the rails. 'Come on,' it hissed, 'or . . .'

Then it stopped, teeth bared.

'What's wrong?'

The Tod's tongue flickered, tasting the air. 'We're too late, sonny.'

Ahead, the silver lines ran into the tunnel, a great mouth opening in the hillside, its dark entrance dripping with brambles and ferns. Inside it, was blackness; a crowded, clinking, restless, fluttering blackness.

11

ICICLES

They were there all right. Horsemen – indistinct in the shadows, but the glitter of their weapons was unmistakable, all colour toned down to a ghostly grey. Pennants and banners floated above them. Shields were slung on arm or saddle-bow. And behind, deeper in the tunnel, other shapes lurked, long and sinuous.

In all the trees of the cutting the ravens came down, silently – a black snow.

'What now?' Alick muttered.

'Not much. You'll have to give it up.'

'I won't!'

The Tod grinned, its eyes on the tunnel. 'That's my boy. We'll doubtless think of something.'

A horseman was moving forward, harness clinking. Slowly his horse came on over the snow, leaving no prints, having no shadow. The rider was helmeted, only his eyes visible. Alick waited, fists clenched. He hadn't come all this way for nothing. He wouldn't give it up. Think of something!

The shining beast stopped. The knight gently dropped the point of his spear an inch from Alick's face, and left it there. The wicked steel menaced his eyes. Still he did not move.

'He wants that tree,' the Tod muttered, unnecessarily.

'He can whistle for it.'

The spear fell, its point touched his chest. Then, eyes impassive, the knight pushed. Alick felt the point push through his clothes, then shove, painfully, against his breastbone.

He stepped back. 'All right. Have the damn thing.'

Slowly, his hand went to his coat buttons. As he took out the tree, dragging each second out as long as he could, the tiny leaves tinkled in the wind, glittering gold and black.

And then, with a bounce and a flutter a raven came from nowhere and landed on the spear, weighing it suddenly down. The horse moved back, uneasy; the knight whipped up his weapon angrily.

It was then Alick had his idea. Both sides, ravens and knights, wanted the tree. To get it was to win. While he had it both sides were against him, united, but if he gave it to one side, the other would fight them for it. Divide and conquer.

Suddenly, he held the tree high, so the moonlight caught it. Every eye swivelled to it, a small, glinting, mystical object. Then he flung it, hard and fast, into the tunnel – or pretended to. Every head turned, seeking the small thing in the blackness of the sky. Alick shoved it back quickly into his pocket. But as he stared he saw to his amazement the flash and glitter of it falling from the stars high over the horsemen into the tunnel's mouth. But he hadn't thrown it!

. Chaos erupted. The knight wheeled and rode. Birds and riders poured into the tunnel; shriek and howl and sword-slash rang in the cutting. For a moment he and the Tod were forgotten. And then, as they watched the black semi-circle in the hill, the change began.

Icicles grew suddenly, swiftly, without sound. Down like a portcullis they fell, like a frozen curtain, spreading and joining and spilling, hard as rock, on to the snow. Sealed with seamed glass, the tunnel's mouth was white and hard.

'Alick,' said a voice. 'Up here.'

High on the embankment, Luke was watching them, hands in pockets. Behind him a white horse nuzzled the snow.

Shoved from behind by the Tod, who was snorting and chortling with glee, Alick scrambled to the top. The horse raised his head and watched him with narrow red eyes.

Luke caught the bridle. 'Can you ride?'

'Not much.'

'It doesn't matter.' Luke swung himself up. 'Just get behind me, Tam Lin will manage us.'

'Put your feet here.' The Tod crouched and clasped its hands. Alick put his foot in, but did not jump.

'Hurry up!' the bent figure snapped.

'Luke. I didn't throw it . . .'

The Tod snorted.

'I know.' Luke was watching the tunnel. 'But you saw it.'

'He means he conjured it up,' the Tod snapped. 'Now, are you getting on this creature or not?'

Alick scrambled up. Once it felt him there, the horse turned its head and paced into the wood. The moon stroked them with brief silver fingers.

'That trick with the icicles,' the Tod declared, 'that was the best ever, laddie.'

Luke nodded, serious. 'It was risky. It could have brought the whole thing down on top of you.'

He sounded tired, Alick thought. He held the conjuror's coat with both hands.

'I didn't know you had a horse.'

'There are a lot of things you don't know,' Luke observed.

'And you've met this horse before, though he might have looked different.'

Alick thought of the face in the shaving-mirror.

'I was glad to see you,' he said. 'I was worried stiff in that church.'

The conjuror shook his head. 'You did all right,' he said. 'Tam Lin was waiting for me, that was maybe an hour after you'd gone. I found your note.' He slapped the horse's neck affectionately. 'I was sore and cold and worried. There was terror running in the wood. Trees were down on every road. You'd been seen running, and in a glamour.'

'A what?'

'A sort of spell. I don't know what they tried, but when I got there I knew you were all right, because

91

of the box. Then someone said you were with the Tod. I stopped worrying after that.'

The Tod, loping at the horse's side, laughed, and bowed with a flourish.

'We tracked you from the lair,' Luke said. 'It wasn't easy.' He and the Tod exchanged a knowing look. 'Now, hang on. We haven't got time to waste.'

As the horse ran, the wood loomed like a black wall in front of them. Before Alick could gasp, they arrowed down a path like a crack in masonry. Clutching Luke's coat he twisted and glanced back, saw far behind them a long red form loping. The fox sped after them, bending its sly, whiskered face sometimes to lick the cool snow. Alick clung on, out of the wind, thinking of his living-room over the shop, with its snug fire and the Christmas tree loaded with tinsel and coloured globes. And his father's present – a pullover and two books and a tin of tobacco – all wrapped up in the bottom of his wardrobe. If I don't get back, he thought, how will he know where they are?

'Alick!' Luke yelled irritably. 'Hold on! You're falling asleep!'

With a jerk he gripped tight, and opened his eyes. The horse slowed and stopped. Alick slipped off, thankfully, and stamped about, banging his arms against his body and rubbing the agonizing chill out of his ears. 'Sorry. I couldn't help it.'

The Tod-lowery ambled out of the trees, grinning, and Luke took it aside, talking quietly. It nodded, waved at Alick, and was gone.

'Drink this,' Luke said, crossing to him. 'It'll wake you up.'

Alick took a swig. Hot, searing liquid struck the back of his throat like a flame-thrower. Gasping, he handed it back. 'Did you make that?' he managed.

Luke laughed. 'I wish I could! It's brandy.' He took a drink and screwed the top on, his hands clumsy with cold. 'Come on. The last lap.'

The next half-hour was the worst. Despite the bitter cold, Alick found it hard to keep awake, and when he did his hunger was painful. That chicken leg must have been hours ago. And not only that – as they came nearer the Greenmere he began to feel that terror that Luke had talked about. Owls flapped about them as they rode; the trees were full of creaking wind; small animals scattered and screeched as they thundered by. On the last part of the path Luke slowed the horse. Progress was difficult. Branches had been torn down and scattered; the spilt and trampled berries were black as blood. As they went on it was harder; whole saplings had been uprooted, and finally a great bank of snow, as high as the horse's head, reared before them. They had to stop.

Luke sat there, silent for a second. Then he whistled, low and clear. The answer came from far off towards Tolbury; the eerie bark of a fox. Luke turned the horse's head. 'The wood is sealed,' he said grimly. 'So we'll have to go another way, one they might not expect.'

The horse whinnied and blew through its nostrils,

then it turned off the path and pushed through some bushes.

'Hang on now, Alick,' Luke said in his firmest voice.

They came out of the trees. There lay the Green-mere, its surface shining strangely. Daintily, the horse stepped down to it, crushing the pine needles and the frosty white stalks of grass. Its forehooves clattered on the Mere. It stepped out, and the polished surface was as smooth and firm as a marble floor. The Greenmere was frozen.

Astounded, Alick gazed down. A perfect reflection of his face stared back at him. The mirror-horse below licked the tongue of its replica.

'Will it hold our weight?'

'I don't know,' Luke said. 'Anyway, we've no choice.'

'And if it breaks?'

'Don't ask.'

12

SEALED

Luke nudged the horse on with his knees. Blowing and tossing its head, it gave him an unreadable look and began to walk. The silver hooves rang on the glassy surface, and strange, wheezing sounds came from the ice, as if it would crack and splinter underneath them. Breath held, Alick waited, expecting any minute the crack, the dark star of water and the sudden toppling. But, despite a few slips, the white horse walked out into the middle of the Mere and stood there, snorting clouds of breath from its nostrils.

'Come on, Tam,' the conjuror murmured. 'Don't listen to them. That's what they want.'

The horse paced, ears pricked. Behind the splintering, Alick could hear it too, a muffled sound, like people shouting to be heard, and banging on some thick door between them and you. Angry, frustrated voices. Then he realized where they were coming from.

Beneath the horse's hooves, beneath the green glass of the ice, shapes moved. Broad hands splayed against the barrier; a host of faces mouthed muffled threats. Alick heard beaks pecking, swords

95

hammering; he looked away, but Luke had already felt his grip tighten. 'Ease up, Alick,' he said gently. 'You're pinching.'

'Sorry.' Alick stared straight ahead. If they fell . . . If the ice splintered up like a row of green teeth and swallowed them . . . but he told himself not to think about it. It was too late now.

Then, like a pistol shot, the ice cracked. Tam Lin staggered; Alick grabbed Luke tight. The ice heaved, jolted apart, a hand came out of it, then a sword, a body in armour, and at that moment the horse put his forehooves on the first cracked reed on the shore. At once Luke kicked him into speed, and behind them, as they rode, the Greenmere erupted with a roar and crash as if some mighty iceberg was smashing through the surface.

Over the soft wet snow they galloped, out of the trees and on to the floundering whiteness of Tolbury Tump. The sky was dark; a thin moon trailed rags of cloud.

Luke jumped down and Alick leapt after him. They fell into the snowy bushes breathlessly, the cries from the lake roaring through the wood. Luke snatched up a stone and struck it against the rock until it rang among the clamour. But the door did not open.

'Try again!' Alick yelled, but Luke shook his head and flung the stone away. 'It's sealed. I expected it.'

The crack of a twig made them spin.

'Tod?'

The long, grinning face slid round a tree.

'Still here?'

'Oh, I had to see this one through.' Tod bit its nails. 'What are you going to do?' Behind him the ring of the hollow was a mass of shadows. Luke ignored them. 'Where's Tam?'

'Here.'

Alick stared in surprise. Into the hollow jumped a tall slim boy, his white hair glimmering in the moonlight. He wore pale clothes and carried a spear; a gold collar gleamed about his neck.

'They're coming,' he said. 'Gold and black together.'

'Open the door!' Alick shouted. The tree stuck in his chest and he pulled it out and flung it down. 'I've brought the damn thing back! What else am I supposed to do!'

'Quiet!' The conjuror put all twelve fingers together and blew on them. 'All right, I'll do it. Tod, Tam, I'll need time. Just five minutes.'

The Tod grinned, 'My pleasure. This should be good.'

'It will be,' Luke glanced at Alick. 'If it works.'

In seconds they were alone. Two sinuous streaks, one white, one red, flashed over the lip of the hollow. Growls and cries and the screams of horses rang around them. Fox and hound flung themselves on the foremost riders.

'No questions,' Luke ordered, before Alick could open his mouth. He pulled boxes of oddments hastily from his pockets. Horns rang below them; green phosphorescent flashes lit the sky.

'Take your boots off. Socks too.'

'What!'

'Do it!'

Grumbling, Alick obeyed. His feet were blue in the bitter air.

'Sit still!' Falling on his knees the conjuror dipped his finger into a box of ointment, dabbed it on the undersides of Alick's feet and then on the tops. It was icy, but Alick clamped his teeth shut and endured it. Luke worked hurriedly, humming and muttering to himself. As Alick jerked his socks back on, the backs of his hands were anointed, then his forehead, his neck, the small of his back – all were dabbed with the icy cream. When it was finished, tiny rings of cold lay on the extremes of his body. As he stood, he could feel the cross of ice creep up and join with swift, stabbing pains.

'Here! Don't forget this.' The Fidchell tree was shoved into his hands. 'Put it back where you found it!'

'What!'

'Back where you found it!' Luke yelled, shoving him to the door. Vivid green lights were flickering in the sky; the screech of a fox and the clang of swords rang down the hillside. Alick hung on to the cliffside, transfixed by cold. The strange hands of the conjuror turned him to face the rock, pushed him hard on each spread hand, each foot, on back, on head. He screamed. The rock softened, welcomed him. Its cold grip folded him in blackness. It gripped his hands, his feet; he could not turn his head. Luke was somewhere, shouting, kneeling in the snow behind him, far, far behind. Down a tunnel of blackness he was sucked, absorbed, and the rock took hold of him and tore him fiercely through.

Outside, a spear clanged against the rock.

Luke stood up slowly, and turned to face the dark ring of horsemen around the hollow.

THE FORTRESS

Alick was lying in dirt and blackness. A spider ran across the back of his neck, and he shook it off as he sat up. Blood ran from a cut on his face. His body felt as if it did not belong to him, as if it had been frozen and thawed again, or gone through some extremity of pain.

The tunnel, he found, standing up, was just as it had been before, a filthy crack in the hill. But the odd thing was that he could see right through the door. He knew it was there, but as he put his hand up it sank in gently, and it was hard to tug out again.

Outside, he saw that Luke was standing with his back to him, hands clenched. A spear lay on the ground. In the dimness round the hollow clustered a great host of shadows, black and formless. Luke was speaking, but no sound came in to Alick. He saw the Tod lope up, and Tam Lin, behind him, picked up the spear.

But what now? Put the tree back, Luke had said, but still Alick hesitated. He couldn't leave them out there. Not like this. He shoved the tree into his pocket and fumbled over the door. There must be a way to open it. His fingers stubbed on hardening rock. No knob, no handle.

Already the lip of the hollow was seething with birds, rising and swirling like black smoke from a cauldron. One of them launched itself at Luke. The conjuror ducked, and Tam Lin stabbed the thing with the spear. Black feathers crashed against the rock.

A lock, a lever, anything! His hands groped. He kicked and slammed the rock in fury. Birds were falling like black rain. The Tod bit and snapped, his lithe body twisting in the air. Luke flung his arm over his eyes.

Nothing! And after all, Alick thought suddenly, why should there be? This was no ordinary door. 'Open!' he yelled, hands flat, commanding. 'Open!'

The rock shuddered, swung; noise erupted from outside. It was a battlefield. As the golden light hit them, the birds screamed; their eyes were gilt studs in blackness. A waterfall of horses roared into the hollow.

Luke must have felt the rock move against him; he grabbed the Tod. 'Leave it! Get inside!'

They dived in beside Alick and threw themselves against the door. 'Tam Lin!' the conjuror yelled. Slowly the great rocks moved together; a white body slithered in, behind it a lance head snapped, a bird's wing was crushed. Then the line of light closed up and sealed tight. Feathers and dust settled.

For a while they sat wearily in a breathless row; Luke and the Tod bleeding on face and hands, Tam

Lin smiling strangely. Finally Alick rubbed tired eyes with his sleeve.

'They can't get in now, can they?'

His voice echoed down the tunnel. Dimly he saw Luke shrug.

'Not through this door. There are other ways.'

He gazed at Alick. 'I told you to go on. We would have been all right.'

'It didn't look like it!'

'It's not us they want. It's the tree.' The conjuror tossed the Tod a handkerchief, and with a grin the creature dabbed daintily at a cut.

'Sorry,' Alick said bitterly. 'Next time.'

'I'm not ungrateful,' Luke said quickly, 'but we've lost time and that's important. Still, it's probably just as well. This part isn't likely to be easy.' He stood up. 'Come on. I'll lead, then you, Alick. Tam last, if you will.'

As they rose, the Tod clapped Alick's shoulder. 'Whatever he says,' he whispered, 'I'm damned glad to be out of *that*, little cub.'

Alick grinned. Then, hands stretched, he shuffled into the darkness. The passage was as narrow and contorted as before, but soon Alick came to realize that the twists were tighter and more sudden, as if somehow the tunnel had shifted and wriggled in the earth. Ahead, in the dimness, Luke's shadow stumbled as he felt his way; behind, the Tod kept a firm grip on Alick's coat.

Not only did the tunnel twist wrongly, but it began to run steeply downhill. Alick knew they should have reached the Fidchell hall a long time ago.

Then Luke stopped. A cool draught moved against Alick's face. 'Are we there?'

His voice rang double. Luke shook his head. 'The tunnel forks in two.'

'That's impossible. It didn't before.'

'Before, Alick.' The conjuror peered into the left-hand tunnel, his words distant. 'Since the Fidchell began, "before" is another world. Which way, Tod?'

The Tod-lowery pushed past Alick and snuffled down the tunnel entrances. 'The left is water,' he said at last. 'The right, fire.'.

Tam Lin tapped the spear on a stone. 'Fire, for me.'

'No,' Luke said. 'We can't go through fire. And we must stay together.'

The pale face moved closer to the conjuror. 'You know I cannot touch the water.'

'Then you must pass over it,' Luke answered, as if he was laughing.

Something happened. Something rustled and flapped.

Then the Tod moved to where Tam Lin had been and picked up the fallen spear. A white bird sat on Luke's shoulder, preening. It sent a delicate downy feather into the darkness.

'If water is the worst thing down here,' the conjuror remarked, edging into the tunnel, 'we'll be very lucky.'

*

At first, the water was enough. It began after only a few steps. Alick's gloves were so wet he had taken them off, and now he could feel the walls turning slimy, and the cold trickle of moisture froze the ends of his fingers. Then his feet began to stick, squelching as he tugged them free. Something cold lapped about his wellingtons.

Grimly they trudged on, splashing downhill. The noise of the stream grew to fill the cavern, and after a while the first wave came over the top of Alick's boots and ran down in an icy cascade into his socks. He groaned.

'What's the matter?' the Tod laughed. 'Cold feet?'

Gritting his teeth, Alick watched the bird take off from Luke's shoulder and fly down the tunnel. Suddenly he realized he was seeing Luke more clearly than before; a faint light was growing ahead, and the conjuror was wading towards it. Just before it flew round the bend of the rock, the bird shone.

'We're coming out,' Luke shouted over his shoulder.

'Out where?' Alick murmured.

'Just about where we are now,' the Tod said. 'And where we have been since we came through that door.'

Alick frowned 'What?'

'Walking and standing still, my lad. They're all the same in the hollow hill.'

Trying to make sense of that, Alick waded round a rock, and stared, astonished.

Before him the stream cascaded out of the mouth of a cave and down a steep, rocky hillside. Below them a network of fields lay white with untrodden snow, and beyond those, a threatening fringe of dark pine forests stretched into the distance. The sky was iron-grey; every tree and hedgerow laden with snow, thick and heavy. A bitter wind whistled into their faces.

Alick shivered. 'It's not possible.'

'No,' said the Tod, splashing past.

'But where are we?'

'I told you. We're not anywhere – or anywhere you could put a name on.' The red paw grabbed his arm. 'Now then. Look at that!'

On the white field stood two pavilions, about a hundred yards apart, their doors facing. Each had a pennant flying from its roof; Alick could just make out the devices. On the black pavilion, a raven, and on the gold, a knight. And between the two tents, facing him on a rocky knoll of its own, a great fortress, iron-grey, its gates wide open.

No one moved in the fields or the pavilions, or on the battlements of the fortress. The windows were staring blanks. Everything seemed deserted. Far over the woods one white bird circled.

Luke was sitting on a rock emptying water from his boots. The Tod scrambled down beside him, out of the wind. Alick followed. He took off his scarf and rubbed his numbed feet, then put the wet socks back on. He could never get wetter or colder than this.

The Tod sniffed. 'Looks deserted.'

'Good. Still, nothing here is as it seems.' Luke stared down at the castle with a smile. Alick tried another question.

'Are we still inside the Tump . . . I mean, is all this inside?'

The conjuror shook his head. 'I suggest you try not to think about it.'

'He means he doesn't know,' the Tod put in.

'Do you?' Luke said.

'Nope. Come on.'

They scrambled down the hill, over rocks and scree, and when they reached the bottom the wind snatched their breath and froze their faces. Alick pulled his hood on; Luke clutched his collar. Only the Tod seemed not to care about the cold. They plunged across the snowy waste, heads bent, struggling forward. Above, the white bird circled.

The field seemed enormous. However far they trudged, the great gates of the fortress came no nearer, and to each side the pavilions swayed and flapped in the icy wind.

It was eerie walking between them. Once, Alick paused and stared at the flapping draperies of the black tent. For a second the whole billowing structure seemed a vast black bird, struggling and flapping in the snow. Then the Tod tugged his arm, and he turned to face the fortress. It was still a long way off.

'I keep thinking,' he said. 'They might come out at us from these tents.'

Luke took no notice. He stopped and listened. A low sound, barely heard, troubled them.

'Thunder,' the Tod said.

'Bees?' Alick tried.

Luke shrugged. 'I don't think so.' He began to walk faster, taking some powder from a box in his pocket and sowing it liberally before his feet.

Instantly, the fortress was nearer. In a few steps they had reached the gates.

14

THE PLAYERS

The gates were wide open. Pure untrodden snow filled the courtyard. Luke paused, and Alick noticed that he and the Tod were looking anxiously along the rows of dark, empty windows. The quiet was broken only by the wind, whistling through the bare cloisters, banging a door somewhere, sweeping dry snow into corners.

'Do we go in?'

Luke nodded. 'It'll be in here somewhere. Is the tree safe?'

Alick put his hand up and touched the small lump inside his coat. 'Yes.'

Tod was looking into a doorway. 'Start here. I'll feel better out of the open.'

As he said it, Alick gasped. 'Look!'

In the faint light the white gates were closing, swinging silently together. Snow jerked from them.

'It's best to be safe,' Luke said, hands in pockets. He grinned at Alick. 'Don't want Them coming up behind us, do you?'

'No . . . Will it do any good?'

The Tod snorted, and Luke did not answer. Alick followed them up the stone steps. It was best not to be surprised at anything any more. Just shut up and tag along.

The steps were broken and dangerous. They wound upwards, past arrow slits that showed deserted courtyards below, and gardens of black, stunted trees. When they came to a corridor they walked down it in silence, and Luke flung open each door as they passed, but found only dusty, empty rooms, with broken windows and snow on the floorboards. No living thing – not a spider, not even an ant. Only, in the last room of all, a small silver fruit, rolling in the draught.

Alick picked it up. 'It's the same as the one I ate in the Tump.' He showed it to Luke. 'Are we near it, the Fidchell board?'

'Near enough!' Luke muttered.

Suddenly he glanced towards the window, so swiftly that Alick looked too, and saw a fire burning before each pavilion, blazing eerily in the snow.

'They weren't there before.'

The Tod was hustling him out of the room. 'We must find the board,' he said to Luke. 'It must be here.'

Luke bit his lip. 'Oh yes, but would we know it if we saw it?' They walked along corridors and up and down countless stairs, through many empty echoing halls. There was no sign of the chequered board, the table, the hall with its central fire. Then at one turn in a corridor a white bird sailed in through a window and became Tam Lin tapping Luke on the shoulder.

'They've reached the gates.'

As he spoke, a heavy thud shook the slabs of the floor under their feet, rumbling away into silence. And then came shouts, the far-off clash of metal. 'Didn't take them long,' the Tod sighed.

Alick was playing with the fruit in his pocket. Quietly, he took it out and put it in his mouth. After all, the first time . . .

The taste was as unpleasant as before. He felt suddenly sick and leaned against a window; a small dirty glass pane, only as big as a book. His eyesight swam, then steadied, and he saw . . . the Fidchell board!

'Look! Down there! What does that remind you of?'

Luke squeezed in beside him. Alick felt his body stiffen. Below them was a small courtyard, paved with black marble slabs. The dust of dead leaves lay on it, but not scattered randomly – it lay in a pattern; a pattern of black and gold squares. Leaves, and no tree.

'How do we get down there?' the Tod snapped. 'There must be a door.'

They clattered down some steps, Alick last, still feeling strange and dizzy. In front of him, the others faded, their voices indistinct. Above, heavy footsteps paced the corridors.

Then Alick saw it, the small door, shimmering in the wall. He pushed it, stepped through, and heard it click behind him.

He was a figure on a black and golden board. It

stretched to the horizon in every direction, flat and unending. And he was alone on it; one solitary figure under a grey sky. Somewhere was the centre, the important square. How could he find it? It would look just the same as any other. He began to walk, and the wind swept across the empty acres and snatched his breath.

Suddenly, he turned. Around him the Fidchell pieces were springing from the earth. Black and gold, glittering — bird and horseman, greyhound, minstrel — as he had first seen them at Talley, worlds and centuries ago. But this time they were the giants, and he was tiny, tiny as an ant on a chequered tablecloth. They towered above him, bestriding their squares, eyes fixed on him. All around him. He was in the middle, in the very centre.

For a moment, Alick hardly realized what that meant. Then, as they began to move, to press closer, to clink and rustle and flap towards him, he tugged the tree from his pocket and ran across the huge blackness of the square towards its centre, the very hub and axis of the great spinning board. Breathless, he felt the black and gold giants crush down on him. He held the tree, its leaves tinkled, a shiver and roar swept the falling darkness. But before they crashed over him he was kneeling, falling, and the roots of the tree touched the black icy soil.

It exploded. It shot upwards and arched over him. Huge and glittering, it erupted into leaf and branch like a firework of jet and gold. Leaves and snow and dust cascaded on his upturned face; leaves that rattled like tin in the sudden wind and uprush, whirling round a great tree, heavy with fruit and stars and birds, its branches tangling in the sky. The ground heaved and buckled; twisting boles and roots snaked around him; a cascade of leaves brushed and smothered his face and became a curtain of gold that he reached out to, and grabbed, and tugged firmly aside.

The Fidchell hall was quiet, and flooded with sunlight. Two men were sitting at the table. One leaned back in his chair, face towards Alick. The other was frowning at the board, chin on hands. A dog lay asleep under the table, and a raven on a gold chain croaked and hopped on the back of one of the chairs.

'So,' said the sprawling man to Alick, 'you're back.' The other looked up, interested. Neither seemed in the least surprised.

Alick stepped forward, and saw the tree on the centre square, exactly between the opposing armies. They all surveyed it, calmly.

The player with the raven sighed. 'It was not a long battle.'

'But some of the moves were interesting,' added the other. He glanced at Alick. 'Don't you think so?' He wore a fine fillet of gold in his hair.

Alick nodded, wary. He rubbed dust and leaves from his coat. 'Where are my friends?'

The players smiled at each other. 'They'll be here,' one said. 'The tree is back, so all the danger is ended.'

'And is the game over?'

'The game goes on for ever, secretly, here with us. You let it spill out into the world. Now you have brought it back.'

The player with the raven stood up. 'And it's time you left.' Whistling to the sleepy dog he walked over and opened one of the three doors.

Impossible breezes blew in, warm and sweet. Bees hummed in strange flowers. Alick saw an orchard, heavy with blossom. A stream ran through it, bubbling over stones, its surface a cloud of dragonflies. A white road led over distant hills.

'Where is that?' he whispered. The players smiled at each other. 'Go and see,' one of them said. 'You know you'd like to. Or perhaps you might prefer this.' Taking Alick by the elbow, he pushed him to the second door. A rose garden, in full bloom. Behind it a house of glass, its roof thatched with bright birds' feathers.

Alick shook his head. 'Where are these places? They look so . . . familiar.'

'Countries of the mind. Your mind. They are whatever you want them to be.'

'And you. Who are you?'

He knew they were smiling over his head. 'Just the players. Watching the ways of the world.'

The third door was very close. He made a picture in his mind, then reached out his hand, turned the knob, and opened it.

The sea.

The sea thundered on rocks somewhere below. Just through the door was grass, short and coarse —

the top of a cliff. Not far out to sea was an island, misty with cloud and seagulls. He took a step closer. He wanted to see the water crash and foam far below. He wanted to step through the door. The player was close behind him, a hand at his back. 'Go on. There's no harm. Just for a look.'

Suddenly Alick stopped. 'No. No. I don't think so.' He turned quickly away.

'You're wise, Alick.' Luke was leaning just inside the curtain, his coat dark with water and dust. 'Don't go in.'

The players exchanged glances. 'He's seen us,' one said. 'He's seen the inside of the hill. You know . . .'

'I know,' Luke interrupted. 'But you can leave that to me. He will never find his way back in here, and if he should tell anyone of this, who would believe him?'

'Are you certain, sorcerer?'

'Quite certain.'

Alick came back and gazed down at the board. 'And if I had,' he said, 'what would have happened?'

'You know, don't you?' Luke moved aside for the Tod and the white dog. 'Nothing. You would walk to the edge of the cliff, gaze out to sea, come back. Just five minutes. But when you went back down into Halcombe you would have been away two hundred years.'

As they walked to the curtain, Alick paused and looked back. The players sat on their carven chairs, the dog asleep, the raven preening its feathers.

Between them the Fidchell board gleamed, its knights and birds and ladies still and cold.

'Goodbye, Alick,' one of them said.

The other shook his head. 'He should have gone through the door, as all the others did.'

'All those tales,' the Tod said slyly as they walked down the tunnel, 'of those people who went into the wood and never came out.'

'You'll never have the chance again,' Luke added.

'What about you?'

The conjuror laughed. 'That's my business — which you are going to stay out of, from now on.'

At the entrance to the hollow, they paused. The door was wide open, the golden glow lighting falling flakes of snow. As Alick looked back down the tunnel the golden pillars stretched into the distance.

'I'll never understand all this.'

The door closed.

'Well,' the Tod grinned, 'the sun's coming. Until next time, sorcerer. And you, young one, I'll watch out for you in the wood. You're the sort that makes trouble, and no mistake.'

With a wink and a wave of its arm it was gone.

Alick and Luke walked slowly home through the wood. The white dog — or whatever it was — trotted along behind them, nosing roots and rabbit holes, just like any other dog. Light grew slowly; the first birds began to sing. Once past the Cross the going was easier; a gritting lorry had been along, strewing bright red gravel. As they came near to Halcombe the church clock chimed six.

'I'm going to catch it now,' Alick muttered.

'I doubt it.' Luke took his hands out of his pockets and blew on them. 'Your father could never have got home.'

'He could have phoned.'

'The lines were down.'

Alick thought about that. 'Good.'

'But he'll be home today. The blizzards are over.'

'Are you sure?'

Luke laughed. 'Quite sure. And Alick . . . don't follow me anywhere again.'

Alick grinned.

'And keep away from the Greenmere, unless you want more warts. Merry Christmas.'

'Merry Christmas, Luke.'

At the bookshop the key was on the ledge over the door. Alick thundered upstairs, turned on all the electric fires and sat in a huddle, shivering and tugging off wet clothes. Then he put the kettle on and went to the telephone.

'Jamie . . .? Yes, I know that's the time . . . Listen. Do you think your mother will make a pair of gloves for me, by Christmas? I know it's tomorrow! But listen, idiot, they're a bit special. They've got to have six fingers. Yes, that's what I said. Six.'

THE
THIRTEENTH OWL

Nick Warburton

For Laura and Susan

with thanks to Gretchen, Tom, Jen, K. T., and Altie

1

Boy Carter was stubbing stones out of the road with his toe. Imogen watched him through the kiln-room window. The glass was dull with clay dust so she'd smeared a clear circle with her thumb. But Boy Carter was concentrating on his stones. He might not have noticed her anyway. Imogen watched the little clouds of dust swirl up round his ankles; saw him bend and sort out the best sized stones to throw at the school wall. They clicked against the flint and flew off at angles.

'I shan't move while you're there,' Imogen said softly. 'I shan't.'

She turned her back to the window and looked round the kiln-room. The shelves of pots, some fired, some not. The heavy sacks, damp with clay, kicked against the wall – subsiding there like bodies. The dust and muddle of it all. Her father's room, full of her father's work. Some of it had been standing on shelves for years. Never fired. Never quite got round to it. Imogen wouldn't let him move them now, even if it crossed his mind.

'I'd like to go out now,' she said to the empty room. 'Please. I'd like to be outside.'

Behind her, very faint, came the shout of Boy Carter's mother, like an answer to her plea.

'Boy, what are you doing? What are you frittering your time on now?'

No reply from Boy Carter. Just the click of stone on flint.

'Come inside this minute,' his mother shouted. 'Get your lump of a self in here or I'll take your father to you.'

A last stone hit the school wall and the road became silent. Imogen smiled to herself, picturing Boy trailing indoors with his head bowed. Getting a cuff aimed at him for the dust on his boots.

'Cuff him,' she said. 'Cuff him one for me.'

She sighed, lifting her shoulders, and slipped out of the kiln-room into the evening light. But too soon. Just a moment too soon. Boy Carter glimpsed her before he was dragged indoors.

'Crack-pot!' he yelled. 'Where you off to, Crack-pot?'

Imogen turned her back to show she hadn't heard. She hurried down the street, head down like a little old woman.

'Hear me, Crack-pot?' Boy Carter called after her. 'Hear what I say?'

Go in, Boy, she thought. Go in and get your head smacked. And she ran the fingers of her right hand over her cheek. Smooth as an apple and then rough, where the scar was. Her fingers traced the line of the scar.

The potter's daughter. A fair face with a scar down

120

one cheek. Crack-pot, she thought. A little crack-pot.

When she reached the lane outside the village she slowed. She was by herself, no one at her back, and she felt happier for it. The lane was deep, between two banks of hedge and ivy, and dusk had already reached it. The sky and the fields still seemed light in the late summer air but the lane was closed in with shadow.

She would turn at the first gate and walk the track across Mr Balik's big field. Make her way slowly back and round so that she could come in at the top of the village, and through the snicket by the church. Boy Carter and all the others would be safe inside. You could take the path across Mr Balik's field. You were allowed to do that. He didn't like it. Sometimes he was working in the fields when Imogen walked past and he stopped what he was doing to watch her walk by. Whenever he was there she pulled her shawl round her head and didn't look to one side or the other. But she always felt him there, pausing in his work, watching her. Making sure that her feet remained on the track and didn't stray on to his land.

Tonight there was no sign of him. Or anyone else. Imogen liked it best like that. Herself treading the ground, the light draining out of the sky, Old Carter's dog barking far away in the village. Probably barking at Boy who was probably aggravating the poor thing. And Boy maybe getting nipped for it.

She began to sing to herself. The crop had been harvested and Imogen passed between two seas of stubble. Her track was marked by the solid prints of work horses, dried in the sun. It cut straight through the field and ended at a clump of old trees. The trees were in a dip to the left, with several ways through them and back on to the upper road at the top of the village. On the right was a blackened barn in the corner of Mr Balik's field. It sagged at one end, as if it had a weight on the roof.

Imogen stopped walking and turned a slow circle on the spot. Looking back at the path she'd walked, then at the twisted trees, and at the barn, moving steadily across her vision as she turned.

Then she saw it.

The owl. Short and upright on a branch which reached towards her like an arm. Watching her. Because of the dip down to the trees it was almost at eye-level. She caught her breath and stopped turning. For a long second they looked at each other.

Imogen, pale and still. The owl steady, a light, glowing brown, its feathers flecked. Imogen's blue eyes narrowed, so she could see all there was of the owl. The owl's eyes black, darker than the dark trees behind it.

The owl hunched to take off. It fell from the branch and swooped down, then up and off to Imogen's right. Its wings were white underneath, both soft and hard, curved like flexing swords in the dusk. It flew in complete silence towards the barn, flickered for a moment and then disappeared somewhere into the roof. Imogen stood and watched the barn until parts of it had faded into the general darkness. But the owl could not be seen again. It was in there somewhere, a fierce life waiting on some beam or ledge. Alone in the barn.

Dad spooned stew into their brown bowls. The bowls were seconds, imperfect, for home use only. The best pots went to the shop for others to buy.

'What's to do this evening, Imogen?' he asked her.

'I don't know. I was thinking, maybe I could make something. From a bit of left-over.'

'Left-over stew?' he said, lifting an eyebrow but not smiling. 'I can't see that there'll be any.'

'Not stew, you soft thing. A bit of clay.'

'Oh, clay. Ay, well make it small and perhaps I'll fit it in the kiln. As long as . . .'

'As long as it's good enough,' said Imogen. 'I know.'

'Do you want to be in on an evening like this?' he asked her.

'I don't mind.'

'You've not been out all day.'

He looked up from his bowl. He didn't make much effort to persuade Imogen to go out but sometimes he thought about it. And she knew he did.

'I was out before supper, Dad. Didn't you miss me?'

'Oh,' he said. 'Of course you were.'

'I took a walk over Mr Balik's field.'

'By the track, I trust. You don't want to meddle with that dry old stick.'

No one in the village wanted to meddle with Mr

Balik. Although there were occasions when they had to. When Mr Balik or his man, Grainger, came for the rents. When he also had a good look round, to check that all was in order.

'Of course by the track,' said Imogen.

'And what did you see?'

'What I usually see. The field. The barn. The usual things.'

Something stopped her telling him about the owl.

After supper Imogen took the oil lamp into the kiln-room and sat herself at one of the benches. She took two or three pinches of clay and worked them between her fingers. The clay was squeezed into a face, an apple, a round-bodied rabbit, but none of these things was satisfactory. She rolled it into a ball again. A crust dried on her hands and she clapped it off, then sat looking at the shapeless lump for a while, wondering how it would end up.

When she started again she had no clearer idea of what it was going to be but gradually it turned itself into a little dragon with lifted wings, its body arched as if it was about to spring.

Then she heard her father's boots scrape over the threshold.

'Imogen,' he said, stepping into the pool of light from the oil lamp. 'It's getting late.'

'Well, I've done all I'm doing tonight,' she told him.

He squatted down and looked closely at the dragon.

'Eh, it's fine, is that,' he said. 'A lizard, is it?'

'A dragon, of sorts.'

'It'll do nicely, Imogen. We can find a bit of kiln space for that, I'm sure.'

She was pleased. Dad didn't put things in the kiln unless they deserved their place. And she liked to see him satisfied with what she'd done. But the little dragon itself she wasn't so happy about. It was all right, but that was all.

She wrapped it in a damp cloth and decided to leave it overnight. See how it looked in the morning. She was sure, though, that she would squeeze it into a ball and start again. Or maybe give up making something this time round. She liked what she made to be perfect and the shape under the cloth wasn't the thing she'd had in mind. This time, though, she couldn't really grasp what that thing was supposed to be.

2

Imogen had no chance to go back to the dragon in the morning. Instead she went with her father to collect wood for the kiln. They went round the back of Old Carter's cottage and Dad sawed up good lengths from the fallen apple tree while Imogen loaded them on to the handcart. There was no sign of Boy but that didn't mean anything. There was no sign that he was far away either.

Boy was easy to avoid when school was on. He had little to say to Imogen and rollicked around with the other boys during play. That was safe enough. And she could sit in her desk during lessons and do her work, with the cracked side of her face angled away to the edge of the room. Mr Popplewell never said anything about it. He never had done, and whenever he looked at Imogen he pretended he couldn't see any scar. Even though she could see in his eyes that he had.

During the long holidays, though, you couldn't be sure where Boy might lurk. You might go for days without seeing him, and then he'd give a whole afternoon to following her around. Taunting her for a reaction like he sometimes did to the dog. He was a year or two younger than Imogen but a world away in sense, she thought.

When the cart was full, Old Carter came out of the cottage to collect the payment from Dad. He wasn't really old. He was probably about thirty. Tall with a red face and sandy hair. They only called him Old Carter after Boy was born and his wife insisted on calling the child Carter too.

'I won't ask much,' Old Carter said. 'The tree's come down and I don't want it cluttering the yard. You're doing me a favour.'

But he made sure he asked for something. And Dad was content to pay, though he kept quiet about how well it suited him. The apple was good, slow-burning wood. It would do nicely for the kiln. And both he and Imogen liked its smell when it burned.

'Come and have something to drink,' Old Carter said when the price was paid. He led the way into the cottage, stooping at the kitchen door and holding his hand out behind him to indicate that Dad should follow.

Imogen hesitated in the yard. She wasn't sure that Old Carter meant her to come in and have a drink. He had a way of not noticing she was there. She went over to the handcart and tidied the apple branches so that they shouldn't fall on the way back to the kiln-room. A pointless job – the rearrangement made them no more secure – but she didn't feel comfortable about standing still in the yard and doing nothing. When she'd finished she sat down with her back to the dog's kennel.

Old Carter's wife engaged herself in a rattling conversation with Dad, complaining about the weather, the dog and Boy. Their voices drifted into the yard.

Then Boy and the dog came scuttling round the side of the cottage and stopped in their tracks at the sight of Imogen. She stared at Boy for a moment and then turned away. He was not looking into her eyes but at her cheek.

'What you doing here, Crack-pot?' Boy asked.

'What's it look like?'

'It looks like nothing.'

'I'm collecting wood.'

Boy walked up to the hand cart and jiggled the branches around.

'This is our tree,' he said.

'Not now it isn't,' Imogen told him. 'It's our kindling. Bought and paid for so keep your fingers to yourself.'

She was prepared to swipe him one. Hoping he might do something that asked for a swipe. He came up to her and dropped to the ground, resting on his elbow and still gawping at her face. The dog nosed Imogen's knee and slunk into its kennel.

'What you staring at, Snotty?' she said.

'How'd'you get that?'

'Mind your own.'

'Does it hurt?'

He was looking at her without taunting this time. Just curious. Imogen felt like an insect on a leaf. She put her fingers to her cheek to cover the scar.

128

'I only want to know,' said Boy.

It was probably the nearest he'd ever been to her.

'I burnt it,' she told him simply.

'How?'

'On the kiln door.'

She remembered. Three years old, following Dad around in the kiln-room. Stumbling over his feet and falling against the kiln door which was open to take out the pots. The searing pain. And her ears filled with the sound of her own frightened scream.

'How can you burn yourself on a door?' asked Boy.

'It's white hot in a kiln. You have to have a glove for a kiln door. Don't you know that?'

Dad had whisked her off her feet and squeezed her to him, cursing the kiln and himself over and over.

Boy Carter sat up frowning and leaned towards her. He put his hand up and tried to touch her cheek. As if Imogen wasn't there. Not a person at all.

'No!' she yelled, twisting her head away.

And she swiped at him. Her fingers snatched up dust and sprayed it in his eyes. Her knuckles clicked against his nose. Boy yowled and looked down at the warm blood dripping on to his palms. There was a clattering of feet behind her and Dad and Old Carter appeared at the kitchen door. Wiping their mouths and blinking in the sunlight.

*

Dad hadn't said much about Boy's bloodied nose. Perhaps he knew the reason for it. Boy's mother had shaken him into the kitchen to put his head in a bowl. She said he'd probably asked for it but you couldn't tell from her cross face what she was really thinking.

In the evening, when Imogen went out into the lanes, she found herself remembering the owl. She turned towards Mr Balik's field, and half hoped that it might be there again, peering into the stubble for prey. She pictured its talons, fixed on the branch. The sharpness of death. They talked about that in church sometimes. About overcoming the sharpness of death.

As she approached the clump of trees where she'd seen her owl, Imogen slowed down. She thought she could discern a pale blur moving against the dark background towards the barn. She couldn't be sure, though. Voices came to her over the field. There were men, down in the corner by the barn. She quickened her step.

Two men, bending and shifting around at the base of the old barn. Grainger, the land manager, in his faded smock, silent and busy as usual. And Mr Balik himself. They were so intent on what they were doing that they didn't notice Imogen. She stopped to watch them.

Grainger was leaning loose bundles of sticks and straw against the barn wall. At first Imogen thought they were trying to prop the old building up. It sagged like a tired bullock and maybe the walls needed some extra support. But not with straw. Straw could only be for another purpose.

'Be a bit sharp, man,' Mr Balik was saying. 'I want this done tonight, not tomorrow.'

Grainger's reply was mumbled into the shadows. He lifted a foot and trod the bundles into place.

'They're going to burn it,' Imogen said quietly to herself. Then shouted out loud.

'No!'

Mr Balik looked up and saw a girl running across the corner of the field towards him. Her fair hair swished from side to side as she ran. Her feet crunched on the stubble.

'No!' she was shouting. 'You can't!'

'What is all this?' he said.

Imogen hurtled into him and clutched his arm to stop herself falling. He shook her off.

'Take your hands off me, girl. What are you doing on my land?'

'You can't burn the barn, Mr Balik,' she said.

'Can't? Who's telling me I can't?'

She looked up into his face which was silhouetted against the sky. His black hair, long and straight, was swept behind his ears where it hung on to his shoulders. He wore a shirt without a collar. A point of gold shone from a stud by his neck.

'I'm sorry, Mr Balik,' Imogen gasped. 'I didn't mean to stray off the track . . .'

'Then you can get back on it. Now.'

'But you don't understand . . .'

He took hold of her wrist and shook her. She would've fallen if his grip hadn't been so firm.

'What do you mean, I don't understand? What are you saying? You come running across my field, telling me I don't understand.'

'No,' she said. 'It's the barn. There's an owl . . .'

But she was too frightened to say properly what she meant. She looked at Grainger, hoping for a word of help from him, but he was bent over one of the bundles. Stopped in the middle of his task, watching Imogen and waiting to see what Mr Balik intended next.

'Please, Mr Balik, don't burn the barn.'

'Good God. I'll burn what I like on my own land.'

'But there's an owl. I saw it flying . . .'

'I want to hear no more. Do you understand, girl? Have you got it clear?'

She took a sharp breath, to stop herself crying, and she couldn't do that and speak. So she simply stared up at Mr Balik and then flinched as his hand darted towards her. He caught her by the jaw, squeezing her till her lips bunched.

'You are on my property,' he said. 'Trespass.'

His hand was large and calloused. He lowered his head to look into her eyes. Imogen saw him open his mouth to speak again. And then hesitate. A cloud of doubt seemed to pass over his face. With a turn of his wrist he twisted her head round, studying her. Whatever he intended to say dried in his throat. For a second the anger disappeared. Then he shoved her away so that she fell backwards on to the stubble and he strode back towards the barn.

'What are you waiting for, man?' he barked at Grainger. 'Get it going!'

Grainger came to life and pushed home the last bundle of sticks with his foot. He took matches from his smock and flicked his wrist to strike one. Yellow flames were sucked into the straw.

Imogen picked herself up and scrambled away, back towards the track. By the time she turned, the flames had taken hold and were licking up to the roof. She stood helplessly watching as the fire cracked and pulled the barn down into its heart. There were blackened ribs against the wall of flame and specks of dark floating into the sky. Smoke folded down into the field and drifted towards her. Her eyes were stinging but she blinked to clear them and focus on those specks. Trying to make out something from the way they moved.

But she couldn't tell. They just looked like specks and there was no life in them.

That night, Imogen loitered in the kiln-room before going in to see Dad. She took a pot and scooped some water from the barrel in the yard. Her eyes were red from smoke and crying and she dabbed at them until they felt fresh. There were also parallel scratch marks on one arm. They must've been caused by her fall in the stubble but she hadn't noticed them until she got home. She was about to cross the yard into the kitchen when she caught sight of the cloth over the little dragon.

'You're not right, are you?' she said, peeling back the cloth. 'Poor thing.'

And she squeezed it into shapelessness again. She saw why it wouldn't do. It was trying to become something it shouldn't be. It shouldn't be a dragon but an owl. Now that she understood that, Imogen wanted to work on it immediately, before this day was over. To work uninterrupted.

But first she had to see Dad. She didn't want him to come looking for her.

The evening passed quietly. When she went up to her room, she lay awake until she heard Dad's tread on the stairs up to the loft. She waited another half hour and then she took the faded grey cloak from the back of her door. Her mother's cloak. Her mother, who was no more to her than a soft brown photograph on the mantelpiece. She held the cloak to her face for a moment and then pulled it round her shoulders and went barefoot to the kiln-room.

The whole village was in darkness. Not that it mattered to Imogen. Outside her circle of lamplight it could have been bright daylight and she wouldn't have noticed. She heard the church clock chime one, then, what felt like a short time later, half-past. And she was standing back from the bench, looking at the owl she had made, feeling it was still not right, when the clock chimed again. Three o'clock.

She turned her back on her work and walked outside. The air was black, almost trembling with unseen life. She waited. Perhaps an owl would call to her. Perhaps the sound of it would make her finish the figure as she knew it must be finished. But there was no owl. Almost no sound at all. It was as if the night were mourning the loss of all owls.

She remembered her own owl, staring at her and hunching to take off. Fierce and wild. Like a cold white flame. She remembered the panic she felt at the sight of the burning barn. That wall of flame.

When she returned to the bench she took up one of the modelling sticks and gouged roughly at the figure's eyes. Two deep holes, imperfectly round. And there it stood. Tiny and red, a piece of solid clay. But with a new life of its own.

3

She woke late the following morning and went straight to the kiln-room to look at her owl again. She feared it might seem lifeless in the daylight. Dad was there ahead of her, cradling it in his palm.

'What happened to your dragon?' he said.

'I didn't like it. I had to make that instead.'

'You were right to change your mind, Imogen. This is better. I'm proper proud of it.'

After the owl had been fired, Dad took it into the shop and stood it in the middle of the shelf in the big window.

'Will someone want it, do you think?' Imogen asked.

'Someone is bound to.'

'To buy it?'

'To buy it, certainly. And the pennies shall be all yours.' He turned from the window and smiled at her. 'It's your work and I'm a fair master, I hope,' he said.

'I don't know, Dad. It might not be right . . .'

'Of course it would. Boy's mother would love that. It'd go with her china pieces over their fireplace.'

Imogen looked at the owl and frowned.

'I don't think I'd like it, though,' she said.

'Boy won't go near it, sweet. He wouldn't dare.'

'It's not that. I don't think I want it to go out of the home.'

'No? Well, maybe it would be hard to say goodbye to it. We'll show it, then, shall we? Show it but not sell it. Eh?'

And he made a card to prop beside it: not for sale.

For several days Imogen did not go out to walk across the fields in the evenings. Didn't stop to watch the birds, didn't sing to herself. The countryside outside the village was no longer a place to go to be alone. She feared that kind of loneliness now. Now she thought of those fields as a place of drifting smoke and sudden violence. A kind of smoke drifting through her own head.

She said little, kept her thoughts to herself. And nobody noticed the difference in her. She was silent, sometimes looking thoughtful. Well, that couldn't really be called a change. That was the way she was. So the difference stayed hidden from others.

At night, those moments in which the barn caught fire came back to her. She saw the broad face of a white owl, looming from side to side, inches away from her eyes. And behind it the flames, forcing it towards her.

Sometimes she saw the owl as she remembered it. A fleeting, silent figure. But at other times it came to her as the little clay figure she'd made. Curiously alive and hovering before her with a rattling of stiff wings. And she would wake and stare into the dark corners of her room. As if she expected it to be perched there somewhere, watching her.

'What is it?' she would ask softly. 'What do you want?'

She listened to the sounds of the night, straining to hear a settling of feathers in the dark.

'I can't help you now,' she said. 'It's too late.'

And when she slept again the owl would return. Sometimes living feather and talon, sometimes the curious, seeing clay. These dreams disturbed her because she hardly knew what they meant. But she wasn't frightened by them.

One night she crept downstairs to the shop. She took her clay owl off the shelf and held it in her fingers. The life it had was what she'd given it. Nothing more. But it comforted her.

'Fortune,' she said. 'I'll call you Fortune.'

Dad was somewhere out in the yard and Imogen thought she could hear the shop bell. She came through to the shop to see but it was empty. She ducked under the counter and went to the big window to peer between the displayed pots. Mr Balik was coming down the street with Grainger trailing a yard or two in the dust behind him. She saw at once it was Mr Balik, his black hair swept back from his high, pale forehead, and she caught her breath. She thought perhaps he'd come to complain about her trespassing the other evening; to find out what must be done about it.

There was hardly anyone else about. Very likely people were staying indoors till the two men had passed. Mr Balik wasn't the sort of man you exchanged pleasantries with. You lived on his land and paid him for it. You didn't stop to chat.

Only one other figure remained in the street. Boy Carter, kneeling by his front step and playing with some mud he'd made. Imogen saw Boy look up, take notice of the dark figure striding down the middle of the road towards him, then carry on playing. She saw him toss little balls of mud into the road. His mouth pouted and opened as he watched them explode.

Imogen was turning away, into the shadows of the shop, when an unexpected movement stopped her. It was Boy, swinging his arm up in a peculiar gesture as Mr Balik and Grainger drew level with him. There was a moment of stillness. Boy was looking up at Mr Balik, squinting with a wide grin into the sun. Then Mr Balik stooped and rubbed something off the toe of his boot with one thumb, and Grainger stepped forward, to give Boy a rough word and send him packing.

But he was prevented. Mr Balik stood sharply and his stick whipped through the air, stinging into Boy's calf. Imogen heard the smack. Another moment of stillness, the squint still frozen on Boy's face.

Briefly, Imogen laughed to herself. He was getting what he'd asked for many, many times. For his silly pranks and stupidity. But the stick was lifted again, high, as if Mr Balik intended more hurt, and Boy tried to make himself small in the road. Frightened, not understanding, Imogen was shocked. Without thinking, she started forward, one hand reaching for the door to the street. But Grainger had stepped between Mr Balik and the boy. He took the stick from his master's hand, quite slowly and gently. Then handed it back to him. Mr Balik took it and immediately turned away. He continued to walk steadily down the street, towards the potter's shop.

This time Imogen did shrink back into the shop, darting under the counter and into the safety of the middle room where she could watch through a crack in the door. Half a minute later Mr Balik pushed into the shop. The bell jangled in the silence and Imogen thought it took far longer than usual to fade away. She held her breath and watched Mr Balik.

She was surprised to see how impassive his face looked. As if he'd strolled down from the big house and nothing had interrupted his progress.

No one came to the sound of the bell so Mr Balik turned to the window and lowered his head to the glass. He looked into the street for a moment or two before his attention was caught by something on one of the shelves. He had his back to Imogen. A broad back, bent as he examined whatever it was that he'd seen. His hands, one of them holding that same stick – Imogen could now see that it had a silver top – rested on his hips. After a moment he straightened and turned, impatiently, looking into the shadows to see if anyone was coming to speak to him. Imogen took a step back and cowered behind the door.

'Shop!' called Mr Balik. 'Where are you, then?'

He rapped his stick on the floor and went back to looking at the things on the shelves. Dad came hurrying from the back.

'Didn't you hear the bell?' he asked Imogen in a hushed voice as he pushed by.

Before she could answer, Dad had continued into the shop and seen that it was Mr Balik calling for him. He wiped his hands on a scrap of towelling and dropped it on to the floor behind him.

'Mr Balik,' he said. 'I'm sorry. I didn't know it was you.'

'I've come for rent, potter. Not to buy.'

'Yes, of course,' said Dad. He called to Imogen over his shoulder. 'Imogen. Fetch the jar, will you, sweet?'

Mr Balik's gaze pierced the gloom and found her out. His face remained expressionless, though. He did not seem to know her. Relieved, she ran into the kitchen to get the money jar. When she returned, Mr Balik was squatting down by the window, tapping his stick against his knee.

'Now I'm here, though,' he was saying, 'I do see something that I like.'

'Yes, sir?'

'But it says "not for sale". So, what can be done?'

Imogen held her breath. Why was Mr Balik looking at her owl? Did he know more about it than he showed in his face? Perhaps he recognized her after all. Remembered the wild girl who shouted at him about owls. And maybe this was a twisted way of bringing the subject up.

'I'm afraid I couldn't sell that, sir,' Dad said as he counted coins out of the jar. 'It's not mine, you see.'

'Really?'

Mr Balik flicked another glance in Imogen's direction. But, again, she could see no recognition in his face.

'No, it's my daughter's and she wants to keep it,' Dad went on. 'So she says. Although I suppose I could . . .'

'No. Let her keep it,' said Mr Balik, pursing his lips.

Dad handed the money to Mr Balik who nodded briefly and turned for the door.

'I could make another, if you like,' Dad said.

'Another? Just like this.'

'As like as I can get it, Mr Balik. Or bigger. I could make a large one for you.'

For a moment Mr Balik stood still and said nothing. He held the shop door open with his stick and loosened a strand of hair from his collar with one finger.

'Yes,' he said softly, almost to himself. 'Yes, make me one like that. Life size.'

'Life size, sir?'

'In fact . . .' He looked up at Dad. 'Make me more than one. A dozen. Can you do that?'

'A dozen? Of course, Mr Balik. Of course.'

'Good. Let me know when they're ready.'

And he left the shop, clattering the door behind him.

Dad's eyes were shining. He looked round for Imogen and smiled broadly at her. A dozen owls for Mr Balik. She couldn't remember him ever getting a job like that before and she was pleased that her little owl had helped it come about.

'Tell me what I just heard, Imogen,' said Dad. 'Twelve owls for Mr Balik. Is that what he said?'

'It is, Dad. Will he pay well?'

'Oh, he will, sweet. He's very fair about such matters, whatever else you might say about him. I think we're about to make our fortune, you and I.'

But beneath his delight at the work, Imogen thought she detected a worry in Dad's eyes. If she hadn't known his face so well she wouldn't have noticed it. That hint of anxiety. I'm not sure I can do it. I'm not sure I can get it right.

4

Throughout the rest of the week, Imogen and her father worked hard on Mr Balik's commission. Dad kneaded the clay and built up the bodies in careful layers. Imogen concentrated on the details, returning to each figure again and again until she was satisfied that it looked right. She had little need to go back to her original owl, though. The image of that was fixed firmly in her mind. At first, Dad wouldn't trust her to do the modelling from her head. He wanted her to keep checking and sometimes, when his part of the work was done, he watched nervously over her shoulder.

'He'll want them exact, Imogen,' he told her. 'It won't do if they're any different.'

'Don't worry, Dad,' she said. 'They're all right.'

'But there's a lot to go wrong, sweet. There's the firing, for a start. The more I think about that the more it worries me.'

'Then we must make another one.'

'Another one?'

'Yes,' said Imogen, concentrating on the clay beneath her fingers. 'We must make thirteen. One for luck. Just in case.'

And that's just what they did.

When they were finished and lined up on the bench in the kiln-room, Imogen told her father to go out into the yard and worry there for a moment or two. She took a piece of wire and scratched a number at random on the base of each one.

'Now, potter,' she said sternly when she led her father back into the kiln-room, 'which is the thirteenth owl? Can you find him for me?'

He frowned and moved slowly down the line, studying each one in turn. He hesitated over first one and then another.

'This one?' he said at last.

'No,' smiled Imogen. 'That's number five. But it wouldn't matter. They're all the same. Twins, or whatever you call thirteen identical owls.'

He laughed at her, standing there so proudly beside her line of owls. He was almost relaxed. But she knew he wouldn't be truly at ease until they were all fired and delivered safely to Mr Balik's house.

'I'm going to sit by this kiln until I know for sure,' he said.

'That's going to be a long wait, Dad.'

'Well, I shan't sleep if I leave them to it so I might as well be in here.'

He took a chair from the kitchen and settled himself beside the kiln. Sideways to the door so he could hear the fire purring to itself. Imogen went back to the house and attended to the shop until closing time. It was a quiet afternoon with few customers. Mr Bailey, the man from The Hope, called to collect three jugs he'd ordered. Boy Carter came lurking outside the window but ran off as soon as Imogen got to her feet and took a step towards the door.

At dusk she locked up and turned the sign round to show they were closed. Then she took her little owl off its shelf and carried it through to the kitchen. She stood it on the window ledge while she cut Dad some bread and cheese and heated him some milk. She placed the food and drink on a wooden tray with the owl. When she took these things out to him, she saw Dad with his head nodding on his chest and the lids of his eyes sliding shut.

'Let me sit here awhile,' she said. 'Nothing will go wrong. And, if it does, I'll know what to do about it.'

'If it goes wrong, Imogen,' Dad said, hauling himself stiffly from his chair, 'you're to call me. At once. Do you understand?'

'Of course I understand. Go inside and rest.'

Alone in the kiln-room, Imogen didn't feel like sleeping. She thought she'd been tired but now found that she was wide awake. She turned the little owl over and over in her hands, thinking of nothing in particular. She looked into the dark holes of its eyes as it turned, and ran her fingers over the curve of its wings.

Then, without warning, she felt it move in her hand.

A tiny pulse of life, as if it was wriggling to be free. She caught her breath and watched it slip through her fingers and dash against the stone floor, exploding in fragments.

Before the shock hit her, she heard another sound. Nearby. A rattling whisper this time, from the kiln.

'Dad,' she said fearfully, but not loud enough for anyone to hear.

The rattling sound came again. And, yes, it was inside the kiln. Imogen picked up the heavy glove Dad used to open the door. She knew she shouldn't do it, knew that the thirteen owls were in the middle of firing. But she had to look. She had to see what was making that noise.

The door swung open for only a moment or two. Imogen glimpsed a block of yellow-white light, broken by the huddled shapes of the dark owls. A fierce heat wafted against her face and she screwed up her eyes to peer into its heart. There was no movement in the kiln. Only sound. That same whisper of a rattle, louder now that the door was open. It was dying on a hiss when a second explosion jumped out at her. A violent crack, deeper and more resonant than the smashing of Fortune.

She slammed the door shut and stepped backwards. Then she ran. Out of the kiln-room and away. Anywhere that was away from that terrible, live rattling sound and the crack that meant that she had maybe ruined Mr Balik's owls.

'Imogen? Imogen, are you awake?'

She was curled up on her bed. Dad was looking down at her.

'I thought you were in the kiln-room,' he said. 'I thought you were still watching.'

She sat up and looked around. Strong morning light was coming into the room. Everything seemed peaceful and ordinary. Boy Carter's small voice was shouting outside somewhere. And his dog was barking back at him.

'You should've woken me, Imogen. If you were tired I'd've carried on watching. I didn't want those owls left by themselves.'

'I got frightened . . .' she said.

'Frightened?'

'Yes, but . . .'

She stopped herself. She didn't mean to tell him what she'd heard but she found she was speaking about it before she was fully awake.

'What was there to be frightened of?'

'Nothing. No . . . It was just dark and . . .'

'Well, it doesn't matter, sweet. The firing's done and your owls are all out on the bench.' He paused and smiled at her. 'And they're fine, Imogen. Every one of them.'

'They're all right?'

'Perfectly. And waiting for you to inspect them. Are you coming?'

He took her down to the kiln-room, bubbling with chatter and relief, and stood aside so she could step in first. The owls were ranged on the bench. A perfect line in the dusty light. Not destroyed, as Imogen had feared. She felt like singing at the sight of them.

'Now,' said Dad, 'here they are. Take a good look at them, young potter, and tell me which one is number thirteen. Pick him out for me.'

She smiled and moved slowly down the line, just as he had done before the firing. Each one was solid and true and as like its brothers as made no difference. Until . . .

A face with a crack across it.

The same deep eyes as the others, the same turn of its head, but a thin crack running diagonally down one side of its flat face.

Imogen stopped and turned back to her father. Surely he knew that one of the owls was cracked? But no. He was still smiling at her. Nodding slightly and smiling in anticipation. To him they were all alike. She reached out her hand, as if to touch the damaged figure, and hesitated. Then she moved on, two places down the line.

'This one?' she said.

She looked at Dad and tried to match his smile.

'No,' he said. 'Or maybe yes. I can't tell. You must look at the numbers on the back.'

The number on the back said nine which seemed to delight him even more. Imogen knew what the number on the cracked owl would be.

5

On the Tuesday morning, Dad wheeled the hand-cart to the front of the shop and they loaded the owls to take to Mr Balik. They put a layer of straw in the bottom of the cart and packed more straw, like blankets, round each of the figures. Dad's face was shining with sweat and concentration as he carried them from the shop to the cart.

'Will he like them, Dad, do you think?' Imogen asked him.

'He can't fail to like them. They're just what he asked for. Twelve fine owls.'

'Thirteen.'

'That's right. Thirteen. Enough for a judge and a jury.'

He breathed deeply and wiped his hands on his trousers. Then he began to push the cart carefully up the hill towards the big house. Imogen walked ahead to warn of holes in the road or chickens which might take it into their heads to dart under the wheels. Several people stopped what they were doing to watch the cart go by. Mr Bailey appeared at the doorway of The Hope with one of Dad's jugs in his hand.

'Where to with that lot, potter?' he called.

'To Balik's,' Dad said without taking his eyes off the road.

When they reached the church there was a flurry of movement somewhere to their left and Boy Carter erupted from the snicket. Dad heaved the handles of the cart round. Boy's mouth gaped with shock and he stumbled over his own feet as he tried to swerve clear. He charged into the side of the cart with his head and shoulders. The cart lurched, balanced on one wheel for a second and dropped down again with a shudder. Boy toppled backwards into the dust. There was a moment's silence while the three of them looked at each other.

'Oaf!' said Dad through his teeth. 'Bloody little oaf!'

It was the first time Imogen heard him call anyone bloody or oaf. She was more startled by that than by Boy's tumbling out of the snicket so unexpectedly. It sounded wrong, even though she knew Boy was all the things Dad had called him.

Dad lowered the handles of the cart and started delving in the straw. He had to step over Boy who was sitting upright in the road and had started blubbering to himself. All those times she'd willed him to hurt himself, to fall off walls and be cuffed by his mother; now that he was here at her feet, wailing like a baby, it didn't seem to mean very much. There was no satisfaction in it.

She ran up to him and pulled him to his feet. It was the first time she'd been close to him since Mr

Balik had beaten him in the street. He was wearing coarse trousers, cut off at the knee, and, as she held him firmly by the elbows, she was able to look closely at the back of his legs. He sagged in her grip. She could see none of the marks she'd been imagining, only streaks of dust on a brownish skin.

'Are you all right?' she asked, meaning the beating but knowing he wouldn't understand. Then she hissed at him, 'Get off. Get yourself off home while you've the chance.'

At the sound of her voice he stopped blubbering and looked up. He blinked, then tried to pull away from her.

'Go on,' she said, shaking him. 'Unless you want to stay here and see what happens next.'

Without another sound he scuttled off towards the Carters' cottage and was well out of the way by the time Dad turned round from the cart.

'Where is he?' he asked.

His face was pale and shiny. He clenched his fists.

'He's run off. Is there any damage, Dad?'

'Not that I can see. But I'm not taking them out for a proper look. Not here in the road. Not with mad ragbags like him about.'

'He didn't mean it,' said Imogen. 'That's just Boy. He's always running his head into something or other.'

'Well, he ought to think before he moves.'

'I'm not sure he's able to, Dad. Let's get these up to Mr Balik's while we can, shall we?'

★

152

They left the handcart at the foot of the broad steps up to Mr Balik's door. Grainger let them in. He was expecting them.

'No,' he said shortly, 'I know why you've come, though I don't know who put it into your heads.'

He turned his back and allowed them to follow him across the hall. It had a marble floor of black and white squares and the air was cool and full of soft shadows high above their heads. Three sets of tall doors led to the rest of the ground floor. One stood ajar, revealing a cream-grey corridor which Imogen found unbearably gloomy. To their left a staircase with iron posts and handrails swept away to a landing and the upper rooms.

When it looked as though they were about to follow him through one of the double doors, Grainger cleared his throat and barred the way.

'Wait here,' he said. 'Mr Balik will come to you.'

He backed through the double doors and pulled them to with a soft click which echoed off the marble.

Dad looked at Imogen and smiled nervously. He wiped his lips with the back of one finger and she thought he looked afraid to break the silence.

'You've brought the owls?'

Speaking before they knew he was there, Mr Balik was striding into the hall in riding boots which clicked over the floor.

'I'll see them now,' he said. 'Where are they?'

'In the handcart, Mr Balik. Outside,' said Dad.

'Bring it in. Grainger, help them. I'd like them all out on the floor.'

Grainger and Dad hurried out to the cart and eased it slowly up the steps. A block of sunlight fell into the hall as Grainger unbolted the tall front door. The light struck Mr Balik, making him narrow his eyes. Imogen saw his high forehead, the swept-back, dark hair. He was, she thought, like the hall they were standing in. Both dark and pale, marble and cool.

Dad pushed the cart to the middle of the hall, leaving a tiny trail of dried grass from its wheels. But Mr Balik didn't seem to notice. In fact, now that there was so much sunlight in the hall, Imogen could see that it was far from clean. There were scatterings of straw in places over the floor and some grey planks of wood leaned against a wall. They looked as if they belonged in some yard. As if they'd been thrown aside a year or more ago and left there.

Mr Balik stood with his feet apart, watching as the first owl was unpacked from its straw and set down for him to see. He made no reaction but Grainger, leaning back on his haunches, let out a soft whistle and looked slowly from Dad to Mr Balik. His face showed the faintest trace of puzzlement.

'Don't stop there, man,' Mr Balik said to him. 'We'll see the lot, if you don't mind.'

'Yes, sir,' said Grainger, but Imogen thought he looked uneasy.

Once or twice, as she lifted a figure carefully out of the cart, she risked a glance at Mr Balik. His eyes moved a little, taking in the details, but his face was set. She couldn't tell what he was thinking.

'What's this?' he said when the last figure was set before him. 'Thirteen?'

'Yes, sir,' said Dad. 'We made an extra. Against something going wrong with the firing.'

'I asked for twelve.'

'Yes . . . I know, Mr Balik. I just thought . . .'

'One's for luck,' said Imogen.

She surprised herself by daring to speak and immediately wished she'd kept quiet. Mr Balik turned to her.

'Luck? Where does luck come into it? I wanted twelve. I did not want extras. These were to be the only owls of their kind. Didn't you understand that?'

'Of course, sir . . .'

'Then why thirteen, man? Don't you trust your own craft?'

Dad was silenced. He waited, with his head bowed, as Mr Balik dropped on one knee to examine the owls more carefully. Minutes passed in silence. Then:

'What's the matter with this one?'

'Which one?'

'This,' said Mr Balik, standing and catching up one of the figures. 'It's cracked. Here, across its face.'

'What?' said Dad. Alarm made him bold and he took the owl from Mr Balik's hand. Mr Balik released it as if he wanted no more to do with it and Dad fumbled it before bringing it up to his eyes to examine it.

'Perfect, they had to be,' said Mr Balik. 'Twelve perfect owls. Are the others all right?'

He got down on his hands and knees, like some urgent animal, to look at the others.

'The cart took a bump,' mumbled Dad. 'On our way up here.'

But Mr Balik wasn't listening. He took hold of the owls one by one, turning them over and studying them closely. Imogen held her breath but he found nothing wrong with the remaining twelve.

'Right,' he said at last. 'Twelve, as requested. You can pay for these, Grainger. But that one . . .' He nodded sharply at the thirteenth owl in Dad's hand. 'That I want destroyed. Do you understand me? I don't want anyone else to see it.'

They weren't sure whether to be pleased or disappointed after their encounter with Mr Balik. He had accepted and paid for his twelve owls – and good money, too – but he'd said nothing about liking or admiring them. And Dad was always more pleased by praise for his work than by payment. He was thoughtful and quiet as they trundled the almost empty cart down the hill again. Getting the job and making the owls had, for all his worries, put some edge and excitement into him. There were heavy coins in his pocket but it wasn't the same.

Whatever the outcome, though, it was a relief to be out of that house. Those tall doors, leading to corridors leading to emptiness; they disturbed Imogen.

When they were almost home, they saw a tall man with sandy hair leaning against the shop door. It was Old Carter, waiting to have a word with them.

'Boy tells me you've crowned him one with your hand cart,' he said.

'I would've done,' Dad told him, 'but he was too quick for me.'

'Why, what's to do?'

'He shot out of the snicket by the church like a rat out of a stack, Carter. Rammed straight into the side of a fully loaded cart.'

'I thought it might be something like that. His mother did too, only she said to come and find out.'

'He didn't mean to,' said Imogen. 'He wasn't looking where he was going.'

'He doesn't know where he's going half the time. His Mother said I was to give you a wigging if you were responsible and pass on her apologies if it was down to Boy.'

'Well,' said Dad, 'it's down to Boy all right.'

'Then I'm sorry for it. Did he do you much damage?'

'Very nearly. He all but put me the wrong side of old Balik. There were a dozen pieces survived the blow but . . .'

'But it was all right, really,' cut in Imogen. 'Mr Balik liked the work.'

'Ah,' said Old Carter. 'So you were on your way to the big house, were you? With the pots, was it?'

'That's right. They were owls. How did you know about them?'

'Grainger told me, though he didn't say they were owls. Said the old devil wanted some kind of work off you.'

'Is that so?' said Dad, a little put out that Old Carter should know so much about it. 'Grainger does talk, then? He said precious little to us.'

'He'll talk if you've got time to wait and listen,' said Old Carter. 'In fact he more or less got the jabbers over these blessed pots.'

'Well, I can't think why that should be.'

'Nor me. Still, there's no point trying to work Grainger out after all those years at the big house. He told me that Balik wanted pottery for each of his outward rooms. He intends to stand them on the window ledges.'

'What for?'

'God knows, potter. There's only him and Grainger up there to see them. Still, I haven't the patience to work out the ways of the rich. And I don't suppose you mind what he does with them.'

'Not now he's paid up, I don't.'

Old Carter shuffled back up the road to report his findings to his wife while Dad unlocked the shop. Imogen took the handcart round the back and removed the thirteenth owl. She lifted it delicately from its straw, carried it into the kiln-room and placed it on the bench.

Fortune was a good name for her little owl, she thought. It would make a good name for this one too. Mr Balik didn't like the idea of there being thirteen owls but, if it hadn't been for the extra one, his order couldn't have been met. The twelfth owl would have been damaged and then it was quite likely that he'd have refused the lot.

Dad came through from the yard and stopped in his tracks at the sight of the clay figure on the bench. He snatched up a sack and tossed it over its head.

'Don't cover it,' said Imogen.

'I'm not just covering it up,' he said. 'This is to stop the pieces flying.'

'Why? What are you going to do?'

'What I said I would.' He took up a hammer and tapped the shaft against his palm. 'Destroy it.'

'No,' said Imogen, catching his arm. 'Don't smash it.'

'I promised, Imogen. I have to.'

'Please. Mr Balik said he didn't want anyone to see it. They won't if I keep it in my room, will they?'

'Keep it?' he said, looking at her with a puzzled frown. 'What do you want to keep it for?'

'Because my little owl was smashed and . . . and I want this one to take his place. To remember things by . . .'

'But Imogen, it's not even right. Its face is cracked. You can't want it.'

She wasn't expecting him to say that. She flinched, just a little, and looked steadily at him. He stared back at her for no more than a moment and then lowered his eyes.

'Can't want it?' she said. 'Because its face is cracked?'

'Yes, well . . .'

He placed the hammer gently on the bench and moved towards the door. 'Perhaps you should take it, Imogen,' he said over his shoulder. 'It's mostly your work after all, I suppose. But Mr Balik mustn't know. You mustn't tell anyone.'

He's afraid, thought Imogen for the first time. Afraid of Mr Balik, and of me.

'I won't say anything, Dad,' she said. 'And, anyway, who is there to tell?'

Fortune, the thirteenth owl, stood on the ledge of Imogen's square window. It looked out, over the red-tiled roof of the kiln-room, towards the fields. Imogen lay on her bed and watched it. By moving her head a little from side to side, she made it appear to sway. Gently, as if it was attending to the movement of some field-mouse or vole in the distance.

After a while, she repositioned it so that its eyes were staring into the room. Deep, black holes in its flat face; but, somehow, not empty. The face had a troubled look. It was lit down one side by the low sun and the fine crack across its cheek appeared to glisten. Almost as if it were moist.

'What's the matter?' Imogen said softly. 'Are you sad?'

The owl looked silently into the room.

Eventually Imogen's eyes closed and through the blackness of sleep the sound came back to her – that rattling undertone she'd heard from the kiln. A tangle of shaken wires, a breeze disturbing the leaves of a silver birch.

She tried to drag herself back to wakefulness but she didn't have the strength. The sound hissed around her room, both inside and outside her head. Dream and reality.

6

A block of sunlight came in at the back door and angled over the kitchen table. Imogen's head was resting on the table when the shadow appeared behind her. So sharp and clear that it seemed to be more than shadow, to have a substance of its own. She felt the cold weight of it on her arm. A shape, falling across the kitchen table and moving its head from side to side. It was the size of a tall man but in its precise outline she could see feathers, the hook of a beak glimpsed before the head turned and the outline was lost.

Imogen could not bring herself to look. The shadow grew across the table in front of her. It obliterated the sunlight. She felt something move to stand behind her.

A broad man in a black suit with the head of a bird. A thin skin, laced with red veins, over the swelling of its eyes. It opened its beak, wide and silent.

The sound that filled her ears was Imogen's own shout. She sat up in bed and leaned forward to prop her head on her knees. It was still dark and the house was quiet.

First there had been the rattling sound from the kiln, as she was falling asleep, then this; a man-bird standing at her back, made blind by skin stretched over its eyes.

Imogen had seen him without turning round. Somehow she'd been high above the kitchen and had seen herself sitting at the table with the man-bird behind her. When she closed her eyes now she could see him again. This time, though, she knew it was only the memory of the dream and not the dream itself. The danger wasn't close. All the same, she climbed out of bed, took her mother's cloak and pulled a chair to the window. She rested her elbows on the ledge, determined to stay awake till she saw the first streaks of light sky above the fields.

The folds of the cloak made a good pillow. She liked the fading grey of it, and its heaviness. It seemed to comfort her and, gradually, the dream began to lose its vividness and slip out of her mind.

The cloak was almost all there was in the house to remind her that once she'd had a mother. Some-times she stopped to look at the photograph above the fireplace, when Dad wasn't around, but it didn't mean as much to her as the cloak. A lady resting a hand on the back of a chair. Not smiling, rather sombre. Imogen was sure she hadn't been as serious as that. The cloak told a different story. It felt like a plump arm across her shoulders.

There were times when she wanted to ask Dad about her but something in his face always stopped her. Some shadow of loss, perhaps. Her mother had died such a long time ago, even before the accident in the kiln-room, and yet he still couldn't bring himself to talk about her.

Before the dawn came Imogen had fallen asleep. 'Are you all right, Imogen,' Dad asked her in the morning. 'You look a little tired to me.'

'Oh,' she said, 'I had a dream. It woke me up.'

'A bad dream?'

'Just enough to wake me.'

She wanted him to ask more about it but he wouldn't. He was centring clay on the wheel; making himself busy. If he'd asked what her dream was about she might've tried to tell him. Part of her wanted to tell him. If she put it in words for him, said it out loud, it might not have seemed so bad. She might even have been glad to hear him laugh it off.

'Did I wake you?' she asked.

'Wake me?'

'Yes. I think I called out.'

'I didn't hear anything, sweet. You know me. I never wake up, even when I'm supposed to.'

Oh yes, she knew him. She knew when he tried not to look at her because he was fussing over a job he normally did without thinking. When he had things to say but wouldn't open his mouth.

In the evening she went out for a walk and Boy and his dog emerged from nowhere and tagged along. Imogen sighed and said nothing. But she noticed a difference in Boy. There were still sidelong glances at her, making her feel as if she were part of some circus, but there was no mockery in them. Perhaps the bang on his skull had knocked the taunting out of him, she thought.

She'd planned to go down the lane and cut across the fields, like she used to do, but the thought of Boy dragging behind her and yattering nonsense all the way made her change her mind. She turned right and headed up towards the church.

'Your mum's looking for you,' she said.

'What?'

'She's looking out the window. See. I think she wants you.'

'No she don't. She just told me to clear out.'

'Oh. I wonder why?'

'Says I've been under her feet. Ted showed me where there's badgers. D'you want to see?'

'No.'

'It's a bit early, though. They don't come out till it's getting dark. You seen old Balik lately?'

'We took the cart up there the other day. Remember?'

'That man's a bastard. A right bastard.'

'You shouldn't say things like that, Boy.'

'He is, though. I heard my Dad say so. He's a right old bastard, he said.'

'You just like saying the word.'

'I don't.'

Imogen didn't argue. If I don't say anything, she thought, he might go away.

'A right, proper old bastard,' Boy muttered darkly.

'Bloody old bastard of a bastard. I hate him. You know what he's done now?'

'What?'

'He told off Ted and his brother to their old man.'

In spite of herself Imogen wanted to hear more about Mr Balik.

'What for?' she asked.

'For poking around his garden.'

'Well, they shouldn't have been there, should they?'

'Didn't do him no harm, though. And it's bloody big enough. It weren't nothing to get stewed up about. What was they doing anyway? Squashing his precious grass flat?'

'It was trespass, though.'

'Oo-er. Tresp-arse.'

'They asked for it, Boy.'

'Asked for it? For him to come flying out and give them both a cut of the lug? Then tell their old man so's he can give them a leathering? Bastard.'

'I'll tell your mum what you say.'

'You won't. You'll have to say it yourself. Then you'll be in trouble.'

'You wait and see, then.'

Boy fell silent for a while. By this time they'd reached the church. Imogen thought about going into the yard but she didn't like the idea of Boy, with his foul mouth and his scruffy dog, following her. So she walked on, out of the village.

In a little while they came to Mr Balik's drive, as she knew they would. She wanted to stop and turn round before they reached it but she couldn't do that without giving Boy a reason. And Boy would nag her for a reason and not be fobbed off with anything that sounded weak or vague.

An iron gate, permanently open and overgrown between two tall pillars marked the entrance. She hesitated outside, looking up the drive. It was overhung with trees, almost like a tunnel, and curved away to the right, up to the big house. The house itself couldn't be seen from the road.

As they stood there, the dog started to whimper. It crouched down on its haunches and rolled its eyes at Boy.

'He wants to run,' said Imogen. 'Why don't you take him into the fields?'

'No. Someone's coming. Listen.'

He dropped to his knees and wrapped his arms around the dog's neck. The jingle of harness came to them through the trees.

'It's Balik,' said Boy.

He picked up the dog and wrestled it into the bushes by one of the pillars. It writhed in his grasp and its whimpering became more urgent.

'Quiet, you daft thing!' hissed Boy, and clamped his hands round the dog's jaws.

Imogen waited. Why should she hide from Mr Balik? She'd done nothing. And she was on the public highway, not his property. Then she heard Mr Balik shout something at his horse, sounding very close. She glanced up and saw a blur of high-trotting

167

front legs, the mass of the horse's neck, twisted and pulled back. And the toe of Mr Balik's boot.

Immediately she shook herself into movement and ran for safety, throwing herself down next to Boy. Her face was pressed into the turf but she didn't dare to move. She held her breath and listened to the thud of the horse's feet pass by.

'He's gone,' said Boy eventually. 'Down the lane and into the village.'

'Why'd you hide like that?' Imogen asked sharply. 'There was no need.'

'Why'd you do it, then?'

She stood up and swiped at the few wet leaves clinging to her dress. Then she looked down at Boy fiercely, as if she might take a swing at him. He remained crouched in the grass. The dog was trying to twist its head free from his grip. He struggled to hold on but it gave a sudden jerk and spilled out of his arms.

'All right, all right,' he said. 'You don't like him either, do you, boy?'

The dog backed away, lowering itself to the ground and yapping.

'No,' said Imogen. 'It's not that. It's not Mr Balik he doesn't like . . .'

''Course it is. Look at him.'

It yapped once more and then sprinted off down the lane, the same way that Mr Balik had gone.

'He's frightened of the place,' said Imogen quietly, not really for Boy to hear. 'He can't abide being near this place.'

Boy jumped up and took off after his dog. His squeaky shouts faded quickly among the trees.

'Come back here! You hear me! Come back, you bastard!'

The sight of Boy's dog, struggling and whimpering outside the gate, kept coming back to Imogen. She wondered whether it had some memory of the place. Perhaps Mr Balik or Grainger had found it sniffing around up there and had chased it off. She could imagine Mr Balik giving the poor creature the toe of his boot. Maybe it was as simple as that, a hazy memory of being frightened.

She didn't think so, though. The more she thought about it, the more it seemed as if the dog had seen something, something that was hidden from everyone else. Some unreal thing, like a figure in a dream.

And Imogen knew what dreams could be like.

On some nights she saw nothing and was only aware of that rattling sound, and sensed unseen things swooping in the black air above her. At other times her dreams were astonishing and vivid; a great wall of fire, sucked towards her down a picture-lined corridor; tiny figures dancing from side to side inside the flames; or the man-bird, also coming towards her, staring at her out of its skin-covered, unseeing eyes. It never made any sound but gaped its beak wide as if it intended to.

When she woke from these dreams, she paced barefoot around her room, or took her chair to the window to wait until morning. She comforted herself by touching the cool flank of Fortune, stroking him gently. He kept her company, looking into the room while she looked out. Once she thought she heard Dad stirring in his room in the loft and seemed to see a thin bar of candlelight under her door. She waited for a knock but none came.

One night, after about a week of this, Imogen woke and didn't know where she was. There was a patch of pale blue light on the floor, in a pattern of twisted squares, and she could feel the roughness of scuffed wood under her fingers. Out of place but familiar. She was in the shop, she realized slowly. Stretched out on the floor, her fingers like claws, her body stiff and arched and her head bent backwards as she stared out of the window at the moon.

In a moment her body relaxed and she felt the world righting itself, becoming ordinary again. And here she was, on the floor of her father's shop, small and foolish. Her head was spinning and she choked, suddenly and loudly, with frustration. She rolled over and sobbed. Her tears soaked into the pale floorboards.

The air was still and heavy and when she got back to her room she opened the window. Then she stretched out on her bed, very weak, and closed her eyes. Immediately she saw the man with the bird head. Standing over the bed like a doctor. But when she opened her eyes she saw nothing.

Not a dream, she thought. I'm wide awake. And there's a sound — a sound in the room.

It was a sound that didn't belong. The hard rustling of plates or tiles settling. Over by the window. Fortune on the ledge, hunched to take off. Moving. Stepping to one side. Stepping back. And rattling his wing tips against the glass.

Imogen sat up slowly. Then, as she was standing, she saw the owl spring.

'No,' she whispered. 'Don't go.'

But Fortune disappeared into shadow and the window ledge was empty, nothing but space. She ran across the room and looked out. The moon, high above a layer of silver cloud, looked bigger from up here. For a moment she remained at the window, feeling as if the emptiness was passing into her body. Then she saw him, perched on the low roof of the kiln-room. And she knew he was waiting for her.

She snatched up the faded grey cloak and padded downstairs again, carrying her boots so she shouldn't wake Dad. As soon as she opened the back door to the night, Fortune lifted from the roof and swooped away again. Over the top of the shop, in the direction of the street. She struggled into the boots and ran round to the street. Almost at once she caught sight of him again, sitting on the thatch of Old Carter's cottage.

She followed him, from roof to chimney stack, from pub sign to fence post, up the street. Fortune kept ahead of her, stopping to wait for her, swaying from side to side, looking at her from his cracked face. And each time he landed it was easy to find him because Imogen knew where he was heading.

Mr Balik's house. Mr Balik himself must've been in there, perhaps awake, pacing up and down, but great as her fear of him was it was not as strong as her urge to follow Fortune wherever he led her. To a window on the ground floor. It was wide open, as if ready for her. She stood beneath it, smelling dew-damp earth and rich, sweet flowers from a nearby bed. The room before her was full of squares and shadows. She saw the sheen of a long table and little else that had a proper shape. Close to her on the window ledge stood a pottery owl but it wasn't Fortune. He was in the room somewhere. She couldn't see him but she sensed it. She stood quite still, not knowing what to do now that she was here.

Then she heard the sharp scrape of metal against brick. Another window being opened. Above her head, on the first floor. She looked up and saw the flicker of candle light and a dark arm holding the window catch. She shrank back against the wall.

'Who is it?' said Mr Balik. 'Who's there?'

His voice was soft but it filled the night. There was no other sound. Imogen saw him lean out of the window. The pale oval of his face against solid blackness as he turned his head slowly, searching the grounds. Her arms and legs began to shake but she stayed where she was, waiting for him to withdraw. Down in the village the church clock began to strike the hour. Before the last chime of two o'clock had faded away, she heard another sound. Inside the ground floor room this time. A rattle and a hiss. And there was a shape swooping at her out of the shadows. Fortune, flying at the open window.

Imogen fell back against the wall and cried out as the thirteenth owl passed over her head, dipped low against the ground and disappeared.

'I see you!' Mr Balik shouted down at her. 'What do you think you're playing at?'

She picked herself up and ran. Straight away from the house, towards the cover of the shadowy trees, her cloak billowing behind her. Mr Balik cursed loudly but she couldn't make out the words. Just angry shouting. Then he stopped. She imagined that he was hurrying through the house, clattering down the staircase or flinging open a cabinet to get to a gun.

At the head of the drive, gasping for breath, she stopped and looked back. No. He was still at the window. Standing there in silence. No more than a shadow in the weak light of the candle. Looking straight at her through the darkness.

Then he shouted again. One long cry, as if he'd been stabbed, but very clear.

'Charlotte!'

7

'You're up late,' Dad said.

There was no lightness in his voice. He wanted to know the reason, suspected he wouldn't like it, but still didn't ask. Didn't even turn round to look at her.

'I was tired,' she told him from the door of the shop. 'I've been walking a lot.'

She hadn't been walking but he wouldn't know that. Or, if he did, he wouldn't say so. She came and stood beside him. He was packing two large plates in a canvas bag.

'These are to go up to the church,' he said. 'Will they be safe in this bag, do you think?'

Imogen didn't answer. Her limbs felt stiff and last night's fear was still inside her. When she'd got home she'd found Fortune back on the window ledge. Cold and still but looking at her as if he wondered where she'd been. Almost disapproving. She'd felt like smashing him. Picking him up in both hands and bringing his head down on the ledge. She'd leaned against her door, picturing this. Hearing the sound. Seeing the fragments scatter over the floor. Then she'd fallen into bed and slept.

'I'll take them if you like,' she said to Dad. It suddenly seemed a good idea to go up to the church.

'All right. But don't take them to the vicarage. Leave them on the old oak chest by the font. The vicar won't want to be disturbed.'

The plates weren't heavy but Imogen packed the bag into the handcart to be sure she wouldn't drop them. She walked steadily up the hill, keeping to the middle of the street where there were fewer ruts.

Sharp memories of last night kept coming to her. Fortune gliding out of the open window. Mr Balik's face in the light of the candle. That name, shouted after her as she ran away. But they didn't come in any sensible sequence. They were like shards, pieces that might make a proper shape if she could put them together. And they were muddled with quite ordinary thoughts.

She found herself wondering where Boy Carter was, whether he was lurking round some corner, waiting with more silly things to tell her. She hadn't bothered to make sure the coast was clear before setting out. And it was too late now. If Boy was watching her somewhere he didn't show himself. Still, she was glad to reach the safety of the church-yard and carry the plates through the heavy oak doors into that cool gloom. She preferred the church when it was empty. On Sunday mornings the pews were full of neighbours looking out of the corners of their eyes and worrying about the tightness of their collars and the neatness of their boots. A stiff, uneasy place on a Sunday.

She took the plates to the black chest by the font and spent some moments arranging them so that the vicar would notice them when he came in and be pleased with them. Then she sat in one of the pews and looked up at the wooden roof boards, so high above her with so much cool air floating in between. She was grateful for that centuries old peace. It made her feel safe.

Then there was a clank at the door.

Imogen sank lower in her pew, conscious that she was sitting where she shouldn't be. Footsteps clicked over the stone floor. And another sound, too. The light tap of a stick. Each sound seemed large and solemn, rising slowly to lose itself in the air of the nave. A figure passed down the aisle; went beyond her place without noticing her. She knew it was Mr Balik, almost before she saw him out of the corner of her eye.

He walked as far as the altar steps and stopped. One foot on the step, his head bowed. Mr Balik didn't come to the church on Sundays. He was notable by his absence, the villagers said. Imogen watched him standing there uncertainly, both hands pressing on his bent knee. Even from the back he looked uncomfortable, as if all the muscles in his shoulders were tensed.

Suddenly, he drew in a long, loud breath and walked briskly back down the aisle. Then, turning his face briefly in her direction, he noticed Imogen. She saw the moment of recognition in his eyes but it was nothing to do with what he'd seen, or thought he'd seen, last night. Yes, the potter's girl; that cracked little thing. That was all. She stood up slowly and looked at him.

'What are you doing in here?' he said, his voice jarring and loud in the silence of the church.

'I've brought some plates. For the vicar.'

He took a slow step towards her. Against the deep colours of the church window his face looked white as stone.

'Tell me . . .' he began and then stopped, looking at her for several moments, like someone emerging from a dream. Almost helpless.

'What?' asked Imogen.

But he shook his head and didn't answer. Then he turned away and walked quickly out of the church.

Over the next two nights the dream returned. But they remained dreams. Fortune did not move again or call her to follow him.

'And I wouldn't go if he did,' she said to herself. 'I shan't go up there again. Ever.'

One morning, she was sitting in the shop, waiting to open and nodding over a book, when a large cart pulled up outside. The cart was familiar enough; it belonged to Mr Robinson who farmed the bit of land north of the village, beyond the big house. But it was unusual to see it stop at the potter's shop. More so to see Mr Robinson himself swing out of it and clump up to the shop front. He shaded his eyes and pressed his nose against the window. When he caught sight of Imogen, he began to work the handle up and down, very deliberately, and mouth words at her through the glass. Imogen tossed the book down and skipped over to unlock.

'We're not open yet, you know,' she said, holding the door so he couldn't pass. 'What's up?'

'You're ready, are you?' Robinson said.

'Ready for what?'

'You're coming with me, aren't you? To Melling?'

'I don't think I am.'

Dad hurried into the shop from the back and took the door from Imogen. Mr Robinson flexed his neck and shoulder muscles and glanced at Imogen as he stepped inside.

'You're early, Basil,' Dad said.

'This is morning, isn't it?' said Mr Robinson. 'I told you I'd be round in the morning.'

'She'll be with you before too long, Basil. I must have a word first, though.'

'It'll have to be a quick one, mind. I'll be starting when I start, ready or not.'

He marched out of the shop and clambered back on to the cart. Taking a watch from his waistcoat pocket, he glanced from it to Dad who was still standing at the door. Then he began to fill his pipe, again very deliberately. Dad shut the door and turned round to find Imogen staring at him. He knew she would be.

'We're going somewhere?' she said. 'You never said.'

'No, I know. I've been looking for the moment to tell you, sweet.'

'To Melling, he said. What for?'

'To see Helen.'

'Why should you need to find a moment to tell me that?'

'It's been a long time since you've seen your Aunt Helen, Imogen. I thought it would be nice for you . . .'

'What's so hard about telling me, though?'

'The air's so good there. By the sea and everything. So they all say and . . .'

'Dad.'

'Look, Imogen, you need to get away for a spell. I don't think you've been at all right these last few days.'

'I've been as right as anything. I've done all my jobs, haven't I? I haven't been letting you down, have I?'

'Of course you haven't.'

'What is it, then?'

For the first time since he'd come into the shop he lifted his face and looked straight at her. There was a film of moisture on his brow.

'You've not slept at all well, sweet, you know you haven't. Shouting and things. I reckon you need a change. It's not been easy to mention.'

'You mentioned it to Mr Robinson. Why couldn't you talk to me?'

'I just didn't. I just did what I thought best. And I've said nothing to Basil, bar that I want him to take you.'

'To take me? Aren't you coming?'

'I can't leave the work, Imogen. Not now. We've just done that job for Mr Balik and we might get others from it . . .'

'You're sending me away.'

'It's not like that at all. I've done this to help you. Don't look at me like that, Imogen.'

Then she ran out of the shop and up to her room. Cursing him and biting her lip. A small brown case had been placed open on her chair. Her best blouse, the one Dad liked, with the wild roses on it, was draped half-heartedly over the end of the bed. He couldn't even pack properly. She slammed the door shut and, without thinking, began to fling some things into the case. The blouse she left where Dad had put it.

She took the case downstairs and threw it into the back of Mr Robinson's cart. She climbed up beside the farmer, her eyes fixed on the church spire at the top of the street. Mr Robinson flipped the reins, clicked at his horse and they moved off.

'It'll be nice, Imogen,' came her father's voice behind them. 'Helen will spoil you.'

She didn't answer, didn't even turn round.

'You're the wrong side of your Daddy this morning,' mumbled Mr Robinson, half to himself. 'I can tell that much.'

When they pulled past the church and left the last cottages behind, warm tears were running down her cheeks. She shifted herself sideways so that Mr Robinson wouldn't know.

8

When she woke, Imogen wasn't sure where she was. She wondered whether she'd gone downstairs again and was in the shop; but it didn't feel at all like that. There wasn't the touch of floorboards. And she was in a bed. She opened her eyes and looked towards the light. There were rooftops outside. This house was much taller than home. And at the window edge there were bricks, not stone. Aunt Helen's house. She saw on the ceiling the even glow of a sea-sky and thought she could detect the breathing of the sea itself somewhere in the distance.

There were fragments of pictures in her head – pieces of dream left over from the night – but none of them was very clear. It was as if she'd been watching them through some kind of billowing curtain. Whatever they were, though, was nothing to do with the old dreams. There were no thin, dancing creatures in walls of flame, no sightless man-bird.

My memories being washed clean, she thought.

She closed her eyes again and, for several moments, forced the old images to return. It wasn't difficult; they hadn't really gone away. It was as if they were just out of sight somewhere, waiting.

When she went downstairs to breakfast, Aunt Helen was bustling in and out of the kitchen.

'Here she is,' she said, smiling suddenly and folding her hands under her bosom. 'Here's my girl.'

Aunt Helen was a small, talkative woman – not at all like Dad – and she had a way of looking directly at people that reminded Imogen of a robin, hopping around by a gardener's spade. Dad always said that she had more than her fair share of the family talk, and it was true. He'd been left with mumbles and moans and the odd sideways comment.

'I don't know why you want to be up so early, Imogen,' she said. 'You're here to rest, you know. You can stay in bed as long as you like. I don't suppose you get much chance to do that most days, do you?'

She hurried back into the kitchen and Imogen sat down at the table. She noticed with a start that Uncle Jack was also sitting there, leaning forward and sipping carefully from a large mug of tea. He gave her a nod of greeting and looked straight down at his breakfast.

'Imogen's come down, Jack,' came Aunt Helen's voice from the kitchen. 'In case you haven't noticed.'

He smiled and gave Imogen another nod. He looked as if he was about to say something but Aunt Helen appeared in the doorway with a jug of milk.

'Don't mind him, sweetheart. He doesn't mean to

be rude. The king himself wouldn't get a word out of Jack before nine in the morning, would he, Jack?'

Jack wiped his moustache between his thumb and finger and raised his eyebrows as if he would answer. But Aunt Helen launched straight into a story about Hobnails, the man who brought the milk.

'He's got it into his head that he has to have a bicycle,' she said. 'To deliver the milk. Well, I explained the nonsense of that to him but you could see he'd already buttoned his ears to any kind of sense. He was the same when he was a kid. Full of far-fetched dreaming but about as quick off the mark as a bullock.'

'Hm . . . hmm . . . uh–huh,' said Jack, nodding and tapping his fork absently on one of Dad's best plates, and gazing through the lace half-curtains as he chewed.

Even when Helen bustled out to the scullery and her voice faded to nothing, the nodding continued. Eventually he swung his coat off the back of the chair and went off to his work down at Melling quay. He winked at Imogen on his way out, though she wasn't sure whether this meant 'goodbye' or 'just listen to your aunt rambling on out there'.

At the end of breakfast Imogen carried the plates out to the kitchen to help with the washing-up but Aunt Helen wouldn't let her do anything.

'No,' she said. 'You're to rest, my girl. And you mustn't put me in trouble with that brother of mine by flitting about all day and every day, finding things to do. If you weren't here I'd have to do things myself so don't you soften me up with help.'

It made Imogen wonder what Dad *had* said to her. Very little, probably. A few hints about being tired and growing up. Then he'd hope that Helen would somehow guess the rest. Imogen certainly couldn't tell from the way her aunt treated her whether she knew anything more or not. She treated everyone the same; people to talk to or specks of dust to flick out of the way while she bustled about the house.

For a long time Imogen had nothing to do but sit around the house, listening to her aunt talking and occasionally getting in the way.

'You're in my dust, Imogen,' she'd say, swiping at the floor with a broom. 'Why don't you sit down somewhere and rest?'

So she took herself off and sat in the kitchen. She stared out at the little back garden for ages, trying to remember things in their proper order, while Aunt Helen swept the stairs and sang a hymn in the background.

The way she'd followed the thirteenth owl up to Mr Balik's house. Why had she done this? She pictured herself doing it, and now it seemed such a foolish and unthinking thing to have done. Then Fortune flying over her head and across the grass to the trees. Not a real owl. She must've imagined that. Fortune had stayed on her window ledge at home. He must've done. She'd been sleepwalking. Like finding herself downstairs in the shop and not knowing how she came to be there.

But Mr Balik, appearing in the candle light at the upper window, that was real enough. And shouting out so strangely, Charlotte. There was no mistake. He'd called that name.

Aunt Helen backed into the kitchen with her broom and Imogen almost turned to her and said, 'Who's Charlotte?'

But, of course, Aunt Helen wouldn't have known anything about it.

After a day or two of resting, Imogen decided that she wanted to go down to the sea. There was some vague memory of it from the last time she'd been to visit Aunt Helen. But she'd been so much smaller then. She thought that it might seem different now. More important, somehow; she wasn't sure how. On several occasions she'd walked around Melling and glimpsed it between buildings. And once she'd even ventured briefly on to the quay with its odd mix of salty air and heavy machinery. But Aunt Helen wasn't happy about her straying too far from home.

'There's nothing down there,' she said. 'Only the grain store and you won't be interested in that.'

'Isn't there anything else at all?' asked Imogen.

'Can't you remember?'

'I was only little the last time I was here.'

'Well, there's boats, which aren't interesting either. And The Anchor, which is. Only The Anchor's a sin hole, Imogen. All Christian souls give it a wide berth.'

'Why?'

'Don't ask. Just make sure you never go anywhere near it.'

'What about the sea, though? Couldn't I get a proper look at the sea?'

'You don't want to do that,' said Aunt Helen. 'That's not entirely safe if you haven't got your strength back.'

As if some watery arm would pull her into the waves.

'I have got my strength back, Aunt Helen. And I can't come to any harm by just walking.'

'You let me be the judge of that.'

Eventually, though, towards the end of the week, she agreed that a gentle stroll might be all right.

'You must take it easy, though, Imogen,' Aunt Helen said.

Except when she passed The Anchor, of course. Then she was allowed to hurry.

So Imogen walked slowly down to the quay.

The grain store was a green tower of wood and corrugated iron. She stood beneath it and looked up. A kind of covered bridge reached out across the path and ended high above the hold of an old coaster. Aunt Helen was wrong about the boats. Imogen found this one fascinating. It sat impossibly in the water, so heavy and solid.

She passed under the bridge, and caught sight of The Anchor a little way along the quay. A squat little pub with thick white walls, its weathered door shut tight. Full of old men playing dominoes, Imogen thought. Not nearly as interesting as the coaster. Although Aunt Helen would probably consider dominoes a danger to the soul.

She reached the stone steps which led to the beach and then trod steadily along the soft sand, keeping her head down. She didn't want to take in the sweep of the sea until she'd left the town far behind her. When at last she stopped, she sat down where the rough grass had made the sand more firm, and looked out, quite deliberately, across the North Sea.

She couldn't remember seeing anything so big. Or empty.

She narrowed her eyes but couldn't tell where sky began and water ended. The sky was a shining pearl grey. The darker grey of the sea came lapping towards her in endless lines of little waves. They ran in, building as if they'd break, and then folding over and falling in on themselves. Sliding back tamely under the mass of waiting sea. Purring and hissing, amounting to nothing. Again and again.

A small boat with an orange sail was moving slowly across the bay. Imogen watched it until it rounded the headland and disappeared. Then she noticed that two or three bright stars had appeared above the layers of pink-grey clouds.

She stood stiffly and began the walk back towards the quay. The little town was showing several golden lights at windows and the land behind it was soft with darkness. It all looked so safe, she thought, and predictable.

Crunching up the damp steps from the beach, she began to walk back along the path in the direction of the grain store. It was about a quarter of a mile away, she guessed. The bulk of the coaster was still resting against the quay, its lights now trembling on the still water. Some men were swinging ropes and busying themselves with the shoot for the last loading of the day. Flecks floated in the yellow light which spilled from the store. The men were calling to each other with faint voices. Such activity, she thought. Everyone busy with his own job, knowing exactly what to do.

As she passed The Anchor the door burst open and made her jump. She heard the wheeze of an accordion inside, and laughter. She slowed a little and, without quite turning her head, looked in. But she saw almost nothing because, at that moment, two men ducked out of the door and blocked her view. They leaned, dark against the white-washed wall, and she felt their eyes pick her out and follow her. One of them mumbled something and the other laughed. She quickened her step, hurrying towards the activity and noise ahead.

She stopped, a little breathlessly, by the bow of the coaster. Its flank was streaked with rust and coils of grimy rope, as thick as a man's arm, were strewn on its foredeck. She breathed the heavy air, a mixture of engine oil and the clean dry smell of the grain.

The scratch of a boot on cobbles made her turn

round. A man was standing a few yards away, facing her in the shadow of the grain store. One of the men from The Anchor. Her heart began to thump and she looked round wildly.

There were three men on the boat. Two were holding the shoot as the last dribbles of grain fell into the hold. The other sat on a box smoking a pipe. He had his back to her. She thought of calling out to him but didn't know what to say. High above her a fourth man was perched in the opening, silhouetted in the square of warm light.

She looked back the way she'd come. No safety there. Only The Anchor with its cheery music, and, in the distance, the steps down to the empty beach. On the other side of the grain store was the alleyway which led up to the town. But that was dark too, and she'd have to pass close to the man in the shadow to reach it.

Imogen took a step towards him.

'Miss?' he said softly.

If he moved she would push him as hard as she could and then run. He swayed, a half motion in her direction, and at the same time there was a shout from above. She looked up and pushed in one movement. Her hands felt the rough material of the man's smock for a brief moment. Then he was stumbling backwards, away from her. And out of the sky something was swooping down at them. A solid black shape, coming down like a striking bird. It brushed the man's smock and cracked on to the cobbles between them. Sparks jagged off the stone.

The man groaned quietly and tried to sit up. Then fell back again and lay still. Imogen sank to her knees and sat down in the road.

There was a pulse of silence before she heard the sailors from the boat running towards them. An orange lamp was swinging through the darkness. When it settled it made a pool of light on the road. Imogen saw the knees and hands of the men and one or two moon-like faces. One of them, she noted without surprise, belonged to Uncle Jack. In the middle of the pool of light, by the fallen man's feet, was a block and tackle, blue-black metal with a thick hook, the size of a small gravestone.

'You all right?' someone said.

There was no answer. Another voice added in a whisper, 'He's like a sheet but he's still breathing. Not a mark on him.'

'It missed the beggar,' said the first voice, 'by a whisker.'

The lamp was held over the man's head. He was blinking and moving his mouth. His face, bright on one side, in shadow on the other, looked puzzled. At the sight of him Imogen caught her breath and the men looked round, taking her in for the first time.

'My God, it's a girl.'

Black shining eyes and a peppery beard loomed out of the darkness at her.

'That's right,' said Uncle Jack, flat and matter-of-fact. 'It's my niece.'

'And who the hell's this character?' said the bearded sailor, turning to the man at their feet.

'I think I know him,' said Imogen quietly.

And she looked again to make sure.

'Yes,' she said. 'His name's Grainger.'

Aunt Helen enjoyed the fuss. The bearded sailor and Uncle Jack helped Grainger into the high-backed chair in the front room. She skipped ahead of them to whisk the cover off it and then darted out to boil the kettle.

'I'm all right,' Grainger told the men testily. 'A bit done in, that's all. I didn't know where I was.'

'You bloody near had your head caved in,' said the sailor. 'If this lass hadn't shoved you . . . well, I don't like to think.'

Imogen was standing by the door, still holding on to the handle. Grainger wiped his mouth and looked at her. His skin was the colour of a candle.

'It is you,' he said. 'The potter's child.'

Uncle Jack was twisting a leather cap in his hands. He looked almost as numbed as Grainger.

'That block and tackle,' he mumbled. 'I did say it weren't right. I did say it should've been looked at.'

The sailor slapped him across the shoulder.

'Come you on,' he said. 'The bloke's in one piece so don't fret about it. I'm off to have a drink,' he added with a wink at Grainger. 'To your health.' Then he pushed his way out of the room.

'I should see what Helen's up to,' said Uncle Jack, and he shrank out of the room.

'I'll come with you,' Imogen added quickly.

'No. Wait.'

Grainger was leaning forward in Aunt Helen's chair, his elbows on his knees, looking down at his feet.

'You was very quick,' he said. 'Like lightning. I reckon I must say thank you.'

'I wasn't that quick. I didn't really see . . .'

'What?'

'Nothing.'

'I'd've been dead. Half an hour back and I could've been a dead man.'

'You were . . . watching me.'

'Yes.'

'I saw you come out of The Anchor.'

'I was watching you. At first I just looks up and sees a pretty girl.'

Because it was dark, she thought. And probably the drink.

'Then I thinks I know who that is.'

He spoke carefully, like a man not used to words.

'I seen you before,' he went on. 'So I went along to see if I was right. And . . . well, the bloody sky come down on me.'

He was grinning down at his boots. A brief, inward grin. It was the first time she'd seen him look other than impassive. And at that point Aunt Helen hurried in with the teapot.

'Jack,' she called over her shoulder, 'go you upstairs and fetch a blanket. No, no,' she added to Grainger.

'Don't you get up. Stay where you are. You've got a touch of the shocks and you'll have to watch that.'

She put the teapot on the hearth and pulled up a stool so she could sit by Grainger's feet.

'Now. I want to know exactly what happened, start to finish. It's no good asking Jack. He puts everything into one sentence. Move yourself in, Imogen. You'll have to do some of the poor man's talking for him.'

The following morning Aunt Helen told Imogen to walk down to The Anchor with some fruit loaf for Mr Grainger.

'Don't go in,' she said. 'Just tap at the door. And you can tell him he doesn't have to stay there. I don't know how anyone could sleep in a place like that. What with all those daft old boys hawking and spitting in the bar all night. There's a bed up here if he wants it.'

'He's not hurt,' said Imogen. 'And I think he likes to keep to himself.'

'That's just what I'm telling you. He's not by himself with half the drinking population of the town beneath his feet, is he? And anyway, he's Mr Balik's man. It's a family connection. In a manner of speaking.'

Imogen said nothing but wrapped the fruit loaf in a cloth and set off for The Anchor. She was still unsure of Grainger and had no intention of inviting him back to the house. Besides, it annoyed her to see Aunt Helen make such a stir over him. As if he were royalty or something. And not because of any grandness in Grainger himself but because of the link with Mr Balik.

You wouldn't fuss over Mr Balik if you knew what I knew, she thought. If you'd seen him lay into Boy Carter for no good reason and stalk through the village like a thunder cloud. And everybody hating the sight of him.

But, as far as Aunt Helen was concerned, Mr Balik was one of the masters. You had to be proud to walk the same path as the likes of him. And if you couldn't pander to the master himself, you pandered to his man.

The front door of The Anchor was shut when she got there and Imogen knocked lightly, hoping no one would come. She was wondering whether to leave the loaf by the foot-scraper when the door opened and Grainger came out.

'Oh,' he said. 'Was you knocking?'

'Yes. I brought this. From Aunt Helen.'

'Right,' said Grainger. He took it awkwardly and, after a moment's uncertainty, turning it over in his large hands, he carried it into the pub. She was left on the pavement, not sure whether he intended to come out again or not.

'Tell her thank you,' he said, re-emerging.

'It's a fruit loaf,' said Imogen. In case you were wondering, she thought.

'Oh.' There was a long pause. 'Look, I'm off back to the village tomorrow. I only come with a load of

Balik's grain. That's why I'm here. He won't come here himself, you see.'

He looked as if he wanted Imogen to say something but she didn't. He cleared his throat and set off across the road. Then hesitated. To see if she would follow, Imogen thought. The tide was out and several silvery banks of sand had appeared where yesterday there had only been sea. He looked out of place, standing there with this expanse of beach and water at his back.

'Well,' Imogen called over to him, 'I suppose I must . . .'

'Them owls,' he said suddenly. And stopped.

Imogen took a breath and crossed the road after him. They began to walk along the quay in the direction of the beach.

'What about them?'

'You brought them up to the house, didn't you? You and your old man?'

'Yes.'

'He did the deal but I heard that it was you actually made them. Was that right?'

'I made the first one.'

'What was it behind them, then?'

'Behind them?'

'Why did it have to be owls?'

She wasn't sure that she should tell him. She hadn't told anyone else so why should she say anything to this straight-backed, silent man?

'There's something about them, isn't there?' he

went on. 'Something a bit funny, if you see what I mean.'

Standing there, so far from home and in such odd circumstances, was like being in another country. On the edge of some desert, perhaps, where ordinary life had somehow stopped. Maybe things were so strange here, she thought, that it would be possible to say something to Grainger. Maybe she could try and see what happened.

'It was when you burnt the old barn down,' she said. 'You and Mr Balik.'

'Ah, yes. I remember that. You came charging down over the field. Shouting at us. Was that something to do with it?'

'I saw an owl in that barn, yes.'

'Burned, was it?' he said, pausing to stare out at the sea.

'I don't know. I thought it might be. That's why I made the model. I made a little model out of a bit of clay. The others were copied from that.'

'Yes?'

'Mr Balik saw it – the model, I mean – and he told us to make some more. Life size . . .'

'Which I know about, yes.'

He carried on walking for a while in silence. Climbed down the stone steps to the beach. Arms swinging steadily by his side, as if he had somewhere special to go.

'I don't know why he wanted them,' said Imogen after some minutes.

'You don't?'

196

'I suppose he just liked the model.'

'I suppose so. Except . . .'

'What?'

'Can you meet me by the road into Melling this afternoon? Near the Cottage Hospital?'

'What for?'

'I want to show you something. Do you know where I mean?'

'Yes, I think so.'

'I'll wait there at two o'clock. Come if you can.'

They stopped walking and faced the sea. Imogen squinted back at the huddle of buildings far behind them on the quay. She waited for Grainger to say something else but he remained silent. For several moments she watched a scattering of little birds with stick legs run about at the edge of the water.

'Two o'clock, then,' he said, turning back. 'If you can make it.'

Aunt Helen wanted to know how Grainger was looking, what he said and whether he was pleased about the loaf.

'He was very grateful,' Imogen told her. She couldn't remember him saying anything at all about the loaf but it didn't feel much like a lie to pretend he had. He probably was grateful. She thought he wasn't used to receiving gifts.

'So what did he have to say for himself?'

'Not much. Hardly anything, really.'

'Well, Imogen, you've been gone nearly the full hour. He must've said something.'

Aunt Helen found it impossible to think of two people spending so long together without indulging in full and wide-ranging conversation. 'Hardly anything' merely fired her curiosity.

'You didn't set foot inside that place, I hope,' she said.

'No, Aunt Helen. I knocked and waited for him to come out.'

'And he's recovered from his mishap?'

'Yes. He's back to normal.'

'Except that he's lost his powers of speech apparently.'

'Well, he never did have much to say for himself.'

'Huh. You and I know too many men like that, Imogen. Nothing to say for themselves because there's not much in their heads, I suppose. Perhaps he'd've been better off if he *did* get a crash on the skull.'

After lunch Imogen asked her if she could go out again. Just for a walk, to get some exercise.

'You can shake the rugs with me. There's plenty of exercise in that.'

'I could do that later. I thought I'd just wander round. See the place while I've still got the chance.'

'See Melling? What is there to see? I'd've thought you'd had enough of the quayside to last a lifetime.'

'Somewhere else, then. Away from the sea.'

'All right. If you must. But I won't be saving the rugs up for you. They'll have to be done when I'm ready.'

Until then Imogen hadn't been sure that it would

be right to meet Grainger again. He wasn't the easiest person to be with. But she said she wanted to go out and now she found that she really was anxious to hear more about Mr Balik. Something to do with the owls and with Melling itself. She avoided mentioning any of this to Aunt Helen and that didn't feel much like a lie either. As she walked up the hill to the edge of town, though, she began to feel uncertain about it. She would have liked her aunt's approval for this meeting.

Just after two she found Grainger sitting on a hump of grass at the crossroads by the Melling sign. He stood up when he saw her and nodded, as if in answer to a question.

'It's further up the hill here,' he said and, just as he'd done in the morning, walked away from her. She hurried to catch him and walked by his side, not too close.

'I come here two or three times in the year,' he said after a while. 'But like I said, Balik never does. It's several years since he came to Melling.'

'Why doesn't he come here?' Imogen asked. Only for something to say. She didn't see why Mr Balik should want to come to Melling anyway.

'This is what I'm going to show you. Look up there, beyond that hedge.'

She saw the grey roof of a large house between tree-tops.

'The house? What is it?'

'It's not my business to tell you this. Balik ain't

never said don't; but I know he wouldn't want me to. Only, there was a lady lived in that house once.'

'Lady?' said Imogen quickly.

'A long time ago, before he ever came to the village. Did you ever hear about that?'

'No,' she said. 'Never.'

'Oh. Only people do talk in the village.'

'Not to me. I mean, not much to me.'

'No. I don't think they know. He told me himself once. A long time ago and when he was in a funny old mood. After a bit to drink, perhaps. It was when I was supposed to come here with the grain but there was some reason why I couldn't. I told him and he said I had to. Said he damn well wasn't going himself.'

Grainger spoke slowly and there were long pauses during which they walked along without saying anything. They reached a five-bar gate which opened on to an avenue of trees. At the top of the avenue was a cluster of flint outbuildings. Beyond them the house itself. Tall and empty-looking.

'Is the lady there now?' asked Imogen.

'No. She sold up and left. I don't know who's in there now. But when she was there Balik knew her well. They had an understanding. You know what I mean? To be married.'

'Married?' Imogen couldn't imagine Mr Balik married to anyone. Or even with an 'understanding' to be married.

'It never came to it, though,' said Grainger, leaning

on the gate. 'He lost her. That's the way he put it. She was lost.'

Suddenly the image of her mother's photograph in its wooden frame came to her. And Dad standing at the kitchen door with his back to her, looking out at the kiln-room.

'Did she die?' she asked.

'No. Not that sort of lost. She just went away.'

'To marry someone else?'

'I don't think so. But she was very young; just a girl. I suppose she might be married now.'

She tried to picture the girl with Mr Balik; tried to imagine them walking through lanes together. Nothing was very clear, though. She could see him, striding seriously along, frowning at the ground, but the girl wouldn't form properly in her mind. Did she walk in silence beside him? Or skip round him, showing him flowers and asking him all sorts of silly questions? Imogen almost saw a long, pale dress swinging along. She couldn't see a face. And anyway, perhaps, the picture she had of Mr Balik wasn't right either. Perhaps he wasn't so gloomy when he was with the girl.

'What has this got to do with me?' she said.

'You see them low buildings up there? A sort of barn and stables? She kept birds in one of them.'

Imogen narrowed her eyes and looked up the avenue. She could make out three rectangles constructed out of flint boulders, with perhaps a fourth tucked away in the background. They were old and heavy, each one topped with a sagging roof of dark slates. No. One roof was a little different from the others. Its slates looked clean and straight, as if it had been rebuilt.

'It was kind of a thing with her,' said Grainger. 'The birds. Hawks, like people used to hunt with. And an owl. He never told me this himself but some of the men at the grain store knew about it. They told me. All Balik ever said was that an owl always put him in mind of this lady. But he said that in drink, too. I'm sure he don't remember speaking of it.'

'A tame owl?'

'No. Of course not. You don't tame birds like that. But it was hers and it must've meant a lot to her. So, when I see the owls you brought up with your old man, well, it put me in mind of this lady. Balik asked you for them, then, did he?'

'Yes. When he came into the shop for the rent.'

'I wondered if he said anything. Told you anything.'

'No. Nothing.'

'It was just a bit of chance, then?'

'Yes.'

He was chewing his lip and staring at the distant house with nothing more to add, it seemed.

'Who was the lady?' Imogen asked eventually.

'Who was she?'

'Her name, I mean.'

'I don't know. It was just before my time with him and he only talked about her the once. He's not the sort of man you ask questions.'

'Why didn't they marry?'

'Don't know that, either,' he said, suddenly looking straight at her. 'Something went wrong. She went her way and he went his. She was a bit of a hot-headed sort by all accounts. But Balik took it hard. Had more to drink than he should. Raged about on his own.'

'But all this was before you knew him?'

'Whatever happened up here was before I knew him. But he was still likely to fly into rages when I come to manage the farmland for him. I thought the birds come into it somewhere but that's only my guess. And you don't know anything about it, either?'

'No.'

'No. I just wondered. He was sort of forgetting about it, as far as I could tell. Sort of settling down, I suppose. Till you turned up with them owls.' He breathed in deeply and looked back at the house. 'Now it looks like it's starting up again,' he said.

When Imogen got back to the house, Aunt Helen was nowhere to be seen. She went through to the kitchen where a series of echoing smacks filtered in from the garden. Her aunt was in the middle of wrestling with the rugs, flinging them over the line and beating clouds of dust out of them. Imogen tapped on the window and waved. She went outside to help.

'Look at all this,' said Aunt Helen. 'Just look at it

all! This is what Jack's walked in from work. There's enough flour in these rugs to make a dozen rolls.'

She sighed and propped the beater against a hedge.

'And what did you find in Melling?' she asked with a sidelong glance at her niece. 'Plenty of mystery and excitement?'

'It's an interesting place if you're not used to it.'

'Oh, is it? You'll have to tell me all about that, my girl. I could just do with a bit of interest.'

'You go in and put the kettle on,' said Imogen with a smile. 'I'll take over for a bit.'

She set about the rugs, glad to make such a noise with the beater that Aunt Helen couldn't ask her any more questions.

9

'And how was old Jack?' Dad asked. 'Still the same?'

'He looked the same but he never said much. I couldn't tell.'

'No. He's a dark old horse, is Jack.'

He chuckled and nodded towards the teapot, meaning did she want another mug? Imogen shook her head. She'd said nothing about meeting Grainger. It was probably all in her aunt's note so it would come up in good time. As much of it as she wanted to tell.

'Aunt Helen loaded you up with supplies, as usual,' he said. 'Fruit loaves and jam and whatever.'

'She likes to do all that. You know she does.'

'I know.'

There was a pause while he pulled a piece of bread from the loaf and squeezed it into a pellet. His features seemed to sag a little. The cheerfulness seeped out of him. He stood up with a sigh. Giving up, Imogen thought. If you can't get what you want by being jolly, you don't know what else to do, do you?

'I hope you were good to her, sweet. She's very fond of you, you know.'

'Did you think I'd be rude, then?' she asked him sharply.

'No. No, of course not.'

'I wasn't. I was truly grateful.'

'You look much better now. I told you a good rest . . .'

'Yes. I know.'

'Helen thinks I don't look after you,' he said.

'She's right,' said Imogen and, when he looked at her, added with a smile, 'I look after you.'

Fortune was still on the window ledge in her room. Facing out, staring at the tree tops, as he had been over a week before. Imogen stood in the doorway for a moment, looking at him.

'Hallo,' she said, and then crossed the room to touch him lightly on his folded wings.

He was hard and cold; more so than she remembered. She let her fingers remain there and closed her eyes. Nothing happened, but she wasn't sure that she expected anything to.

'I'm coming to bed,' she told him. 'It tires you out, sitting on a cart for hours with old Basil Robinson, looking at fields. If anything happens,' she added slowly, 'I won't be afraid. I won't mean to be afraid, anyway. If I see anything. Or hear anything. I'll just keep still and listen. And see what happens.'

The night passed peacefully, though. Imogen was aware of Fortune, standing there in the shadows, silent and watchful. But he had nothing to say to her. No dreams came. Nothing at all.

In the morning his silhouette against the window square was the first thing she saw. Her lips were sticky and closed after sleep. She opened them to speak to him but changed her mind. Suddenly, she felt it would be a silly thing to do. Making him seem like some old toy, like the rag-doll she'd stopped talking to last year.

Life returned to normal. Helping Dad with the usual duties in the kiln-room and the shop. Walking past the empty school and thinking, dully, that she would be back there soon, to complete her last few weeks as a pupil. She remembered sitting on the beach and watching the expanse of the sea that made everything in the village seem so small and ordinary. But watching the sea was stuck in the past. Not last week but some distant, unreal time. She felt it had nothing to do with her now. And that incident with Grainger – the fear of him following her, the moment when she'd pushed him, his strange story about Mr Balik – all that seemed unreal too.

She walked past Old Carter's cottage one afternoon and Boy was sitting on the step with his arms round the dog's neck. Out of habit she veered away from him but he looked up and called to her.

'Hallo, Imogen. Where've you been, then?'

'Away. Nowhere special.'

'The seaside?'

'Maybe.'

He jumped up and fell in beside her. The dog crouched and sprang, yapping at his heels.

'Can't you keep him quiet?' she said.

'He's all right. He don't mean nothing. You're just saying hallo, aren't you, boy?'

'Hallo, dog,' Imogen said coldly. She narrowed her eyes at the dog, wondering whether, perhaps, they shared some secret.

'I went there once,' Boy was saying. 'To the seaside. There was nothing to do.'

'That's nothing different. You don't do anything here.'

'I do. I helped with the harvest.'

'I expect that's why it took so long this year,' she said.

'It didn't take long, Imogen. It was the normal time.'

Too dim to see the joke, she thought. She gave him a withering smile and headed for the shop.

'Is your old man down for the cricket?' Boy called after her.

'What?'

'The cricket up on old Balik's lawns.'

'I don't know anything about any cricket.'

'There's tons you don't know, then, isn't there? The vicar's bringing a side from the cathedral. Ted says God's playing for them so it's not fair.'

'Don't be so stupid.'

'Going in first. W. G. God. With a big long beard.'

Imogen laughed, in spite of herself. 'If you didn't have such a solid wooden head, you'd be wicked, you would,' she said.

'That's not wicked, Ginny. That could be true.

God can do anything so He could play cricket for the vicar if He wanted to. Then your old man would have to bowl to him.'

'If he's playing.'

'He is. Grainger asked him to last week.'

'Then why did you ask, if you know so much?'

'Just to see,' said Boy turning and wandering off.

Imogen let herself into the shop where Dad was wiping plates with a cloth and stacking them on a shelf.

'What's he been on about?' he asked. 'Has he been saying things to you?'

'Just going on in the usual way,' she said, passing straight through the shop.

'I could have a word with his mother. She'd sort him out.'

'No, Dad. It's not like that,' she called from the kitchen. 'He's only talking. He says you're going to play cricket against God and the vicar.'

'He said what?'

Dad set down his plates and put his head round the kitchen door, but Imogen was already out in the yard, and still smiling to herself. It was the first time anyone from school had called her Ginny.

After supper, Dad sat himself at the kitchen table and began to dab white liquid on a pair of old cricket boots. Imogen left the plates to drain at the sink and came to watch. She'd never seen the boots before. They were made of canvas, stiff and streaked greenish and pale brown at the toes. The hard leather of their soles shone and was curved like the bottoms of boats.

'I didn't know you ever played cricket,' she said, leaning over him to light the oil lamp.

'I used to. When you were a kiddie. Don't you remember?'

'Not a thing. Are you any good?'

'Grainger says I'm the only man that can turn a ball properly,' he told her. 'Must be the clay. Working with my fingers all day.'

She sat opposite him and watched him work. The thought of the cricket match pleased him; he was almost talkative.

'It doesn't make any sense,' Imogen said. 'How can you turn a ball?'

'You impart spin on it.' He picked up a cup to demonstrate. 'Flick it in your fingers, like this, and it'll deviate off the pitch.'

'Like that? It'd fly off all over the place.'

'Not if you know what you're about it wouldn't.'

'Will you beat them, then?'

'We shall see. It won't be easy. The vicar played at Cambridge as a youth and clergymen can be devils with bat and ball, Imogen. Anyway, it's not the winning that counts. It's a social occasion. People get together and talk.'

'About cricket?' she laughed. 'That shouldn't delay them much.'

'About all kinds of things. It can be a very relaxed affair, can a match like this.'

'Can it? On Mr Balik's land?'

'I don't see why not.'

Of course, Imogen knew she'd have to go to the match. For Dad's sake. The thought of Mr Balik seeing her, though, on his lawns and so close to the house, was an uncomfortable one. The next morning she decided to take a walk up the hill to look at the house from the roadway. Just to look, to see how she felt about it. She had no intention of setting foot on Mr Balik's land a moment before she had to.

It was a quiet morning. There was no one about. She stood by the gate and looked up the drive. Then she remembered, you could see nothing of the house from here. Not when the trees were in full leaf. Just the drive leading into a green tunnel. She stayed there for a moment, looking and thinking. There were no odd feelings, no foreboding.

If I was a dog, she thought, it might be different.

She was about to return to the village when she caught sight of a figure standing under the trees in the drive. Not moving, but looking at her. After a moment of uncertainty, she saw that it was Grainger. She was sure that he recognized her but he gave no sign, not even a nod. He simply lowered his head and began to walk briskly away, down the curve of the drive towards the house. He was almost out of sight when he stopped, turned round and came back, just as briskly, in Imogen's direction. It reminded her of standing outside The Anchor with him; how he crossed the road before he could bring himself to say anything.

As if he can't speak at all when people are near, she thought.

And now he came to a halt, still a couple of yards off, still safe on Mr Balik's land, with the open gate a barrier between them. Even so, he was close enough for Imogen to make out the wiry grey hairs on his cheeks and lines like cracks running down from the corner of his mouth.

'Hallo, Imogen,' he said awkwardly.

She smiled at him. 'Are you all right now, Mr Grainger?' she asked.

He shuffled round, ignoring the question or perhaps not even hearing it properly, and looked off into the trees somewhere.

'You got some spare time?' he asked. 'To look at something in the house?'

'In the house?'

'Not indoors. Something you can see from the windows.'

'I don't know.'

'Balik won't know. He's out,' he said, and looked directly at her.

So Imogen stepped warily off the public highway and joined him in Mr Balik's drive. She followed a pace or two behind Grainger, her eyes fixed on the house as it came steadily into view. First a flat, grey corner of façade against the sky. Then a black square of window. The top of a column. Carving; leaves or something. She thought that was odd, somehow out of place. Carved to please someone's eye, yet almost out of sight.

'There,' said Grainger, stopping so abruptly that she almost ran into him. 'See?'

'What?'

'That window.'

He was pointing at a ground floor window. At first Imogen could make out nothing but the sheen of glass across several small squares. She moved a little to one side. The window became dark and she knew for certain that it was the dining room. She recognized the owl she'd seen on that night. It had been moved, placed against the glass, not quite in the middle of the ledge. It looked small and dainty against such a slab of black.

'You see it?' said Grainger.

'Yes, but . . .'

'It's facing out. Looking at us. Is that right?'

'I don't know.'

'I mean, is that how it's supposed to be?' His voice was urgent and he didn't wait for an answer. 'And look there, too. And there. And there.'

He jerked his arm from window to window. At each one stood one of the owls, facing outwards, its back to the dark of Mr Balik's house.

'You don't see it, Imogen? He always had them on them window ledges. Tidily placed, all looking square into the rooms. Now they've been moved. Turned round to face the grounds.'

'That's not strange, though,' said Imogen. 'It's what I've done.'

'What?' He looked sharply at her. 'You done it?'

'No, I mean . . . I don't think there's anything

wrong with it. If I had owls I might have them like that. So they can see the trees and things.'

Grainger shook his head and she thought he was going to laugh at her for being so fanciful.

'Not shoved there any old how, you wouldn't, girl,' he said. 'See how he's done it. Just turned them round and stuck them against the glass. And look here.'

He strode away from her, towards the house, and leaned up to place the flat of his hand on one of the dining room windows. Imogen moved closer to look. She felt safer by Grainger's side.

'See this one?' he said. 'He's banged it down so hard it's cracked the pane. I'll have to see to that but I can't say anything to Balik, can I? It's like telling him, look what you've done. Like asking him what he's up to.'

'I don't know what to say, Mr Grainger.'

'You can't explain it to me?'

'No.'

He breathed in deeply through his nose before adding, 'Well, there's other things, too.'

'What other things?'

'Writing.'

'Writing?'

'He sits up half the night writing stuff on paper. And then screwing it up and burning most of it. Why should he take to doing that?'

'I don't know.'

'And shouting. The night before last. I come out of my room at the back to fetch something from the kitchen, and there's shouting going on in the dining room.'

'Mr Balik shouting?'

'There's no one else here.'

'But it was him?'

'Of course it was him. Yelling out something or other, like he was scared. I couldn't make it out. And there was no one else about, that I'm sure of.'

'What happened?'

'Nothing, as far as I could tell. I didn't hang around to ask. Then, in the morning, I goes through the house and sees these things, all moved.' He paused and looked at her. 'Thought you might know something about it.'

'I'm sorry Mr Grainger,' she said firmly. 'I don't understand either.'

'No,' he said and looked at her in silence for a moment. 'I didn't know who else to talk to, though. Things go from bad to worse with him, you see, and I don't know how they'll end up.'

'I'm sorry,' Imogen said again.

There was nothing more she could say to Grainger. She could see that it perplexed him and she wanted both to help and to understand for her own sake.

'One more thing,' he said, shrugging as if, now that he'd asked her, it didn't matter any more. 'In the workshop.'

He set off round the side of the house and Imogen followed reluctantly. As soon as she lost sight of the drive she became anxious that Mr Balik might return. She could picture him riding up to the front door, swinging from the saddle and shouting for Grainger. Finding her there. The surprise and anger in his face.

The workshop was an old wooden shed which slouched against the back wall of the house. It looked as if it had been dumped there until a better place could be found for it. The planks of the old door were dark and rotten from contact with the damp ground. Grainger ducked his head and went in.

'Wait there,' he said. 'I won't be a moment.'

Imogen peered after him into the gloom. Grainger's private place. It suited him, she thought. A floor of trodden earth; a heavy bench, solid like the stump of a tree that had grown there; a scattering of tools; shelves of tins and jars. In one corner she noticed a pot of brown glue like the one Dad kept in the kiln-room. She waited, heard Grainger clear his throat, glanced back at the corner of the house, expecting Balik to appear at any moment. She wanted to run. Her nails were digging into her palms. She called Grainger's name but couldn't make it loud enough for him to hear.

Eventually he emerged with a small parcel of blue sugar paper which he held out to her. She didn't know whether she should take it.

'Apples,' he explained with a nod. 'Good 'uns. He won't miss 'em.'

'Thank you,' she said uncertainly.

'A couple for you. And one for the potter. If he likes. Tell him we're in for rain.'

'In for rain?'

'That's right. The pitch could turn a treat.'

He grinned at her, showing two brown teeth. Then went back into the shed.

On the Friday evening, the day before the match, Imogen went up to her room and saw at once that the window was ajar and that the ledge was empty. She thought that perhaps she had opened the window herself but she knew that she hadn't touched the owl. She looked quickly, helplessly round the room. It had not been disturbed. She went down to the kitchen again.

'What's the matter?' asked Dad, looking up from a book and seeing something wrong in Imogen's face.

'Did you go into my room today?'

'Why should I do that?'

'Did you?'

'Of course not. I don't go to your room unless I tell you first. You know that. Not since . . .'

He didn't finish but she knew what he was trying to say. Not since that time he'd half-heartedly tried to pack for her trip to Melling.

'Is anything wrong, sweet?'

'I was looking for something,' she said.

'What?'

'It doesn't matter. It's not important. I just thought . . .'

'Do you want me to look for you?'

'No. It'll turn up.'

She went back to her room and stood at the window, looking out at the trees and the roof of the kiln-room, listening keenly. The night was still. There was a muddle of distant singing from The Hope but no other sound.

On that other occasion, when Fortune had flown out into the night, there had been the rattle of his wings, a disturbance which seemed deliberate, as if he'd wanted her to know what he was doing. This time there was only absence and silence. She reached for her mother's cloak on the back of the door, as she had done before. Then stopped, let her arm drop. What was the point of going outside now? The only place to look for him, she felt sure, would be Mr Balik's house and she couldn't go there until Dad was asleep. That might be another hour or so. And supposing she did go. What could she do up there? What could she achieve? She would be powerless. A witness, perhaps; nothing more.

She stretched out on her bed, fully clothed, and stared at the ceiling.

Maybe he's simply gone, she thought suddenly. Maybe Fortune didn't mean to come back.

10

Grainger's promise of rain came to nothing. The Saturday of the match was bright and clear. Imogen was putting together some food to take with them to Mr Balik's grounds.

'There's been a heavy dew, though,' Dad called down the stairs. 'Might prove beneficial, I suppose. Give a bit of grip to the soil. And the sun'll make a nice day of it, won't it?'

Imogen didn't answer. She packed the sandwiches into a basket and thought about the thirteenth owl. Missing him. Now that he'd gone, now that she knew he wasn't waiting on her window ledge, the day felt dull, as if a mist had closed on it. Dad's voice and the familiar sounds of the plates, the knives and forks against the kitchen table, all seemed muffled and more ordinary than they had been before. But relief was part of this, too. The sense that a vague worry had been removed. The world had become safe again; safe and predictable.

Dad clattered downstairs and appeared before her at the kitchen door. Dazzling, almost like an angel.

'Well,' he said. 'Do I look the part?'

He held out his arms awkwardly, allowing Imogen to inspect him. She laughed in spite of herself.

'Very smart,' she said. 'You look too white to be running around and sweating. What's that round your waist?'

'That tie. You know, the one Helen gave me.'

'Oh Dad . . .'

'I know, I know, but I'm never going to wear it round my neck, Imogen. And I don't like to tell Helen I've never even had it on, and I don't like to lie . . .'

'So now you can say you've worn it, in all truth?'

'And that it looked the proper thing.'

He smiled widely and started to turn round on his heels, so she could see the back.

'Yes, very smart,' she said again. 'You could go off and get married in an outfit like that.'

Stupid, she thought to herself as soon as she'd said it. A stupid thing to say. She glanced at the fading photograph above the kitchen fireplace. A quick look, then away again. Dad stopped turning, just for a second, with his back still to her. He lowered his head and she saw his neck stretch. It was brown and pitted, like the cover of their bible. When he turned back to her again he was smiling. Not quite the same, but still smiling.

'We'd better go,' he said. 'I want a good look at the opposition before we start.'

'The very sight of you will strike fear into their hearts,' she told him, reaching up to straighten his collar.

★

A pitch had been prepared on the wide lawns to the back of the house and a large marquee erected in a space between two flowerbeds. Dad went off to talk to the rest of the team, leaving Imogen to find a place to sit. She walked slowly round the boundary, looking for somewhere out of the way, hoping that she would see no signs of Mr Balik. She was so intent on this that Boy had shouted to her twice before she noticed him.

'You come to learn a thing or two, then, Imogen?'

He was leaning against the trunk of a poplar, tugging at an impossibly long boot lace. She wandered over to him.

'Are you playing, too, Boy?'

'I am now. They were a man short.' He didn't look up. He was concentrating proudly on his lace. 'Old Grainger come down and asked me himself.'

'You? They're still a man short, then, aren't they?' she said with a wide-eyed look he couldn't see.

'No. That's what I'm saying. It's me. I've filled in.'

'Of course.' She smiled at him. 'Good luck, Boy,' she said and began to walk away again.

'Oi. Ginny. Look at this.'

When she turned round she saw him jumping about, crashing both feet down flat and hard, and grinning fiercely.

'A good bit of tresp-arse this is. Eh?'

'We're all invited,' she told him. 'It's not trespass if you're invited.'

'I don't care. I just like treading on his grass. I only wish he could see it.'

'He might see it, the way you're carrying on. Everyone else is looking at you.'

'He's not going to see, though,' Boy said, stopping. 'He's gone away for the day.'

'Where to?'

'Melling. So Mr Grainger said.'

'Melling? Are you sure?'

'I'm always sure. Anyway, why shouldn't he be there?'

'I just didn't think he ever . . .'

'What?'

'It doesn't matter. Good luck, Boy. I hope you do well.'

Imogen was glad that Mr Balik wouldn't be around; but knowing where he'd gone made her feel uneasy. Why Melling? Didn't Grainger say he never went to Melling, that he hadn't been there for years? So why had he gone there today? If he wanted to keep out of the way of the crowds at the cricket match he could've gone almost anywhere; out into the fields, even somewhere in the depths of the house. But not Melling.

She found somewhere to sit where she could keep her back to the high, grey walls and blank windows of the house. Even with the master out of the way, she didn't want to see it every time she lifted her head to watch the cricket.

Grainger went in first for the village, holding himself straight and still and gently patting his bat on the ground. Everyone was turned his way; the fielders, the watchers spread round the boundary with their boxes and rugs, even the ring of dark trees behind them. There he stood, the imposing centre of a green circle, not at all like the Grainger Imogen was used to seeing.

Everything became still as the game started. The only movement was the soft tapping of the bat on the ground and the leaning run of the bowler hurrying in to the wicket. Imogen hardly saw the ball leave the bowler's hand. She heard him grunt as he swung his arm, saw Grainger lift on to his toes then turn and look over his shoulder. The ball appeared, bobbling down towards the boundary, and only then, it seemed, did Imogen hear the chock of its impact on the bat.

'Yes,' shouted the batsman at the other end. Grainger loped up the wicket and the match was under way.

As it unfolded, Imogen tried to take an interest in the cricket but she found it impossible to tell which side was winning. Instead she became distracted by the efforts of Mr Bailey who was supposed to be scoring. From time to time he would run backwards and forwards to the large black scoreboard, then stand still with his eyes shut and one hand clasped to the top of his head as he tried to remember the score.

'Score-board! Score-board!' figures in white yelled to him from the distance. 'Try to keep it up to date, will you?'

Whenever Imogen looked back to the cricket a clergyman with a boyish face and shiny black hair seemed to be bowling in a cartwheel of arms and legs. Occasionally he managed to get a ball through to rattle the stumps or to thump against someone's legs. Then he would lift both arms in the air and twist round to shout like a pagan at the umpire. At other times Grainger would move forward, make a seemingly gentle arc with his bat and the ball would go scudding over the grass to the boundary.

The day wore on like this, the odd flurry of excitement and long stretches of repeated rituals. Dad went in to bat, swung one ball away to the trees for four and sent another steepling into the sky. Their own vicar placed himself beneath it and waited with his hand cupped before his face. Imogen heard the slap of the ball against his palms, saw him buckle a little at the knees. And Dad was out. He trudged back to where the village team had scattered their gear, nodding briefly to the vicar as he passed but not looking in Imogen's direction at all.

Boy's turn came last. The black-haired clergyman slowed his run considerably but still managed to send a ball into the pit of Boy's stomach. Both teams gathered round him and several clergymen ruffled his hair. He then went back to the crease, closed his eyes and nicked the next delivery over the wicket-keeper's head. The ball skimmed over the grass towards Imogen. A rural dean, his face red and shiny, came galloping after it. He was running straight for her, baring his teeth as if he meant to savage her.

When he saw his chase was useless, he struggled to a standstill. The ball trickled over the boundary and Imogen bent to scoop it up and toss it back to him.

It was at that moment, as the ball was about to roll into her hand, that she sensed someone move behind her. A shadow appeared on the grass to her left. More than a shadow, in fact; darker, as if it had a substance of its own. She stood slowly and turned round.

Mr Balik, in a long black coat and dark riding trousers, shielding his eyes against the sun.

The world seemed to slow down. She felt the leather of the ball in her fingers. Mr Balik, silhouetted in a gap of blue between the corner of the house and a line of trees, moved his head. Imogen couldn't see his eyes but she knew he was looking at her.

'Young lady. Young lady, can you hear me?'

The rural dean was calling to her. The top of his head was pink with sweat and he was holding out his hand for the ball.

'Oh, yes,' she said blankly. 'I'm sorry.'

He might've been standing there for minutes. She couldn't tell. She smiled at him, saw his eyes take in the scar on her cheek as he smiled back.

As the clergyman galloped back to the game, Imogen turned her head and saw Mr Balik out of the corner of her eye. He was still looking at her. Then there was something small and solid bisecting the patch of sky above his head.

A curving, steady flight, from the trees to the

house. Like an omen, a shooting star. Not silver on black as a star should have been, but some dark thing against the bright day-blue.

Mr Balik twisted round and looked up, too. But he couldn't have seen anything. The sky was empty again.

Shortly after that Boy was bowled and the players all came in for lunch.

'Eighty-four to get,' said Grainger striding towards the marquee. 'They won't find it easy if we can keep it straight. They'll have to fight hard for it.'

Imogen followed him and stood at the entrance, looking through the pale gloom for Dad. She saw him perch astride a bench and tap a place for Boy to sit next to him. The sun on the canvas made their faces appear blue, almost as if they were under water.

'Put yourself down there, Boy,' said Dad. 'Eat with the men. That four of yours might yet decide the whole thing.'

Imogen was relieved to see him laugh. He didn't look as if he needed the company of his daughter. Mrs Carter hurried past her with a plate of sandwiches.

'That master of yours turned up after all,' she said to Grainger. 'I thought you told us he'd be at Melling all day.'

'I did, because he was. So he said to me, anyway.'

'Well, he's back.'

'Then I'd better see what he wants.'

Grainger's face assumed his usual frown. If he felt

that there was anything to worry him about Mr
Balik's early return, he kept it to himself. He clambered awkwardly out of his place and headed in the
direction of the house. Again Imogen followed him,
this time keeping her distance so that he wouldn't
notice her. She saw him take the path through the
circular herb garden and step down on to the lower
lawn. Then stop and look up.

Mr Balik was standing at an upper window. His
face stood out against the darkness of his coat and
the room behind him. Grainger was familiar with
that look, knew better than to interrupt. He turned
and went back to the marquee. Imogen shrank
back and let him pass.

Between his fingers Mr Balik was holding a sheet
of paper. After a second he closed his fist on it,
screwed it into a ball and tossed it aside. Then stood
there, looking out at distance. Not taking anything
in. Below him on the ground floor, she could see
one of his owls at the dining room window.

It stood on the ledge as if it, too, were staring out
at nothing.

During the afternoon, the vicar's team were all out
for eighty, four runs short, and Dad took four of the
wickets. Four wickets, including that of the vicar
himself. He described each one to Imogen, endlessly,
as they collected up their things and left the ground.

'I paid the vicar back for catching me out,' he
said, his eyes sparkling. 'The ball shot off like I
was bowling on a pebble beach, Imogen. Do you

understand what I mean? The way the ball deviated from its line?'

'Yes, Dad.'

'I shall feel the stiffness tomorrow, you can bet on that. Worth it, though. Worth every ache and pain.'

She was hardly listening but he was too pleased with his afternoon's work to notice. They entered the tunnel of trees over Mr Balik's drive. Several paces ahead of them Old Carter walked with Boy who was trailing his sweater along the ground behind him. Beyond them, just passing through the gate and turning into the lane, were the vicar and Mrs Carter. As Dad rambled on, Imogen looked up to see a dark movement, a flutter against the pale canopy of leaves. The same dark movement she'd seen earlier, above Mr Balik's head, only clearer now, bigger.

Something had settled on the iron gate.

No one else saw it. Old Carter had stopped to remonstrate with Boy. Dad was staring down at the ground while he talked.

Imogen couldn't stop herself calling out.

'Look,' she said. 'On the gate.'

'What? What is it?'

But almost at once the bird lifted off again. That familiar leap, the hunch and then the take-off. It swooped up the drive towards them, over their heads and out of sight towards the house.

'Did you see it?'

'Only just,' said Dad. 'A crow or something.'

'No. Not a crow. It was an owl.'

'Couldn't have been, sweet. It's too early for most owls.'

'But it was. I saw it.'

'The only sort you'd see in daytime,' Dad said resolutely, 'would be little owls and that would be too big for a little owl.'

He hadn't seen it properly but that didn't matter. He didn't want to believe that it was an owl. Imogen said no more about it. She wondered whether he was right. A crow, and not an owl. Perhaps she'd seen a crow and her imagination had told her it was an owl.

Old Carter was waiting for them to catch up.

'Nice bit of bowling, potter,' he said. 'They couldn't tell ball from grass when you were on.'

'Thank you, Carter. I did my best.'

'Well, it was good enough. A famous victory, I'd've said. It should help to keep the Church's feet on the ground.'

The two men walked side by side and Dad began to tell Carter all about the capturing of his wickets. Boy fell in beside Imogen.

'I took one in the belly. Did you see?'

She didn't answer.

'Nearly got me in the pills, too. Didn't think vicars were supposed to do things like that. What's the matter?'

'Boy, did you see that bird on the gate?'

'Just now? Yes. Why?'

'It really was there?'

''Course it was. Then it flew up to Balik's place.

You can go anywhere when you're a bird. That'd be good, that would. If I was a bird I wouldn't go anywhere near . . .'

'What was it?'

'What?'

'What sort of bird was it?'

'I don't know . . .'

'It was an owl, Boy. You saw it. You were closer than we were. You must've . . .'

'It couldn't have been an owl, Imogen. It didn't have proper feathers. And it was all kind of shiny.'

11

She went up to her room, closed the door carefully, and it began to happen just as she feared it would. The dream came back more fiercely than ever before.

She stretched out on the bed but knew she wouldn't sleep. She only had to close her eyes for the images to swoop around her head.

The man-bird in black, with its gaping, silent beak.

The flames in corridors.

And Fortune muddled in with it all.

He was leaning forward and swinging his head from side to side. Mr Balik was there, too. Looking out at her from the upstairs window. At times his face took the place of the man-bird's face. Instead of the beak there was Mr Balik's mouth, wide open and shouting but making no sound. A point of gold at his collar, shining in the dark. The skin tight over bulging eyes in a face that was both Mr Balik's and the man-bird's.

And then the eyes began to split, like the skin of a chestnut. Suddenly there was blackness staring out at her and all around her a low, throbbing sound. It was a humming, singing noise but there was no word behind it, nothing that made any human sense.

Nevertheless, Imogen understood what it meant. That it was calling her.

It was only when she stopped at the end of Mr Balik's drive that she realized that the sound had disappeared and the night was quiet. Cloud cleared from the face of the moon for a moment and made the grass between her and the house a silver-grey. She looked back over her shoulder and wondered whether she should go home again. It felt wrong to be here. Why had she come? Nothing made any sense.

Then she noticed that one of the dining-room windows was open and she knew that Fortune was inside somewhere. That, at least, made sense.

She moved out of the shadow of the trees and made quickly for the house. Her cloak flapped heavily behind her and she felt a few warm drops of the promised rain on her hands and face. By the time she reached the window it was raining steadily. There was darkness and emptiness inside the house.

She waited for a while, thinking hard but deciding nothing.

Then she reached up, hooked her fingers over the ledge and pulled herself in. Her boots scrabbled at the wall and then she was tumbling into the room. One elbow struck the floor with a thud. She lay there for a second or two, listening, and looked around the room.

It was large. High and narrow, with only one or two pieces of furniture: a solid, carved sideboard near to where she'd fallen; a long dining table and some tall-backed chairs, all black as iron. She stood up carefully and began to walk round the table. There were several sheets of paper scattered across it. Some screwed into balls. Matches and a stub of candle. A pen and an ink stand.

No sign of what she was looking for.

'Fortune?' she said. No more than a breath.

The only other sound in the room was the beating of rain on the windows. She couldn't see him.

At the far end of the table were two plates, abandoned half way through a meal. Soft white in the gloom. She was looking at them when her foot pressed on something and she couldn't prevent herself putting her full weight on it. It slipped and crunched, like a man's hand. She froze and looked down.

Bones.

'Dear God,' she said quickly to herself.

But they were chicken bones, tossed on to the floor and left there, and she shut her eyes and sighed.

Then a shriek. A blade of sound cutting the night. Filling the room, shriek and echo almost in the same moment.

Where? Where from?

Imogen cried out and twisted round. She saw a rounded, gravestone shape by a circular mirror on the sideboard. Something like a lowered head, looking at her. She saw the dark of eyes, the arch of a back in the mirror. Had she found him? Was he looking directly at her now?

For some moments everything remained still. Then there was a violent disturbance of air, coming across the room towards her. It lifted a sheet of paper from the table and floated it to the floor.

Imogen cowered, throwing up her arms to protect her face. But nothing touched her. For an instant a kind of darkness hung above her head before rising and passing over to the window ledge behind her. When she turned she saw Mr Balik's owl, and next to it a kind of pulsing shadow, seeming to step from side to side.

'Fortune,' she said softly.

Then the movement stopped. She peered through the gloom but all she could see was the ordinary pottery owl, motionless on the ledge. By itself.

'No. Don't leave me,' she called.

She ran to the open window, catching the chicken bone with her foot and spinning it across the floor to clatter against a chair leg. She leaned right out of the window and called again.

'Where are you?'

There was no answer. Warm rain hit her face in thick drops and the smell of soaked earth rose up to her. Nothing moved behind the curtain of falling water.

She turned back to the room, almost crying with frustration.

'Why have you brought me here?' she said, dropping to her knees. 'What is it you want?'

On the floor before her was the sheet of paper which had fallen from the table. She picked it up. Scratched across the top in black ink was a single word.

Charlotte.

Imogen felt for the matches and lit the stub of candle. She breathed deeply once or twice. The circle of pale light on the table calmed her.

I shouldn't be feeling like this, she thought. Not here. I don't belong. Mr Balik's house. His words on paper. I should go home and mind my own business.

But she knew she had to stay. And read what she had found, what she had been led to.

She sat down, slowly and deliberately, and spread the paper on the table in front of her.

Charlotte. And, beneath it, a line gouged with such force that it had torn through the paper, and a block of black ink words in an urgent, neat hand.

Charlotte.

I have spoken your name again. I have said it out loud. I did not want to — I was afraid of the sound of your name — but it has been forced from me.

Charlotte.

After all these years I have been back to Melling. I rode there myself this morning, feeling sick at heart the nearer I got. I knew you would not be there. I do not know where you are but I knew I would not find you in Melling.

Every day since I destroyed your life I have thought about you. Many times I have asked the Lord to forgive

235

me for what I did. He has not forgiven me. I have tried to forget but that does not work. Now I am making myself remember.

I wish you had cursed me for my sin. Your curse would have been easier to bear than your silence. But it is your silence that I deserve. It is what I have been living with all this time, the memory of that day and your silence.

Charlotte.

At times I have thought of looking for you, to confess and tell you of the remorse I feel. There is no courage in me, though. I was afraid of the look I might see in your face and I could not do it.

Lately I have been haunted by another fear; the fear that you are no longer alive. I cannot explain why I feel this. I do not understand it myself. That is why I am writing to you now. A letter I have started over and over again but will never send.

I see images of fire in the night, terrible images of fire and birds. I have imagined a bird at the window behind me. It seemed so real, flapping at the window as if it was trying to beat its way inside. It has caused me such torment that I could not think properly, did not know what to do with myself.

This is why I rode over to Melling. To make myself suffer. To punish myself with the sight of the place where we had been happy. And your name.

Charlotte.

Today I stood at the end of the drive and looked at your house again. I remembered the things I had said to you; how I had wanted you to be perfect, to belong to me, to be tamed. And I remembered that night; when I shouted at you for not being what I wanted, and ran out of the house with my head full of my own anger.

I made myself remember everything I did.

How I ran blindly into the stable. How I snatched a saddle from its peg and threw it down in my rage.

I saw it all again.

The oil lamp falling against the bale of straw. The sudden sheet of flame. And me standing there, a hopeless coward, not knowing what to do.

Oh, Charlotte.

I saw your birds tethered to their perches and beating their wings in panic.

I should have stayed in that fire and tried to save them. It would have been better to stay and be eaten up by the flames.

I remember the terrible silence the last time I saw you. How you would not look at me.

Charlotte.

Oh, Charlotte . . .

12

Imogen sat for some while staring at the paper, unable to move or think at all clearly. She was feeling small and full of shame at what she had done. Then she heard a sound outside the room. A board cracking under a footfall, very sharp. She brought her hand down abruptly on the pale flame. The room became darker than ever and hot wax burnt into her palm. She dropped to her knees and crawled under the table, pulling up the hood of the cloak to hide her yellow hair.

The door opened and a shimmer of light came into the room. A candle trembled in the draught from the window. Two or three heavy steps across the floor. Her arms and legs began to shake and she squeezed her hands between her knees.

'What is it?' That familiar, dark voice, very low. 'What do you want?'

Imogen held her breath as Mr Balik strode round the table to the open window. He paused and turned slowly so that Imogen could hear his boots scrape minutely on the boards.

'You?' he said softly.

She stood up, as steadily as she could. Her heart

was pounding but there was nothing else she could do. She'd have to face him now. Then she saw that his back was to her. Still staring out of the window. No. Not out but at the window. At the pottery owl, motionless on the ledge. He didn't know she was in the room with him.

She turned to look for the door. Moved slowly towards it, slowly. And hit the back of a chair with her arm. The chair dragged across the floor, loud and sudden. Mr Balik jerked round, saw her and held the candle up. A lemon glow across the dome of his forehead. For a second they faced each other.

'Oh God,' he whispered. 'It can't be.'

He was staring at her as if she were somehow unreal. She wanted to look away but couldn't.

'What do you want from me?'

The silence was unbearable but there was nothing Imogen could say to him. It was as if two shadows faced each other.

'Speak to me,' he said, his voice low and trembling, his face full of pain and helplessness. 'If you can't forgive me, say something.'

The rain outside and nothing but rain.

'God save me, you're . . . you aren't alive any more. Is that why you've come? Because you're . . .? Have you come to punish me?'

The candle fell from his hand and spluttered out on the table. He stumbled away from her, backwards, awkwardly swinging his arm. It struck something behind him. The owl on the ledge. It teetered, rocked against the window, scratching the glass as it slid down and toppled to the floor.

And smashed. A high, sharp crack on the floor. The scattering of fragments.

Following by a roaring sound. Part shout, part scream, as if something in Mr Balik had cracked, too.

He ran to the door, barging it open with his shoulder. Imogen heard his footsteps on floorboards, then on marble, then running up the stairs. The shouting faded into the depths of the house.

She hadn't moved since Mr Balik had turned to look at her. Now she was alone she groped for one of the dining chairs and sat down. She felt that she should do something. But what? A second crash sounded from somewhere above her head. Another owl, she guessed, smashed from its ledge. Then another. He was raging through the house, breaking them all.

A long sigh shook her body, as if she'd been holding her breath all this time, and she began to sob. She had no control over what was happening in this house and yet she felt that she was responsible for it. She didn't belong, and she knew things she had no right to know. The madness that had taken hold of Mr Balik was because of her. She'd followed Fortune up to the house and she'd brought destruction with her. The owls destroyed, Mr Balik destroyed, and in time she would be destroyed, too.

Another explosion sounded upstairs, a high-pitched cracking sound followed almost at once by the booming of a vast drum as something hit the floorboards. For a while she heard nothing but then there came the sounds of quick, sudden movements in one of the upstairs rooms. Followed by silence again.

She felt her way carefully to the door of the dining room and looked out. She recognized the hall where they'd first brought the owls, all those weeks ago.

She could just make out the pattern of squares on the floor. The old planks still propped by the wall. Rain was washing down the tall windows, smearing everything inside with a weak, grey light. A broad marble staircase led up to deep shadows. And out of these shadows came a white face, as if it had no body. It began to move smoothly down the stairs. Became clearer, Mr Balik carrying something like a rod against his shoulder. At first Imogen thought it was his silver-topped stick but it was more solid than that, with the dull sheen of metal.

She shrank back as he crossed the hall and threw open the double doors. A gust of lurid wind and rain blew in. He stepped outside and the doors banged to behind him.

Then Imogen was alone in the house. There was a release of silence all around her and the whole place suddenly seemed empty.

She backed into the dining room and felt her way to a window at the far end. From there, she thought, she would be able to see where Mr Balik was going. All she could make out, though, was a blur of movement behind diagonal canes of rain. Stooped and moving fast somewhere to the right. Towards the marquee, perhaps. She pressed her face against the glass but nothing was clear. All moving things seemed to be branches and shadows tossing in the wind.

Let him go, she thought. He's made this trouble for himself. Stay where you are and let him go.

She turned back to the table and stood for a while, touching the rim of one of the plates with her fingers. Looking down at it and thinking.

He has destroyed the owls and he will destroy you. Leave him alone.

On the other side of the room the shards of broken owl were scattered across the floor. She sensed them there in the darkness. Ruined.

She remained at the edge of the table for several moments, poised between two states of mind, the need to stay where she was and the need to act. She pictured Mr Balik stumbling blindly through the rain. Pictured the silent pieces of shattered pottery. The images came and went in her head.

A man in driving rain, a broken owl. Over and over.

Then, almost without thinking, she found herself hurrying towards the dining room door, blundering against a chair, running desperately across the hall.

Outside, the rain was toppling out of a black sky. It soaked through her cloak in seconds and made her slip as she ran. She reached the lawn by the marquee and stopped. There was thick mud down one thigh and the length of her arm, though she couldn't remember falling.

She saw Mr Balik's bowed back a few paces ahead of her. He was kneeling in the middle of the lawn, like a man at prayer, a penitent. She called his name but her voice was snatched away by the wind. She was about to shout again but something made her hesitate.

Surely it would be wrong to go stumbling up to him now. To break into his thoughts and tell him . . . What? She didn't know how to tell him who she was, why she was there.

Maybe it's best he thinks I'm someone else, she told herself. Best for him and best for me.

But as she watched she saw his back straighten. He seemed to feel her presence and he twisted slowly round to look at her through wide eyes.

His bunched fists gripping a shot-gun.

Its muzzle forced under his chin.

Not a man at prayer at all.

'Let me go.' His voice was low and rasping. 'I'll pay for what I've done. Let that be enough.'

'Mr Balik, no . . .'

Imogen took a step forward and sank to her knees, close enough to touch him now. He stiffened and tightened his grip on the gun.

'Keep away from me!'

'Can't you see?' she said, pulling back her hood. 'I'm not Charlotte. You've got things wrong . . .'

He stared back at her with water washing over his

face. The rain bore down on them out of the darkness with a steady, beating sound.

'Mr Balik, it's me. Imogen. From the potter's shop.'

'Imogen . . .'

'You know me. We brought you the owls, Dad and me.'

One hand unfolded from the gun and he lifted it carefully to Imogen's face. She let him touch her lightly on the chin. And trace the scar on her cheek with his cold fingers. He studied her face like a man in a trance.

'What's happened to you?' he whispered. 'Your face . . .'

'I had an accident. When I was little.'

'No . . .'

'Yes, Mr Balik. My name is Imogen. I was burnt.'

'Burnt? In the fire?'

'No, no. On the kiln door. Here in the village. You know who I am.'

'The potter's girl,' he said to himself, and then frowned uncertainly. 'What are you doing here?'

'I don't know. There was . . . something calling me here.'

'Calling you? Who was it?'

'It wasn't a person, Mr Balik. I . . . I can't explain . . .'

'You must. Tell me what it was.'

'It was like an owl.'

'An owl,' he said slowly. 'Yes.'

His voice was weak and distracted. He lowered

244

his head and looked at the gun resting against his chest. Imogen saw his white fingers trembling against the barrel.

'I've seen it, too,' he said.

'Please, Mr Balik . . .'

She lifted her hand gently towards him. Held it still. He watched her place it over his fingers.

Then, somewhere behind them, she heard the splash of heavy footsteps. Out of the corner of her eye she saw the huddled shape of Grainger hurrying towards them over the wet lawn.

'Wait,' she called without turning round.

Two, three heavy seconds hung between them before Mr Balik released his grip on the gun. He looked with astonishment in his eyes from Imogen to Grainger.

'Will you help me?' he mumbled. 'I don't know what I'm doing here.'

All Mr Balik's strength seemed to have left him. He hardly knew where he was and Grainger had to carry him in his arms like a child. He took him into the house and up to his room.

'You go ahead,' he told Imogen. 'Open the doors for me.'

Mr Balik's room was large and cool with a high ceiling. Imogen waited at the door while Grainger lifted his master on to the bed.

It took great strength, she thought, to move him as gently as that.

Out of the corner of her eye she saw something

245

curved and jagged, like a piece of jawbone, in one of the corners. She guessed it was part of another broken owl.

Grainger took the corner of the coverlet and wiped mud and rain from Mr Balik's face.

'We'll leave him to himself for a bit,' he said, steering Imogen out into the corridor.

He closed the door softly behind him. Then sighed and narrowed his eyes at her.

'I can't tell you why I'm here, Mr Grainger,' she said firmly before he could speak. 'It's no good you asking.'

'Then you'd best go home, Imogen. And hope he forgets all about this.'

But she knew that Mr Balik would not forget, any more than she would. She also knew that she could not go home. There was one more thing that had to be done before she could leave the house that night.

Grainger stood an oil lamp on the dining room table. Next to it he placed the pot of brown glue Imogen had asked him to fetch from his workshop. Then he watched in silence as she gathered up the shards and fragments from the floor and arranged them in the pool of light.

'Is this what you must do?' he asked quietly.

'It is.'

'And it must be done now, must it? At this hour of the night?'

'I think it must, Mr Grainger, yes.'

'Then I'll say no more.'

It was slow and careful work and Imogen had no notion of how long it was taking her. Time seemed to have stopped moving. Her fingers wanted to hurry but she wouldn't let them. She had to do this properly.

Eventually the pieces were put together and there was a complete owl standing before her on the table. Then she took some of the glue and made a paste of dust and splinters which she smeared into the largest fissures running through its body. Grainger stood beyond the light and watched her in silence.

'So,' he said. 'It's finished.'

'Yes. One owl to begin with. It'll do for now.'

'It'll do well. Good as new.'

'Oh no, Mr Grainger. It's not that.'

Imogen knew that, if you looked closely at it, you could see a jigsaw of cracks and crazes across its body. It would never be as good as new again. She rubbed her eyes with the back of her hand. The rain had stopped and there was a yellow grey light at the windows.

Weak sunlight fell on the stairs and across the landing. She stood for several moments at the door to Mr Balik's room, watching him. His face was even paler than usual and there were thin strands of black hair stuck to his forehead. She couldn't tell whether he was awake or not until he spoke.

'I don't know what you're doing here,' he said, 'but I'm glad you came. I mean, I'm glad that it was you and not . . .'

'I know, Mr Balik.' She paused and took a breath. 'I . . . I think I know more than I ought to.'

'Do you?'

'About Charlotte, I mean . . .'

'Oh. The letter.'

'Yes. I'm sorry. I . . .'

'It doesn't matter.'

'I shan't say anything, Mr Balik.'

'No.' He smiled a faint, inward smile, not intended for her, and opened his eyes. 'I can't see you if you stand there with the light behind you.'

She stepped into the room and pushed the door to behind her.

'Look,' she said, holding up the owl for him to see. 'I've brought this for you.'

'What is it?'

She moved a little nearer. He blinked, to clear his eyes, and half lifted a hand, as if he wanted to touch it but didn't have the courage.

'Mended?' he said.

'Yes.'

'You did this?'

'Yes. You left it smashed, and now it's fixed.'

'Why did you do it?'

'It was something that had to be done. Can you see? Broken and mended. And better for it.'

'Better for it? How can it be?'

'It's not perfect any more. I know that. But that's not what I mean. It's different now, not like it was before. You can see the story of what's happened to it.'

Mr Balik remained still for such a long time that Imogen began to wonder whether he'd forgotten she was there.

'Put it down on that chest,' he said at last.

She placed it in a patch of light the shape of the window, and stood aside while he looked at it. Trying to see its story. How it had been in pieces, and was now a complete owl again. Imperfect but whole.

'The others can be mended, too,' she said. 'In time, if you agree to it.'

'Broken and mended,' he said to himself softly. 'Yes. The others, too.'

Grainger walked down the drive with Imogen and would have escorted her all the way home. She stopped by the iron gate, though, and said she'd prefer him to leave her there.

'Well,' he said, 'I imagine you know best.'

'Thank you for all you did, Mr Grainger.'

'For what? I haven't done nothing.'

'You helped me. You didn't ask why I came and you didn't make me leave.'

'That's what I say. I didn't do nothing.'

He nodded briefly and turned back up the drive. Imogen watched him go and then began the walk back to the village. Her cloak was still damp with last night's rain, heavy on her back. She was very tired, she realized.

When she reached home, she could hardly remember passing through the village. Whether anyone had been about, whether she had been seen. Scooping some water from the pitcher, she took a clean, cold drink and sat for a while at the kitchen table.

The light in the kitchen dimmed as someone came in from the yard and stood in the doorway. Her father. She recognized the scrape of his boots, the way he hesitated.

'Imogen?'

She didn't answer, but lifted her head a little to show that she'd heard.

'I've been out to look for you. I didn't know where you were.'

'I went for a long walk,' she told him flatly. 'There's nothing to worry about.'

'Good.' She heard him move behind her, clear his throat. 'Are you all right?'

'Yes, Dad. Just a bit tired.'

'Only, I found these,' he said, leaning over her and putting some pieces of pottery on the table. They rocked quickly for a moment, then settled.

Fortune. Broken in two along the line of the crack.

'Is this what you've been looking for?'

'Yes,' she said. 'Where did you . . .?'

'He was in the yard, by the kiln-room. I don't know how he came to be there.'

She turned round, saw his hand on the back of the chair, and closed her own over it.

'I'll mend him, Dad. It'll be all right,' she said. 'I'm sorry if I worried you.'

'I was worried, Imogen. I've been walking around all morning thinking about things. Then, when I came back and saw your owl out there, I started to get a bit . . . frightened.'

'Frightened? What of?'

'I don't know. About losing you. You weren't in your room and I thought you might've . . . that you'd . . .'

'What?'

'Like I say. That I might've spoiled things and lost you.'

'No. You haven't, of course you haven't.'

'No,' he said and suddenly bent down to kiss the top of her head.

WORDS OF STONE

Kevin Henkes

For Jennifer

I would like to thank colleagues at Bishop Otter College, Chichester, and John Taylor of the BBC, for their help and support

1

BLAZE

Blaze Werla buried Ortman before breakfast. It was the fifth of July, and already the day was white hot. Blaze peeled off his T-shirt and tossed it on the hard ground. He shovelled quickly and furtively, making a small, neat hole the size of a basketball. When the digging was through, Blaze knelt, and using both arms and cupped hands, filled the hole back up, covering Ortman forever. There was something fierce about the manner in which Blaze worked – the determined line of his mouth, the tension that rippled across his back. Dirt stuck to Blaze's sweaty body like bread crumbs; his damp red hair clung to his forehead in ringlets. Blaze slapped the ground flat with the palms of his hands, making a thudding sound and remembering all the other burials, glancing at the nearby stones that marked them.

Burials. There had been four others before Ortman. (Not counting his mother's.) The small graves formed a partial ring around the huge black locust tree on the hill near the highway behind Blaze's house. First there had been Benny. Then Ajax. Next Ken. Then Harold. And now Ortman. Blaze wondered what he would do once the circle was complete. Where would he bury then? He was ten years old. Would he still need to do this when he was twelve? Fifteen? He hoped not. He was tired of being afraid.

Blaze stood and stamped the dirt over Ortman one last time. He picked up the stone he had chosen earlier that morning and held it for a few seconds, as if it were a large egg containing precious life. He had chosen the stone because of its markings: pale mossy blotches that looked like bull's-eyes. Blaze set the stone down firmly in place. 'Goodbye, Ortman,' he whispered. Blaze backed up, scratched the scars on his ankles with either foot, ran his dirty hand through his hair, and stared at the grave site until the crescent of stones blurred before him, becoming a broken pearl bracelet around the arm of a tree it bound.

On the way down the hill toward home, Blaze was already creating someone new in his mind to take Ortman's place. Someone who would be big. Someone who would be tall. Someone who would be fearless. Someone who would be everything Blaze was not.

Blaze was slight, with small feet and hands. He thought his fingers resembled birthday candles, especially compared to his father's ample, knuckly ones. At school, Blaze was the shortest student in his class. His identity with many kids from other grades hinged solely upon his size and his red hair. His hair was so distinctive, in fact, that passersby often turned their heads to take notice. His clear blue eyes had a similar effect on people. Freckles peppered Blaze's cheeks and the bridge of his nose. His eyelashes were full and as transparent as fishing line. And – he was fearful.

Blaze swatted at the leafy, waist-high weeds that surrounded him and thought, I am a contradiction – my name is Blaze and I'm afraid of fire. And fire was only the beginning of a long list of things that made Blaze's head prickle just thinking of them.

Fire. Large dogs. Wasps. The dark.

And then there were the other things. The more important things. The really frightening ones. Nightmares. The Ferris wheel at the fairgrounds. The Fourth of July.

Blaze fixed his attention on the drooping slate roof of his house in the near distance. 'Come on . . . *Simon*,' he said over his shoulder into the warm breeze. 'Let's go eat.'

'Morning, Blaze,' Nova called pleasantly when she heard the screen door open and gently close.

'Morning, Grandma,' Blaze said, entering the kitchen. He walked to the sink and began washing his hands methodically with liquid dish soap, making a thick lather that worked its way up his arms. Ortman's dead, he said matter-of-factly in his head, watching a tiny pinkish blue bubble rise from his hands. Now I've got Simon.

Blaze didn't believe in imaginary friends the way he truly had when he was younger. He didn't set places for them at the table or make himself as small as possible in bed to leave room for them. He didn't talk to them out loud when anyone might hear. But every July he formed a new one. It was habit as much as anything else.

In a way, he compared it to Nova's practice of saying 'Rabbit, rabbit, rabbit' for good luck on the first day of each month. It had to be her first words spoken or else it didn't work. Nova was far from superstitious, and yet, if she forgot to say it, she seemed annoyed with herself all morning.

Blaze also compared it to the relationship his father had with God. Although he told Blaze many times that he didn't really know what he believed, Glenn said that he prayed every now and then. He talked to God when no one else was around.

Glenn had his version of God. Nova had 'Rabbit, rabbit, rabbit.' And Blaze had Simon.

'Well, what can I get you for breakfast?' Nova asked mildly.

Blaze had been looking out the window towards the hill. He turned and faced his grandmother. 'Scrambled eggs, please,' he said. And Nova hummed while she made them. At the stove, with her back to Blaze, Nova's wispy moth-coloured hair looked just like a dandelion right before you make a wish and blow it. But nothing else about Nova was wispy. She was generous in both size and spirit.

Breakfast was Blaze's favourite meal of the day, and the kitchen was his favourite room in the house. Towels, pots, pans, and various other cooking utensils hung on hooks from the walls and ceiling, reminding Blaze of the buy-and-sell shop in town. Four wide windows let in enough sunlight to balance the clutter. In the early morning, the dramatic shadows of the suspended spatulas and ladles spilled down the flowered wallpaper like stalactites. Or were they stalagmites? Blaze could never keep them straight. He had confused them on his final science test of the school year only last month.

During the summer, Blaze always ate breakfast with Nova, just the two of them at the thick, round oak table. Nova unerringly sensed Blaze's moods; she knew when he wanted to talk and when quiet seemed to be what was needed. If Nova wasn't asking Blaze questions or maintaining a peaceful, necessary silence, she was humming (as she was now); that meant she was deep in thought. Blaze was certain that Nova's low murmuring that morning was due to the cucumber beetles she had been battling in her squash patch. Books and magazines on organic gardening were stacked on the counter by the sink like dirty dishes.

Humming. Then silence. Then only the sound of silverware playing against china.

'I don't know how you do it – getting up at this hour when you don't have to,' Glenn said, suddenly appearing in the kitchen doorway.

'Hi, Dad,' Blaze said with a start, surprised by Glenn's unusually early jump on the day. His eyes skated up to meet his father's. Ordinarily breakfast was long finished by the time Glenn made it out of bed.

'Morning, Glenn. Eggs today?' Nova asked.

'Just coffee.' He padded barefooted across the cracking linoleum and reached for a mug from the cupboard. Glenn was tall and big-boned. His straight blond hair fell into his eyes and barely grazed his shoulders, hiding the ringed birthmark on the back of his neck. It was purple and looked like Saturn. When Blaze was mad at his father, he pretended that the birthmark meant that Glenn was really an alien from outer space. 'So what's on the agenda for you two today?' Glenn asked, filling his mug. He sat at the table precisely halfway between Blaze and Nova.

'Cucumber beetles,' Nova said. 'I'm going to try to lick them with a mixture of vanilla and water. It's a trick I read about in one of my magazines,' she added, working her fingers as if she held a spray bottle.

'And you?' Glenn said, looking at Blaze.

Blaze shrugged. 'Nothing really.'

Glenn rubbed his steel grey eyes and yawned, his wide unshaven jaw opening and closing like a machine. 'Want a ride into town? You could call someone from school.'

'Nah,' Blaze replied, wrinkling his nose and shaking his head.

'I'll take you to the lake or the park. Anywhere you want to go.'

'The moon?' Blaze joked.

Glenn yawned and chuckled at the same time.

'I think I'll just mess around here,' Blaze told him.

After rubbing his eyes again, Glenn massaged the space between his eyebrows. 'Just don't think too much,' he said slowly, turning his mug on the table and winking. 'It's not good for you.' He rose with his coffee and headed towards the back door. He stopped at the sink and leaned against it momentarily. 'Oh, by the way . . .' he said. He thrust his hand deep into his pocket and pulled out something small. He flung it gently across the tabletop. It was an old rusty skeleton key. It stopped right beside Blaze's plate, kissing his fork. 'I found it yesterday,' Glenn said. 'For your collection.'

'Thanks,' Blaze answered. He watched Glenn disappear down the hallway, the key floating on the fringe of his vision. His ankles itched. Blaze knew that Glenn wouldn't give him keys if he knew why he saved them.

But here was a new one. Right before him. An ancient thing. It might be my best one yet, Blaze thought. The key's sharp metallic scent tickled Blaze's nostrils. He scooped it up and fingered it, and it seemed to burn in his hand. Blaze wondered who it had once belonged to, what lock it would release, whose door it might open.

It would be a typical July day. Glenn would spend it in the sagging garage that he had converted into a studio, emerging at dinnertime flecked with paint of all colours. Then he'd return and work again until very late, maybe until dawn. Unlike most fathers, Glenn was home all day in the summer. He was a high-school art teacher who devoted his entire vacation to painting large canvases that Blaze liked, but didn't quite understand. Nova would bustle about the kitchen and her garden – concocting, canning, weeding, pruning, and trying to exterminate cucumber beetles for all time. And Blaze would wander throughout the house and around the hill, occasionally talking to someone that no one else could see.

And it would be a typical July night for Blaze. In bed, he would will himself not to dream. Or, at least, not to remember his dreams when he awoke. He would take the library book from his nightstand, open it halfway, and place it beside him to look as if he had been reading. His mason jar filled with his lost key collection would be on the floor within reach. Then, his lamp still on, Blaze would settle in among his nest of four pillows, wishing and waiting for morning light.

2

BLAZE

When Blaze woke up the next morning his chest ached with strangeness. He had been dreaming. It was a dream he had had before. In it a maze of black snakes burst into flames at his feet while he struggled to open a door. The door was held tightly closed by a series of locks. His mother's voice came from behind the door. Sometimes in the dream he would have a key. But even when he did, it would never work.

Don't think about it, Blaze told himself.

His dreams were always so vivid during the summer. He might not remember having a dream for months, but come July they would return. It was peculiar the way that worked.

Blaze blinked and looked around. His room focused about him, becoming familiar and touchable. The library book from the night before was now closed and neatly placed on his nightstand, his bedside lamp turned off. Although he had never actually seen Nova or Glenn do these things, he had often sensed a presence – passing as a shadow, removing the book, turning off the light, tugging the bedclothes up under his chin, touching his forehead, pulling the door closed.

Blaze sat up and swung his legs out from under the sheet. It was dawn. A gust of wind caused the loose window screen to flutter and the faded plaid curtains to balloon and collapse. The curtains had worn thin in many places and were at least as old as Blaze. So was the large, multi-coloured oval rug that covered most of the floor. But nearly everything else was relatively new in comparison. The bookshelf, the bed, the nightstand, the dresser. Blaze could still remember the old blue-striped wallpaper, but now the walls were white. He had picked the paint himself. Snowflake, it was called on the paint chart.

It was several summers earlier that Glenn had urged Blaze to redecorate his room. 'I could paint the solar system on your ceiling,' Glenn had suggested. 'And we could buy some of those neat glow-in-the-dark stars to stick on.' Glenn paused, tapping his fingers on his chin. 'We could redo the walls, too. This wallpaper's not the greatest. We'd have to clean this place out first, though. Get rid of some of this old baby stuff.' As he spoke, Glenn gestured vaguely toward the toys, knickknacks, and books that crowded Blaze's shelves, drawers, closet, and the dusty space under his bed. Things he had long outgrown. 'What do you think?'

Blaze was looking at his prized possession – a plastic Noah's ark replica – perched atop the low overstuffed bookcase. 'Okay,' he answered reluctantly, not wanting to disappoint Glenn.

'Great!'

'But can I keep my ark?' Blaze's voice was urgent.

Glenn hugged him. 'Of course,' he said into his son's red hair.

Blaze picked the ark off the shelf and clutched it tightly. 'And can we just paint the walls and ceiling white? No solar system?'

'You bet,' said Glenn.

Blaze figured that the lighter the walls and ceiling were, the lighter his room would be at night.

Blaze still had the ark. He kept it tucked safely under his bed. Out of sight if a friend from school came over. Now he pulled it out and brought it to the window. Resting one end of it on the sill, he held it in place with his stomach and drew open the curtains to glance at the hill. He did this every morning. But that morning there was something different. Something very strange. Something so strange that Blaze stepped back from the window in surprise, causing his ark to fall. It cracked in half at his feet, little animals scattering across the floor like the pieces of a shattered glass.

A chill hit Blaze in the small of his back and spread to his neck. Written with stones on the broad, mowed stretch of the hillside was the word REENA. Blaze felt hazy and anxious. His heart rattled. He closed his eyes and counted to ten before opening them again. Nothing had changed. Squinting, Blaze leaned on the windowsill, his nose pressed to the screen, then pulled back. The word was still there. It seemed to fill the window. The window seemed to fill the room. Blaze was smaller than ever.

REENA.

'Who did this, Simon?' Blaze whispered. His first thought was to wake Glenn, but something deep and instinctive led him in another direction. Temporarily forgetting his ark, Blaze slipped into some shorts, a T-shirt, and shoes. His hands shook, fumbling with his laces and getting tangled in the folds of his shirt. But, once dressed, he managed to move quickly and quietly so as not to wake anyone – melting down the stairs, tip-toeing throughout the house, and then pushing up the hill with all his might.

When Blaze stopped, he was gasping for air. He doubled over – hands on knees – and tried to breathe evenly. His breath felt warm on his skin. He lifted his head. The letters were enormous up so close. Impulsively, Blaze shoved stone after stone aside with his feet, scrambling them so no one else could read the word. A few he heaved with his hands; they tumbled down the slope. A round and smooth stone with green rings on it caught his attention. It looked exactly like the stone he had chosen to mark Ortman's grave. He examined it closely. Recognized it.

'Oh, no,' Blaze said, stunned all over again. The sky and the grass changed places in his vision as he raced for the black locust tree. After stumbling twice, he used his hands in an animal-like fashion to help him move without falling.

He wanted to cry. His stones were missing. All

five of them. Whoever had written REENA had used them to help construct the letters. Blaze circled the tree a number of times, raising a cloud of dust. Then he sat resting against it, thinking. Waiting. Without the slightest idea of what to do next. A group of crows swooped down nearby. They strutted in a chaotic formation, their calls long and raucous. In a sudden beating of glossy black wings, they took off again. Up, up, up they flew, and Blaze watched, feeling as if he were sinking.

3

BLAZE

Blaze spent the morning in his bedroom, feeling unconnected. He was fixing his ark with Elmer's Glue. While he waited for the glue to dry, he gathered the small animals he had dropped earlier and played with them – first grouping them by colour, then lining them up in a row. He held a memory of doing this with his mother, Reena. He remembered placing the pairs of animals – elephants, giraffes, bears, sheep – on one of the inner braided coils of the rug in his room, following the rug's contour, curving the line of the procession until it formed an oval. Reena and Blaze in the middle. Now there was only one of each plastic animal. When Blaze was five and Reena died, he took one animal from each pair and smashed them with a brick behind the house. Because the ark was his favourite toy and he wanted to punish himself somehow. Because a pair of anything didn't seem right.

Periodically, Blaze peered out of the window, turning his gaze from left to right, checking for another message in stone. He was continually relieved when he found only the remains of the first, still strewn haphazardly across the hill like popcorn on a theatre floor. Who did it? He kept asking himself that question. And he kept coming up with no answer. Although Blaze knew in his heart that neither Nova nor Glenn had done it, he toyed with the possibility.

Nova. She rarely left the house or garden, except to go grocery shopping. It was unusual for her to complain, but Blaze knew that by the end of the day her thick legs were puffy and sore. She often had to elevate them with pillows. Once, she said she had the legs of a ninety-year-old woman, even though she was only sixty. Her legs reminded Blaze of maps – bumpy blue veins connecting feet to knees like crooked highways. When he was younger, Blaze had found comfort in running his fingers over the bulging veins. Compared to them, the scars on his ankles seemed insignificant. The pinkish skin on his ankles was rippled, as if tiny worms were trapped underneath. It was as if twisting snakes were trapped under Nova's skin. Her legs didn't stop her from cooking and gardening with a passion, but trudging up the hill and rolling stones around to spell the name of her dead daughter was surely the last thing she would do.

And Glenn? It wasn't his style. Glenn was a private person. And anyway, it was hard enough to coax him from his studio for dinner or a telephone call on a summer day. Blaze knew he wouldn't take time away from his painting to do something like this.

Who then?

Not his classmates. None of them lived this far

out in the country. (Blaze was the first one picked up and the last one dropped off by the bus each school day.) And although Blaze didn't have a best friend, he was treated with genuine fondness by students and teachers alike. He was smart, but not the smartest. Shy, but not the most shy. He was ninth fastest in his class. And he was considered by some to be the best artist in the entire school. He could draw nearly any popular cartoon character upon request.

There were only two fellow classmates that Blaze didn't like – Teddy Burman and Chelsea Kurz – but they both liked him, so they were out of the question. Teddy was a tiresome braggart and Chelsea was a tireless brown-noser.

At Alan B. Shepard Elementary, Blaze was often called Big Red (a nickname that didn't bother him at all), even by Mr Wiebe, the principal, who'd always try to ruffle Blaze's hair if he spotted him among the noisy throng that paraded past his office on the way to and from recess.

Floy Stark was a possibility, but a vague one. She lived alone on the other side of the hill in a tidy, boxlike house the colour of celery. She was about Nova's age, maybe younger. Sometimes Blaze lay on the hill and watched the Stark house. Nothing interesting ever happened. Floy did ordinary things like hang laundry on the clothesline, wash windows, cut the grass, and play fetch with a terrifying German shepherd she called Gary (who was, thank goodness, usually chained safely to the garage). That was about it.

Blaze couldn't think of anyone else. 'Help me, Simon,' Blaze said, flopping onto his bed like a fish. Pressed into his hand was a tiny plastic bird, wings outstretched, anticipating flight. He lay on his back, staring at the ceiling, trying to weave a plan. And remembering.

Soon after Reena died, Blaze, Nova, and Glenn went to a therapist together. Blaze couldn't remember how many sessions they had gone to, but he would never forget how uncomfortable he felt at them. 'She looks at me like I'm an ant on a stick,' Blaze told Glenn and Nova meekly, after what turned out to be their last session. They were walking across the parking lot toward their car. Blaze inhaled deeply, so happy to be out of Dr Zondag's office. He sniffed his sleeve; the lemony smell of the office still lingered and he waved his shirt-tail in the air.

Glenn and Nova shared a long glance.

'It's really important to talk about things, you know,' Glenn said cautiously, leaning against the car, jingling his keys.

Blaze nodded. He waited for Glenn to unlock the door, then crawled into the back seat. The late afternoon sun spilled into the car, creating sharp-edged shadows. Blaze moved his hand in and out of the warm light.

They stopped at a drive-in restaurant on the way home. Before they ordered, Glenn turned in his seat and leaned over toward Blaze. His head was touching the roof of the car, pulling his hair to one side as if he had slept on it funny. 'We don't have to go back,' Glenn said slowly. 'But you have to promise that you'll always ask me anything you want to. Even if you think it's silly or stupid. I want you to always be able to talk to me.' Glenn ran his hand along the back of Blaze's neck and rested it on his shoulder. 'Mom would want it that way.'

Semis and cars rolled by on the highway while they had dinner. Blaze ate nearly half of his hamburger and he almost finished his junior chocolate shake – something he had never done before. He slurped his shake so quickly he got a headache. The pain thrilled him and he tried it again, egged on by his sense of relief.

As they pulled out of the driveway and threaded into the stream of traffic to go home, Glenn said, 'Nothing's too big or too small to tell me or ask me. You know that.'

Blaze *did* know that. And yet he couldn't bring himself to tell Glenn about what he had seen on the hill that morning. For several reasons.

First, he was beginning to wonder if he had only imagined it or dreamed it. (That's what he wanted to think.)

Second, if it hadn't been a dream, would Glenn believe him anyway? Considering that Blaze had already jumbled the stones so that the hill looked as it always did?

Third, he was still shy when it came to talking about Reena with Glenn sometimes, even though he knew that he shouldn't be. Sometimes his unspoken words were almost tangible, he was so close to talking. Sometimes he stopped himself because he didn't want to take a chance on making Glenn sad. Blaze had seen Glenn cry once when Reena was ill. It had made Blaze feel as small as a dot and completely afraid. Now and then Blaze heard Glenn and Nova talk about Reena in what Blaze thought were sad, hushed voices. Of course, Glenn said sad things about Reena to Blaze, remembered things with him, but Glenn always initiated the conversations. That was the difference. Blaze didn't want to ask or say something about Reena if he couldn't be absolutely certain that the time was perfect and that Glenn would want to talk about her. Even at school if Blaze didn't understand something, he'd often try to figure it out by himself rather than raise his hand and ask a question.

And then there was the other reason. The eerie thought that he was trying to suppress. The thought that his mother was somehow responsible for writing her name on the hill outside his bedroom window.

It was then that Blaze decided to handle this thing on his own. (With Simon, of course.) Maybe he hadn't been able to ride the Ferris wheel on the Fourth of July. Again. But this was surely a way to prove his bravery. He would get to the bottom of this. Blaze didn't want to be afraid any more.

4

JOSELLE

Joselle Stark dried her eyes with the back of her hand. 'No, I'm *not* crying,' she called fiercely. She was crouched on the ivory wicker clothes hamper in her grandmother's narrow bathroom. She wound her arms tightly around her knees and rocked back and forth. The hamper creaked and sagged in rhythm.

'Joselle? What are you doing in there?'

'I'm coming, Grammy!' Joselle scooted down and looked at herself in the mirror on the back of the door. I'm a mess, she thought, sniffling. Her dark brown hair hung in tangled strands around her face, one untamed clump falling over her right eye. 'I wish my hair would cover my *mouth*,' she muttered, flipping her hair back. Joselle's teeth were perfectly shaped, but they were sizes too big for her mouth. In fact, her teeth were so big, it took a conscious effort on Joselle's part to keep her mouth closed. Piano keys, she called them. And she had the nervous habit of bringing her hand up to her mouth, pretending to play a tune on her teeth, humming as she did.

Joselle wasn't fat, but her knees and elbows were

dimpled like a baby's, and her arms and legs looked meaty. She was wearing an extra-large raspberry sweatshirt with the sleeves cut off; it hung to her thighs. The circles under her eyes matched her clothing in colour. Joselle knew that her grandmother's eyesight wasn't terrific, but she knew that her grandmother wasn't blind, either. She hoped her grandmother wouldn't be able to tell that her eyes were bloodshot. Joselle stuck her tongue out at herself in the mirror. She flushed the toilet for effect, unlocked the door, and marched into the hallway, her red rubber thongs slapping crisply against her feet.

'What were you doing in there, sweetie?' Floy asked.

'Grammy, you're old enough to know what goes on in a bathroom,' Joselle replied, walking away, an agonized look on her face.

'I'm also old enough to know when someone's been crying.' Floy grabbed Joselle by the shoulders and spun her around. Floy was strong, despite her petite size, her grip unflinching. 'You *were* crying.' She drew Joselle against her chest. They were so close, Joselle could feel two heartbeats.

Joselle started to cry again. 'I hate and despise my mother,' she sobbed into her grandmother's sleeveless lavender shift.

'I know, I know,' Floy soothed. 'Come to the sofa. Let me do your eyelids.'

Floy settled into the low end of the worn velour sofa and Joselle lay down, her head on her grandmother's lap, her eyes closed firmly. Although their visits were seldom and sporadic, the instant Floy touched Joselle's eyelids it was as if they had never been apart. 'I've done this for you since you were a baby,' Floy said.

'Since forever,' Joselle whispered.

'Relax,' Floy said, as she gently stroked Joselle's eyelids over and over. 'Your eyelids are the colour of my needlepoint lilacs.'

Joselle couldn't have cared less about lilacs. Or needlepoint. Her mother had abandoned her. The Beautiful Vicki had taken off with her boyfriend Rick to 'get away to try to be happy for a while without any interruptions.' The more Joselle thought about it, the more upset she became. Her body shook; tears slid down her cheeks.

Her mother had done stupid, impulsive things before, but this was by far the worst. And the stupid, impulsive things usually had to do with men. Life would be going along just fine until The Beautiful Vicki became interested in someone new. As her interest escalated, so would her time away from Joselle and so would her rash behaviour. Before Rick, Vicki had been involved with a man named Bert. This was late last summer. Bert had come into the restaurant where Vicki worked and charmed her completely. Bert was all she could talk about. It wasn't long before he moved in.

Before Bert, Vicki and Joselle had watched 'The Mary Tyler Moore Show' in reruns every weekday night after the ten o'clock news. Since it was summer, Vicki didn't mind if Joselle stayed up so late. It became ritual. Every night 'Mary Tyler Moore'. Every night cream soda. Every night microwave popcorn sprinkled with Parmesan cheese. Every night Vicki and Joselle sprawled on the futon, the little electric fan turning side to side, cooling them off as they licked their cheesy fingers clean and laughed at Mary Richards and Rhoda Morgenstern. Every night the hypnotic light of the television flashing across the walls of the dark, dark room like a fire in a cave.

'This is my all-time favourite show,' Vicki would say.

'We could watch it all night,' Joselle would add, scooching closer to her mother. 'If it was on all night.'

But as soon as Bert came, everything changed. No more 'Mary Tyler Moore' (he preferred M*A*S*H and Vicki let him watch it). No more microwave popcorn with Parmesan cheese and cream soda alone with Vicki. No more comfortable routine.

'He helps pay for the groceries and the electric bills,' Vicki would tell Joselle. 'And besides, he makes me happy.'

'He doesn't make *me* happy,' Joselle would counter. 'And you hardly spend any time with me any more.'

'I've spent more time with you than with anyone – nearly my whole life.'

'What about "Mary Tyler Moore"? You even said it was your favourite show.'

'So I changed my mind.' Vicki sighed, exhaling

frustration, losing patience quickly. 'M*A*S*H is real. Watch it – you might learn something.'

Joselle was ecstatic when Bert finally moved out about four months later. In a matter of weeks, things settled back to the way they had been, and Joselle and Vicki's spats were few and far between. But then Rick entered their lives, and the cycle began repeating itself.

A small part of Joselle seemed to understand what made Vicki change from being the mother she loved to being the mother she didn't. But she was always unprepared when it happened. Joselle brought her hand up to her mouth and began playing 'Strangers in the Night' on her teeth.

'Listen, it won't be so bad,' Floy said, competing with the melody. 'I'm sure your mother will be back soon. You'll like it here. And anyway, it could be worse – that little Werla boy from around the hill doesn't even *have* a mother.'

Suddenly Joselle stopped humming and crying and trembling. She sat up and stared at Floy with great astonished eyes. 'You mean that skinny redhead I saw sitting on the hill this morning doesn't have a mother.'

Floy nodded.

'Tell me, tell me,' Joselle demanded, snatching her grandmother's hands and squeezing them like sponges. She hoped that the skinny redhead's life story would be worse than hers. She hoped that it would be absolutely dreadful.

★

Joselle listened hungrily. She hung on Floy's every word until even the smallest incident blossomed into full tragedy in her mind. And there was tragedy enough, with or without the aid of Joselle's imagination.

The boy's name was Blaze Werla. And his mother had died when he was just five years old. Of cancer. 'Her name was Reena,' Floy said, doing Joselle's eyelids again. 'She was so young.'

Reena. Joselle liked the sound of the name. She thought it was kind of exotic and sexy. She repeated it softly, drawing out the long E sound like a bird call. *Reeeeena.*

'She died in the middle of the summer,' Floy continued 'when it was hot and muggy. She had long, thick red hair, and I remember thinking how sad it was when she lost it.'

'Lost her hair?' Joselle said, her eyes widening.

'From the treatment. Chemotherapy, it's called,' Floy explained. 'It made her hair fall out. She wore pretty scarves then. Bright ones. The last time I saw her, she was resting on a lawn chair in their yard wearing a chartreuse scarf that was knotted at the top of her head.'

Joselle imagined the scene: the exotic and sexy Reena was so thin you could practically see every bone in her body. Blaze, her tiny son, was weeping hysterically, picking clumps of her hair off the ground and stuffing them into his pockets. The confused husband (who Joselle knew *nothing* about) was hiding behind a nearby bush staring into space like a lawn ornament.

Floy sighed deeply, regaining Joselle's attention.

'Go on, Grammy,' Joselle ordered.

'Oh, sweetie, let's talk about something else. Let's talk about something happy.'

'If we did that, I wouldn't have anything to say.'

'Oh, Joselle!'

'At least tell me more about the boy,' Joselle said in her best supplicating voice.

'Well,' Floy said, shrugging, 'he's quiet and small and he's about your age. He looks a lot like his mother to me. I remember about a year after Reena died, there was an accident at the fairgrounds. A fire. He burned his legs on the Fourth of July and spent the rest of that summer wrapped in bandages up to his waist. Poor little thing. Of course, he's fine now. I don't really know him, but I see him alone up on the hill a lot. From my window. He must like it up there. So you see,' Floy added, 'you're not the only one with a complicated life.'

'What's that mean? Complicated?'

'Oh, I don't know. Confusing, I guess. Mixed up.' Floy took her glasses off and cleaned them in her dress. 'But enough of him. Let's talk about you.'

'No way,' Joselle replied quickly, getting up and clapping her hands. She was thinking about the word *complicated*.

'Well, then, why don't we unpack your bags and get your things organized?' Floy suggested cheerfully. 'I'm just so glad you're here with me.'

Joselle wanted more details (What about the funeral? What about the father? Did he remarry? What did Blaze's legs look like when they were burned? What did they smell like? What did they look like now?), but she figured that she'd work them out of Floy eventually. And the things that Floy wouldn't reveal or had forgotten or didn't know, Joselle would simply have to make up. And they would be the most awful things of all.

5

JOSELLE

Joselle paced about Floy's small house, surveying every corner like a cat. Since she was going to be staying here for a while, she needed to reacquaint herself with the way things looked, smelled, and felt. Joselle moved from room to room, shoving chairs and floor lamps an inch or two in random directions, leaving her mark. She rearranged Floy's Hummel figurines, turning some so that the backs of the children's heads with their odd peaks of hair faced outward.

'Just be careful with those,' Floy warned, hovering over Joselle's shoulder, referring to the Hummels. 'They're worth money.'

Joselle discovered Floy's nail polish, and they took turns painting each other's fingernails and toenails. Joselle was intrigued by the names of the colours: Rambling Rose, Cherub Frost, Iceberry. She wanted each nail to be a different colour, but Floy didn't have that many bottles and some were empty.

'You look racy, Grammy,' Joselle said, having a giggle fit.

When their hands and feet had dried, Floy made popcorn and Joselle strung the kernels with a needle and thread, making necklaces. The necklaces reminded Joselle of Hawaiian leis, and the popcorn reminded her of her mother. Joselle laced the garlands around her neck and did a rhythmic hula dance for Floy. Floy found it humorous until Joselle carried the joke to extremes, bumping her rear end into the furniture as part of her dance. Joselle gyrated until she became dizzy, falling into an end table. One of Floy's Hummels – a round-faced girl gazing dreamily at a book – wobbled and nearly fell.

'That's enough,' Floy scolded. 'And those popcorn necklaces are making grease stains on your shirt.'

Joselle blushed with shame. 'Leave me alone,' she snapped, her eyes pinpoints of anger. She tramped to the front window and rolled herself into the drape. She stared blankly out the window, twizzling a strand of her hair.

After dinner, at the window again, Joselle noticed movement on the hill. It was the red-haired boy. Blaze Werla. Joselle watched him intensely until the window turned blue with the onset of night.

Later, on the sofa that was her bed now, Joselle regretted the meanness that she had shown Floy. At that moment she loved Floy more than anyone. 'I'm sorry, Grammy,' she whispered into the lonely night. The only one who heard her was Gary, Floy's German shepherd. He trotted over to Joselle from the kitchen, his tail wagging like a wind-up toy. He rested his head on her pillow, and she kissed him between the eyes. After a reciprocal lick, Gary folded himself up into a knobby sack on the floor beside her.

Gary's hairy body and pointy ears made Joselle think of her mother's boyfriend Rick. She wondered where the two of them were. How far they had driven. How long it would take before they wrote or called.

It had only been a few days since The Beautiful Vicki had informed Joselle that she needed a vacation. And Joselle would never forget that fateful day. Joselle had taken a felt-tip marking pen and drawn black stripes along the edges of her teeth to make them look even more like a real piano keyboard. 'Look, Vicki,' she had said to her mother excitedly. 'You know, the black keys.' Joselle pointed to her mouth and opened wide to reveal her handiwork.

'God, Joselle,' Vicki had replied, throwing down her magazine in exasperation and grabbing Joselle's wrist. 'It's things like this that make me – '

Joselle could fill in the blank many ways – crazy, want to send you away forever, regret being a mother.

Vicki pulled Joselle into the bathroom and brushed her teeth for her until her gums bled. 'It's not a permanent marker,' Joselle tried to explain.

But all Vicki kept saying was, 'I could scream. I could just scream!' It was then that Vicki announced that she and Rick were going to take a trip. By themselves.

Joselle stayed in the bathroom, alone, crying,

rocking on the toilet. There was greenish grey spittle all over the mirror and on the sink. Joselle knew she would always hate that colour. Minty greenish grey.

It wasn't easy getting comfortable on Floy's old sofa with so much to consider. Joselle played her tongue against her teeth and gums and tried to focus on something stupid and safe. The sofa. Joselle imagined that it had been handsome when it was new – red and firm and plush. Now the dye had faded to a dirty wine colour. It was soft, but lumpy. And the patchy raised pattern that was supposed to be roses reminded Joselle of bald mutant camels that were more hump than anything else. But soon the pattern resembled the fabric of one of Vicki's skirts. And then it resembled the upholstery in Rick's car. It took a while, but Joselle finally nestled deep into the cushions, wrapped in a thin blue blanket, tight as a parcel. Tomorrow I will show Grammy how much I love her, Joselle thought. And I will complicate the life of Blaze Werla.

6

JOSELLE

'Thank you, Joselle,' Floy said, smiling. 'That was a wonderful breakfast. Where did you learn to cook so well?'

'Omelets are easy,' Joselle said triumphantly, as she wiped the table with a dishcloth. 'And I cook a lot at home. If I didn't, I'd starve to death.'

Floy leaned back in her chair, saying nothing, the veins in her neck pulsing. The conversation seemed to have ended.

Floy looked older to Joselle that morning, and her face and neck had a bluish cast to them as though her skin had turned translucent and light were shining through. Floy had always been thin, but the older Joselle became, the thinner Floy appeared to be. Almost breakable, like blown glass.

'It's true,' Joselle said finally. 'I *would* starve. Especially since Rick and The Beautiful Vicki took a class at the community college on developing your ESP potential. They lounge around on the futon for hours – which is hardly unusual – and they go into trances to explore other countries. The trances really freak me out. I used to sit and watch them, wondering if they'd be home in time to fix me dinner.

Now I just fix it myself. I've gotten good at it.' Joselle was playing with crumbs in her hand, and only then did she notice that her hands were still dirty from her secret prebreakfast task. Little crescent moons of dirt shone through the places on Joselle's fingernails where her nail polish had chipped away.

'Well, you can cook for me any time,' Floy said, working at a spot on the tabletop with her thumb.

'I know The Beautiful Vicki's your daughter,' Joselle said, glancing at Floy nervously. 'And I – ' she said, then hesitated a moment, deciding to change the direction in which her comment was headed. 'And I was just wondering what I could make you for lunch.'

'We've got all morning to decide,' Floy said. She rose from the table and reknotted the ties of her bathrobe. 'Just tell me one thing – why do you call her The Beautiful Vicki?'

'Because that's her name. And she is.'

Floy turned around to face the sink, and her entire body began to move as if small waves rippled under her robe. Joselle was certain that Floy was crying, and her heart dropped as she pulled Floy towards her. But as their eyes met, Joselle's heart became weightless; Floy had been holding back laughter. 'The Beautiful Vicki – that takes the cake,' Floy managed to say between shrieks. 'Well, I always thought she should be a beautician. Lord knows she spends enough money on cosmetics.' Floy poked Joselle with her elbow and howled. They pressed together in hysterics.

While Floy went off to shower and dress, Joselle stayed in the kitchen. She opened the silverware drawer and pulled out every teaspoon and table-spoon. She looked at her face in each one. On the back of the spoons, her face was thin and long and right side up. On the other side, her face was wide and upside down. She moved the spoons at varying distances, distorting her face. She was amazed that each time it worked the same – upside down on the inside, right side up on the outside. Vicki had shown her this trick years ago, and Joselle still tested it wherever she went.

Joselle licked a spoon. My mother is smart, she thought.

They had been eating ice cream at the kitchen table right before bed the night that Vicki had pre-sented Joselle with this minor marvel.

'It's magic!' Joselle had said.

'Try another spoon,' Vicki suggested.

Joselle tried every spoon in the house, wide-eyed and mystified.

'Does it only work with chocolate ice cream?' Joselle asked.

Vicki opened the refrigerator. 'Let's see,' she said.

Laughing, they tried jam, cold leftover tomato soup, and maple syrup. They tried milk and orange juice, spooning them out of bowls. They tried peanut butter straight from the jar and sugar right out of the sugar bowl.

'*Every* spoon is magic,' Joselle told Vicki, her voice

cracking with excitement. 'No matter what you're eating with it. Every spoon in the *world*.'

They did the dishes together that night, the radio blaring. They played with the suds and serenaded one another using the spoons as pretend microphones. It was after midnight when Vicki finally kissed Joselle goodnight and tucked her in.

'I love being a single girl with you,' Vicki whispered.

'Me, too,' said Joselle. She had closed her eyes, lulled by Vicki's voice. She was asleep in minutes.

Joselle put the last spoon in its proper place and closed Floy's kitchen drawer. She wondered how her mother could be so perfect sometimes, and other times be as far from perfect as possible.

Joselle was pleased. She had accomplished everything she had set out to do for the entire day, and it wasn't even 9:00 A.M. Not only had she shown Floy how much she loved her by making her breakfast, Joselle had also made Floy laugh harder than she had ever seen anyone laugh. But more importantly, Joselle had done something daring and original. Something that she thought could shake up someone's life. She wasn't exactly sure why she had done it – except she sensed that if she could make someone else more confused than she was, the weight of her own emotions might be lifted. It was worth a try. 'Misery loves company,' Vicki often said. The idea had begun during the night as a tiny seed that kept growing inside her until she was consumed by it and there was absolutely no way to fight it.

It was amazing how everything had come together so easily. Floy had said that he spent a lot of time on the hill. She knew his mother was dead. And she remembered that there were rocks and stones on the hill. In the weak light before breakfast, Joselle had done something that she hoped would complicate the life of Blaze Werla. She knew that if the situation were reversed, it would surely complicate hers. Joselle giggled with delight. She played the themes from 'The Brady Bunch' and 'The Mary Tyler Moore Show' on her teeth.

She was in the bathroom with the door locked, sitting on the clothes hamper. When she had finished her tunes, Joselle began decorating her thighs with ball-point-pen tattoos. At first she was going to put them on her arm, but she didn't want anyone to see them. So she settled on her thighs – so far up that they would only be visible if she were naked. And no one ever got a glimpse of her in that condition.

REENA was the first tattoo she gave herself. She was using her four-colour pen and chose blue ink, pressing so hard that it hurt. Beneath it, she drew a rose in red ink and a leaf and thorns in green. It looked professional. She admired it. REENA.

This was the second time she had written the word *Reena* that morning. She wanted to write something else with stones on the hillside in a day or two. She practised on her thighs. In black ink she wrote FIRE! And then in red she wrote YOU'RE ON FIRE, encasing the letters with jagged flames.

Just then Floy pounded on the door. 'Joselle, are you upset in there again?' she asked.

Joselle hopped off the hamper, made sure her tattoos were concealed, unlocked the door, and greeted her grandmother holding her pen as if it were a cigarette. 'I've never felt better, Grammy,' Joselle said, grinning. She waltzed down the hallway blowing pretend smoke haughtily. 'By the way,' Joselle said, stopping and turning towards Floy, 'what do you think is the worst way to die?'

7

BLAZE

The air was dizzy with insects. And Blaze was dizzy under the black locust tree. He had been twirling himself about, his arms outstretched like a propeller, until he was too unsteady to stand. He fell to the ground, and everything continued to whirl.

He had been talking to Simon in his head. About his mother. One piece of information for each full turn. Making a game of it.

She died when I was five and a half. *Turn around.* The last thing we did together was to ride the Ferris wheel at the fairgrounds. *Around.* She was already very sick. *And around.* It's my last memory of her. *Faster.* She was wearing a pink scarf. *Faster.* And there were blue rings under her eyes. *Faster, faster, faster . . . stop.*

Blaze looked straight up. Things were slowing down. He was shielded by a gigantic green canopy that shimmered as the wind blew, throwing shadows across his body. The pieces of sun that filtered through were so bright they hurt his eyes. For a couple of weeks in the spring, the canopy was white and fragrant. And on a clear moonlit night with a breeze, the canopy was silvery, as if made of stars rather than leaves or blossoms. He never thought you could love a tree, but he did. The black locust was perfect – except for the thorns that spun out from the branches like teeth, making it nearly impossible to climb. Blaze took a deep breath. Summer afternoons on the hill smelled of heat and dirt and grass and weeds and laziness. And – lately – of vigilance, caution, suspense. Blaze felt like an alarm clock just waiting to go off.

It had been two days since Reena's name appeared on the hill. Blaze had reconstructed his semi-circle of stones around the tree, each marker in its proper place. The other stones he left dotting the hillside here and there. Everything looked exactly as it should, and yet there was a peculiar feeling in the air, as if someone or something strange were lurking nearby. Blaze circled the tree several times, then glided down the hill towards home in a zigzag fashion, his legs scissoring the sunlight.

He waved to Nova, who was bending over in her garden. She stood tall and waved back, calling out his name from beneath her wide-brimmed straw hat. Blaze turned and cut across the lawn, angling toward Glenn's studio. Blaze often peeked in one of the huge windows to see what his father was working on. He tried to be invisible and quiet, careful not to disturb Glenn.

Glenn painted large canvases crammed with a multitude of figures and objects that were out of proportion in reference to one another. A man might be holding a plum swollen to the size of a basketball, or a woman might be walking a dog that was as large as a horse. Dragonflies and airplanes with the same dimensions flew side by side. Everyone in Glenn's paintings seemed detached, lost in a cool, claustrophobic dreamworld. There was often a red-haired woman in Glenn's paintings; Blaze knew that she was Reena. Sometimes Blaze spotted himself in his father's work – a pale, reedy boy hiding in the background among trees or floating in the air like a cloud. He liked that. It made him feel proud.

At the end of the school year Glenn would build wooden frames and stretch enough canvas to last the summer. Blaze would help. Blaze's favourite part was attaching the canvas to the wooden frames with Glenn's silver staple gun. It was heavy, and Blaze had to concentrate and push hard to get the staples into the frames as deeply as possible. The staple gun had a nasty little kick that jolted Blaze's arm, and it made a whooshing noise that reminded Blaze of getting a vaccination. Sometimes Glenn had to remove the staples and Blaze had to try again. Blaze noticed that it became easier each summer. He was growing stronger.

After the canvases were stretched, they had to be gessoed. Blaze helped with this, too. He had his own brush. Father and son would work together in the hot studio, perspiration beading above their lips like moustaches, first brushing the gesso in one direction, letting it dry, sanding it, then brushing it in the opposite direction, letting it dry, sanding it, brushing again, repeating, repeating, repeating. Canvas after canvas after canvas.

After a couple of days of work, the studio was filled with about a dozen taut, white rectangles of various sizes, just waiting to be painted.

'This is either promising and exciting, or scary as hell. It all depends on how you look at it.' Glenn would always say something like that as he stared at the empty fields of white laid out flat on the studio floor like perfect rugs. It would often take him a few days to actually begin. And then he would work passionately, as though painting were as important as eating.

Earlier that summer, their annual ritual completed, Glenn gave Blaze one of the canvases. 'It's about time you had a real canvas to work on.'

Blaze was dumbstruck. He loved to draw and paint, but he usually worked with coloured pencils on newsprint tablets, or with watercolours on the back of heavy, dimpled paper that Glenn had done studies on. Most often, he drew television cartoon characters from memory, or he copied panels from comic books. 'I don't know what to paint on it,' Blaze said. Cartoon characters didn't seem important enough for a real stretched canvas.

'I'll let you use my paints and brushes when you think you're ready,' Glenn said. 'Do some sketches first.'

The canvas was hidden away, leaning against the wall in Blaze's closet. He was waiting for a good idea. Something worthy enough.

Glenn worked in oils, and Blaze liked the way the combination of turpentine, linseed oil, and varnish smelled. When he reached the open window, Blaze inhaled deeply.

He heard laughter and froze. Glenn and a woman Blaze had never seen before were standing face-to-face in front of Glenn's easel. They were both barefooted. The woman had long greyish blond hair that fell to her waist. She was wearing a thick shiny band around her upper arm and an orange sleeveless dress that moved like water in the breeze that swept through the studio. Blaze watched them kiss. He considered closing his eyes, but intensified his gaze instead. Now Glenn stood behind the woman and coiled her hair into a nest on top of her head. He pulled a pencil out from behind his ear and positioned it in the woman's hair so that the bun stayed in place. Blaze had to catch his breath.

Glenn had dated other women before. A few – particularly a nurse named Carol – Blaze had liked. She talked openly and comfortably with him, and she gave him small gifts – shells, pens and candy bars. She wasn't afraid to touch Blaze's arm or lightly rest her hand on his shoulder, but she never hugged or kissed him as if she were trying to be his mother. Carol didn't come around very long, however; maybe two months after Blaze had met her. And Blaze never asked why.

Some of the women Glenn introduced to Blaze made him feel squirmy and shy. They often looked at him with wide pitiful doll's eyes and their voices dripped with a sweetness that said, Oh, you poor motherless boy. His self-consciousness grew in their presence.

Blaze stared at this new woman. There was something different about her. He sensed that she would be around for a long time. And he wasn't exactly certain how he felt about that.

8

BLAZE

It took some prodding, but Nova convinced Blaze to go.

'I think you'll be sorry if you don't,' Nova said from the pantry. She entered the kitchen with a jar of her homemade pickles.

'But *you're* not going,' Blaze replied, eyeing the picnic basket that sat on the kitchen table bulging with good things to eat.

'Too much walking. And I wasn't really invited anyway,' Nova said as she reorganized the contents of the basket. 'I think your father would love for this to be just the three of you.' Jars, small bags, and plastic containers fit together like the pieces of a puzzle. 'This Claire woman must be special. It's odd of him to want you to meet her so early on.'

Blaze didn't exactly know what Nova meant by that comment. And Blaze didn't tell Nova that he'd already seen the woman.

Nova tucked some silverware and striped cloth napkins into the basket and nodded approvingly. 'There's too much food for just your father and Claire,' she said, wiping her hands on her faded gingham apron. 'I really want you to go,' she added, her eyes doing half the talking.

Blaze fingered through the basket, looking at the food again. He could see pickles, plums, potato chips, devilled eggs, brownies, iced tea, and chicken. 'Okay,' he said. 'For you.'

During the drive to the lake it seemed to Blaze that Glenn and Claire were smiling every other minute. The smiles broke across their lips like bubbles, and, more often than not, erupted into laughter. Glenn and Claire already appeared to be comfortable and familiar with each other – which made perfect sense, because Claire worked at the high school with Glenn.

'Claire teaches Art Metals,' Glenn had told Blaze that morning. 'You know – rings and belt buckles. Things like that.' They had been folding an old blanket to use on the picnic. Glenn and Blaze each held two corners, the blanket drooping between them. The piping was coming loose in Blaze's fingers, threads giving way. They drew near to meet, and as Blaze handed his corners to Glenn, he noticed a slightly amused look in his father's eyes.

Glenn also told Blaze how much he admired Claire's artwork. She made jewellery, but her speciality was small ornate boxes of gold and silver, delicately clasped and lined with dark velvet. 'Last year was her first year teaching here,' Glenn had explained. 'And I really want you to meet her, Blazer.'

Glenn seldom called his son Blazer – only when he was wildly happy after completing a painting successfully, or on the rare occasion that he had had too much to drink. Neither was the case that morning.

Blaze shifted around in the back seat. He rolled the window up and down. He fussed with the collar of his shirt and pulled it higher around his neck. He fiddled with the handles of the picnic basket. Finally they arrived. Blaze was relieved to be out of the car and into the open air that was busy with a myriad of sounds – birds, insects, and the laughter and voices of other people.

They found a shady spot on the grass to spread the blanket, secluded a bit from the crowd on the beach. The sun sequined the lake and Blaze squinted when he looked at it.

'Isn't it beautiful?' Claire said to no one in particular. She had long legs and arms that she moved gracefully. When she sat down, the skirt she wore over her swimsuit billowed and fell like an umbrella opening and closing.

'You are,' Glenn said softly, touching one finger to Claire's sandalled foot. 'And you are, too,' he said loudly, looking at Blaze. Glenn raised and lowered his eyebrows comically. Then he winked at him.

Blaze could feel himself blush. 'Da-a-a-ad,' he said.

Throughout lunch Blaze tried to steal glances at Claire. His eyes flitted quickly from one detail to another. Yellow-green eyes. Long streaky blond–grey hair that made him think of animal fur. Skin tanned dark as tea. There was so much to take in, Blaze had to remind himself to chew.

They talked about art and the high school and what a good gardener and cook Nova was. They talked about books and recipes and Blaze's teachers from last year. They talked long after they had finished eating. Claire told Blaze that she had grown up in Chicago and that she liked being in Wisconsin now. Then they talked about art again. Glenn said that he wished he could make enough money painting. He wished that he didn't have to teach. He couldn't think of anything better than the luxury of being able to paint every day without worrying about mortgage payments and bills. And Blaze thought of his own blank canvas.

Although Claire and Glenn tried to include Blaze in the conversation, he tended to nod a lot and give one-word answers and comments. He was busy observing and being shy. He found himself watching Claire's hands.

When they had picked up Claire at her apartment, Blaze had been surprised by the seriousness of her handshake. As Glenn introduced her to Blaze, she held his hand in hers for a long moment as though she really meant it. Her hand had been warm. His had been cold.

After a while they went swimming. Blaze was leery about going in water over his head, so when they did finally go in deeper water, he rode on Glenn's back while Claire floated beside them.

Periodically Claire would swim ahead and then somehow end up surfacing behind them. She'd pop up out of the water, dripping and blinking. Her eyelashes were beaded with water droplets and they sparkled. Her colour was high, her movements quick and sure.

'Look at that,' Blaze said to Glenn.

Blaze had spotted a wiry towheaded girl and a big bald man not far from where they were. The girl climbed onto the man's shoulders, then jumped off, making an enormous splash. She did it again and again, her laughter growing louder with each jump.

'Want to try it?' Glenn asked.

Blaze tensed, but said, 'Yes.' His response surprised him. And he even asked Claire to watch.

'We should go a little farther out,' Glenn said.

Glenn crouched.

Claire watched.

And Blaze climbed onto Glenn's shoulders, holding on like a clamp. Glenn's birthmark was visible between strands of his hair, between Blaze's thumbs. Blaze hesitated. He took a deep breath, closed his eyes – and jumped.

Blaze's hands were in fists as he hit the water. Then they opened up. And so did his eyes. And so did his mouth. He took a breath under water.

When Blaze surfaced, he was coughing. He grabbed Glenn.

'Are you all right?' Glenn asked, carrying Blaze to shallow water.

Blaze shivered. 'Yeah,' he said. He coughed some more. 'I just swallowed some water.'

'That was some jump,' said Claire.

Blaze didn't say anything for a moment, and then he told them quietly, 'Maybe I'll just sit on the beach for a while.' His throat and nose and eyes were burning. He shivered again.

'Want company?' Glenn asked.

Blaze shook his head no. He was embarrassed.

Blaze walked the length of the beach looking at stones. Then he sat at the water's edge, poking his toes at the bubbly fringe that lapped about him, wishing that he knew how to swim.

'Bored?' someone said.

Blaze turned with a start. It was Claire. She wrapped her towel around herself and sat down.

'Where's my dad?' Blaze asked, trying to cross his legs in a manner that would hide the scars on his ankles.

'Over there,' Claire said, pointing.

Blaze watched Glenn with a combination of pride and envy. Glenn sliced through the water, his arms cutting perfect angles, his head turning rhythmically.

'He's good,' Blaze said. 'At swimming. You are, too,' he added.

'I didn't know how to swim until I went to college,' Claire said. 'I could hardly float before that.'

'Really?'

Claire nodded and narrowed her lips. 'It was one of those things I always wanted to do, and always put off. I still want to learn how to play the piano and speak French.' She paused. 'Is there anything you really want to learn how to do?'

Blaze was paralysed by the question. There were so many things he wanted to be able to do. But they would seem so simple to anyone else: Go to sleep without the light on. Go out for the basketball team at school. Pet a big dog without shaking. Ride the Ferris wheel alone.

Sweat dripped down Blaze's face. He touched one corner of his mouth, then the other, with his tongue. 'I'd like to fly,' he managed to say. 'I've never done it.'

'In an airplane, or on your own like a bird?' Claire asked, smiling.

Blaze laughed, relieved a bit. 'Like a bird,' he said, relaxing.

'Me, too,' said Claire. She closed her eyes and threw her head back, stretching. She hugged herself. 'Wouldn't that be wonderful?'

Two children, holding hands, ran past Blaze and Claire, splashing them.

'You know, that jump you did out there was good,' Claire said, her eyes following the children down the sand.

'*Really?*' Blaze thought it had been terribly clumsy, not to mention all his coughing.

'Good jump,' Claire said. She ran her fingers through her hair. 'Good jump,' she repeated, her face slanted upward as though she were talking to the sun.

They stayed on the beach, side by side, silently.

Without realizing it, Blaze had untucked his legs and begun rubbing his ankles. The blister-smooth skin was vivid in the sun, the rippled areas emphasized like tiny raised cursive writing. Suddenly, Blaze noticed that Claire had been watching him; he saw her looking at his ankles. When their eyes met, Claire didn't turn away; she just smiled naturally.

And then, for some reason, Blaze told her about the fire.

How he had been waiting in line to ride the Ferris wheel on the Fourth of July after Reena died. How there had been a short circuit. How the electrical wires that lay at his feet sizzled and jumped like snakes on fire. He told her about the awful smell in the ambulance. Even about the paramedic who tried to comfort him by telling him that both his father and mother could ride with him to the hospital. And how – during a confusing minute – he asked for Reena, even though she was dead.

When Blaze finished he felt numb and weightless. He thought he might rise off the beach and drift above the lake like fog, the way he did in his father's paintings.

9

BLAZE

'Well, what do you think?' Glenn asked. They were driving home after dropping Claire off at her apartment.

Blaze shrugged. 'I don't know,' he said. 'What do *you* think?'

'I like her,' Glenn answered, lightly tapping out a rhythm on the steering wheel. 'I like her a lot.' Glenn looked sideways at Blaze. 'Is that okay with you? I'd like it to be.'

'I guess,' Blaze replied. 'She's pretty.'

'She is, isn't she?' Glenn said, smiling. 'And smart and artistic and nice . . .'

'Are you going to marry her?'

Glenn let out a quick laugh. 'Not tonight,' he said, joking.

'No, really, are you going to?'

Glenn lowered his voice. 'It's too early to tell. But I know that we have a lot in common. We have a good time when we're together, too.' He paused. 'I've known Claire for a year at school now . . .' His voice trailed off. And he smiled a big smile again.

Blaze thought it was a goofy smile, like the smiles he drew with crayons when he was three. It made

Blaze feel good to see Glenn so happy. And at the same time it was scary. What if Glenn *did* marry Claire Becker? What would their life be like? How would it change?

Blaze watched the passing clouds, searching for different shapes in them: a car; a cow; a wizened, bearded man. It had only been hours since he had told Claire about the fire, and already he regretted it. Why had he revealed so much to a near stranger? Claire was pretty; was that why? At least he hadn't told her everything. He hadn't told her about the skin grafting or how hard he had cried. And he hadn't told her *why* he had been waiting in line for the Ferris wheel.

'Do you mind if we stop at the grocery store?' Glenn asked. 'I should pick up a few things.'

'Okay,' said Blaze.

Glenn hummed in the parking lot. He raced Blaze up and down the aisles. And, laughing musically, he plucked oranges from a display and tossed them to Blaze directly in front of a sullen-faced man who shook his head and clucked his tongue disapprovingly.

After grocery shopping they stopped for ice cream. Sitting on the curb in the muggy afternoon air, spumoni dripping down his wrist, Blaze wished that he could see the future. He wished that he could see ahead to the end of summer, to Christmas, to the following summer. He wished that he could know for sure what would be happening to his family. He wished he knew what was happening now.

Blaze's mind was muzzy. He was thinking about his mother. He rolled over on his stomach and his bed squeaked. Sometimes he would forget exactly what his mother looked like, and he would have to study a photograph. Sometimes what he could remember was clouded. Sometimes he and Glenn would look at old photographs and mementos together, and it would make Blaze feel calm and edgy at the same time.

After a few minutes, Blaze flipped over on his back again. He thought of the fire and the Ferris wheel and Claire and what he *hadn't* told her . . .

Reena rode the Ferris wheel with Blaze shortly before she died. It was the last thing they did together before Reena went to the hospital for the final time. They were at the fairgrounds on the Fourth of July. Glenn watched and waited while they rode. It was a small Ferris wheel, part of a small fair that came to town every July. There were rides and game booths and bright billowy tents where food was sold. Two weather-beaten wooden soldiers marked the entrance. They looked like the unwanted toys of a giant, dropped into the trees and forgotten.

The next year he wanted to do it by himself. For her. It was something he had to do. It was very important to him. He begged Glenn to let him try it. It was a small Ferris wheel, made for children, so

Glenn said yes, bought him a ticket, and watched and waited again.

But Blaze needed the help of a friend. So he made one up. Benny was his name. Blaze whispered to Benny while he moved closer and closer to the man taking tickets. That was the year of the fire. Of course, he didn't go through with it *that* year. So he buried Benny. And then came Ajax.

Goodbye, Benny.

The following year Blaze had to ask to go to the fairgrounds. 'Are you sure you want to go?' Glenn asked. Blaze was sure. 'We can just walk around,' said Glenn.

Blaze hadn't heard Glenn and Nova talking about insurance money and doctor bills for a long time. And Glenn told Blaze that a different company was running the fair now. The big wooden soldiers were gone, but there was still a Ferris wheel. It looked enough like the one he had ridden with Reena to count. It was small, with wire cages that spun gently as the wheel rotated.

'I want to try it,' Blaze said.

'Okay,' said Glenn. 'Let's do it.'

'I want to try it alone,' said Blaze.

Glenn let him try.

But it was more difficult than he thought it would be. He worried about the Ferris wheel itself. He remembered the cords that had caught on fire. He thought about his mother. He couldn't do it. Ajax didn't help. 'I changed my mind,' he told Glenn. 'Can we get something to eat?'

Goodbye, Ajax.

He tries every year. He doesn't want to be afraid.

Goodbye, Ken.

He stands in line, but turns away at the last minute. He goes on other rides.

Goodbye, Harold.

Now that he's old enough to go to the fairgrounds with some of his classmates, he sneaks off alone to the Ferris wheel. Unsuccessful every time. Or if his classmates want to ride the Ferris wheel, he says, 'I have to go to the bathroom – do it without me.' Or 'I'm going back to the games for a while. Meet me there.'

Goodbye, Ortman.

Every year that he can't ride the Ferris wheel, he buries his old friend and gets a new one.

Every year he tells no one.

Every year he digs another hole.

10

BLAZE

Blaze had a dream that didn't frighten him, but time and place and all other particulars escaped him. He stared listlessly at a spot on the ceiling in his bedroom, trying to make the dream come back. But he could only remember a foggy, pleasant feeling, and he tried to hold on to it, grabbing his chest as if the feeling were touchable and could be hugged like a pillow.

After looking out the window and checking the hill (no new words of stone), Blaze dressed and went down to the kitchen for breakfast. Nova made pancakes for him. She served them with butter, blueberries, and powdered sugar. Blaze played with the blueberries, forming a letter C with them on the top of his stack of pancakes.

'Do you like her?' Nova asked.

'Who?' Blaze said. He spread some of the blueberries to the edge of his plate.

'Claire, of course,' Nova replied. 'Who else would I mean?' She smiled at Blaze and her cheeks became a farmer's field of wrinkles.

'I'm not sure,' Blaze answered, raising his fork, a blueberry speared on each tine. 'But I think Dad's in love.' The word sounded funny to Blaze: *love*. He wrinkled his nose.

'Love's not such a bad thing.'

'I know, I know,' Blaze said, tossing his head from side to side. He smiled at Nova. 'You really wouldn't care if he got married again?'

'I'd love it, and I mean it, and you know it. We've talked about that before.'

'Would you still live with us?'

Nova shook her head yes. 'But don't you think you're jumping the gun? Slow down a bit. Eat your breakfast.'

He ate and he thought. He thought that Nova was the most calm person he knew. And the smartest. And the nicest. He thought about going to rummage sales that afternoon with Glenn and Claire; Claire was looking for old furniture to fix up for her apartment. He thought about being short and wondered how tall he would be when he was fully grown. And he thought that he wanted to eat another pancake. And he did.

After finishing breakfast and helping Nova with the dishes, Blaze walked up the hill to the black locust tree. He seemed drawn there as if by a magnet. It would be a hot day. Earlier there had been a milky haze on the hill that burned off, but the air was still heavy. Dew glittered on the tips of the grass. As he approached the crest of the hill, Blaze swung his arms back and forth, pretending to cut through the heat. When he reached the top, he stopped suddenly.

Within the border of the grave site were more

messages. This time the words were formed with small stones and pebbles, each letter only a few inches tall at most. The stones spelled YOU'RE ON FIRE and FIRE! The words were written in an arc near the trunk of the black locust tree. The exclamation point that ended it was long and wiggly like a worm.

'Come on,' Glenn coaxed, slapping the upholstery beside him. 'We're running late.'

'I'm not going with you,' Blaze said slowly, his eyes narrow because of the sun.

'What's up?' Glenn asked. He had been waiting in the car for Blaze, the motor idling. He was ready to pick up Claire and had been signalling Blaze by honking the horn.

Blaze shrugged. He didn't feel like talking. He knew the words would catch in his throat, possibly making him cry. He also knew that he never wanted to see Claire Becker again. Now there was no doubt in his mind who was responsible for the words of stone. Claire Becker. A swift internal pull convinced him this was the truth. He had told Claire about the fire, and she had used the information for a cruel joke.

Glenn turned off the ignition. 'Are you okay?'

'I think I ate too much for breakfast,' Blaze said, holding his stomach. 'It's not a big deal, but I think I should stay home.'

'Would you rather I stayed home, too? I can call Claire.'

'No,' Blaze said. 'You should go.'

313

'Okay,' Glenn said, almost like a question. 'I hope you feel better.' He started the car again. 'See you later,' he called.

Blaze waved. He had figured out who had written the words of stone. But what would he do now?

11

JOSELLE

Joselle was examining a scab on her knee when the phone rang. She jumped up to get it, but since the only phone in the house sat on the end table beside the rocking chair where Floy happened to be planted, her chances of answering it were next to none. After a pleasant hello, Floy's voice took on an icy edge. Joselle knew instantly that The Beautiful Vicki was on the line. Floy's face seemed to deflate and her lips pursed. Nearly everything about her became tight, and yet she cradled the phone against her shoulder and continued to work on her needle-point. Her fingers moved like dancers, pushing and pulling, bringing a garden to life with thread. Lilacs, tulips, and daffodils bloomed between her hands. Her silver needle glinted and Joselle thought of sparks. Even when Floy sighed heavily or rolled her eyes, her fingers continued to flow at the same rhythmic pace.

Joselle picked her scab while she listened. Then she drew her knee up to her mouth and bit off the scab. She swallowed hard and licked her wound.

'How can you afford that?' Floy asked. 'What about your job at the restaurant?'

Joselle could feel her heartbeat quicken. She began playing 'The Star-Spangled Banner' loudly on her teeth.

'Don't worry about Joselle,' Floy said. 'Good *heavens*, of course you should talk to her. Just a minute.'

Floy handed the receiver to Joselle.

'Joselle?' Vicki said.

'Hi,' Joselle answered reluctantly, flexing her toes inside her shoes.

'Sorry I didn't send you a postcard or call sooner. . . .' There was an awkward pause. 'Uh, Rick and I decided we'd like to see the ocean – the Pacific Ocean. So we're going to be gone longer than we thought. It's a far way from Wisconsin, you know. But anyway, your grandmother's glad to have you there. And – don't worry – I checked it out with the restaurant. They'll give me my job back when I get home.'

'Why can't I come with you?'

'Come on, Joselle. We're already on the road. And Rick doesn't want this to be a kid's vacation. We need a break. *I* need a break from *you*. You know how we get when we're together too long. This is good for you, too.'

Joselle didn't want to pay attention any more. She tried to twirl the phone like a baton, but dropped it on the floor. She picked it up, hesitated a moment, then spoke into the receiver very clearly. 'I might have blood poisoning,' she said, curling her lip. 'But if anything happens I'm sure someone will be able

316

to locate you.' Without waiting for a response, she gently hung up the phone.

Joselle and Floy looked at each other.

'I don't want to talk about it,' Joselle said, turning her eyes away.

'Me neither,' said Floy, placing her needlepoint on the end table and standing. She grabbed her sweater from the back of the chair and draped it over her shoulders. 'The mall's open late tonight. Let's go shopping.'

The air in the mall smelled stale – of popcorn, smoke, sweat, and perfume – but it was a hopeful smell; it carried with it the prospect of new things to take home. When Joselle shopped at malls with Vicki, they rarely bought anything. They purchased most of their clothes at resale shops. Vicki tried to convince Joselle that the clothes from Retro Fashions and Goldie's Oldies were more chic anyway, but Joselle knew that Vicki couldn't afford shopping at the other stores. And yet they went to them on a regular basis 'just to look'. Joselle disliked the whole routine because she often saw things that she wanted badly, knowing full well that she couldn't have them. She'd pout all the way home, bewildered by the injustice of it all. She referred to this practice as 'visiting clothes'. Last year for Mrs Weynand's language arts class, Joselle wrote an essay about 'visiting' a pair of tight, stone-washed jeans so many times that she became best friends with them. Mrs

Weynand said the essay showed a great deal of creativity but was lacking in other areas – namely grammar, spelling, and punctuation. She gave it a C-minus.

Joselle felt only slightly guilty that Floy was spending so much money on her. But Floy was the one pushing certain items, as though an extra pair of tights or some dangly rhinestone earrings could fill Joselle up until there was no room for unhappiness. When Joselle expressed an interest in a fuchsia tank top, Floy insisted that she have the black-and-white striped one, too. And Floy wouldn't take no for an answer when she saw the way Joselle's eyes widened as she stroked a peach cashmere sweater that had buttons like pearls.

'You'd look beautiful in that,' Floy said, scooping it up and holding it in front of Joselle.

'Grammy, I was just looking,' Joselle said, turning away. She had seen the price tag. She knew how expensive it was.

'It's got your name written all over it,' Floy said. 'Just think how envious your classmates will be next school year.'

Joselle considered this and felt herself weakening. Even Sherry Gerke, who often made a point of criticizing Joselle's wardrobe in front of anyone who would listen in the girls' rest room, would have nothing but good things to say about *this* sweater. It was classy. Joselle cackled to herself.

'Okay, Grammy, you win,' Joselle said, throwing up her hands. 'I'll take it.'

As they marched up to the checkout counter together, Joselle had to concentrate hard to keep her fingers from crawling onto Floy's arm and tugging the sweater away from her.

'Forget the bag,' Joselle told the clerk. 'I'm wearing it!'

Floy nodded approval.

'Thanks, Grammy!' Joselle shrieked. 'Now you're sure this is okay?' she added in a very serious voice.

'Yes,' Floy answered. 'A good splurge every now and then does wonders.'

But Joselle repeated the question over and over because she had noticed the way the corner of Floy's mouth had twitched upward, forming a thick indented comma deep in her cheek as she wrote out the cheque to pay for the sweater.

'If you ask me one more time, I'll start calling you a broken record,' Floy finally said, swatting Joselle softly on her behind. 'Come on, we need to find some nail polish before the store closes.'

On the drive home, the stars were brighter than Joselle had ever seen. And the evening smelled of grapes. Fireflies dotted either side of the highway as if there had been too many stars for the sky to hold and some had spilled downward. Joselle rubbed the buttons on her new sweater, pretending that they were tiny stars that had lost their light. And then, because she wanted the way she felt at that precise moment to last forever, she stuck her head out the window and gulped the air that rushed at her face, hoping that it would work some kind of magic inside her. Hoping that it would make her life perfect in every way.

12

JOSELLE

Joselle woke up with a headache, and there was a pinching sensation behind her eyes. She blinked her eyes quickly and steadily, hoping the feeling would stop, but all it did was intensify the dull pain and make her see double for a minute. Gary heard her stir and raised his head. He slept on the floor alongside the sofa every night now. Right by Joselle. He nudged her hand with his nose until she petted him. Simultaneously, he wagged his tail and yawned twice, like an echo. Joselle covered her face with her arm. 'I feel bad, but you smell worse,' she told him.

Despite the heat, she had slept in her new sweater. It had transformed her ratty cotton nightgown into the elegant party dress of a princess. Joselle slid off the sofa and pirouetted to the kitchen, trying to work off the way she felt. Gary snapped playfully at the frayed edge of her nightgown as though her dance were a game created especially for him.

Now, on top of having a headache, Joselle became dizzy. After sitting at the table and counting to one hundred, she thought that food might help. She made a three-minute egg, a piece of toast, and a cup of tea with four spoonfuls of sugar and enough milk to turn the tea pale and lukewarm.

After breakfast, Joselle felt better. Floy was still asleep, so Joselle tried extra hard to be quiet. Joselle wondered if Floy couldn't pull herself out of bed because she regretted spending so much money on Joselle. Joselle pictured her grandmother flat in bed, lethargic as a wet wool blanket, exhausted by the shopping spree and clutching an overdrawn cheque book. The thought nagged at her, and it just got worse when she retrieved all her purchases from the closet and spread them out on the sofa. There were two pairs of tights, two tank tops, a bikini, earrings, socks, four bottles of nail polish, and, of course, the sweater. Joselle knew that if The Beautiful Vicki hadn't phoned about her prolonged trip the sofa would be empty. Floy would never have permitted Joselle to buy the bikini or the dangly earrings. They would have been completely forbidden if Floy hadn't felt sorry for Joselle. Maybe she thinks she's partially responsible, Joselle said to herself. After all, Vicki's her daughter.

Joselle had a fashion show. She tried on each new item and paraded around in front of Gary. He cocked his head, his ears alert, his tail sweeping the floor. But somehow the effect had worn off for Joselle. Last night, in the dressing rooms at the mall, she had been electric with anticipation. She had sniffed everything she tried on, intoxicated by the scent of newness. And on the ride home, buried beneath the shopping bags, her happiness had been a dazzling white spot. Now, sitting on the floor, picking Gary's wheat-coloured hair off her rainbow-print bikini, Joselle was a brightly swirled, empty lump of self-pity. She could have gulped enough air last night to fill a hot-air balloon and it wouldn't have mattered. No magic had been worked. Her life would probably never be perfect.

With only her bikini on, Joselle's ball-point-pen tattoos were visible on her thigh. They had worn off a bit, so she took out her pen and wrote over them again, carefully tracing each letter. REENA, FIRE! YOU'RE ON FIRE. And then she added a new one: ORPHAN. And she wasn't entirely certain if she was referring to Blaze Werla or to herself.

The distance between Joselle's house and the Pacific Ocean seemed endless. After the fashion show, Joselle discovered a road atlas on Floy's bookshelf, and her finger followed the red and blue lines that indicated highways, weaving across the country until they ended at Route 101 on the coast. The number of miles that separated Wisconsin and the ocean was so staggering, her finger quivered. On the map, the crisscrossed network of roads looked like a maze – much too disorienting for Vicki to negotiate. Joselle hoped that Rick was doing most of the driving.

At least Rick was a good driver. In Joselle's opinion, Rick's only other talent was turning his eyelids inside out. It was one of the most disgusting things Joselle had ever seen, but he was very good at it. Another disgusting thing about Rick was his hair. The hair on the top of his head was okay — short, brown, straight, thick. But the hair on the rest of him wasn't okay. It sprouted from the backs of his hands and from under his shirt collars like twisty forests. The sight of it made Joselle want to throw up. Rick was rangy and languid. He hunched his shoulders frequently, and a perfect pimple flourished on the bridge of his nose. Vicki said that Rick was good at his job; he was an electrician. But Joselle thought that he was too absentminded and too interested in ESP to be working with things as dangerous as power sources and currents. She hoped that he would never rewire their house.

Sadly, Joselle envisioned Rick and Vicki lost and confused in Nebraska or stranded on some dirt road in Wyoming. And yet, ironically, part of her wished that the car *would* overheat, that they *would* run out of gas, and that they *would* get flat tyres. A minute later, she wished them a speedy, safe trip, and she longed for Vicki so intensely that her eyes turned misty.

Joselle had never been out of southern Wisconsin, and she realized how small an area this was compared to the rest of the country, not to mention the world. She and Vicki lived in a small brick ranch house in Kenosha. Floy lived in the country outside of Madison. They were only a few hours apart by car, and yet they only saw each other two or three times a year. And it was nearly always Floy who did the visiting. If I ever make it out of the Midwest I'll probably faint, Joselle thought. Her father, who she had only seen once, supposedly lived in Texas. She never heard from him, and Vicki cringed whenever his name was mentioned, so Joselle didn't bother thinking about him very often. And she never asked Vicki to talk about him – that was hitting below the belt and she knew it. She could be awful, but not that awful. Joselle owned one photograph of him that she kept in the bottom of her sock drawer. The photograph was dog-eared and slightly out of focus, but Joselle could make out a man who she thought looked devastatingly handsome or evil as a snake, depending on her mood. His name was Jerry Hefko, and in the photo he was posing on a motorcycle wearing sunglasses and a red bandanna on his head. Dense black curls hung to his shoulders. Although neither Joselle nor Vicki had ever used Hefko as a last name, Joselle had secretly carved JOSELLE HEFKO on one leg of the kitchen table with a paring knife when she was seven and furious at her mother for something or other.

'Why do people live in certain places?' she asked Gary, staring at Texas.

Gary tipped his head and knitted his brow.

'I mean, why wasn't I born in New York or Miami? Someplace glamorous?'

'Planning a trip?' Floy asked in a voice thick and raspy with morning, startling Joselle. She shuffled across the floor in her fuzzy slippers.

'Nope,' Joselle said, closing the atlas and replacing it on the shelf. 'I was just killing time waiting for you to get up. Sleepyhead.'

325

Between stretches and yawns, Floy banged around the kitchen making coffee.

'I checked on you five times, you know,' Joselle said. 'I wanted to make sure you were breathing.'

Floy flicked her wrist and glanced at her watch. 'It's only seven-fifteen. This is when I always get up. How long have you been awake?'

And only then did Joselle realize how early she had gotten up. She figured it had been hours since she awoke. 'I don't know,' is all she said.

Floy sipped her coffee, savouring every drop, as though it eased some discomfort. Her cup sounded like a tiny bell when it clinked against the saucer. 'I thought I'd cut the grass today. If you're not too busy, I could use some help.'

Joselle's chin crumpled. She hated yard work. 'Well, actually,' she said, 'considering everything that's been happening to me lately I think I might need time alone today to contemplate my future.'

Floy only nodded and looked away, her deep-set grey eyes focusing on the coffeepot.

'I'm probably helping you by *not* helping you,' Joselle offered, her voice confident and round. 'I'm usually much more trouble than I'm worth.'

The lawn mower roared in Joselle's ears, but she walked right past Floy and toward the hill undaunted. Sometimes she hated herself for the way she treated people, for her selfishness. And yet, she seemed to have no control over her behaviour. It's not my fault I am the way I am, she thought.

The sky was the blue of a baby's blanket and the clouds looked like massive heads of cauliflower. Joselle slapped her thigh and whispered, 'Orphan.' She couldn't decide if she should write the new word with stones as she had done with the other words or try something different. She wondered how Blaze Werla had been reacting to her messages. She hoped he was going crazy with confusion. Maybe this time I should write the word and then hide behind a bush and wait till he appears, she thought. Maybe I could see him cry.

But as it turned out, Joselle's plan was not workable. She skipped to the top of the hill and stopped suddenly, frozen. Blaze Werla was crouching beside the big tree. And before Joselle could move, their eyes met. And locked together.

BLAZE

The first time Blaze saw her, the hair on the back of his neck prickled. Although the sun was shining, he swore that she had no shadow, and despite the fact that she stood perfectly still and there was no wind, her dangly rhinestone earrings jiggled, making thin music. Her eyes appeared to be entirely black — like hard, shiny pieces of liquorice. They were so hypnotic, Blaze had to work at forcing his eyes to break contact with hers. When she came closer he noticed that she smelled dusty, like a ladybug. And then she smiled. Her smile did anything but put him at ease. Her smile was enormous and glassy and sharp.

'Big teeth,' was all he managed to say, walking backward as if in a trance.

The girl thrust out her hand, her fingers grazing Blaze's chest. 'I'm Joselle Stark,' she announced grandly.

Blaze's fingers felt dwarfed and breakable in hers. She had the grip of a man.

'The old lady that lives over there is my grand-mother,' Joselle said, pointing toward Floy Stark's neat, square house. 'I'm staying with her for a bit while my mother explores the Pacific Ocean. She's kind of a scientist – my mother. My grandmother's just a grandmother.' While she spoke she tossed her head and flared her nostrils. 'So,' she said, 'who are you?'

Blaze could barely speak. His words cracked and melted. 'My name is Blaze,' he finally offered in a scratchy whisper.

'That's an odd name.'

Blaze shrugged and scuffed his shoes.

'You're so *little*, too,' Joselle said in a thrilled voice, rumpling his hair. 'And if it wasn't impossible, I'd swear you were shrinking right before my very eyes.'

Looking down, Blaze scanned his entire body, checking to make sure that he wasn't, in fact, becoming smaller. And then, as though he had no control over what he was saying, words spilled out of his mouth like the beads of a breaking necklace: 'I'm the smallest in my class. I am every year.'

'No kidding,' Joselle said sarcastically. 'It wouldn't take a brain to figure that out. Unless you go to school with midgets.'

Blaze only fidgeted, regretful.

'Well, who cares anyway?' Joselle said, marching in place. Then she strutted around the black locust tree like a queen. 'All I can say is – just look at this view! I've never been up here before. It's tremendously fantastic.' She cleared her throat. 'I just arrived today, you know,' she said, turning her head towards Blaze, her eyes thin as slits. Because she wasn't looking ahead, Joselle tripped over one of Blaze's stones. Dust rose, veiling her as she stumbled and fell. Her knees and hands were streaked with dirt.

'Are you okay?' Blaze asked shyly, lightly nudging the stone with his shoe.

'I'll live,' Joselle answered, her face bunched. And then suddenly her mood swung and she smiled again. This time gleefully. 'Hey, look, I'm injured,' she said merrily, pushing her knee at Blaze. Marking the middle of her knee was a perfect drop of blood. 'It's an enchanted liquid ruby,' Joselle whispered. 'Now we're true friends. Forever.'

Blaze pulled the edge of his T-shirt into his mouth and bit down, and because he was breathing so hard, his mouth sounded like the wind. 'I'd better go,' he said tentatively, moving away. In his mind, he was already home, lying on his bed with the door closed.

'Come back tomorrow,' Joselle called. 'You have to. Same time. Same place.'

Blaze ran all the way down the hill. As he tore through the weeds and grass, his arms making huge loops in the air, he felt as though he were emerging from a terrible and wonderful spell.

Thoughts of the girl stayed with Blaze all afternoon like a film on his skin. She baffled him and intrigued him. His mind strayed to her even as he set the table for dinner. He saw her face in each plate and bowl. Her teeth and her eyes materialized vaguely on the china like the Cheshire cat.

The day had grown hotter and hotter, so they were going to have a big salad and gazpacho. 'Too hot to use the oven today,' Nova repeated as she moved around the kitchen. Her skin had taken on a sweaty sheen. When she turned from reaching for the large wooden salad bowl in the cupboard, her forehead glistened and Blaze noticed damp saggy half-moons under her arms on her thin housedress. The heat didn't bother him nearly as much as it did Nova.

Glenn was slicing hard-boiled eggs for the salad. It had been just over a week ago that he had introduced Claire to Blaze and Nova. Since then, he had been spending a considerable amount of time doing domestic things: helping to make dinner, washing dishes, shopping for groceries. He wasn't painting nearly as intensely as he usually did.

'I'm going to freshen up before Claire arrives,' Nova said. She flapped her dress and sighed. 'Too hot,' she murmured on her way upstairs to change clothes.

'You seem quiet,' Glenn said to Blaze.

'Not really.'

'Well, then talk to me,' Glenn said as he arranged the eggs on a ruffly bed of various lettuces from Nova's garden. 'How are you?'

'I dunno,' Blaze answered, and it was purely the truth. He didn't know. And if *he* didn't know, how could he give his feelings a name and discuss them? He had too much to think about. Claire. And now Joselle Stark.

'I understand how you might feel about Claire,'

Glenn said. 'I do . . .' He smiled his assurance and squeezed the back of Blaze's neck.

'I know,' Blaze replied, hoping that he sounded cheerful and cooperative. But Glenn couldn't understand. Blaze hadn't told him about the words of stone.

At first it had made perfect sense that Claire had been the one to write them. Blaze had told her about the fire, and the next morning the words appeared. But since then Claire had acted completely normal – whatever that meant for someone you hardly knew.

Although Blaze had tried to avoid Claire, she still treated him kindly, which puzzled him. Even if he had been ignoring her throughout an entire meal, she would present small gestures – a look, a grin, a compliment – that would cause Blaze to drop his silverware.

'I have something for you, Blaze,' Claire said when she arrived. 'Come to my car.'

It occurred to Blaze that he could pretend not to have heard her. He could just walk past her into the kitchen to get something to nibble on while he waited for dinner. He followed her to her car.

'Your dad told me that he had given you a canvas to work on. I thought you might like to have your own paints.' Claire opened the car door and pulled out a box the size of a portable TV. She placed the box on the ground and opened it up so Blaze could see inside. 'I know you have watercolours, but these

332

are acrylics. They're my old ones – I don't use them any more.'

There must have been thirty tubes of paint. Blaze could tell that some of the tubes had been used, but others looked brand new.

'I know your dad would let you use his oil paints in his studio, but this way you can paint in your own room if you like. Whenever you want. And you can clean up with water. They're easy.'

'Thank you,' said Blaze. He turned the tubes in his hand, reading the names of the colours.

'The brushes are in here,' Claire told him, picking up a long, thin manila envelope that was tucked in the side of the box. She took out one of the brushes and pretended to paint in the air. Her wrist moved gracefully, round and round. 'Well, I'm going to see if Nova needs any help in the kitchen,' Claire said, handing the brush to Blaze.

'Thank you,' Blaze said again.

'You're welcome.'

Blaze carried the box to the porch and sat down. The tubes of paint reminded him of party favours frozen in various stages. The kind that unroll as you blow into them, then collapse on themselves as the air escapes, curling up. Blaze was familiar with most of the colours because of Glenn: cadmium red, alizarine crimson, burnt umber, cobalt blue, yellow ochre. He pretended to paint in the air as Claire had done. He was beginning to get excited about starting his canvas.

His certainty that Claire was responsible for the

words of stone had been a knot lodged inside his chest. The knot was gradually loosening. Blaze was glad that he had waited, that he hadn't said anything to Glenn.

'*Was* it my imagination, Simon?' Blaze asked. He wanted to convince himself of that. He told himself it wouldn't be surprising, given that it was July. His dreams were proof of the power of his imagination.

He would wait. He would push it out of his mind. After all, he had something new to concern himself with: Joselle Stark. She had said they were true friends – and yet they barely knew each other. If they *did* become true friends, maybe he could tell her about the words of stone. Maybe she'd know what to do.

A spider hanging motionless in its web caught his eye. The web was a perfect, intricate hexagon strung between two posts of the porch railing. Blaze didn't like spiders particularly, except from a distance. He pictured Joselle Stark approaching this spider easily and touching it with her finger. Blaze knew he would go to the hill tomorrow. He wondered if she would be there.

14

BLAZE

'For the first couple of years of your life, you were probably no bigger than a salt shaker,' Joselle told Blaze, cupping her hand and holding it out to indicate size. 'In fact, it's probably a miracle you lived. I'll bet your parents have photographs from when you were three, but they tell you they were from the day you were born.' Joselle brushed a tangle of hair away from her eyes. 'Parents do things like that,' she added crisply, snapping her fingers.

Blaze wondered exactly what Joselle meant. She confused him completely, but at the same time she spoke with such authority that he was compelled to accept as true everything she said. 'I was little, but not *that* little,' he mumbled at last, blushing a bit, opening and closing his fists.

'Believe what you have to,' Joselle said, shaking her head.

It was only their second time together. They were sitting beneath the black locust tree, within the semi-circle of Blaze's stones. He hoped that Joselle wouldn't ask about the stones, or worse, move them. Whenever Joselle poked at them with her foot or gazed at them for what seemed like a long time,

Blaze felt a small tremor in his leg. He could never explain his stones to this curious girl who reminded him of wild, impish, confident children he had only known in books.

'Want some?' Joselle asked, lifting the necklace of popcorn she was wearing over her head and offering it to Blaze. 'Popcorn. Fresh popcorn,' she called, making her voice sound important.

'Thanks,' said Blaze, pulling off a few kernels. Bewitched, he handed the necklace back. Each time he chewed and swallowed, his teeth creaked and his throat tickled.

'I always get the hulls stuck on my teeth. And always my tooth with the micro-dot,' Joselle said.

'What's that?'

'It's this teensy-weensy thing printed on my tooth with my name, address, and birthday. You can't even see it with the naked eye. I used to think it was really neat until I realized it would only do any good if they found me dead. You know, to identify me.'

Blaze tried to absorb this, but his mind kept stumbling on the word dead. It made him shiver. And of course, he thought of his mother. He could see an image of her, memorized from a photograph, so clearly among the leaves above him that he thought he could make the image stay there forever. But the breeze fluttered, the leaves stirred, and she disappeared. 'My mother is dead,' he heard himself say.

For once, the girl seemed to be at a loss for words. Wrapped in absolute silence, Blaze watched her. Joselle twisted her popcorn necklace, then pushed and pulled pieces of popcorn as though she were moving counters on an abacus. She appeared to be so deep in thought that Blaze wondered if he could see what she was thinking in the air around her if he looked hard enough.

'Well, you're not the only one,' she suddenly blurted out, one large tear sliding down her face. 'My father is dead.' She placed her necklace over Blaze's head, draping it crookedly across his shoulders. 'Welcome to the orphans' club,' she sniffed. 'The saddest club of all.' Then she kissed his cheek sharply and quickly before vanishing behind the slope of the hill.

15

BLAZE

'That's about all I know,' said Nova. 'But if you like her, it would be nice to have someone to play with. Someone so close.' She moved her basket up a few feet and continued picking beans. The plants were heavy with pods that ranged in colour from milky yellow to emerald. The sizes and shapes varied, too. Some beans were huge and so swollen they looked surreal. Others were narrow and small and straight as nails. 'Is she here for a long visit, or a short one?'

'She didn't say exactly,' Blaze answered. He was sitting in the row next to Nova eating a bean. Mist tickled his eyes when he snapped it. 'Her father died,' he said.

'I wasn't aware of that,' Nova said. She really didn't know much about Joselle Stark. Or her mother. 'I'm not even too familiar with Floy,' Nova told him. 'We greet one another, but that's about it. I guess the hill is big enough and our houses are far enough apart to keep our lives separate.' Nova took off her hat and fanned herself with it. 'Would you like to have Joselle over for lunch?' she asked. 'Egg salad sandwiches? With homegrown beans and homegrown lettuce?'

'Not today. But maybe sometime.' Would Joselle say yes if he asked her? Possibly. After all, she had kissed him. Blaze had never been kissed by a girl before. Just thinking about it made his heart anxious. And he thought about it a lot. No one had ever been so interesting to him before. And to have Joselle confide in him about her father bonded them.

When Nova finished picking her row, she pointed to the tomato plants. 'I've got more tomato plants this year than ever. If they all ripen, we'll have enough tomato sauce and chili relish and salsa for the entire town,' she said. She heaved her basket of beans into her arms and sighed. 'I'm going inside to start blanching these. And I'm hoping that my legs don't fall off first. Bad circulation,' she added matter-of-factly.

Blaze watched Nova trudge through the garden and across the lawn. Her thick, corded veins seemed to pulse with each step. Blaze wandered over to his favourite corner of the garden, glancing over his shoulder at Nova until the back door shut behind her. In the corner, a stand of sunflowers formed a wall. Slivers of blue, blue sky shone through the lattice of leaves and huge drooping yellow flowers. When the wind hastened, Blaze could smell the basil, which was planted in a raised bed near the sunflowers. Sometimes he'd pick some of the basil leaves and rub them on a small patch of his arm near his wrist, tinting it green. Then, periodically throughout the day, he'd bring his arm up to his face and inhale deeply. Last year, he had hung a big bunch of basil from the doorknob in his room; the room smelled wonderful for nearly a week. It was amazing to Blaze that everything that was so alive and leafy and aromatic and productive in Nova's garden had begun as tiny seeds. The whole process was one of the most hopeful things he knew. Thinking about Joselle Stark was hopeful, too. Blaze wondered how long she would be staying with her grandmother. He hoped she'd at least stay until school started in the fall.

Blaze wanted to do something special for Joselle because he felt so badly about her father. He wanted to give her some kind of gift. He lay down under the sunflowers, trying to think of something appropriate. It wasn't long before he fell asleep, dreaming, as the morning crept away slowly without him.

The only things of value that Blaze had to offer Joselle were his lost key collection and his Noah's ark. He didn't think he could bear to part with the ark – and besides, he could picture Joselle commenting on how infantile it was – so he gladly put that thought out of his mind. The key collection would also be hard to give up, but not having it around would be something he would just have to get used to. At any rate, the lost key collection wasn't serving its purpose. Blaze had collected the keys and kept them near his bed while he slept with the secret hope that they might open the locked doors that often appeared in his dreams. Usually Reena's voice came from behind the doors, calling him. It was a stupid idea anyway, Blaze thought. A real key can't open something in a dream.

He looked at each key carefully, trying to remember where it had been found or who had given it to him. When he placed the mason jar that held the keys in a box and sealed it, he had a premonition that he would wake up in the middle of the night, panicked and needing the keys. 'I hope I'm doing the right thing, Simon,' he whispered. Regretfully, he wrapped the box in the comics from the previous Sunday's newspaper, tied a limp bow on top with red yarn, and held it tightly on his lap until he knew he was ready to meet Joselle on the hill.

As she opened the box, Blaze detected first amusement, then baffled uncertainty in Joselle's look. After a moment she shrieked lustily and said, 'Oh, I get it – you think you have the key to my heart.' She batted her eyelids and preened herself, obviously enjoying her remark.

'It's not a joke. It's a present.'

'Oh, piffle, piddle,' she said airily. 'Don't be so serious all the time.'

Blaze tried to explain his feelings about Joselle's father, but only got frustrated.

'Let's play a game,' said Joselle, barely allowing Blaze a word. 'It's called Personal Scent. It'll just take me a minute to get ready.'

Blaze watched Joselle. She unrolled the top of a brown paper sack from the local grocery store and opened it up. The bag was soft and crumpled from use, from being held by sweaty hands. One by one, Joselle took out small glass bottles of various sizes filled with different coloured liquids. She lined them up between them like a tiny fence.

'Like I said, the game is called Personal Scent. And I, Joselle Stark, am Keeper of the Scents.' She shook the mason jar, rattling the keys. The sound was grating. 'The game will now begin!' she announced. She placed the mason jar in the bag and moved it aside.

With a dainty flick of her wrist, Joselle chose one of the small bottles. She unscrewed the tarnished metal top and rubbed a generous amount of some of the clear golden liquid on her arm. She replaced the bottle and chose another one. This one was filled with a cloudy liquid tinted a suspiciously bright blue colour. Joselle leaned over toward Blaze and splashed his shirt with it. She was so close that Blaze could practically taste the perfume she was wearing. It was overpowering and sweet.

'Now smell yourself,' Joselle instructed.

Blaze did as he was told.

'That is your personal scent. Now you have to become a different person – someone who would smell like that.'

Blaze was confused. His face was blank. 'I don't get it,' he said, mindful of Joselle's delight and discouraged that he didn't understand.

'Watch and learn,' Joselle said. She sniffed her arm. 'This is a beautiful, flowery perfume,' she com-

mented, her eyes half closed. She sniffed her arm
again, then inhaled and exhaled luxuriantly. 'I am
definitely a Veronica,' she said, speaking with a lilting
accent. 'Veronica Marsdale. And I am someone's
perfect mother. Picture me wearing a carnation pink
dress and lipstick that's thick and cakey in a nice
way.' She leaned toward Blaze again and whispered
into his ear. 'Who are you?' she asked, still speaking
as Veronica.

Now Blaze understood how to play, but it took
him a minute to come up with something. He fidgeted with his hair while he thought. The bright blue
liquid was a dreadfully spicy after-shave. 'I am Bruno
Slobkin,' he finally said in his deepest voice, flexing
his muscles. He smiled to himself at this notion.

'Ha!' Joselle screeched. 'That's good! That is really
good.'

That afternoon, shaded beneath the black locust
tree, Joselle, Keeper of the Scents, rubbed and
sprayed Blaze and herself with various perfumes,
colognes, and after-shaves. They even used leaves,
dirt, and berries. And depending on the particular
mixture of smells, they became different people:
famous movie stars, characters from books, or simply
people they made up themselves.

Blaze laughed until his side ached and he had to
massage it. He could not remember when he had
laughed so hard.

Periodically throughout their game, Joselle – hand
in mouth – would hum theme songs from television
programmes and make Blaze guess what they were.

'Why are you pretending to play music on your teeth?' Blaze asked, after successfully naming a tune.

'Because my teeth are as big as piano keys,' Joselle said. 'And it's a special talent.'

'How long have you been doing this?' he asked in his Bruno Slobkin voice.

'Since the very day I was born, sweetheart,' she answered, speaking with a pronounced southern accent.

During a particularly quiet moment when Blaze was trying to come up with the name of a song, he almost told Joselle about the words of stone. But he stopped himself for some reason. He just couldn't force the words out.

After they had been playing for quite some time, Joselle asked suddenly, 'Can I come over to your house?'

'I don't know,' said Blaze. The growing effect of their concoctions was light-headedness. He experienced a fluttering in his stomach, too. 'I'd have to ask my grandma first.' He stared at his knees. 'And my dad. Maybe tomorrow would be better, or something.'

'Then come over to mine,' said Joselle. 'You can call your grandma to let her know where you are.' She gathered her belongings into her paper sack, her little bottles falling together and clinking against the mason jar.

Blood beat in Blaze's ears. He watched her get up and start to walk away.

'Come on,' said Joselle. 'Are you part statue?'

344

'I can't go,' he said.

'*Why?*'

The way she said it, and the way she looked at him, made him feel invisible. 'I'm afraid of your grandma's dog,' he admitted shyly.

'Gary?' Joselle's eyes widened and she stretched her mouth in an exaggerated fashion. '*Gary?*'

'He's so big. And sometimes at night I can hear him bark all the way over at my house.'

Joselle approached him and grabbed his arm as if she were going to pull him down the hill behind her. She clucked her tongue. 'Silly,' she said. Then she looked right at him, and as she did, Blaze saw something register in her eyes, and he felt something change in her grip. 'You're *really* afraid of him, aren't you?' she asked, her voice serious and quiet.

Blaze nodded.

'Don't worry. Gary's just a pussycat. I'll introduce you properly and teach you to like each other. He smells awful, but that's his only bad point. And we don't smell so great, either. He'll like you.'

'Really?'

'I promise,' she said, waving him along. 'What are friends for?'

16

JOSELLE

Something was shifting and changing inside Joselle. It didn't happen all of a sudden, but gradually, over the course of long, hot summer days. It was a feeling she couldn't exactly describe, except to say that it was private and dense and tight. She felt as if she owned something wonderful that no one else in the whole world knew about. She first became aware of the feeling the afternoon she taught Blaze how to pet Gary.

'I can't do this,' Blaze had said, backing away.

'Yes, you can,' Joselle told him.

Gary romped forward, pulling his chain taut, his tail wagging fast and hard.

Joselle petted Gary and commanded him to sit. Then she stood behind Blaze and slowly pushed him toward Gary. She could feel him shake. 'Stay,' she said to Gary. 'Now give me your hand, Blaze.' She guided his hand, gently forcing it along the back of Gary's coarse head, again and again.

Blaze made a small sound in his throat.

'See, it's easy.'

'Kind of,' Blaze said.

Joselle suspected that it wasn't easy at all for Blaze,

and she moved her hand with his like a shadow, nudging it along when he hesitated. And as she did, something occurred to her. He needs me, she thought. Blaze Werla needs me.

The following day the feeling washed over her again. She was showing Blaze the spoon trick. They were on the hill.

'I don't believe it,' Blaze said, excited.

'It works every time,' said Joselle. 'Really, truly. Give it a try.'

Blaze took the spoon from Joselle and moved it in front of his face. Closer, closer, farther away. Then he turned the spoon over and moved it again. 'I'm always upside down on the inside,' he commented. 'And right side up on the outside.'

Joselle nodded thoughtfully. 'I told you. It's one of the small wonders of the world.' And that's when the feeling struck. Watching the expression on Blaze's face, Joselle thought she knew how teachers must feel after they've successfully explained the mystery of long division.

A few days later, Joselle experienced the feeling under completely different circumstances. She wasn't helping anyone; she was being waited on by Blaze and Nova. She had been invited to Blaze's house for lunch. She was so impressed by the smells of fresh-baked bread and home-made cookies, by the matching towels with rickrack trim, by the flowers in coffee tins lined up on the counter, that afterward she couldn't even remember what day it was, and she

actually danced around the table and offered to wash
the dishes.

Perhaps it was Nova's bread that had done Joselle
in. It was absolutely wonderful. Vicki and Floy were
both partial to store-bought bread, the bleached
white kind that is so puffed up with air and preser-
vatives that it looks and smells like something
kindergarteners are given to express themselves cre-
atively. Occasionally Joselle would form little balls
with her bread, and using the dull, knobby ends of
the silverware, shoot them around the kitchen table
billiard-style.

'You elevate the concept of playing with your
food to new heights,' one of Vicki's boyfriends had
commented once.

'It's better than eating it,' Joselle had replied,
striking a cereal bowl with a small greyish wad.

One afternoon after she had eaten several meals
and snacks at Blaze's house, Joselle asked Nova,
'When was the last time you bought bread at a store?'

'I can't remember,' Nova answered. 'Baking bread
is a cinch – and it's one of life's greatest pleasures,'
she added, smiling.

'I help with the kneading sometimes,' Blaze said.

'You don't buy frozen or canned vegetables, either,
do you?' Joselle asked.

'Not usually,' Nova replied. 'I freeze and can
myself. Why?'

'Just checking,' Joselle said, spreading butter on a
slice of warm whole wheat. She licked her fingers,
feeling drunk.

The feeling came back to Joselle even when she didn't expect it, even when she was alone. She wondered if she was falling in love with Blaze and his family. Was that possible?

She still experienced what she called 'the hollow feeling' or 'the Sunday afternoon feeling', but it seemed to come less often. She associated the feeling with The Beautiful Vicki.

Joselle used to think that she would end up alone. A spinster. Not a timid, frail woman with blue hair and lacy dresses, but a feisty woman who wore young, stylish clothes. A woman who could take care of herself. But now she wasn't so certain. Maybe living in a family could really work.

Sometimes Joselle tried to see herself through Blaze's eyes. Depending on her mood, she would see a fat, loud girl who, strangely, played music on her teeth. Or a strong, beautiful girl capable of mesmerizing boys and their families.

Each morning Joselle awaited the arrival of the mail. And each morning she was disappointed. She'd run to the mailbox at the edge of the road as soon as the red, white, and blue truck puttered away. With her eyes closed, she'd open the mailbox and reach into the dark space greedily. Without fail, her hope quickly disappeared; there was never anything addressed to her. After slamming the mailbox shut, she'd kick dirt all the way back to the house, and then toss the bills, letters, and advertisements for Floy carelessly on the kitchen table. She cursed her mother under her breath. The Beautiful Vicki hadn't sent even one postcard. She hadn't telephoned again, either. If Joselle thought about her mother long enough, she became so worked up she was convinced that her bones would twist out of their sockets and snap into sharp pieces.

'I didn't get anything from her either,' said Floy one morning when Joselle looked especially disappointed.

'Well, you're not her daughter,' Joselle said testily, pulling her chin.

'I'm her mother.'

'That's different,' Joselle said. She made a paper airplane out of a ShopKo circular. The lines of her folds and creases were precise as cut glass. 'Maybe it's your fault she is the way she is,' Joselle said, giving Floy a challenging look. Joselle sent the plane toward the garbage pail in a perfect arc, but it careened off course at the last minute and landed in Gary's water dish. Joselle pretended that the plane was an arrow and that the water dish was her mother's black heart.

'Try not to worry about your mother too much,' Floy said softly, drumming her fingers on the counter. 'She has the annoying habit of being happiest when those who love her the most are upset.'

Floy's words confused Joselle, and she tried to make sense of them as she ran over to Blaze's house. She knocked fiercely on the door.

'Hi,' said Blaze through the screen, looking gauzy. 'What do you want to do today?'

Joselle pulled the door open a crack and squeezed inside. 'It doesn't matter,' she replied.

And it didn't. She just wanted to be there.

They began spending more and more time together. And when they parted at dusk, Joselle eagerly awaited morning when they would join one another again – usually on the hill.

Sometimes Joselle called him The Boy with the Apricot Hair. And sometimes she called him Blazey. But mostly she called him Blaze.

Sometimes Joselle wanted to tell Blaze everything about her life. But she didn't. She held back. What if he didn't like what he heard? What if he found out that she had written the words on the hill with stones? She had no idea how he had reacted to them – except that someone had always dismantled them. Would he still want to be her friend?

Sometimes Joselle wanted to know everything about Blaze's life. But she decided not to ask too many questions. She fabricated what she didn't know. And the history and circumstances she invented for him were exactly what she wanted them to be.

Sometimes Joselle liked to be alone with Blaze on the hill – playing with the hot, hot sun beating down on them, or sitting quietly against the black locust tree like bookends in the cool shade. And sometimes she liked to be with his entire family at their sturdy, round kitchen table. Blaze and Nova and Glenn and Claire.

Sometimes Joselle wished she could live with them.

Sometimes she wished she were Blaze.

17

JOSELLE

'Ha!' Joselle shouted, storming into Blaze's bedroom, taking him by surprise. She was struck enough by Blaze's expression to add, 'It's okay. I didn't mean to scare you.' She joined him on the braided rug, plopping down so heavily that the walls seemed to vibrate. Although Joselle had spent a fair amount of time at Blaze's house, she had never been in his room before. She looked around, collecting details and storing them away. 'Your grandma let me in. She told me I could come up here. Second door on the right.'

Blaze seemed particularly quiet. His cheeks reddened as he abruptly scooped up the toy he was playing with. 'Let me just put this away,' he said, talking so fast that Joselle had to decode his words, taking a few moments to understand him.

'What have you got?' Joselle asked, reaching around Blaze's arm and picking up a handful of small plastic animals. A camel, a swan, a goat.

'It's this stupid old toy I used to play with,' Blaze replied. 'I was just looking at it.'

'It's a Noah's ark,' Joselle announced. Without asking, she grabbed the toy out of Blaze's hands and scrutinized it. 'I hate to tell you this, but it's defective – there are supposed to be two of every animal and you've just got one.'

Blaze only nodded.

'Well, it fits, doesn't it? It's a Noah's ark for orphans.' Joselle broke down completely with spasms of laughter, holding her belly with both hands. She quieted down quickly, however, since Blaze only averted his eyes and remained silent. Not even a flicker of a smile touched his lips. 'I was trying to be funny, but I guess I'm about as funny as a big fat cinder block.' She handed the ark back to Blaze and began picking at the cuticle of her thumb. 'Sorry. Really,' she said as gently as possible, offering the words as a gift.

Today is turning out to be a bad day, Joselle thought. First, no postcard from The Beautiful Vicki. Again. Then, I took it out on Grammy. Again. And now Blaze thinks I'm a dope. I shouldn't have joked about being an orphan. And I never should have lied about my father being dead in the first place.

She was sorry about that, but in a sense he *was* dead. At least to her. If she told Blaze the truth now, he'd hate her for sure. And that wasn't what she wanted at all. She wanted to be friends with Blaze Werla. Very best friends.

How many lies had she told Blaze? It was hard to keep track of them all. She had lied about her father. Lied about her mother being a scientist. She had lied about when she arrived at her grandmother's house, so that Blaze wouldn't think she had had

354

anything to do with the words of stone. And the words of stone were a kind of lie, too. She wished she had never written them.

Blaze had been the perfect candidate for deceit, and Joselle had gladly taken advantage of his innocence. Pinpricks of regret ran up and down her legs. No more lies, she told herself. No more words of stone. Joselle made a promise to herself never to lie again. She vowed to be honest in every way until the day she died, or as long as she possibly could. Which wasn't very long. Because as soon as Blaze's back was turned, Joselle sneaked the tiny plastic fox that Blaze had overlooked from beside his dresser and slipped it into her pocket. She couldn't stop herself. *This* is the last dishonest thing I will ever do, she said to herself. Ever, ever, ever.

After shoving the ark under his bed, Blaze pulled his bedspread down until it touched the floor, hiding the ark entirely. He appeared to be more relaxed now. 'I can't play with you today,' he said. 'I've got to go with my dad and Claire.'

'Where?'

'Claire is selling her artwork at a fair. My dad and I are going to help her.'

'Can I come, too? Please? If I'm there it'll be more fun.'

Blaze seemed to blossom. 'Let's ask,' he said, already out of the door and in the hallway.

The stairs sounded hollow as Joselle pounded down them. She caught up to Blaze and nearly knocked him over, she was moving so fast. She extended her left arm, placing her hand on his shoulder to stop herself. Her right hand was in her front pocket, her fingers wound tightly around the tiny fox. The fox was nearly weightless, but felt heavy against her leg.

From the instant Joselle slid into the van with Glenn, Claire, and Blaze, she pretended that they were her father, mother, and brother. Buckled safely into her seat, she watched them fondly. She studied Glenn first, deciding quickly that she approved of every part that formed her new father. Longish blond hair, big hands, thick wrists, scratchy voice. How are you supposed to feel about a father? she wondered. Or a brother, for that matter?

She knew a bit more about mothers. But Claire seemed very different from Vicki. Vicki was surely beautiful; she worked hard at it with lipstick and eyeliner and curlers and manicures and hair spray. Claire didn't appear to be wearing any makeup, and her hair was simply pulled back into a ponytail with a red rubber band. But she looked beautiful, too. Her features were larger than Vicki's, but more stately, as though she belonged in a painting hanging in a museum in Paris. The Beautiful Vicki would be more at home on the cover of *Cosmopolitan*.

Joselle loosened her seat belt slightly and leaned forward, her chin resting against the front seat. This is my perfect family, she said to herself. When Joselle closed her eyes, she saw them (herself included) etched onto the backs of her eyelids. An aerial view.

The four of them formed a rectangle that crept along the highway slowly and silently like a small toy. She basked in her newfound feeling of belonging all the way to the art fair.

Claire had rented the van because she needed room for her artwork and her display booth. Neither her car nor Glenn's would suffice. The van was silvery grey, and Joselle imagined that it was a sleek limousine taking them to a very important private party.

Claire was driving, but Glenn helped to check for traffic as they veered into the parking lot. When he turned his head from side to side, Joselle noticed the circular birthmark on the back of his neck. 'One world,' she said aloud, wanting to touch the birthmark with her finger.

'What?' asked Blaze.

'Oh, nothing,' said Joselle, blushing. 'I was just talking to myself.'

Joselle and Blaze helped Claire and Glenn set up the display. Glenn and Claire did most of the work. Joselle tried to look busy, but she couldn't keep herself from holding her head high and gazing about loftily at the people who passed by. They all just assume that we're a family, she thought happily.

Joselle didn't know very much about art, but in her opinion Claire's work was exquisite. Claire was selling pins, barrettes, and a few of her boxes. Everything was gold, silver, bronze – and glinting. Claire's work made Joselle think of royalty and perfection and miniature heirlooms people tuck away in secret places that aren't found until years later.

A particular barrette shaped like a fleur-de-lis caught Joselle's attention. She looked at it longingly. She pictured her hair swept back off her face and fastened by the shiny golden swirls. She pictured strangers stopping to get a better look, transfixed by her beauty.

'Come on,' Blaze said, tugging on Joselle's sleeve. 'Let's go spend the money my dad gave us for lunch.'

There was so much to choose from. They bought hot dogs, soda, popcorn, and – best of all – cotton candy, whipped and spun onto paper cones like fancy pink hairdos. Joselle loved how cotton candy melted when it touched her tongue. She ate hers and nearly half of Blaze's. Her teeth ached from all the sugar.

'This is fun,' Blaze said.

'Yeah,' said Joselle. 'But I think I ate too much.'

They were seated at a picnic table, among many, under a large yellow tent. The sunlight shone through the tent, casting a jaundiced look onto everything.

'Want to walk around?' Blaze asked.

'Let's just sit a while longer,' Joselle said. 'We can watch people.'

'Okay.'

Joselle played with the soggy paper cone from her cotton candy. 'Did you ever wish you were someone else?' she asked.

Blaze shrugged. 'Not really.'

'I do, sometimes,' Joselle waited for Blaze to ask:

who? But when he didn't, she continued. 'Is there anything about yourself you'd change if you could? Is there anything you don't like?'

Blaze shrugged again.

'I'd get rid of these awful teeth, if I could,' Joselle said, pointing to her mouth. 'And I'd like to be smaller. Like you.'

'I wish I was *bigger*,' Blaze said. 'And I don't like my scars. From the fire.'

Joselle played dumb. 'What scars?'

Blaze got off the bench and walked over to Joselle's side of the picnic table. 'These,' he said, turning his ankles and nodding. 'I was in a fire one Fourth of July. I got burned – so did three other kids. It wasn't *that* bad. They did some skin grafting. I think they could do more if I really wanted them to . . .'

Joselle leaned over and touched Blaze's right ankle. 'They're tiny,' she said. 'I'd take your scars over my teeth any day. I always wanted a scar. They make you look brave.'

'Really?'

Joselle nodded. 'Yeah.'

'You wouldn't lie to me?' said Blaze.

'Never,' Joselle replied, feeling her cheeks turn pink as polished apples. 'Let's go,' she said, rising abruptly from the bench and running toward the crowd.

'Wait up,' Blaze called.

They wove in and out of the artists' booths. Sometimes Joselle ran ahead and hid behind a tree or a group of people, then rushed out in front of Blaze. Small red flags flapped in the breeze.

'Look!' Joselle said suddenly, bending over. 'A lucky penny.'

'Let's see,' said Blaze.

Joselle handed the penny to Blaze. 'It's yours,' she said, 'on one condition. You have to tell me your wish.'

Blaze's little fingers curled and uncurled around the penny. 'Right now?'

'Think about it and let me know. But if you don't tell me, it won't come true. True, true, true,' Joselle called, running ahead again, dodging in and out of the crowd.

Throughout the afternoon, Joselle was content to sit and observe. She watched Claire interact with the shoppers and browsers. And she watched Glenn holding Claire's money box, making change when he needed to. But when she and Blaze went back to the refreshment stand to get something for Glenn and Claire to eat, Joselle did more than observe. When a boisterous man cut ahead of Blaze in line, Joselle elbowed him. 'Excuse me!' she said crisply. 'My friend was here first.' She felt very protective.

It wasn't until they were driving home at sunset that Joselle remembered that she had taken the fox from Blaze's room. And it dawned on her why she had done it. With the fox in her possession, she might have a kind of power over Blaze. It might add strength to her wishes concerning him. Unlike the key collection he had given her, the fox's where-abouts were unknown to him; that's why it was powerful. The fox represented her secret life with Blaze's family, the life that played out in her head.

There were occasional periods of silence as they rode. But they weren't awkward. They were breaks in the conversation in which time stood still, in which everything was suspended except Joselle's watchful eye. Even so, the ride was going much too quickly for Joselle. She wanted this day to last.

It was Blaze who broke a particularly long silence as they neared Floy's house. 'Here,' Blaze whispered, his voice as quiet as insects' wings. 'You found this. It really belongs to you.' He gave Joselle the lucky penny. 'And you don't even have to tell me what your wish is.'

The penny floated on the sweaty creases of Joselle's palm. She was touched. She pushed the penny into her pocket with the fox. Then she opened her mouth and tapped 'When You Wish Upon a Star'. Her fingers smelled metallic.

Blaze joined in on his own teeth. They played it together, smiling, until the van pulled up to Floy's front porch.

18

JOSELLE

'How was your day?' Floy asked, head poised, waiting. She had been leafing through a magazine. It lay open on her lap.

'It was the best day of my life,' Joselle said. She flung herself onto the sofa, her arms spread out over her head like a giant V. She sighed dreamily.

'I'm glad you had a good time,' Floy said. 'Tell me about it.'

Joselle lay motionless on the sofa. She couldn't tell Floy. If she did, wouldn't Floy feel terrible? Wouldn't it bother her that her granddaughter could have more fun with someone else's family than she ever could with her own? 'I can't exactly explain it,' Joselle said finally. 'I mean, it wasn't *that* great. It was okay.' Her lip flickered. She forced a laugh and got up to go to the bathroom. 'I've had better days. For sure.'

Floy closed her magazine. 'I can't keep up with your thoughts,' she said.

In Joselle's dream the moon was blue. And then it became a penny. And then it vanished. She sat up in the middle of the night with Blaze's words on the tip of her tongue: 'You wouldn't lie to me?' And her answer haunted her: 'Never.'

She rose from the sofa and walked to the front window. There was no moon. It was raining. Water streamed down the window as though she were under the sea. She felt regretful. Joselle pulled her purse out from beneath the sofa. She searched for her four-colour pen.

While the slow steady rain tap-tap-tapped against the house, Joselle darkened the ball-point-pen tattoos on her thigh. When they faded, she would darken them again. She would keep them as a reminder. She would keep them until she told Blaze the truth.

About everything.

The words of stone.

Her father.

Her mother.

The tiny fox.

Joselle placed the lucky penny under her pillow. She wished that when she told Blaze the truth, he would forgive her. She wished that she had a million lucky pennies; she felt she needed that much luck.

When Joselle woke up again, it was still raining. She put on her bikini and ran up and down the front sidewalk several times. The rain chilled her, and goose bumps sprouted on her arms and legs. But she felt much better, exhilarated.

She came inside, towelled off, and wrapped herself around a steaming cup of tea. Floy's door was still closed to the morning, so Joselle was very quiet. She wanted to get out of the house before Floy got up. She pulled her extra-large white T-shirt over her damp bikini. The shirt fell to her knees, covering the tattoos easily. She wore her new sweater, her dangly rhinestone earrings, her red rubber thongs. She brushed her hair back into a ponytail as Claire had done yesterday. Joselle's ponytail wasn't nearly as long as Claire's, but she thought it looked smart, and with her hair away from her face, her earrings were more visible. She left a note for Floy by the coffeepot.

Puddles dotted Floy's lawn like scattered mirrors. But Joselle didn't mind. She hopped off the porch and skipped across the soggy yard toward Blaze's house, her feet sliding in and out of her thongs. Floy's umbrella shielded her like an enormous lavender flower.

She didn't feel brave enough today to tell the truth. She just wanted to see her friend.

BLAZE

The steely smell of rain was in the morning air.
Blaze liked rainy days. 'That's the artist in you,' Nova
said time and time again. 'Most creative people like
grey weather.' Blaze didn't know if that was true,
but he knew that Glenn also liked dark, stormy days.
And according to Glenn, Reena had felt exactly the
same way.

Reena hadn't been a painter, but a writer. She
had majored in English in college. Before Blaze was
born, she had taken a job with the local newspaper,
writing book reviews. After Blaze was born, she
stayed home with him, hoping to write a novel one
day. Glenn said that Reena was never satisfied with
her attempts at a novel and therefore had never kept
any of them. Sometimes Blaze pretended that his
mother *had* written a book. A book that could be
checked out at the library. A book with secret refer-
ences to him.

Blaze's train of thought was broken by a series of
loud knocks on the door.

It was Joselle. She smiled radiantly and waved at
Blaze, then flew off the porch into the rain. Instead
of holding her umbrella above her, she swung it

around, turning circles with it, dancing. She raced about like a top – spinning, twirling, laughing.

'Come out!' she yelled, waving. 'It's fun!'

Blaze opened the door and stepped onto the porch. It was pouring. He could see that Joselle was soaked already. He could see her bathing suit beneath her T-shirt and sweater.

'Come on!' she shouted.

Blaze hesitated, thinking. It was only a summer shower. Nova wouldn't mind. He took off his shoes and sprang from the porch, cringing from the shivery rain. He joined Joselle in a large muddy puddle.

Joselle put her umbrella down and grabbed Blaze's hands, pulling him into her dance. 'I'm drenched,' she said, giggling, kicking her leg out playfully.

And then he saw it. His mother's name written on Joselle's thigh. He could see it through her wet, wet T-shirt which was plastered against her skin. And he could see parts of other words. All the words of stone curving around her leg in ink of various colours.

Blaze jerked his hands out of hers harshly. They stood face to face.

'What's wrong?' Joselle asked.

'I want my key collection back,' Blaze said between quick, shallow breaths, his voice shaking with anger. It was all he could think of to say.

Joselle didn't answer, her face uncomprehending. Blaze could feel the silence in his belly.

Holding his breath, Blaze tried to calm himself. He squinted and concentrated, his eyelashes becoming veils that filtered things and blurred them. But it did little good; he just kept seeing the words of stone as they had appeared on the hill. He felt ashamed for being such an easy target, someone so easily tricked.

'You wrote the messages on the hill, didn't you?' he asked. 'You wrote my mother's name.'

'Oh!' Joselle said, glancing down at her transparent shirt, understanding. She covered the words with her hands and pulled her legs together. 'No. I mean . . . yes.' She looked away. 'I'm sorry,' she said. 'It was just a joke. I didn't mean anything bad by it. And I stopped doing it once I got to know you.' She knitted her fingers nervously. 'Really.'

'I thought you were my friend,' Blaze said. His voice cracked. His fingers were extended on both hands like the points of stars. They whirled around his legs as he spoke. 'Just get out of here.' He gave her a hard mean look.

'You don't like me any more,' Joselle whispered, turning sideways, hiding her face. 'I'm *sorry*,' she reminded him, turning back, flipping a loose piece of hair out of her eyes. She didn't look at him directly. 'Please, don't hate me.'

For a fraction of a second everything became razor sharp to Blaze. The pores on Joselle's face, the liquid of her eyes, each strand of hair, each drop of rain. Everything was so clearly defined that it hurt Blaze's eyes to rest them on anything.

In that instant, Blaze rushed toward Joselle and pushed her down as hard as he could. He hit her once across the shoulders. 'Get out of here,' he said. 'Just get out of here.' And then he grabbed one of the round buttons on her sweater and pulled it off, thread trailing behind it like a fine tail.

He didn't see her face again. He watched as she rose from the ground, picked up her umbrella, and scrambled across the driveway toward Floy's house without looking back. And that's when he started to cry.

By early afternoon the rain had passed and the sun was shining. Birds chirped and skittered through the ribbons of water in Nova's garden. Barefooted and shirtless, Blaze spent the rest of the day tagging along behind his grandmother while she weeded, or sitting by himself in small spaces: his closet, under the porch, between a pile of bricks and the outside wall of Glenn's studio.

'You seem to be miles from here,' Nova said, cocking her head so Blaze could hear her. 'Are you feeling all right?'

'I'm fine,' Blaze replied, gazing at a clump of nasturtiums until it became the sun.

Alone, resting against Glenn's studio wall, it occurred to Blaze that he had never pushed anyone the way he had pushed Joselle. He had never hit anyone, either. Or purposely ruined something that belonged to someone else. The button from Joselle's sweater reminded him of what he had done. Perhaps it always would.

But no one had ever made him feel so stupid

before. No one had ever humiliated him the way Joselle had. No one had ever been so mean. He couldn't believe she had done it. And he couldn't believe that he had accused Claire in his mind.

He wished he hadn't shown Joselle his scars. And he shuddered to think that he had nearly confided in her about the words of stone.

Now he felt as though he should have known. But how could he have known? Joselle had lied about when she had arrived at her grandmother's house. And when he had met her on the hill, she had told him that she had never been on the hill before. She'd probably lied a million times, he thought.

Or was there another part of him that suspected Joselle all along? If there had been, he just kept pushing it deeper and deeper inside himself until it virtually vanished. He had wanted to like her so much.

During the past couple of weeks, Blaze had started to feel as though he had been friends with Joselle forever, but now he didn't know what was true. He didn't know what to believe.

Sitting alone, Blaze realized something else: he hadn't thought of Simon in days. Had Joselle taken his place?

Between his fingers, the button was as smooth as candy. He put it in his mouth and sucked on it.

20

JOSELLE

'I hate you,' Joselle said to her reflection in the living room window. 'I hate you, I hate you, I hate you.' When she turned off the lamp on the end table, her reflection disappeared and everything was dark. Joselle remained by the window; it was past midnight, but she knew it was useless to try to fall asleep. By now she was beyond the point of crying. After dinner, in the bathtub, she had cried so much that her eyes were swollen and raw. So was her thigh. She had scrubbed the ball-point-pen tattoos with a vengeance so that the few remaining lines were as faint as thin spidery veins. 'I hate you,' she repeated. Joselle pinched her arm right above her wrist until she couldn't stand it any longer and there were red dents from her fingernails in her skin.

She felt the way she did at school when she hadn't prepared for a test, only much worse. An overwhelming sense of panic and frustration would fill her head like a storm, making it nearly impossible to sit still at her desk. What was the best thing to do? she'd always wonder. Guess, and most likely answer the questions incorrectly? Or leave the lined answer spaces empty? She'd weigh the odds in her mind, nearly always opting for leaving the test completely blank except for her name – which she would spend most of the period working on, carefully printing each letter with decorative touches. That made things for her teachers more complex, more baffling. Most of her teachers regarded her with suspicion and wrinkled noses, as if she were some kind of specimen that was hard to categorize.

Once, when she had completely forgotten about a vocabulary test for Mrs Weynand's language arts class, Joselle felt compelled to approach Mrs Weynand with a sincere hug and explain how awful she felt. But she knew that that would never work; there was too much history between them for Mrs Weynand ever to think of Joselle as anything but trouble. A constant inconvenience.

But this wasn't a test at school. This was more important.

Joselle needed someone to talk to. She hadn't told Floy about what had happened at Blaze's house, because Floy's patience was wearing thin. Upon seeing the wet, dirtied cashmere sweater – twigs and weeds sprouting from the sleeves – Floy threw her arms up in exasperation. Her eyeballs rolled back and her mouth popped open like a fish when she noticed the missing button. 'You'll never be able to match that pretty button,' she said, yanking the sweater toward her to get a better look and releasing it with a snap, as though a mannequin were wearing it, not a person. 'I'm not even going to ask what you've been up to. Just get yourself showered

and cleaned and dried. And give me the sweater,'
Floy added. 'I'll try to fix it up.' Then she sighed
heavily and shook her head. Joselle knew that she
was fast becoming the same person in her grandmother's eyes that she was in the eyes of her teachers.
Anyway, Floy was surely asleep by now. And Gary
was little consolation.

Joselle needed her mother.

On the end table, resting against the lamp, stood a
framed photograph of Joselle, Vicki, Floy, and Floy's
mother, Alice. The photo was taken in the hospital
on the day that Joselle was born. 'Four Generations
of Women,' Joselle had called the photograph once.
'I'd call it "Four Generations of Fighting and Head-
aches",' Vicki had retorted. Joselle thought it was
odd that she had such a vivid memory when it came
to Vicki's hurtful comments. She shrugged to herself.

Although Joselle's great-grandmother Alice died
before Joselle had formed a memory of her, Joselle
sensed a strong connection to her. In the photograph
Alice's heart-shaped face was a lacework of grooves;
Vicki's was flushed and young. Floy appeared stern
and uneasy, and Joselle was a chubby bundle the
colour of a bruise. It was too dark to see the photograph clearly, but Joselle knew it like she knew the
image of George Washington on a dollar bill.

The only information that Joselle had about her
great-grandmother was from photographs and from
stories Vicky and Floy had told her. When she was
younger, Joselle had thought of Alice as a guardian
angel, a bent, wrinkled woman who lived inside the

crack in Joselle's bedroom ceiling. Someone who was able to see and know all things. Someone who would emerge upon request to rescue and comfort Joselle. As routine, Joselle used to say good night and good morning to the crack every day. It didn't take Joselle very long, however, to come to the conclusion that the crack was only damaged plaster and that her great-grandmother could never, ever truly help her.

Once, when Joselle lost one of Vicki's favourite earrings and was sent to her room as punishment, Joselle called for Alice. 'Here, Alice! Here, Old Grammy!' she cried. At first she waited patiently, sitting cross-legged on her bed, her head tilted upward. When Alice failed to respond, Joselle climbed onto her dresser and removed the curtain rod from the window frame. Using the curtain rod as a tool, she chipped away at the ceiling until bits of plaster dusted her bedspread like snow and she knew at the very bottom of her heart that what she was doing was not only pointless, but would only get her into more trouble.

In the moonlight Joselle wandered. From room to room she roamed without purpose. After she had walked through every room (except Floy's bedroom) several times, Joselle found herself back in the living room beside Floy's rocking chair, staring down at the telephone. With the telephone cord spiralled around her, Joselle dialled her own number. She wanted Vicki to magically answer the phone and say: 'Hello, sweetie! Of course it's me. I'm having all the calls forwarded to me in California. Whatever it is you want, I'll do. I'll be on the next plane home if you need me.' But all she heard was the faraway sound of a dull bell in an empty house. Joselle let the phone ring and ring and ring. She pictured her mother and Rick running along the beach, the orange-and-pink sun dropping into the Pacific Ocean behind them. She pulled the cord across her face, placed it in her mouth, wove it between her fingers. She was all set to hang up, when suddenly she heard a sleepy, but familiar, voice bark, 'Hello? *Hello?* Who *is* this?'

Joselle hung up the phone without saying anything. She fell into the rocking chair. After the initial shock passed, she cried in rhythm with the movement. Back, forth. Whimper, sniffle. She cried quietly at first, like someone at a movie. But then she began to rock faster and cry louder. When she thought that she might completely lose control, she sprang from the chair and barged into Floy's room.

'Grammy,' she sobbed. 'Grammy, help.'

21

JOSELLE

While Floy talked on the telephone, Joselle sat on the floor behind the sofa. The longer Floy talked, the louder her voice grew. 'I don't care if it *is* one o'clock in the morning,' Floy said. 'What are *you* doing home? Your daughter and I were led to believe that you and your friend were somewhere out west.'

Twisting this way and that way, Joselle tried to hear better, tried not to hear, tried to see Floy's expression, tried to hide her own eyes so she couldn't see a thing. Joselle heard Floy say, 'What do you *mean*, you've been home all along?' and 'I don't care what you call it, I call it lying,' and 'Too bad the word responsibility isn't in your vocabulary,' and 'You'll never change,' and 'Nothing's ever your fault, is it?'

By the time Floy slammed the receiver down, she was shouting. Her 'Goodbye!' made Joselle cringe.

'Well,' said Floy, her face pinched with anger, 'The Beautiful Vicki strikes again. She thinks her wishes are more important than your needs.'

Joselle hated talk like this; it meant nothing. She wanted facts. She gave Floy a searching look. 'What are we doing?' she cried. 'What's *happening*?'

'I'm taking you home where you belong.'

'Right now?'

'Right now. I won't be able to sleep. You won't be able to sleep. We might as well.' Floy bent down and kissed Joselle on each cheek. 'She was home the entire time. The Pacific Ocean thing was just one of her stories.' Floy inhaled deeply. So deeply that Joselle thought that Floy might suck in the whole living room. She let out the breath slowly and steadily. 'Come here, Joselle,' Floy said, her voice changing, turning lighter, almost airy. 'Let me do your eyelids one last time.'

Within minutes after having her eyelids done, Joselle was packed and they were on the road. Floy was in such a hurry that she and Joselle kept their night-gowns on. Joselle wore a sweatshirt over hers.

Joselle's sweater was lying on a towel on the back-seat. It was still wet. Earlier that afternoon, Floy had washed it by hand and sewn on a flat, mismatched, dove-coloured button. 'It's the best I can do,' Floy had told Joselle. When they passed a street lamp, Joselle turned in the car to look at the sweater. It was no longer a perfect thing. It was limp and dull. Now it truly belongs to me, she thought regretfully.

The night was thick and black and full of motion. The white painted lines on the highway slashed through the darkness as if they had been cut with a monstrous knife. There were only a few cars on the road, and when Joselle spotted one she wondered where it was going. She was going home. It may not have been under the best of circumstances, but Joselle Stark was going home.

Joselle's bags were in the boot, but she kept her purse and her knapsack on the floor between her feet. In the knapsack were her new clothes, the lucky penny, Blaze's key collection, and the fox she had taken from his Noah's ark.

Blaze Werla.

What could she do about him now? Would he ever forgive her? How could she have been so stupid? Why had she danced in the rain?

A small part inside her wanted to forget him – put him out of her life completely, throw his things into the trash when she got home. But she knew that wasn't possible. She had already added him to her life. Most people she trusted ended up breaking her heart into a million pieces. Blaze was different. Why did she have to go and ruin everything?

'I've got something for you,' Floy said, interrupting Joselle's thoughts. 'Grab the wheel a minute. Traffic's light.'

Joselle leaned over and clutched the steering wheel. She turned it ever so slightly, testing it, feeling the power. Floy had never let her do this before and it surprised Joselle. The highway curved gradually and Joselle manoeuvred the car expertly.

Floy fished under the seat for a minute and came up with a small, flat bag. 'Here it is,' she said. She slid the bag onto Joselle's lap and grabbed the wheel, pushing Joselle's hands away. 'I bought this the night we went shopping at the mall. I paid for it while you were in the dressing room. I thought I'd keep it and give it to you when you needed it most.' Floy flipped the overhead light on.

It was a scarf. A beautiful scarf. It was black, bordered with a network of birds of all kinds, printed in gorgeously bright colours. Every colour Joselle knew. And even some she couldn't identify by name.

'Thanks, Grammy. I love it.' Joselle stroked one of the birds. 'I love you,' she told Floy.

'I thought it would look nice with your new sweater. Jazz it up a bit.'

A lump formed in Joselle's throat. She wanted to say more to Floy. Apologize for getting the sweater dirty. Thank her again for the scarf. She started to cry.

'I know you don't understand everything your mother does,' Floy said. 'I don't understand, either. But I know she loves you.' Floy rubbed Joselle's knee. 'Let's just drive,' she said. 'Let's just drive and think.'

Joselle had a lot to think about. The Beautiful Vicki topped her list. But if Joselle thought about her mother too long, she was overcome with sadness. She tried to keep the sadness moving. Joselle pictured the inside of her body as a pinball machine. And she willed the sadness – the little steel ball – to stay in motion, moving around and around throughout her. Never stopping. If it stopped, she might explode.

Her mind drifted back to Blaze. He may have been the best friend she ever had. If nothing else, she knew that she had to return the key collection and the tiny fox. It was just a matter of time. Joselle remembered so clearly the night that she had thought of the words of stone, how impressed she had been by her own brilliance. And when she had first looked at Reena's name on the hillside, she had felt so elated that her toes tingled. Thinking about it all now caused her stomach to sink. She had set out to complicate someone else's life, and ended up complicating her own.

And that's when she took her pen from her purse and hiked up her nightgown. I'M SORRY, Joselle wrote on her thigh. And – I'M BACK. And she knew that she would be back. She was counting on it. Floy glanced over, clicked her tongue, and flicked off the overhead light. 'Just drive and think,' she said again, softly.

After putting her pen away and readjusting her nightgown, Joselle folded and unfolded the scarf on her lap. Then she wound it loosely around her neck and knotted it above her heart, tossing the ends casually off to the side. Even in the darkness, the birds on the scarf were so colourful, so vivid, that for a brief moment Joselle was certain that she heard them sing. A wild throaty song.

22

BLAZE

The bedroom simmered with stale heat. Joselle was standing at Blaze's window, looking out toward the hill. She was wearing a skirt that reminded Blaze of a tulip, upside down. The skirt changed colour constantly – green to blue to grey. And everything wavered. She was intent, her body firmly fixed to the window frame like a statue. Blaze wanted to see what she was seeing. Was there a message on the hill? He tried to run toward her, but could only move in slow motion, as if he were moving through deep water. By the time he reached the window, Joselle had leaped out. He leaned over the sill, but she was nowhere to be seen. She had disappeared into a blinding yellow light. But her voice came from all around – above, below, and from within. 'I'm everywhere,' her voice said, echoing in his head like a bell, making his ears ache. 'I'm everywhere.'

When Blaze woke up, his sheet was pulled over his head, and the room was sizzling with the summer sun.

For days after the incident in the rain, Blaze didn't see Joselle at all. But then he hadn't gone up to the hill since then, and he wasn't exactly sure if he wanted to see her anyway.

He spent a good portion of each day preparing to paint the canvas that Glenn had given him at the start of the summer.

Blaze had decided to try to paint in a manner similar to Glenn's. He would paint a surreal landscape. Blaze knew that people rendered realistically weren't his speciality, so he thought he would choose different objects to represent people he knew. He would have the objects floating in a night sky, stars all around. Anything was possible in the darkest part of the night.

Lying on his bed, Blaze made a list of the people he wanted to include and the objects that might represent them.

DAD – a paintbrush, his birthmark

GRANDMA – a cucumber beetle, green beans, tomatoes, a flower.

MOM – my ark, the Ferris wheel

Should I include Joselle? he wondered. Or Claire? Or myself?

He added to the list.

JOSELLE (maybe) – a spoon, the button, stones

CLAIRE (maybe) – *long* hair (*not red*), a silver barrette

ME (maybe) – my key collection, my ark, the Ferris wheel

Some things could stand for more than one person, Blaze realized. A paintbrush could stand for Glenn or himself. Or even Claire, seeing as there were brushes in the box of paints she had given him. His ark and the Ferris wheel could stand for Reena or himself. His key collection also symbolized Joselle, since she had it now. And Joselle's button represented both of them, too; it was hers, but it was in his possession. We're all linked in certain ways, he thought.

He sketched on paper first. While he worked, Blaze remembered the day he had told Joselle that he wanted to be an artist when he was older.

'A famous one?' she asked.

'I don't know,' he replied, shrugging. 'Just an artist.'

'*I'm* going to be famous,' Joselle told him, smiling.

'At what?' Blaze asked.

'At whatever I want,' Joselle answered. 'Currently I plan on being a famous doctor, or at least a surgeon of the heart or brain.'

Even though Joselle was on his mind, he decided to concentrate on Glenn and Nova and Reena. Soon, a large paintbrush, green beans, and a tomato circled a full moon. And so did an ark with animals spilling out across the sky.

When Blaze sketched the ark, he set the real one on the floor in front of him. That's when he discovered that his tiny fox was missing. He looked for it under his bed, in his closet, and in all his drawers. I'll find it later, he said to himself.

He worked and reworked his ideas until he was satisfied. Then he smeared charcoal on the back of his drawing, taped it to his canvas, and traced over the drawing. Now the image was on the canvas. He left enough space for other objects he might include later.

With his paints like a box of candy before him, Blaze sat in his room waiting to begin. 'Beginning is the hardest part,' Glen always said. Blaze surely felt that now. He waited and waited and waited. He wasn't yet ready to make a mark on the canvas with paint.

The next day Glenn asked Blaze, 'Where's Joselle? I haven't seen her around lately.'

'I'm not sure,' Blaze answered, trying to be as vague as possible.

'Maybe she'd like to come for dinner, too?'

'Oh, not tonight,' Blaze said.

'Okay,' said Glenn, absently. He was poking at the fire in the outdoor grill with tongs. Claire was coming for dinner. They were going to have bratwurst.

Blaze was wary of the fire. He stood at a distance and squinted his eyes. He could feel the heat and smell the lighter fluid. Blaze crossed his arms, rubbing his elbows tentatively. His ankles felt itchy. The air above the flames rolled and flickered as though he were looking through waves. It was mesmerizing.

Blaze had asked to invite Claire. It was his way of trying to make up for the times that he had ignored her. Glenn's eyes had glinted when Blaze had suggested it. 'Good idea, Blazer,' he had said, placing his hand on the back of Blaze's neck and holding it there for a moment.

After dinner, Blaze found a few minutes when he and Claire were alone.

'I wanted you to come for dinner,' Blaze told Claire softly. The kitchen table stood between them, a flat brown space. They had already cleared the table of dirty dishes and rinsed them. Water dribbled down Blaze's arm. He wiped it on his pants. 'It was my idea.'

'I know.' Claire's mouth was a perfect circle when she finished saying the word know. And her expression was so bright his head spun.

Before Claire left, she came to Blaze's room to say good night. The door was open, but she knocked and waited in the hallway.

'You can come in,' Blaze said, sitting up. He had been lying on his bed. His Noah's ark was on its side, capsized atop a rumpled mess of bedspread waves. The animals were scattered, adrift among the creases of the sheets. He had been wondering (as he often did) about what happened to all the animals that were left behind, all the animals that weren't allowed into the ark. Did they all drown? And how many animals *had* been left? Hundreds? Thousands? Millions? The waters of the great flood must have stunk, he reasoned. And what about the *people* left behind? That was the worst part about the story of

Noah's ark. The part they never really tell you about. What happened to all the people?

'I just wanted to thank you for inviting me tonight,' Claire said.

'That's okay,' Blaze replied. His cheeks turned hot. 'This was my favourite toy when my mother died,' he said, picking up the ark and offering it to Claire. Their fingers touched in the exchange.

'It's nice,' Claire said. Nodding toward an animal, she said, 'May I?'

'Sure.' Blaze handed her the tiger. 'I had twelve kinds of animals, but just yesterday I realized that my fox is missing. I keep this in the ark to take its place. Until I find the fox.' He held up the round, lustrous button from Joselle's sweater.

'No foxes.' Claire looked quietly, then gently placed the ark and the tiger at the foot of Blaze's bed. 'Well, I should go, but I just wanted to thank you. It was nice to see you again. And thank you for letting me look at your ark. It's an interesting story, don't you think? Mysterious.'

Blaze could only nod in agreement. Mysterious was right. He almost pulled his canvas out of his closet to show Claire, but changed his mind.

'Good night, Blaze,' Claire said from the doorway. Her face was in shadow, but her long, ringed fingers waved in the light, catching it and sending it back like miniature comets.

'Night,' he answered. He listened to her oddly rhythmic footsteps pattering down the hallway. She's skipping, he thought, thrilled by the sound and thrilled by the picture it created in his head: a tall adult doing what he had only seen little children and his kindergarten teacher do. Blaze fluffed his pillows and wedged them behind his back. 'See you soon,' he whispered.

23

BLAZE

Because he knew he would have to face Joselle sooner or later, Blaze walked up and over the hill to Floy's house and rang the bell. Gary charged for the window and barked so fiercely Blaze shuddered. After a long minute Floy answered the door, opening it just a crack and blocking Gary with her spindly legs.

'Hello, Blaze,' she said, her bespectacled nose protruding through the small gap between the door and the doorjamb.

'Hi,' he said shyly, trying to keep an eye on Gary. 'Can I talk to Joselle?' he asked, twiddling his fingers nervously. 'Please?'

'She went back home,' Floy replied. 'It's been a few days now. I don't know what Joselle told you, but she was only here for a short visit. For all I know, she told you she moved in here.'

Suddenly Blaze felt lonely. 'She didn't say goodbye.' The boldness of his voice surprised himself.

The door opened wider as Gary quieted down. Blaze could see Floy entirely now. She was wearing a sleeveless white housedress patterned with deep red roses, and she held a magazine in her hand. Her pockets were overflowing with tissues.

Gary slipped past Floy and trotted out onto the porch. He rubbed against Blaze. Blaze scratched Gary behind his ears, trying to remain calm, trying to remember everything Joselle had taught him about dogs. After circling Blaze twice, Gary made himself comfortable in the shady corner of the porch.

'Well, to be truthful,' Floy said, 'I ended up taking Joselle home in the middle of the night. It was a sudden departure.'

'Is Joselle okay?' Blaze had carried the button with him. He felt for it in his pocket and pressed it into his leg. He looked at Floy intensely, seeking an answer.

'Oh, sure. I didn't mean to mislead you. Don't worry about Joselle. She's fine. Joselle's Joselle.' Floy swatted at a fly with her magazine. 'Listen,' she said, 'do you want something to eat?' She stepped aside and gestured for Blaze to enter the house. The sweep of her arm pushed the door open all the way. 'I think I've got some cookies. Store bought.'

'No, thank you,' Blaze said politely, moving slowly off the porch. He backed up to the railing and leaned against it. 'But – but is she coming back?'

'Oh, she'll be back. As a matter of fact, she ran off at the mouth about you to her mother. She told her mother that she wanted to live here, she liked you so much. Her only true friend in the world, she called you.'

Blaze blushed completely and uncontrollably.

'It'd put me away for sure,' Floy said. 'Having her live with me.' She sighed and rolled her eyes. Then her eyes welled. 'You know Joselle. She's a handful. But a sweetheart, despite all her troubles.' She laughed, and it seemed to Blaze that it wasn't exactly a joyful laugh.

Blaze cleared his throat.

Gary stretched and yawned. A long wheezy yawn followed by heavy panting.

'She really likes you,' Floy continued. She was blinking her eyes quickly, as though she had something in them, irritating them. 'It's the only time I've ever seen her so interested in another child.'

Looking down, Blaze played with his feet, waggling his toes; his shoes seemed sizes too small. 'If you talk to her, will you tell her I said hi?'

'I sure will. And you say hello to your father and your grandmother for me. Funny, we live so close and never see each other.'

Blaze said that he would. Then he went up to Gary and petted him, cooing to him as he stroked his sides, the way Joselle had shown him. Gary's tail wagged briskly, and Blaze hopped off the porch.

'You're a nice young man,' Floy called. 'I'd like Joselle to be around you more. Thank you. Thanks a lot.'

'Bye,' Blaze said, turning back toward Floy for a moment before running home, his heart booming.

He had gone to Floy's with the intention of demanding the return of his key collection, and now he didn't even care about it; he only missed Joselle.

He had thought and thought about how he could ever forgive her, and already it was done.

Several mornings later Blaze rose to discover a small wrapped box outside his bedroom door. A note was attached. It said, *I made these for your ark. Love, Claire.*

Blaze opened the package and found a pair of shiny bronze foxes, no larger than an inch in any direction. Blaze picked them up. He hadn't told Claire that he owned only one of each animal. Of course she'd assume there'd be two. The foxes sat on Blaze's palm, heads low, tails curled slightly sidewise. He moved his hand, examining the foxes from every angle. The details fascinated him: delicate lines to indicate fur, the holes that served as eyes, the teensy upturned peaks that formed the pointy noses. The foxes were more sturdy and heavy than Blaze's plastic animals. More beautiful, too.

He looked at the foxes for so long that they became huge. So huge that there was barely enough room in the world for anything else.

Something wasn't right.

Blaze peered at the drawing on his canvas from various distances, tilting his head this way and that way. He still had not begun to paint. He thought of asking Glenn for help, but he wanted to do this all on his own. To make it work.

Blaze had considered adding objects to represent Claire and Joselle to the painting right from the start. And that's exactly what he decided to do.

Claire would be easy. He drew two foxes as expertly as he could, looking carefully at the statues from Claire. He drew them on the underside of the full moon, flying, reaching out and up and toward the ark. The only pair of animals on the canvas.

Joselle was more difficult. But after about an hour of thinking and sketching, it became obvious; with only a few changes, the large, round full moon could also serve as Joselle's button.

It seemed right. Everything circled the button-moon the way Blaze's summer seemed to revolve around Joselle.

He knew it wasn't perfect, but he felt as ready as he would ever be. And so he began to paint.

24

BLAZE

It was August. School would be starting soon. Blaze and Nova were at the cemetery, tending the flowers beside Reena's grave. Glenn had been working with them, but decided to go for a walk. 'I'll wait for you by the car,' he told them. It was parked at the side of the highway.

'Dad doesn't like it here, does he?' Blaze said. He was pulling handfuls of weeds and piling them into Nova's basket.

'I think he was just ready to leave,' Nova said. 'It *is* taking me longer than I thought it would, but I wanted to cut all the roses back.'

'Sometimes it's scary here,' Blaze told her as he watched withering rose petals flutter to the ground.

'Sometimes.'

'And sometimes it's just quiet.'

'I think you're right.'

While Nova finished working with her clippers, Blaze ran his hand over his mother's name. REENA PREHN WERLA. No matter how hot it was outside, the stone felt icy to his touch. The chiselled edges of the letters numbed his fingers. Sometimes he'd press his hand against the stone until an impression was left on his skin. He'd watch it vanish like breath on a window.

When he was in the second grade, Blaze had found a picture of a cemetery in a big book at the school library. He couldn't remember the name of the book, and although he had looked for it again several times, he never found it. The picture was of four boys sitting on tombstones, riding them as if they were horses. The boys were wearing hats and blowing trumpets, as Blaze recalled it. The picture frightened him the day he saw it, and he always thought of it when he came to the cemetery. He could never do what the boys in the picture were doing. But he could imagine Joselle doing it. He saw her clearly. Joselle — hopping onto a gravestone, clicking her heels and whooping, wearing a loopy grin on her face and an outrageous hat on her head. It didn't seem wrong for Joselle.

Blaze took Joselle's button out of his pocket and rolled it along Reena's gravestone. When it fell onto the ground, Blaze picked it up, wiped it off on his shirt, and tucked it into his sock. Sometimes he kept it there, sometimes in his wallet, sometimes in a pocket. But he always carried it with him now, wherever he went.

'We'd better go,' Nova said. She leaned on Blaze as she got up.

'It looks nice,' Blaze remarked, helping his grandmother gather her things. He felt sleepy all of a sudden, and yawned.

'Give me your hand, Blaze,' Nova said. She held it until they reached the car.

Being at the cemetery had given him the idea to go to the hill. He walked around the black locust tree, weaving in and out of the stones.

Blaze thought about the burials he had been responsible for: Benny's, Ajax's, Ken's, Harold's, Ortman's. And everything went fuzzy for a moment. In some ways the whole idea seemed childish to him. Had it always? Or was this some new feeling? He wondered how changes take place in people. He wondered if people knew when things changed in their minds any more than they could feel their bones or hair growing.

Blaze took the five stones, added one for Simon, and formed a letter *J* with them as best he could near the black locust tree.

He hadn't seen Joselle since the morning in the rain.

He wondered if he'd ever see her again.

When Blaze painted, hours could pass without his knowing, and he could vacillate between complete satisfaction with his work and total disappointment within that time over and over again.

It had taken Blaze weeks to finish the canvas. He had gotten to the point where he just couldn't do anything else to it. And yet, he didn't want to show it to Glenn or Nova or Claire. He didn't want to explain what anything meant.

Blaze signed his name in the lower right-hand corner of the canvas, using little white dots of paint to form the letters.

On the last Saturday in August, Blaze woke up feeling exceptionally buoyant. He and Glenn and Claire were going to the county fair. They would be leaving early and making a day of it. Blaze was out of bed and dressed in minutes. He went to the window and threw open the curtains. The morning was shiny with rain from the night, the air breathtakingly clear. Above the hill, the sky was a radiant blue, and beneath the black locust tree on the slope of the hill were stones. The stones were white moons that bled together. They spelled: I'M SORRY.

Blaze stared at them until all the sounds of the morning quieted to nothing – the birds, the clock, the wind. Then he pinched himself to verify that he was, in fact, awake and alive, and bounded down the hallway to Glenn's room.

He'd have to explain some things to Glenn, but Blaze felt that he could handle that. There was a lot of telling to do, but he'd only say as much as he needed to for now. Blaze had simply told Glenn and Nova that Joselle had gone home. He hadn't told anyone about the words of stone. Maybe he'd even show Glenn the painting.

Blaze's footsteps were much too loud for early morning, but he didn't seem to notice. He reached Glenn's bedroom and stopped, loosely holding the doorknob. He didn't know where to begin. He thought for a minute, then slowly opened the door.

'Dad,' he whispered excitedly, 'get up. I want you to look at the hill.'

It was a good place to start.

Other great reads from **Red Fox**

Top new fiction

LETTERS OF A LOVESTRUCK TEENAGER
Claire Robertson

'I'm Gilly Freeborn and I'm nearly fourteen and I've got problems . . .' Her chest is as flat as a pancake, her sister's a mean, selfish man-eating piranha, her best friend's turned traitor and – *argh!* – she's fallen in love with The Vision. What's a girl to do? Turn to Alexa Deehart of course, agony aunt of *The Bizz* magazine . . .

0 09 94252 1   £3.99

SWITCHERS
Kate Thompson

Tess is a Switcher – she can change shape to become any animal she chooses. She always thought she was unique, but not any more. Tess meets another Switcher, Kevin, and together they have powers they never dreamed of . . .

0 09 925612 6   £3.99

MIDNIGHT'S CHOICE
Kate Thompson

With Kevin gone, Tess is feeling ever more lonely and isolated from everyone around her. Then she senses a call to which she has no resistance, and finds herself in the middle of a dilemma. For now she has found a new friend, and has a very difficult decision to make – a choice to change her life forever.

0 09 925613 4   £3.99

CHILD OF THE MAY
Theresa Tomlinson

No one is ever going to crush fiery Magda's independent streak. She yearns for the thrill of adventure and when her chance comes . . . she's going to take it. This stirring sequel to The Forest Wife continues Theresa Thomlinson's compelling account of life amongst the outlaws in Robin Hood's Sherwood Forest.

0 09 969231 7   £3.99

THE
MENNYMS
BOOKS
SYLVIA WAUGH

'Brilliant' *Independent*

'Weird, witty and wonderfully original' *Guardian*

'Extraordinary' *Sunday Telegraph*

Sylvia Waugh's extraordinary debut novel about the Mennyms, a family of life-size ragdolls, won the 1994 **Guardian Children's Fiction Award.**

The Mennyms - Granny and Granpa, Vinetta and Joshua and their five children - are far from ordinary. They've kept a secret hidden for forty years, a secret to which nobody has even come close. Until now...

THE MENNYMS   ISBN 0 09 930167 9   £2.99

MENNYMS IN THE WILDERNESS ISBN 0 09 942421 5   £2.99

MENNYMS UNDER SIEGE   ISBN 0 09 955761 4   £2.99

MENNYMS ALONE   ISBN 0 09 95577 1   £3.50

and coming soon!
MENNYMS ALIVE   ISBN 0 09 955781 9   £3.50

The MENNYMS books by Sylvia Waugh
Out now in paperback from Red Fox

ADVENTURE

The Adventure Series by Willard Price

Read these exciting stories about Hal and Roger Hunt and their search for wild animals. Out now in paperback from Red Fox at £3.50

Amazon Adventure

Hal and Roger find themselves
abandoned and alone in the
Amazon Jungle when a mission
to explore unchartered territory
of the Pastaza River goes off course...
0 09 918221 1

Volcano Adventure

A scientific study of the volcanoes
of the Pacific with world famous
volcanologist, Dr Dan Adams,
erupts into an adventure of a
lifetime for Hal and Roger....
0 09 918241 6

Underwater Adventure

The intrepid Hunts have joined forces
with the Oceanographic Institute to
study sea life, collect specimens and
follow a sunken treasure ship trail...
0 09 918231 9

South Sea Adventure

Hal and Roger can't resist the offer
of a trip to the South Seas in search
of a creature known as the
Nightmare of the Pacific...
0 09 918251 3

Arctic Adventure

Olrik the eskimo and his bear,
Nanook, join Hal and Roger on
their trek towards the polar ice cap.
And with Zeb the hunter hot on
their trail the temperature soon turns
from cold to murderously chilling...
0 09 918321 8

Safari Adventure

Tsavo national park has become
a death trap. Can Hal and Roger
succeed in their mission of liberating
it from the clutches of a Blackbeard
deadly gang of poachers?...
0 09 918341 2

Elephant Adventure

Danger levels soar with the
temperature for Hal and Roger as they
embark upon a journey to the equator,
charged with the task of finding an
extremely rare white elephant...
0 09 918331 5

African Adventure

On safari in African big-game
country, Hal and Roger coolly tackle
their brief to round up a mysterious
man-eating beast. Meanwhile, a
merciless band of killers follow in
their wake...
0 09 918371 4

It's wild! It's dangerous! And it's out there!